CITY

OF

NOPE

THE EXCOMS THRILLERS NO. 3

ALSO BY BRETT BATTLES

THE JONATHAN QUINN THRILLERS
THE CLEANER
THE DECEIVED
SHADOW OF BETRAYAL (U.S.)/THE UNWANTED (U.K.)
THE SILENCED
BECOMING QUINN
THE DESTROYED
THE COLLECTED
THE ENRAGED
THE DISCARDED
THE BURIED
THE UNLEASHED
THE AGGRIEVED

THE EXCOMS
THE EXCOMS
TOWN AT THE EDGE OF DARKNESS

THE REWINDER THRILLERS
REWINDER
DESTROYER
SURVIVOR

THE LOGAN HARPER THRILLERS
LITTLE GIRL GONE
EVERY PRECIOUS THING

THE PROJECT EDEN THRILLERS
SICK
EXIT NINE
PALE HORSE
ASHES
EDEN RISING
DREAM SKY
DOWN

THE ALEXANDRA POE THRILLERS
(with Robert Gregory Browne)
POE
TAKEDOWN

STANDALONES
THE PULL OF GRAVITY
NO RETURN
MINE

For Younger Readers

THE TROUBLE FAMILY CHRONICLES
HERE COMES MR. TROUBLE

CITY
OF
NOPE

THE EXCOMS THRILLERS NO. 3

BRETT BATTLES

ONE

AT TEN P.M. SHARP, the prerecorded bell echoed throughout the factory floor of Building 17. In the large room, workers leaned back from their assigned machines, muscles aching, minds numb. For those assigned to this particular building, it was their fingers that hurt the worst.

Gloria Ortega attempted to ball her hands in hopes of relieving some of the pain, but to no avail. It wouldn't have mattered anyway. Her pain wasn't going anywhere. Too much time pushing garment segments through the sewing machine as fast as possible to ensure she reached her daily quota.

Gloria and the workers around her remained in their chairs, waiting until they were cleared to leave. Silent. Eyes forward. No one wanting to see their own despair reflected in the face of another.

The two inspectors, who had arrived just before the bell, walked down the rows and stopped at each station, one in front and one in back. Given that there were about a hundred workers, it could be thirty minutes before the last station was checked and its worker allowed to return to the dorm for a cold dinner and much needed rest.

Gloria was in luck today. Her machine was in the front third of the building, only two rows away from where the inspector started. She watched him move from machine to machine, making sure quotas had been met. After each post-count nod, a worker would rise on shaky feet and make his or her way to the door. If a quota had not been met, the inspector would turn on the red light hanging above the offending station.

The worker would have to spend however long it took to finish not only what was owed, but a penalty of an additional half of the daily quota. There had been days when Gloria returned to the factory in the morning to find a worker still at his station, finishing from the day before. He would then remain for the new shift, until he either completed his new quota or collapsed from exhaustion.

The inspector approached Gloria's station. He was a wiry man who spoke Spanish with an accent she thought might be Colombian. He looked into her box of completed items and counted the pieces she'd sewn. It wasn't her first box of the day, of course. As earlier ones were filled, they had been checked, the number of finished pieces marked on a sheet hanging in front of her machine, and a new box had replaced the old one.

Though nervous, Gloria kept her eyes downcast and her body frozen, showing as much deference to the inspector as possible while he rifled through her work. She knew she had made her quota a box earlier, but was well aware the inspectors weren't always scrupulous. If they didn't like a worker or were in a bad mood, they might turn on the red light anyway.

When the inspector finished, he cleared his throat, wrote a number on her sheet, and gave her the nod.

"Thank you, sir," she said, but he'd already moved on.

Standing was a torture. Though only twenty-two years old, she felt three times that most days of late.

She and the others in the sewing room were allowed to stand and stretch for three minutes, two times a day—the first at ten a.m., then again at five p.m.—and given a fifteen-minute break at one p.m. for the bathroom and lunch.

Gloria had been in the chair for over five hours, and her hips and knees screamed at their sudden use. Not even her ankles escaped the feeling of abuse. They felt stiff and swollen as she shuffled toward the growing line of her colleagues at the exit.

The pathway outside Building 17 was enclosed by a chain-link cage, creating a corridor that, because of the rain pouring through the chain-link, had turned into a field of mud. The pathway was part of an intricate network of passages, with gates that could be opened onto other similarly caged routes, which were controlled at all times by the facilities management. The current pathway led directly to her dorm.

The large, barn-like building rang like a thousand agitated cymbals from the rain pelting its tin roof, the sound almost deafening as she entered. The evening table was set up near the door, and behind it stood one of the guards, watching to make sure each person took only one of the small plastic boxes containing the cold dinners, and one of the tiny cups containing two ibuprofen tablets.

Gloria knew even a full bottle of pills wouldn't make a dent in her pain, but she took her tabs. On the way to her bunk—the bottom mattress of a stack of three near the middle of the room—she grabbed a tin cup from the stack next to the barrel of water and filled it. When she'd first arrived, she'd avoided drinking from the barrel as much as possible, sure that it would make her sick. But one could go without water for only so long, and since none of the others seemed to be affected, she'd given in. Now she drank at least two glasses every night, and another one in the morning.

As she neared her bunk she glanced over at Ricardo's bed. His was the bottom of a stack the next row over. He was hunched over his food, rocking slightly as he ate. He did that sometimes. It was his way of "dealing with the shit," he'd told her.

She hadn't meant to become friends with him. She hadn't wanted to become friends with anyone. One night, not long after her arrival, she'd woken up crying to find him leaning down next to her bed. She had jerked away, startled.

"It's okay," he said. "You called out in your sleep. I just wanted to make sure you were all right. Nightmare?" His Spanish sounded Central American, and later she would learn he was from Honduras.

Gloria had hesitated before nodding.

Ricardo smiled. "Don't worry. We've all had them. But you should try not to be so loud. If a guard hears you, or someone complains, they'll punish you. Trust me, you don't want that."

"I-I'll try," she whispered.

"Good. Get some sleep. Morning comes fast."

"Thank you."

Their interaction had lasted less than a minute, but it was the most warmth she'd felt from someone since…before. Since that night, their friendship had grown. Because conversation was discouraged, they'd steal moments when they could—on the walk to and from Building 17, when passing one another in the dorm, in the small area outside the toilets. Mostly it was at night when everyone else was asleep. Somehow, he always seemed to know when she was awake.

She'd said he reminded her of her uncle Hector.

"Is that good or bad?"

She'd smiled. "He's my favorite."

Ricardo was always there to cheer her up and make her forget—if only for a moment—the hell her life had become. In the past week, though, his mood had turned more somber than usual. Tonight, it was worse than ever. But she knew why.

"Hey," she whispered. "Do you want my pills?"

At thirty-one, Ricardo was nine years her senior. He always seemed to be in more pain than she was, though he tried to hide it.

It took him a moment before he glanced at her, shook his head, and returned his attention to his food. There was no warmth in his eyes. No happy-to-see-you smile. No sense at all that he even knew who she was.

Before his mood had completely soured, he'd told her his son's fifth birthday was approaching. Now, come midnight, it would be here. She wished she could think of something to say that would help him through his misery, but what did she know about being a parent?

She climbed onto her bunk and picked at the food she so desperately needed.

Thirty minutes later, when the lights went out, she lay there, exhausted but unable to sleep. Her thoughts were a jumble of half-sewn garments, fenced-in walkways, and

14

crammed sleeping quarters, all wrapped in the odor of too many bodies in too small a space.

She could still hardly believe that answering an ad had led to this.

A little more than six months ago, she'd left her small hometown for a job in the larger city of Villahermosa. Unfortunately, five months later, her employer went out of business. She'd looked for another job, but no one wanted her. So, when she read the listing in the newspaper under REAL WORK REAL MONEY, she had called the number immediately and set up an interview with the recruiter, who would be in Villahermosa for only a few days.

When she arrived, she was escorted into the office of a smiling, middle-aged man in a nice business suit. He waved her into a chair on the other side of his desk, telling her his name was _Señor_ Galvan.

He asked her a series of questions: her age (twenty-two), her health history (nothing wrong, as far as she knew), her relationship status (single).

He seemed particularly pleased with this last answer. "Never married?"

"No, sir."

"Do you live with your family?"

"I rent my own room."

"Why not with your family?"

"They live in Benito Juárez, not here."

"I see. A big family?"

She shrugged. "Not so big. My mother, older sister, and younger brother."

"And your father?"

She tried to keep her pain from her face as her heart clenched. "He died two years ago."

"I'm so sorry."

"It's okay."

"So, you're here all by yourself?"

"Yes. Is my living situation important?"

"In a manner of speaking."

It was at this point he'd told her the job was not in Mexico, but in Costa Rica. A new resort hotel on an island in the gulf, just off the coast. "We are looking for candidates who we feel could be trained to become managers."

This was so much better than anything she'd been hoping for, so of course she had jumped at the chance.

Ricardo had told her he'd answered a similar ad, though one for a high-paying construction project in Argentina.

Both had been lies.

While being transported to their work sites, they'd been drugged and woken here.

Wherever here was.

Everything they had with them—phone, jewelry, passports, even the clothes they'd been wearing—had been taken from them and replaced by the drab uniform they all now wore. They were told what was expected of them, and incidents of disobedience would not be tolerated. They were to do their job and nothing else.

For Gloria and Ricardo, that job was sewing garments from seven in the morning until ten at night, every day of the week.

Gloria heard someone slip out of bed and tiptoe toward the toilets. She raised her head.

The silhouette walking down the aisle looked like Ricardo. He seemed to be carrying something, which was odd since no one had anything.

Knowing he must be suffering, she quietly got up and followed him toward the back of the dorm. Ricardo always helped her when she was at her lowest. She wanted to do the same for him.

Rain continued to rattle the roof, almost drowning out the snores of the weary and the cries of the hopeless that arose here and there in the room.

Ricardo entered the toilets. She sneaked to the doorway and heard a thump, followed by a faucet coming on for a second before cutting off again. She decided it was safe to peer in.

The bathroom lights were on timers that allowed them to be on only during waking hours. But there was always enough light streaming in through the narrow windows that lined the top of the outer wall to let someone do their business.

Since there was no privacy here, she could see the whole room from where she was. But she didn't see him anywhere.

Confused, she took a step inside.

A hand clamped on her mouth and an arm grabbed her around the chest. She struggled, but her weakened state didn't allow her to put up much of a fight.

"Quiet," Ricardo whispered.

When she realized it was him, she relaxed.

Slowly, he raised his hand off her mouth and released her. "What are you doing here?"

"I thought you might need...someone to talk to."

He frowned. "I'm fine. Go back to bed."

On the ground behind him was the bundle he'd been carrying. "What is that?"

"Nothing. Please, Gloria. You need sleep."

She could see what looked like a bread roll sticking out of the top. "You're...you're going to try to escape, aren't you?"

The look on his face was all the answer she needed.

"You can't," she said. "It's impossible." Her mind raced for words to make him stay. "They'll...they'll catch you. They'll punish you. Ricardo, don't."

He closed his eyes, and she thought she had gotten through to him. But when he reopened them, his expression hardened. "I have to."

"It's too dangerous."

"Someone needs to get out. Someone needs to find people who can help us."

"Fine. But let it be someone else. Not you."

He looked at the ground, blinking tears away. "I'm going."

"Why?"

She could barely hear his response above the rain. "I promised him."

His son.

"Ricardo, no. Please," she said, knowing her plea would

be useless but unable to stop herself.

He put a hand on her cheek and smiled. "I'll get help. You'll be home soon."

She almost grabbed his hand, to never let him go, but she didn't move.

"You can help me, if you want," he said.

"Help?"

"Yes. Stand by the door, and if you see someone coming, tell me."

She looked at the doorway, then back at him. "But how are you getting out? The windows are too small."

He smiled again. "Will you do it?"

She wanted to scream *no* to make him change his mind. She knew it wouldn't, though, so with a sigh, she said, "Okay."

"Thank you. Don't worry. You'll see me again soon."

She positioned herself inside the doorway, from where she could see the main route anyone would take to the toilets, and also what Ricardo was doing.

"Clear?" he whispered.

She nodded.

He walked to the sink in the far corner and carefully climbed onto it. Gloria was sure it would break from the wall, but it held. Ricardo reached up and pulled off one of the boards near the top of the wall. Behind the board was a narrow hole to the outside. If Ricardo believed he could crawl through it, he was crazy. And yet, that was exactly what he did. The months of limited rations had made him thinner than she realized.

There must have been something on the other side he could stand on, because after he was through, he leaned back in and grabbed the board from where he'd left it sticking up from the sink. He gave Gloria a smile, then raised the board and put it back in place.

She stood there in the doorway, staring at the empty bathroom, until she heard footsteps coming from the dorm.

A middle-aged woman shuffled past without even glancing at her. Good thing, too, or the woman might have seen the tears streaming down Gloria's cheeks. Then again, the woman might have thought nothing of it. Everyone in the dorm cried.

THE LIGHTS CAME on at six a.m. sharp.

Gloria doubted she'd had more than three hours of sleep, all bad. Every time she drifted off, she'd woken soon after, thinking Ricardo's escape had been a bad dream. But all it took was a glance at his empty bunk to know the truth.

She joined the breakfast line out of habit, not hunger. As always, she was given two stale buns and three pieces of cheese. Occasionally they would receive a hard-boiled egg, too. Not today, though. She was tempted to give everything to someone else, but she knew her body needed it.

At 6:45 the bell clanged twice, and she and her dorm mates lined up at the exit. Five minutes later the door opened, and they began their walk to Building 17.

The storm had moved on, leaving a steamy, clear morning, the kind Gloria used to love. Now it was just another day, in what was becoming an infinite string of identical, endless days.

Not identical, she reminded herself. Ricardo wasn't here today.

Within two minutes of leaving the building, a murmur arose from ahead. Gloria craned her neck and saw the turn to Building 17 closed off.

"Keep moving," one of the guards who patrolled the top of the cages called down. More words followed in languages other than Spanish, for the prisoners who didn't speak it.

The procession moved down a route Gloria had never taken before. Another two turns, and they came to a stop.

Again, she craned her neck to look ahead. A closed gate was keeping them from continuing. On the other side of the gate, people dressed similarly to her and her fellow workers were moving down a path perpendicular to her group's.

After the last person walked by, a minute passed before the gate opened.

"Keep moving," the guard above ordered again.

Gloria's group resumed walking.

It felt like they went an entire kilometer before they

reached another closed gate. For the next several minutes, gates rose in front of them and closed behind them, guiding them through small sections of the moveable maze until they found themselves in a pen just large enough for all of them to fit. Once the final person had entered, the gate behind them closed, locking them in.

The pen was only one of dozens filled with flocks of hopeless workers, separated from one another by empty chain-link corridors. Gloria knew she had been living in hell, but until this moment she hadn't realized its extent. There were hundreds of other prisoners, maybe even a thousand.

The pens all sat on a slight upward slope. At the bottom of the slope was a platform, like a stage. Standing at the front edge of the platform, facing the pens, were two dozen armed guards. More guards were spread on top of the cages, looking down into the pens.

Gloria leaned toward a woman next to her, who had been a prisoner longer, and whispered, "Have they brought you here before?"

The woman glanced at her, a blend of fear and sadness in her eyes, then looked back at the platform without saying anything.

Off to the right, one of the last still-empty pens began to fill.

What the hell is going on?

Gloria didn't have long to wait for her answer. A voice blared from a speaker, "Do the work. Do not cause problems. These are our rules. They are not difficult. If you stick to them, you will always have food and a place to sleep. You all know this. You also know if you do *not* stick to the rules, there are consequences."

While translations played over the sound system, four men moved onto the stage. Three wore black masks. The fourth was completely naked and hung limply between two of the masked men.

Gloria stopped breathing.

No. It can't be.

After the naked man was brought to the center of the stage,

the one who hadn't been holding him up grabbed the man's hair and tilted his face up.

"Oh, God," Gloria whispered.

It was Ricardo.

"This is a worker from Building 17."

Gasps rose from the people around Gloria.

"Last night, he tried to leave us without asking. *No one* leaves without our permission. And those that try will be caught."

The words were repeated in several languages.

"What have we taught you?" the voice asked.

All those who spoke Spanish said in near unison, "Disobedience will not be tolerated." Even Gloria, as shocked as she was, couldn't help but mouth the words that had been drummed into her.

After the non-Spanish speakers had repeated the exercise, the man holding Ricardo's hair let go, pulled out a gun, and placed it against the back of Ricardo's head.

"No," Gloria said, loudly enough to get a few glances from those nearest her.

"Disobedience will not be tolerated," the voice said.

The man pulled the trigger.

Gloria fell to her knees.

The lady she'd spoken to earlier grabbed her around her back. "Get up. You don't want them to see you like this. Get up."

Another woman helped pull Gloria to her feet.

"Unless you want that to happen to you, too, you can't let them know how much it affected you," the first woman whispered. "They may think you helped him."

I did help him, Gloria thought, but said, "Thank you."

The woman's expression softened. "Did...did you know him from *before*?"

"No. Just from here."

"Well, that's something, then. Best now to forget him."

Gloria had no idea how she could do that.

"The time you have missed at your workstations will be

added to the end of the day," the voice on the speaker said. "The workers of Building 17 will be on half rations for one week. Follow instructions and return to your stations. Disobedience will not be tolerated."

The pens were released one by one, the pathways converted to lead each group to its assigned building.

Gloria had no memory of walking to Building 17. No memory of sitting at her machine. No memory of making her quota, though she must have. After Ricardo was killed, the only thing she remembered was lying in her bed that night, staring at his empty bunk, and knowing there was no way she would ever get away from here.

No way any of them would.

Two

THE EIGHT BALL rolled toward the side pocket, its momentum slowing.

"Too soft," Dylan Brody said. "Sorry, boy-o, looks like Ireland gets this one."

"Patience," Ricky Orbits said.

The ball inched closer to the hole, then stopped right on the lip.

Dylan stepped toward the table to take his shot, but Ricky held out a hand, stopping him.

The ball teetered on the brink for another second before gravity pulled it into the pocket.

"Ha!" Ricky yelled. "I believe this one is *mine*." He picked up the cue ball. "Rematch?"

Dylan glared at him. "You're a cheat."

"How's that?"

"You've had more time on this table."

Ricky set the rack on the blue felt top. "Sounds like you're just making excuses. You play one table, you play them all."

"That there is a load of shite and you know it." Dylan looked over to where Liesel Kessler sat at a nearby table, thumbing through a magazine. "Back me up. He's got the home-court advantage, right?"

Without glancing at him, she said, "Ricky is right. You are making excuses."

Dylan stared at her, slack-jawed. "Tell me I'm hearing

things, because you couldn't have just sided with Ricky."

"Hey, loser racks 'em," Ricky said. "Let's go."

The Administrator touched the control pad and the image in the main monitor switched from the *Karas Evonus*'s game room to the midship deck, where Rosario Blanca and Ananke were stretched out on lounges, soaking up the last bit of the setting sun. Ananke wore a pair of wireless earbuds, her head rocking slightly to whatever she was listening to. Rosario was reading the Spanish translation of *The Girl with the Dragon Tattoo*, which she'd requested when the team returned after the job in Bradbury, Washington.

Instead of having the team disperse to their homes, the Administrator had suggested they come back to the ship, where they could enjoy a little downtime together. "You've only been together on missions so far," he had told Ananke. "I think it would be beneficial for you all to hang out in a less stressful situation."

The *Karas Evonus*, a converted cargo ship, had been designed as the team's mobile headquarters, and except for the first few days after they were all recruited, they had spent very little time on board.

Ananke had floated the idea to the others, and when no one objected, the Administrator had flown them back to the Bay Area. They had been on board for three days, and he was pleased to see the cohesiveness they'd been building in the field grow even stronger during their time off.

The days of sunbathing and playing pool couldn't last forever, however.

Sitting on the Administrator's desk were files containing information on several potential new missions. In a few minutes, he would be presiding over a meeting with the Committee to decide which mission would be chosen. Until that morning, he had intended to push the Toronto project. It wasn't particularly sexy, but the damage done by the scammer organization known as MIRA needed to be stopped. To do so permanently would mean infiltrating the organization to identify all the players before the whole enterprise could be brought down.

But another file had altered his intentions.

The only question was whether he could convince the committee to see it the same way.

A soft *bong* signaled it was almost time for the meeting. The Administrator activated the screens on the wall in front of him. Because the Committee still had two empty slots, only five of the monitors glowed with the countdown to connection. When it reached its end, the images of Committee members Sunday, Monday, Wednesday, Friday, and Saturday appeared.

"Ladies and gentlemen, welcome," the Administrator said.

They talked first of the slots that needed to be filled. The Administrator said he would have a list of vetted candidates within a few days. He did not, however, mention that the list would be preapproved by Committee member Monday, the man who was secretly behind the formation of the Committee and the Project, and was the real power when push came to shove. There were a few other small business matters before the conversation turned to the real reason they had convened this evening.

"Has everyone had time to read the brief I sent?" the Administrator asked.

There were nods and a few yeses.

"This seems fairly straightforward," Committee member Sunday said. She was a Korean entertainment mogul who managed, among others, several of the top K-pop music groups. As a preteen, she and her father had attempted to escape their former home in North Korea. The only reason she'd made it was because her father had sacrificed his life by diverting the attention of the soldiers who'd been closing in on them as they were about to cross the border. Experiencing the unjust death of a loved one was a prerequisite to being on the Committee. "This business with MIRA in Toronto seems the smart choice."

"I agree," Friday said. His qualification was a sister who had been on Pan Am Flight 103 when a terrorist bomb took it down over Lockerbie, Scotland.

"What about this problem in Naples, Italy?" Wednesday said. He was the only member of his family to survive China's

Cultural Revolution.

The Naples mission was the least attractive to the Administrator, but he remained silent. He was not an actual member of the Committee and did not have a vote. His job was the day-to-day running of the Project.

He was not surprised when Monday repeated something the Administrator had told him during their pre-meeting briefing. "I think Naples can be handled without deploying the team. But I defer to the Administrator on that."

The Administrator acted as if he was giving it some thought before saying, "It will take a little work, but I think we could find a solution that does not involve Ananke's team. Would you like me to look into that?"

The matter was put to a vote, the results unanimous in favor.

"What about this Julio Gutiérrez matter?" Monday said, as if he hadn't given it any thought until now.

Sunday frowned. "There's not much here."

"Perhaps not," the Administrator said, "but if you do decide the team should pursue this item, we have enough on Gutiérrez to get started."

"This is developed from the information learned on the Bradbury mission?" Monday asked.

Monday was referring to the mission Ananke and her team had just finished. A wild one, involving a trio of white supremacist cousins, human trafficking, human *hunting*, and a missing woman—Tasha Patterson—who'd uncovered what was going on. Ananke had made a copy of the information Tasha had gathered for the Administrator before giving the original disk to the FBI. Gutiérrez was the black marketeer the cousins used to sell their human product.

"It is," the Administrator said.

"I thought the government would be handling this."

"They haven't discovered this piece of information yet. But even if they had, they're overwhelmed by the leads they've already uncovered on Patterson's disk and would likely not get to this for some time."

That piece of information concerned a large group of

individuals kidnapped and then sold via Gutiérrez over the last two and a half years.

"I don't like that we only have the one name to go on," Wednesday said. "It could very easily be a dead end."

"It could," the Administrator said. "But—"

"I wasn't finished," Wednesday said.

"My apologies."

"But while I may not like it, and it *could* be a dead end, it seems like this is something we should follow up on. We're talking about one hundred and twenty-seven people. If we can help them, we should."

For the next fifteen minutes, the Committee debated the merits of the remaining mission choices. When it came time for the vote, the tally was two for Toronto and three for Julio Gutiérrez. Committee rules dictated that missions must be approved by four members—a majority with seven voting members. Even with only the five, rules were rules, and four were still needed for passage.

It was agreed they would reconvene in twenty-four hours to vote again.

"Thank you for your time," the Administrator said, swallowing his frustration. "Until tomorrow."

One by one the Committee members disconnected, until only Monday was left.

"That did not go as planned," the Administrator said.

"It's the nature of what we've started here," Monday told him.

"I understand that, but…"

"But time waiting is time wasted?"

"Exactly," the Administrator said, no longer able to hold back his anger. "If something happens to any of the hundred and twenty-seven because we have delayed, then that will be on us."

"If that were the case, then anything that happens to anyone on every job we reject is *on us*. We did not kidnap those people, nor did we sell them."

"You're right. I apologize."

"Don't. I appreciate your passion. And while I might

27

disagree about blame, I agree with you that this is the job we need to do." He paused. "Let me work on the others. If I can't turn one vote then I should quit right now."

"Thank you, sir."

"I'll contact you when I have news."

The Administrator spent the next several hours making sure everything was ready to go whether they went after Julio Gutiérrez or took on the Toronto scammers. At 11:15 p.m., Monday called back.

"I've taken the liberty of moving tomorrow's meeting up to eight a.m., your time."

"Will we have the votes?"

"We will."

The Administrator took a deep, relieved breath. "Thank you. Do you think it would be out of order for me to start things moving now?"

"I think it would be out of order if you didn't."

ANANKE AND THE others spent a relaxing evening aboard the *Karas Evonus*, starting with an excellent dinner of grilled salmon, roasted asparagus, and fresh French bread, followed by an impromptu eight-ball tournament.

Ricky, cocky from his continuous bludgeoning of Dylan on the table that afternoon, had suggested it. But much to his and the others' surprise, Liesel turned out to be a bit of a pool shark. Ricky didn't even get a shot off the first time he played her. When he demanded a rematch, she had let him break, and after he missed a shot, she ran the table again.

"It's okay," Dylan said to Ricky. "I'm sure with a little more practice, you might even sink a ball next time."

Ricky sneered. "Ha. Ha. Well, the least you ingrates could do is to take me out to a bar and buy me a drink."

Unlike the other team members, Ricky was restricted between missions to the alcohol-free *Karas Evonus*. If he hadn't agreed to that, he would have been promptly dropped back into the prison from where the Administrator's people had pulled him out. But he could go ashore as long as he was in the company of other team members.

"Not me," Liesel said. "I am going to bed."

Rosario uncurled from her chair. "Me, too."

"I'm with them," Dylan said. "Let's do it tomorrow." He followed the two women toward the stairs down to the living quarters.

"Ah, come on. It's still early!" Ricky turned to Ananke, who had started to rise. "Sweetie, please. One drink."

She frowned at him.

"What?" His eyes moved around as he reviewed the last several seconds. "'Sweetie?' I didn't mean anything by that. It's a term of endearment. For friends, you know. Like a sister."

Rolling her eyes, she said, "Good night, Ricky."

Years ago, there had been a short and regrettable few months when they were a couple. "Back when I'd been dumb," Ananke would tell people. She'd smartened up soon enough.

It had not been her idea to have him on the team, not that she'd had a say about that, but if she'd been asked, she would have told the Administrator, "No way." Ricky was a pretty damn good tracker—probably one of the best—but his interpersonal skills, particularly when it came to his dealings with women, left a ton to be desired.

She had to admit, though, in the less than a month that the team had been working together, he'd improved. Especially after the last job in Bradbury. At times he seemed contemplative, and there were moments of what she could only call unprompted kindness that she'd never seen in him before. She wasn't about to offer him a spare key to her room—that would *never* happen—but sometimes she wasn't completely repulsed by his presence. That was progress.

She heard the pool balls crashing together in the rec room as she headed down the stairs, and knew Ricky was getting in some practice in hopes that his next encounter with Liesel would go differently. Ananke doubted it would. Liesel had not even come close to missing one of her shots, and hadn't looked like she was even trying that hard.

Through the porthole window in her room, Ananke looked across the bay at San Francisco, twinkling against the skyline. Maybe tomorrow night they *would* all go into the city. Ricky wasn't the only one who would enjoy a night on the town.

She pulled the curtain, turned off the overhead light, and turned on the little reading light next to her bed. She was in the middle of *Lust for Life*, the Van Gogh biography by Irving Stone, and thought she could knock out another chapter or two before sleeping.

Her estimate turned out to be too ambitious. Only a couple of pages in, she fell asleep with the book on her chest and the light still on.

ANANKE DREAMED OF her uncle.

Which was weird, because she hadn't seen him in years, and hadn't thought about him in almost as long. It was the Van Gogh book's fault. Her uncle was a painter, abstracts mostly, things she never seemed to understand. In her dream, he was painting *Starry Night*, but the canvas was gigantic and the colors were all…not wrong, just different. A greenish swirling sky over hills of black and red. And the moon and the stars, silver. Bright silver. So bright she had to put her hand in front of her eyes so that she wouldn't go blind.

"Turn it down," she told him. "I can't see anything."

"You can see it," he said. "Just look."

"It's too bright."

The ground around her rolled gently, as if that was exactly what it was supposed to do.

"It's too bright," she repeated, moving her hand again.

A sting of pain.

Ananke's eyes blinked open. She'd apparently been moving her hand in the real world as well, and had knocked into the hot reading lamp that was still on.

She winced and rubbed her hand. This caused the book to slide off her chest onto the floor.

"Dammit."

As she grabbed for it, she nearly tumbled out of bed. Not because she was clumsy, but because the ship was moving.

She got on her knees and pulled the drapes away from the porthole.

San Francisco had been replaced by an endless expanse of

ocean under a partly cloudy night sky. No lights anywhere.

She checked the time—2:17 a.m. Plenty of time had passed for the *Karas Evonus* to sail out of the bay. And given that her berth was on the starboard side with no land in sight, they were either heading west toward the heart of the Pacific, or south along the California coast.

She pulled on her sweats and shoes and hurried out of her quarters. The common area outside her room was lit by only a handful of floor-level lights and was unoccupied. She headed up the stairs, through the rec room and dining area, and onto the midship deck where she and Rosario had been chilling out earlier.

A good five miles off the port side were the looming shadows of the coast, dotted here and there by the lights of small towns.

"And here I was beginning to wonder if I was the only one who noticed."

Ananke whirled around to find Dylan stretched out on one of the lounges.

"How long have you been out here?" she asked.

He shrugged. "Forty-five minutes. Maybe an hour."

"And you didn't think to wake me?"

"Oh, I thought about it. But what difference would it have made? It's not like you would get anyone to turn this thing around."

"Dylan!" He was right, but that wasn't the point.

"Sorry, boss. Next time I will. Promise."

She looked back at the coast. "Any idea where we are?"

"Somewhere off the coast of California."

"Thanks, Magellan. Pretty much figured that part out for myself."

"Ah. Well, then, specifically? How should I know? This is your country, not mine."

She walked to the port railing and searched the landmass for a hint of their location, but there wasn't much to see beyond the silhouette of mountains.

"Ananke," Dylan said.

When she glanced over her shoulder, he pointed toward

the *Karas Evonus*'s bow.

For a few moments, she couldn't figure out what he wanted her to see. Then she realized one of the stars was moving. She walked back toward the center of the deck, her eyes on the growing light.

Because the wind was blowing toward land, she couldn't hear anything until the light was less than a quarter mile away. The sound was intermittent at first, there for a moment and then gone the next, but soon the *whoop-whoop-whoop* of helicopter blades were too loud to drown out.

"Visitors?" Dylan asked.

"You got me."

They watched the aircraft approach and slowly fly over their heads. The ship's superstructure blocked the helipad at the stern from view, but that was obviously the aircraft's destination.

The lights in the rec room suddenly came on, followed by the loud but not unpleasant tone over the intercom that preceded announcements.

"My apologies for waking you," the Administrator said over the speaker. "Please gather in the conference room in ten minutes."

The tone sounded again, signaling the end of the announcement.

"I guess the holiday's over," Dylan said.

"So it would seem."

ANANKE AND DYLAN reached the conference room first. A few minutes later, Rosario shuffled in, looking half awake and not happy about it. Liesel came next, dressed and appearing ready for anything. Ricky, naturally, was last, rolling in with less than a minute to spare, wearing gym shorts and a Beastie Boys T-shirt and holding a steaming cup of coffee.

When he noticed the others staring enviously at his mug, he nodded back toward the door. "Back off, vultures. I made a whole pot."

"Which you conveniently left downstairs," Dylan said.

"You're welcome. For the coffee *and* the exercise you'll

get grabbing a cup."

The monitor on the wall at the end of the table flickered on, revealing the Administrator.

"Good morning, team," he said.

"Barely morning," Rosario said.

"My apologies for that. As you may have surmised, I have a new mission for you."

"It's in Hawaii, right?" Ricky said. "Please say it's in Hawaii."

"I'm sorry, Mr. Orbits. The mission, as far as I know, has no connection to Hawaii."

"Well, you're just the bearer of good news, aren't you? How about you see if you can round us up a job that does?" Ricky smiled and looked around, as if expecting the others to voice their support, but Ananke was the only one looking his way, and that was to silently tell him to shut up.

"I'll keep that in mind," the Administrator said.

He glanced at something below screen level, and his image was replaced by a still photograph of a fiftysomething man, with wavy, shoulder-length, salt-and-pepper hair. It was a candid shot, taken when the man was in mid-laugh. His skin tone gave him a Mediterranean vibe, but he could have been Brazilian or Argentinian. He was dressed in a suit but wore no tie, the top three buttons of his shirt undone, helping sell the air of easy confidence that clung to him.

"This is Julio Gutiérrez. He is your initial target."

"Initial?" Ananke asked.

"We believe that he will have information that will lead you to the actual focus of your mission."

"And that is?"

"You'll be given briefing packets once you're airborne."

"Airborne?" Ricky said. "Something about this ship I don't know about?"

"You have twenty minutes to pack. Your gear is already waiting in the helicopter. Liftoff is at 3:10 a.m."

"Helicopter?" Ricky said.

"Good hunting," the Administrator said, then the monitor clicked off.

THREE

UNLIKE THE MEETING, Ricky was the second to board the helicopter, beaten there only by Ananke. Since arriving on the *Karas Evonus*, Ananke had kept her bags ready, and only had to change into travel clothes before making her way to the helipad.

"Where do you think we're going?" Ricky asked. "Arizona? Texas? Ooh, I hope it's Texas. I could really go for some good barbecue."

"I have no idea."

"Come on, just guess. It'll be fun." His eyes lit up. "We should start a pool!"

"We're not doing a pool."

Dylan climbed into the cabin. "A pool for what?"

"For where we're going," Ricky said. "What do you think? Twenty bucks each?"

"We're *not* doing a pool," Ananke repeated.

Dylan glanced at Ananke, then said to Ricky, "Maybe we shouldn't."

"Should not what?" Rosario asked, sticking her head in.

"We're doing a pool on where we're going. Twenty bucks each."

Before Ananke could admonish him again, Rosario said, "What has been taken so far?"

"I'm taking Texas," Ricky said. "Go big or go home, right?"

"Oh, for God's sake," Ananke muttered.

"What about you?" Rosario asked Dylan.

Dylan glanced at Ananke again.

She waved a hand. "Go ahead."

Dylan smiled. "Well, I was thinking maybe it's Mexico."

The guess caught the others by surprise. So far their missions had been limited to locations in the US, specifically California, Nevada, and Washington State.

"That is not fair," Rosario said. "Mexico should be mine." Mexico was her home country.

"So what?" Dylan said. "Does that mean I can only pick Ireland? Because I'm positive we're not going there."

"I'm going to have to back Dylan on this one, Rosie," Ricky said.

She turned to him in full glare. After a moment, she said, "Fine. I will take Florida. Wait, Ananke, what did you take?"

"I'm not taking anything."

Ricky gave Ananke a back-me-on-this glance as he said, "Because she's the judge. If no one's right, then she decides which is closest."

"Aren't I lucky?" Ananke scoffed.

Liesel arrived two minutes later, and, after Ricky explained what they were doing, said, "I do not gamble."

"It's not *really* gambling," Ricky said. "It's just a little friendly game to pass the time."

"That will cost me twenty dollars if I lose."

"*If.* You've got a one-in-four chance. That's pretty good odds."

"So, it is not gambling, but I have pretty good odds?"

"Wait…hold on. You can't use my words against me that way."

From an overhead speaker a male voice said, "Good morning, ladies and gentlemen. We'll be lifting off in a moment. Please make sure you're strapped in."

The door to the passenger compartment slid shut.

"Okay, so it's just the three of us," Ricky said. "Texas, Florida, and Mexico. Sixty to the winner."

"Technically it is forty to the winner," Rosario said.

The rotors began turning.

Ricky said something, but his voice was lost in the whine that suddenly filled the cabin. When no one responded, he grabbed the headphones hanging above his seat and motioned for the others to do the same.

As much as Ananke would have preferred to listen to the engine, she pulled her set on.

"Last chance to get in on this," Ricky said, his gaze bouncing from Ananke to Liesel.

"I do not gamble," Liesel said.

"No, thanks," Ananke said.

The helicopter lifted into the air and raced southeast, toward the coast.

A light blinked on the panel separating the passenger area from the cockpit, then a flap opened between Dylan's and Rosario's seats and out slid a tray. On it were five manila envelopes.

Rosario got to them first, tossing envelopes to Ananke and Liesel, before handing one over to Dylan and sailing the fourth to Ricky.

The two men ripped the envelopes open and rifled through the handful of pages inside. At about the same moment Ricky's enthusiasm vanished, Dylan whooped in triumph.

"Pay up, my friends!" Dylan said.

"We're headed to Mexico?" Rosario said, still looking for the right page.

"No," Ananke said. "Panama."

"Whoever's closest wins," Dylan said, beaming.

"No one likes a gloater," Ricky said.

"Did you read this?" Liesel asked, pointing at one of the sheets. "'Through a series of shell companies, Julio Gutiérrez arranged for the purchase of one hundred and twenty-seven people from Devon Rally and his cousins Dalton Slater and Leonard Yates.'" She looked up. "They must have learned this from the info Tasha gathered."

The mission in Bradbury, Washington, had been a wild one, involving human trafficking, human *hunting*, and a missing woman—Tasha Patterson—who'd uncovered what was going on and inadvertently kicked off the team's involvement in the matter.

"Is that true?" Rosario asked.

Ananke looked at the brief. "It certainly looks like it."

"Well, I'll be damned," Ricky said. "So, what's the mission? Free these people?"

"Find them first," Ananke said, reading more. "Gutiérrez is just a middle man. We need to find out where he sent everyone."

Ricky shrugged. "We grab him, put him in a dark room, and beat the holy hell out of him until he talks. That seems reasonable, right?"

"Tell me," Ananke said. "If we did that, what happens if the people Gutiérrez was playing middle man for find out what we've done before we find them?"

"It was a joke. I swear."

"It says here that Gutiérrez leads a very active social life," Rosario said. "He's supposed to be attending an art gallery opening tomorrow night. Uh, I guess, actually tonight. And he's apparently throwing an after-party at someplace called Club De Gaf. Oh, and listen to this, 'Gutiérrez lives on a yacht called the *Angelina*, currently moored in Marina Flamenco.'"

Ananke flipped to the map. A marker denoted the marina. It was on Flamenco Island and was connected to the coast by a causeway from a section of the city called Amador.

"A guy like this, I'm betting his boat has an excellent security system," she said. "Rosario?"

"I will see what I can find out."

The rest of the information consisted of more background on Gutiérrez, a list of the missing people, identified not by name but a string of letters and numbers, with their gender and age and no other information.

"Ladies and gentlemen," the pilot said. "Just a heads-up that we will be landing in a few minutes. You will find the bags that were preloaded in the storage locker at the back end of the aircraft. Please make sure to grab these and take everything with you when you leave. Thank you for flying with us today."

Ananke looked out the window. They were over land now, and though the area directly below was dark, there was a circle of softly glowing lights ahead. The helicopter flew straight toward it, until it materialized as part of a single runway, private airport. The aircraft set down in the center of the landing strip.

The rotors remained turning as the team disembarked. Dylan, Liesel, and Ricky dealt with the gear bags, while Ananke walked over to the solitary man standing next to an extra-long golf cart.

"Good morning," the man said, extending his hand.

Ananke shook it. "Good morning." Names were not exchanged or expected.

As the others joined them, the man said, "If you all don't mind traveling with some of those bags on your laps, I should be able to take everyone in one trip."

Once the team was on board, the man drove them to the end of the runway, where a private jet waited.

"You all have a great flight," the man said.

Like with the helicopter, the jet's cockpit was closed off from the passenger cabin. Having flown in many similar planes, Ananke and Liesel retracted the staircase and shut the door before joining the others, who had already strapped into their seats.

"Hello from the cockpit," a female voice said. "If one of you will punch the call button on the panel between the seats to let us know you're ready, we'll get this baby into the air."

Ananke pushed the button.

"Fantastic," the woman said. "There's a galley in back if you get hungry. Flight time is just under seven hours."

The engines whirled to life.

"What is it with these middle of the night, happy pilots?" Rosario asked.

If anyone had an answer for that, it was lost in the roar of the jet as they sped down the runway.

A FEW MINUTES before one p.m., the plane touched down at Tocumen International Airport in the eastern part of Panama City. When the plane stopped near the small aircraft terminal, a car bearing a Panamanian official drove out to meet them.

"*Bienvenido a Panamá,*" the man said as Ananke descended to the tarmac.

"*Gracias.*"

"*Su pasaporte, por favor.*"

Ananke handed him an American passport in the name of Pauline Suarez.

The official made a show of studying the info page and comparing the photo to Ananke, then smiled and stamped the appropriate page. "*Gracias,*" he said, handing the booklet back. He looked at Rosario, who had deplaned after Ananke. "*Su pasaporte, por favor.*"

After everyone was processed, the official said, "*Que disfrute su estancia,*" then climbed back into his sedan and drove off. As the Administrator's brief promised, there had been no mention of checking their luggage.

While the team unloaded the gear, a dark gray Range Rover and an older Ford sedan arrived. The driver of the SUV exited his vehicle and walked to the sedan. As soon as he climbed in, the Ford drove off.

"Look it over," Ananke said to Dylan and Rosario.

They headed over to the Range Rover. While Dylan opened the driver's door and poked his head inside, Rosario attached a small device to her phone to detect any tracking bugs on the vehicle. They weren't expecting any trouble yet, but it was always best to be sure.

As Dylan and Rosario carried out their inspection, Ananke and the others loaded their bags into the back of the vehicle. Ananke then walked to the front of the vehicle, where Dylan had popped the hood and was looking at the engine.

"So?" she asked.

"Everything looks good." He shut the hood. "Engine's in great shape. Full tank of gas and fully functional GPS."

"Good. Rosario, how we looking?"

"It appears to be clean. I will spot-check it as we drive." Though rare, some bugs were designed to go dark during a scan.

"All right, everybody inside," Ananke said.

"Shotgun!" Ricky called.

Ananke stared him down as he tried to open the front passenger door. With an annoyed grunt, he backed away. "Fine. But I get a window seat."

"You will sit in the middle," Liesel said. She opened the back door and stood to the side so he could get in. Rosario was already sitting by the door on the other side.

"Come on," Ricky said. "I'm bigger than both of you."

"Get in the car," Ananke told him as she climbed into the front passenger seat.

"This really isn't fair," he said, but he ducked inside and scooted to the middle.

"If it makes you feel better, you can all take turns, okay?" Ananke said.

"A little better, I guess."

Dylan drove them into the city to the Sheraton Grande, where they would be staying. It was only five blocks from the art gallery Gutiérrez was due to visit that evening.

They each took a quick shower and reconvened in the living room at 2:20 p.m.

"We have just under six hours until the gallery opening," Ananke said. "So, we're going to have to divvy up assignments. Dylan, you'll check out Gutiérrez's yacht."

"Cool."

"See if you can also find an alternate means for getting out of there that doesn't involve driving down the causeway," she said. The road was a potential bottleneck, and if they ended up going in that direction, she didn't want to get trapped on it.

"You mean you want me to find a boat."

"You catch on fast." She looked over at Ricky and Liesel.

"I want you two to check out the art gallery. Get me lots of pictures. When you've finished, do the same with that club where they're having the after-party."

"Got it," Liesel said.

"Okay. Let's get moving."

"Wait," Ricky said. "What are you and Rosario doing?"

"We're going shopping."

FOUR

HENRIETTA WAS SURPRISED her hands were shaking. She glanced at the paper for the hundredth time, rereading the address she'd already memorized. The pencil scratches comforted her, helped ease her anxiety, like the rosary her grandmother used to clutch whenever she felt anxious.

Henrietta was close.

So close.

Her sister, Gloria, had come to Villahermosa to work and, when she could, send money home. Henrietta, as the oldest, should have been the one to go, but she was better suited to taking care of their mother and their brother, Alfonso, who was only fifteen. Gloria was the adventurous one. The one who relished trying new things.

She would call every Sunday, telling them of life in the big city and how well things were going. Then suddenly the calls stopped.

The first couple of missed Sundays, the family wrote off as Gloria being busy. The next, they were more annoyed at her silence than concerned, thinking she had probably met a boy who was monopolizing her time. After a fifth Sunday with no contact, they could no longer fool themselves into believing nothing was wrong. At their mother's urging, Henrietta and Alfonso had come to Villahermosa to make sure Gloria was all right.

The day they arrived, they learned the business where Gloria worked had closed several months earlier. They spent the next week searching for anyone who knew Gloria, talking to whomever they could, and showing her picture whenever someone would listen.

But day after day, they heard "I don't recognize her," "doesn't look familiar," "I may have seen her but that was months ago," and "If she wanted you to find her, she would have told you where she was."

Finally, when it seemed all was lost, Alfonso had found a woman who said she'd known Gloria fairly well. According to the woman, Gloria had looked for work after she lost her job but kept getting turned down. Her luck changed when she answered an ad in the paper and was offered a position at a resort.

No, the woman didn't know the name of the resort. And no, she couldn't remember in which paper the ad had appeared.

She assumed Gloria was at the resort now, having a wonderful time and making good money.

Had she heard from Gloria since she left?

Well, no, but she hadn't expected to. They were casual friends, not writing friends.

When pressed further, Alfonso got her to narrow down the time frame of Gloria's interview to six or seven weeks earlier—right around the time the Sunday calls had stopped.

Henrietta and Alfonso had spent another couple of weeks tracking down newspapers published in that date range. It was Henrietta who'd discovered the ad. But when she called the number, she'd received a message saying the line had been disconnected, increasing a thousandfold her sense that her sister was in trouble.

With no other leads, Henrietta and her brother went to the newspaper office and spoke to the person in charge of ads. The overweight, sweaty man listened for only a few moments before stopping them with a wave of his hand. "I'm a very busy man. Unless you want to buy an ad, you're wasting my time."

He ushered them out of his office, ignoring their protests, and closed and locked his door.

One of the other employees in the department took pity on them and listened to what Henrietta had to say. The man said,

"Let me see what I can find out. Give me your number and I'll call you when I know something."

Though Henrietta had a phone, it had long ago run out of minutes, and she didn't want to use their meager funds to buy more because once the pesos were gone, that was it. Thankfully the man agreed to meet with her the next day.

The next twenty-four hours seemed to last forever. As much as Henrietta tried to remain positive, the thought that the man would uncover nothing kept running through her head. She forced herself to smile for Alfonso's sake, saying things like, "By this time tomorrow, we'll know where she is" or "I have a good feeling about this."

She slept very little that night, and despite the fact they weren't due to return to the newspaper office until after lunch, she was up and ready to go before the sun rose.

When the time finally came, she had Alfonso wait outside the building. If it was bad news, she wanted to process the information first so she could be strong for him. She approached the ad sales counter and asked for the nice man by name.

"Ah, you're back," he said.

"Yes. Were you able to find anything?"

He scanned the sales room before handing her a piece of paper. "Look at it later."

"What's on it?" she asked as she put it in her pocket.

"The address where the interviews were held."

"This is the company's office?" she asked, hardly believing it.

But his grimace told her that her excitement was premature. "We see this address a lot. I believe it's a place that rents temporary space."

"Temporary?"

"Yes, like for a company from out of town here to do some recruiting."

"Oh." That made sense. If Gloria had interviewed with a resort company, there would be no reason for them to have a permanent office here. "Do you know the company's name?"

"I'm not sure it will be much help, either. The only thing

we have on record is TAS. I don't know if that's a person's initials or the name of a company. I'm sorry. That's all I could find. I should get back to work."

"Thank you. Thank you so much."

She hurried out and collected Alfonso, then headed to the address, telling him along the way what she had learned.

Despite the newspaper man's attempt to manage her expectations, the closer they got, the more Henrietta's anticipation grew. Perhaps the company wasn't there anymore, but surely someone would be around who knew about it.

She wanted Alfonso to wait outside again, but he wouldn't have it this time. He accompanied her into the office of the company that managed the building.

She asked the receptionist if she could speak to someone about a recent tenant.

"Which tenant would that be?" the woman asked.

"I think they might go by the letters TAS."

While the woman tried to hide it, there was no missing the cloud that had flitted through her eyes. "Please, have a seat."

As Henrietta and Alfonso stepped away from the counter, the woman made a phone call. Less than a minute later, a middle-aged man with a friendly face entered. The receptionist pointed at Henrietta and her brother, and the man walked over.

"I understand you have questions?"

"Yes," Henrietta said. "About one of your former tenants, TAS. I was wondering—"

"They no longer have an office here."

"I realize that. I'm—"

"What do you know about them?"

"Nothing. That's why we came here. I'm trying to locate them."

The man frowned. "You and me both."

"They offered my sister a job and we haven't heard from her since."

The man looked suddenly uncomfortable.

"Please, sir. We're just trying to find her and make sure she's all right."

He stared past her a moment before looking at her again. "I'm sorry," he said, his tone warmer. "I really don't have any information."

"Not even an address for their main office?"

"The address they gave us was false. I'm not sure they even have a home office."

"But…you must know something."

"I know they were supposed to be here for six months, but only paid me for a month before they disappeared."

"Disappeared?"

"I came in one morning and they were gone. No warning. No explanation. And no money for the rest of their lease."

Henrietta blinked. "What…what about a phone number?"

"Disconnected."

Tears gathered in her eyes. This couldn't be a dead end. It just couldn't be.

The man seemed to consider something. "Wait here."

He was gone for nearly five minutes. When he returned, he handed her a slip of paper. "Here."

Written on one side was a phone number. "I thought you said their number was disconnected."

"It's not theirs."

Her brow scrunched together. Instead of elaborating, the man mumbled a goodbye and walked back into the bowels of the building.

Henrietta contemplated going after him, but she was sure he would say nothing more. "Come on," she said to Alfonso and headed outside.

"I don't understand," Alfonso said once they'd left the office. "Whose phone number is that?"

She glanced at the paper. "I don't know."

"Are you going to call it?"

The area code was 55—Mexico City. Calling it would cost them some of their precious cash. But that didn't matter if it got them closer to finding their sister.

They located a pay phone in the lobby of a hotel. Henrietta laid out several coins on the shelf under the phone, not sure how much the call would cost. She dropped a coin in the slot and tapped in the number. A prerecorded voice told her how much more she needed to pay, and she inserted the necessary amount.

Given their recent string of luck, she wouldn't have been surprised to find it was disconnected, but the line rang.

"Hello?" The voice was male and impatient.

"Hi, um…"

"Who is this?"

"I, uh, I was given your number, by a man in a, um, rental office."

"Rental—" He went quiet for a beat. When he spoke again, his tone switched from impatience to intense interest. "In what city?"

"Villahermosa."

Another beat. "TAS?"

Henrietta's breath caught in her throat. "Yes. TAS. Are you with TAS? Can you help me?"

"No, I'm not with TAS."

"Oh," she said, disappointed.

"Why are you interested in them?"

"They-they gave my sister a job, and since then we don't know what happened to her. We're trying to find her. Please, if you know something—"

"'We?'"

"My brother and I."

This time the silence lasted so long, Henrietta was worried the connection had been lost.

"They took people from me also," the man said. "Are you in Villahermosa now?"

"Yes."

"You need to come to Mexico City right away."

Two tickets to Mexico City would use up nearly half of what they had left, but she didn't give it a second thought. "We will be on the next bus."

FIVE

THE MAN WHO had been on the phone was named Ramon Silva. Henrietta called him again when she and Alfonso reached Mexico City. He gave them an address and told them to take a taxi.

"It's okay," Henrietta said. "We will just use the city bus."

"That will take hours and you're likely to get lost. Take the taxi."

"I, um…"

"What is it?"

She didn't want to tell him about their lack of funds, for fear he wouldn't be interested in helping someone of their status.

"We will be there as soon as we can," she said, and hung up.

She asked around about which route to take. A bus driver explained they would have to take four different buses to get there. He wrote the routes on a piece of paper and pointed them in the direction of the bus stop where they could grab their first ride.

Silva's warning that the trip would take hours was dead on. By the time they exited their last bus, they had been in the capital city for nearly four hours, and the sun had been down for nearly half of that.

They got lost twice before they reached the door with the correct address beside it. The neighborhood was much nicer than the one Henrietta and her siblings were from. Not super-rich nice, or even very rich. She'd seen those kinds of neighborhoods on TV. This was a comfortable neighborhood, one of steady jobs and good meals and potential.

She pressed the buzzer.

Hearing footsteps approaching from inside, she grabbed Alfonso's hand. He wasn't always great with affection these days, but he made no move to let go.

The door pulled inward, revealing an average-sized man with gray-flecked black hair.

"Henrietta?" he asked.

She smiled. "Yes."

"I'm Ramon. And this is your brother?"

"Alfonso," she said.

"Pleased to meet both of you." Ramon stepped to the side. "Come in, come in."

As they entered, Henrietta realized she needed to up her assessment of Silva's standing. Even from the entry hall, she could see it was a beautiful, well-decorated home.

"I was beginning to wonder if you were ever going to make it," Ramon said, closing the door. "Did you have any problems?"

"No, sir. It was just a long trip."

He looked them over, making Henrietta extremely conscious of their plain, well-worn clothes and dusty shoes.

"You both must be hungry."

Alfonso didn't even try to hide his feelings. "We haven't had anything to eat since breakfast."

Henrietta wanted to poke him for saying that, but Ramon didn't seem to mind.

"Then we should do something about that," he said.

He led them into a kitchen four times larger than theirs back home, and pulled several items out of a refrigerator. Within ten minutes he had heated up some rice and chicken and sliced some fresh tomatoes.

"Something to drink?"

Alfonso opted for a Coke, while Henrietta was content with a bottle of water.

"Let's take those plates into the other room," Ramon said.

Henrietta expected Ramon to guide them into a dining room, but he led them into a living room where, to her great surprise, fourteen other people were sitting, on the sofa and

48

chairs.

"Everyone, this is Henrietta and Alfonso," Ramon said. "Maybe we could make some room for them."

A couple sitting on either side of an end table stood and moved across the room. Henrietta and Alfonso hesitated.

"It's okay," Ramon said. "No one's going to bite you."

Alfonso headed over to the chairs, but Henrietta didn't move.

"What's going on here?" she asked.

"Have a seat and I'll explain everything," Ramon said.

Henrietta reluctantly followed her brother. Once she was seated, Ramon lowered himself onto a wooden chair.

"Let me introduce you to everyone," Ramon said. He motioned to the couple who had given up their seats. "This is Raul and Sonya Jimenez. Raul's brother has been missing for seven months."

Henrietta stared at the couple.

Ramon gestured at a woman on his left. "This is Lena Ochoa. Her daughter has been missing for five months." He moved on to the two young men on the other side of her. "Jesús and Pablo Martinez. Their mother has been gone for over a year."

The introductions continued. Most were relatives of the missing, though a few were friends. Lastly, Ramon pointed at himself. "And my daughter and her husband disappeared ten months ago."

Henrietta looked around the room. "They were…they were all taken by TAS?"

"The TAS name has only been used for the last several months," Ramon said. "When my daughter and her husband met with them, they were known as Vista Opportunities. But it is the same thing."

"How do you know that?"

"I didn't at first. But I eventually figured it out as I started to find others with similar stories. When I learned they were going by TAS, I began searching for where they were conducting interviews. Any time I heard they were in a city, I would go there, but so far they've been gone by the time I arrive."

"So, you leave your number in case others come looking?"

"If there is someone I can leave it with, yes. Several of our...members have come to us that way. Like you."

"Do you...do you know where they have been taken?"

"Not yet. But the more of us who work on this, the closer we are getting. Tell us, how long has it been since your sister disappeared?"

"Almost two months."

"Not so long, then."

Henrietta's eyes narrowed. "No! *Too* long."

"I didn't mean anything negative by it, just that your sister's lucky you're already looking. Many of us didn't realize something was wrong until much later."

"I don't understand," Alfonso said. "Why is everyone here tonight? Were you having a meeting?"

Several people smiled.

"No," Ramon said. "When they heard you had contacted me, those who were close enough came to meet you."

"To let you know that you are not alone," Lena Ochoa said.

"Those who were close enough?" Henrietta said. "There are more of you?"

"Those here represent only a quarter of the missing we've found out about so far," Ramon said.

"A quarter? Have you gone to the police?"

A man across the room—Jesús or Pablo—said, "Have you?"

Henrietta grimaced. "They wouldn't listen to me."

"They wouldn't listen to any of us, either," the other brother said.

"But with all of us together, surely they'll listen."

Ramon smiled sympathetically. "How much money do you have in your pocket right now?"

"Why?"

"Please. How much?"

"I'm not telling you that."

"Would it be a fair guess to say that if you had taken a taxi like I told you to, you would have almost nothing left?"

Henrietta didn't reply.

"I'm sorry I suggested that. I forget sometimes…"

"What Ramon is trying to say," Lena said, "is that most of us are more like you than him and have very little. The police don't listen to people like us."

For the first time, Henrietta realized that, while everyone was neatly dressed, their outfits were mostly old and worn, like her dress. Ramon was the only exception, but his finer garments were subdued in color and style.

"What about the media?" Henrietta asked. "With so many of us, they would listen and could make something happen."

There was an uncomfortable silence.

"What?" she asked.

Ramon said, "We thought about that, so much so that we almost did it."

"What stopped you?"

"What if the kidnappers saw the report?" a woman named Juanita Prieto asked. "Would they just return everyone? Or might they do something…worse…so that they're never found."

Henrietta hadn't considered that.

She looked at Ramon. "So, you don't have any idea where they've been taken? Or-or if they're even still alive?"

"They're alive," Sonya Jimenez said. "Don't ever think they are not."

"But how can you know?"

"Because I do."

Ramon walked over to the wall where a piece of cardboard, two meters high by twice that long, was leaning. He carried it over and turned it so that Henrietta could see the side that had been hidden.

The left half was dominated by a map of Mexico, dotted with red stickers, each with a different number written on it. Below the map was a numbered list of names. On the right side was another map, this one showing the entire western hemisphere. It had more numbered stickers, some yellow and some blue. Since there was no room below the map, running beside it was another list. This was not of people's names, however. Some of the numbered items were one or two words long. Henrietta recognized a few names of places, but many of the phrases meant nothing to her. Other items had longer descriptions next to them, some written too small for her to read. A few were simply a string of numbers.

Ramon had one of the Martinez brothers hold the display, and retrieved a couple of items from a side table's drawer.

"Raise it higher, please," he said.

The man lifted the cardboard until the bottom was about waist high.

Ramon stepped up to the list of people and added the number 42 to the end with a black marker. He looked back at Henrietta and Alfonso.

"Your sister's name is…?"

"Gloria. Gloria Ortega."

He wrote GLORIA ORTEGA next to the number. He then put a red sticker on the map beside Villahermosa and wrote 42 on it.

Henrietta's mouth had gone dry, but her eyes most definitely had not, as a tear ran down her cheek.

"What's the other map for?" Alfonso asked.

Henrietta wiped her face, grateful for the intrusion of her brother's question.

Ramon stepped over to the right side of the display. "These represent clues we've uncovered. The yellow dots are places that we think might have some promise. The blue are ones we are less sure about."

"Let's be clear," Lena said. "We aren't *sure* about any of them."

"True," Ramon said. He motioned to the map. "Could be none of this means anything. But it's all we have right now."

"How did you come up with this?" Henrietta asked, her voice raspy.

"Piecing together little things each of us knew. Talking to people who were in the area where interviews took place. A few of us have even visited some of the locations."

"Thanks to Ramon," Sonya Jimenez said. "If it wasn't for

him, we couldn't do any of this."

Ramon looked embarrassed. "We all help how we can."

"Do you think you're getting close?" Henrietta asked.

Ramon shrugged. "There is no way to know."

"Tell them about the plan," the Martinez brother not holding the cardboard said. "She could help."

"Yes," Juanita said. "She could do it."

The others chimed in enthusiastically.

"Help with what?" Henrietta asked.

After Silva got the others to quiet down, he said, "We have an idea about how to find out exactly where our loved ones have been taken. But unless you both want to officially join with us, I think it would be better if you didn't know the details."

"I want to join," Alfonso said. He looked at Henrietta. "We both do, don't we?"

"Um…" she said.

Everyone in the room was looking at her.

It wasn't that she didn't want to join them. She was just so overwhelmed by everything that she didn't know how to respond.

"Henrietta," Alfonso said. "Tell them." He put his hand on her arm. "Tell them you want to join."

His words snapped her out of her daze. She swallowed hard and nodded. "If it will help find Gloria, I'll do anything to help."

Six

The Present

THE HOUSE OF Cali by Marianna Ramirez was what one online review called, "Only the best of the best." Another said, "When I die, I want to be buried in one of Marianna's creations." A third was not quite as kind: "Needlessly expensive, overly trendy garbage."

Ananke and Rosario walked into the shop, with the attitude of two women who were used to spending money in places such as this.

A twentysomething woman who had been straightening a dress on a stand walked over. "Can I help you?"

"I doubt it," Rosario replied. Ananke had asked her to take the lead. "We are looking for something…" She touched one of the garments. "Better than this."

A middle-aged woman farther back in the store perked up and headed over.

"Good afternoon, ladies," she said. "I am Marianna Ramirez. What exactly is it you are looking for?"

Neither Ananke nor Rosario indicated they'd made the connection that she was the designer and presumably owner of House of Cali.

Rosario considered her for a moment. "We have some parties we will be attending and are looking for…something interesting. But I don't see anything here like that."

"Of course not. We don't put *everything* out. Our best items are saved for special customers. What type of parties are we talking about?"

Rosario sneered. "The fun kind."

"Of course. I'm sure I have just what you're looking for. May I show you?"

Rosario shared a look with Ananke, who gave it a moment before nodding. Rosario smiled weakly and said to the designer, "Please do."

That was how they ended up on an antique couch in the private showroom at the back of the store, sipping sparkling water.

A set of five lights faded up, illuminating the space in front of the couch. Marianna returned from whatever room she'd disappeared into.

"My apologies for making you wait. I wanted to make sure I picked out only things you'd be interested in."

"Can we get this started, please? We have other things to do."

"Of course."

The woman pushed the remote she was holding. A moment later, two women sauntered into the room and walked into the pool of light. The first wore a red, skintight dress, with a plunging back and an asymmetrical hemline. The other was in a white dress with a high neck and oval cutout that started at the top of her rib cage, ran between her breasts, and ended just above her belly button. Its hemline was also uneven, but shorter than the red one. To complete the outfit, this model had on a pair of dark brown, lace-up, knee-high boots.

Marianna described the fit and feel and talked up how stunning it would make them look.

"Better," Rosario said, "but…"

"Oh, this isn't all. May I?"

Rosario nodded for the show to continue.

DYLAN DROVE THE Range Rover out to Flamenco Island and parked behind a small row of stores just west of Battery Newton, part of the old Fort Amador that had been built to protect the Panama Canal. From there, he walked along the main road, past the hill the battery was on, and over to Marina Flamenco, where Gutiérrez's yacht was berthed.

After picking up an ice cream at a small convenience

store, he strolled along the edge of the marina, blending in with the few dozen others who were taking in the sea and the boats and the beautiful day. Many were shooting pictures, so when he stopped here and there to snap his own, no one took notice.

He didn't know exactly where the *Angelina* was docked, but the Administrator's brief had contained a picture of a similar vessel made by the same company. It was large and sleek, shouldn't be hard to pick out.

He scanned the marina. Out of the nearly one hundred boats, only a handful were even close to the size he was looking for. He zoomed in on those he had a good angle on, checking the names on the hulls, but came up empty.

He walked on. When he was about three quarters of the way around the marina, he finally spotted it.

"Damn," he said under his breath, instantly in love.

Sixty meters long, with a dark blue hull and alternating white and blue upper levels, the *Angelina* sat on the surface like a tiger ready to pounce. All Dylan could think about was how cool it would be to get her on the open water and see what she could do.

The ship was tied to a spur dock, sticking out from the pier at the east end of the marina. The pier ran parallel to the rock-and-sand seawall that closed off the marina from the ocean, about six meters of water separating them. All the spurs protruded from the opposite side of the pier, but there was one very interesting item on the seawall side—a bridge connecting the two.

He increased the magnification on his phone and swept the deck of the *Angelina*. He could see some movement through the windows on the lowest visible level, but there wasn't enough light inside the boat to make out more than a few dim shapes. No one was on the decks at the moment.

He took another few minutes to familiarize himself with the area before heading back to his car to take care of his second task.

RICKY AND LIESEL decided to split their assignment. She would take the art gallery, while he checked out the nightclub where the after-party would take place.

In Ricky's opinion, nothing was sadder than a nightclub in daylight. A, it was closed, which he would have considered a crime when he was a few years younger. And B, the sunlight exposed all the tacky design elements that looked cool at night.

Club De Gaf was a sterling example of this. Set off a busy street, it lived in a standalone building covered in black paint that had been sprayed with other colors that Ricky bet glowed in the dark.

Sadder still were the shallow pools of water surrounding the walkway to the main entrance. At the moment, their fountains lay still, but given the abundance of spouts, Ricky guessed they provided some sort of cheesy synchronized water show.

He counted four cameras at the front—two focused on the double-door entrance, two aimed at the walkway between the shallow pools—and three more along the side of the building where a small parking area was located.

Ricky took several pictures then circled the block, looking for a back way to the building. He found an alley, snapped a few more shots, and continued around until he reached the office building directly behind the club. On the ground floor was a beauty shop, with a sign in the window saying the store would reopen in thirty minutes. Ricky wasn't interested in the shop but the glass door next to it. It led into a darkened hallway that looked like it went to the back of the building.

The door was unlocked. He entered and took the stairs up to the roof. From the back of the building he had a perfect bird's-eye view of Club De Gaf.

Another pair of cameras was mounted on the back of the building, one pointing down at the rear doorway, and the other set for a wider shot. He took pictures of the alley and the club, then zoomed in and took a close-up shot of the camera. The angle was wrong to pick up the brand, but he had no doubt Rosario would be able to identify it just by looking at it.

He texted Liesel.

Done here. You?

Her reply came fifteen seconds later.

Not yet.

He checked the map. The art gallery was a ten-minute walk away. He sent another text.

Heading to you.

THE DIEGO CAMPOS Gallery was located a few blocks from the hotel, between a high-end men's shop and a *carnicería*. A neighborhood in transition apparently, though it looked to Liesel like the butcher was doing a fine business and wouldn't be leaving anytime soon. The building the gallery was located in backed up to the building on the next street over, so there didn't appear to be a rear entrance.

All that information was well and good, but what Liesel really needed to do was get a peek inside. Unfortunately, the gallery's windows were covered by white paper.

She texted Ananke, explaining the situation. Ananke had laid out her plan only in the most general terms, so Liesel wasn't sure if she should avoid being seen by anyone at the gallery or play it a bit looser. Ananke gave her permission for a more direct approach, giving Liesel a backstory to use.

Liesel did some research on her phone before walking up to the gallery door. As she suspected, it was locked. She knocked on the glass.

Inside, someone shouted, *"Ya cerramos!"* The store was closed.

Liesel knocked again, rapid and insistent.

This got a set of footsteps moving in her direction. The person fumbled with the paper covering the glass, then gave up and opened the door several inches. The face that looked out belonged to a stressed-out woman in her twenties.

"Ya cerramos," she repeated.

"I'm looking for Carla Nunez," Liesel said in English, asking for the gallery's manager. Though she did speak Spanish, it would be to her advantage if the gallery people didn't know.

58

"Ah, um…*un momento*."

The woman disappeared, shutting the door. Several moments passed before steps returned. Again the door opened, but wider than before, revealing a woman a good twenty years older than the first one, and considerably more put together.

"May I help you?" she said in lightly accented English.

"Carla Nunez?"

"Yes."

"My name is Sandra Li," Liesel said. "I'm head of security for Claus Schneider." She paused before adding, as if it should have been obvious, "Of Schneider-Ferber Chemicals."

The woman blinked. There was little chance someone in her capacity would not know who Claus Schneider was. The notorious German playboy had recently inherited his family's company after his father had passed away from a heart attack, meaning he was now a notorious, even richer German playboy. Because of his new position, his social life had dimmed somewhat, and his name was making fewer and fewer appearances in the tabloids.

"Of course," Nunez said. "How may I help you, *Señorita* Li?"

"*Herr* Schneider will be arriving in Panama City in a couple hours and has expressed interest in attending your opening this evening." Liesel glanced past the woman. "It *is* still happening tonight, correct?"

The woman could barely contain her excitement. "It most definitely is. We would be honored for *Señor* Schneider to join us."

Liesel had had plenty of experience doing this kind of thing for her late boss, Hans Wolf, and knew exactly how to push the right buttons. "Of course you would. But before *Herr* Schneider can even decide if he will come, I need to do a security check of the premises and give him my okay."

"What? Oh. Oh, yes." Nunez opened the door wider. "Please, come in."

The gallery was about three times as long as it was wide, with free-floating walls scattered throughout, breaking up the space. Pictures hung on these and the walls running down both sides of the room. While much of the artwork was already in place, several paintings were still leaning against the wall, needing to be hung.

At the front and back were long wooden tables draped with colorful cloths. Sitting on and around the tables were boxes of beer and wine, waiting to be unpacked. Liesel assumed food would be provided, too.

"We are just putting up the final touches," Nunez said. "So please excuse the mess."

Liesel nodded. "Is this the only room?"

"Uh, no. There are two toilets in the back, and a storage area. And my office, of course."

"I'll need to see those."

The gallery owner smiled. "Follow me."

As they headed toward the back, Liesel scanned the space, taking in not only the pictures but the help putting them up. There were ten people total, mostly college-aged kids. The paintings looked to be a blend of the fantastical and the real— a mundane city street featuring an open doorway to a magical world, a farmer working a field while something unearthly hovered above him, a normal-looking little girl walking her...Liesel wasn't sure what the animal was, only that it wasn't real. According to the info cards mounted on the wall next to the canvases, the artist was Miguel Miguel, from Argentina. Liesel had been to plenty of art openings, and had seen enough to know Miguel Miguel's work was the real deal, even if his name was not.

They passed through a doorless opening at the back into a corridor about five meters long. On the right were two doors, with symbols indicating they were men's and women's toilets. The opposite wall had a single door, half a meter before the end.

Nunez started toward the solo door but Liesel said, "One moment, please."

She entered the women's bathroom and took a look around. There wasn't anything of interest, but it was important to keep up the appearance of her lie.

When she exited, she walked over to the men's bathroom,

knocked, and said in English, "I'm coming in." The room was deserted and she stepped back into the corridor. "Please continue."

The door on the left wall opened to another corridor. It, too, had three doors, but in opposite order—two on the left and one on the right. The last one confused Liesel. As far as she knew, the wall it was mounted in was the back of the building and should have been pressed up against the building behind it. Did it lead straight into the other structure?

"This is my office," Nunez said, opening the first door on the left.

The room was about three meters square, just enough room for a desk, a filing cabinet, and two bookcases shoved against the wall. Though everything was nice and tidy, it had the feel that if just one more item was added, the place would explode in a shower of papers and splintered wood.

"Will this be unlocked during tonight's event?" Liesel asked.

"No. It is always locked unless I am inside."

"It wasn't locked right now."

Nunez smiled, conceding the point. "We are not open for business yet. Plus, when we are setting up an exhibit, there is always a lot of in and out. It will be closed tonight, I promise."

Liesel didn't really care if it was or not, but again, appearances. "How many people have keys?"

"Two at the moment, three tonight."

Liesel raised an eyebrow.

"My assistant, Gisele—she's the one who answered when you knocked—and I always have a key. During events, I give one to my security guard, Geraldo."

"You have worked with him before?"

"For years."

Liesel nodded, as if the woman's assurance satisfied her. If this had been a real security scout, it would not have, and Liesel would have done a background check on the man. "We can move on."

They reentered the hall and stepped over to the next door. Nunez had to pull out a set of keys for this one.

"Storage room," she said as she unlocked the door. "This door is always locked, no matter what."

She pushed the door open, reached inside, and flicked on a light. The room was twice as long as the office, and at least four times as wide. It was occupied by a mix of shelves and stands for holding multiple paintings, and a work area for framing. There were perhaps two dozen paintings, wrapped and stored in the stands.

Liesel stepped into the room, eyes narrowing. "This is wider than your showroom."

"It is. It goes behind the clothiers next door."

"I see. Do you often keep paintings here?"

Nunez shook her head. "Those are mostly pieces that were hanging before and will be moved to a secure facility in the next hour or two. The others have been purchased by clients who will be attending this evening and have requested to pick them up."

Liesel moved farther into the space and looked around. "Any other ways in or out?"

"No. This is the only exit."

"No way anyone in the clothing store can get in here?"

"Only if they hammer through a—"

A buzzer sounded in the hallway behind them.

"I need to get that," Nunez said. She motioned to the door. "Do you mind?"

"Not at all. I've seen enough."

They returned to the corridor, where Nunez walked over to the door on the back wall, unlatched the two deadbolts, and pulled the door open. Standing in what turned out to be another interior space were three men and two women, each holding trays or other closed containers.

"*Pasen, por favor*," Nunez said.

The group entered in a fragrant cloud of spices and meat. The caterers, apparently.

While Nunez led them toward the main hallway, Liesel stuck her head out the doorway through which the caterers had just entered. A long, dimly lit corridor ran to the left and right, far longer than the width of the space Nunez rented. In fact, far longer than the space of her shop and the two on both sides combined.

"*Señorita* Li?" Nunez called.

Liesel leaned back inside. Nunez was looking at her from inside the other corridor.

"Where does this lead?" Liesel asked.

"To an outside door at the end of the block. It's how we get deliveries."

"May I take a look?"

"Oh, uh, I guess that should be okay. There's a doorstop just inside. Put that between the door and jamb so you can get back in. I need to make sure the caterers know what they're doing. I'll be right back."

"Thank you."

Nunez gave her a businesslike smile and let the other door shut.

Liesel stepped into the delivery corridor and snapped several pictures, then headed toward the far end. The well-worn concrete walkway was cracked but relatively even, though she wouldn't want to roll a cart carrying anything fragile on it.

As best she could tell, the wall to her right was the true back of the building. At some point, the building's owners had carved this service corridor out of the backs of the ground-floor businesses and put doors every ten or so meters, giving those tenants access. It had probably been his or her way of making the rental spaces more appealing.

The door at the very end was extra wide and swung inward with surprising smoothness. Beyond it was a turnout from the street, large enough to fit three cars in a pinch. No real loading dock but, in essence, that was what it was.

Liesel's phone buzzed with a text from Ricky. She let him know she wasn't done, then shoved the mobile back into her pocket. Just inside the doorway was a chunk of concrete about the size of a human foot. After using it to block the door open, she walked out to the road.

A side street, not too busy. She took pictures and headed back inside.

The corridor and the side street could be an effective

escape route if they needed it. Of course, she had no idea what Ananke's plan was. She reentered the back area of the gallery and met up with Nunez in the hall where the toilets were.

"Everything to your satisfaction?" Nunez said.

"How did the caterers enter at the other end? Or is the outside door left unlocked?"

"No, it locks automatically. We gave them a key this morning. And before you ask, I will get it back from them before the opening."

Liesel nodded, said nothing else.

Nunez escorted Liesel back into the main gallery, shooting hopeful glances in her direction. As they neared the front door, she said, "Is there anything else I can show you?"

"I believe I have seen all I need to."

After a slight hesitation, Nunez voiced the question Liesel knew she really wanted to ask. "Can we expect to see *Señor* Schneider this evening? We are very honored he is even considering attending."

Another unreadable smile from Liesel. "Thank you for your time."

"Of course," Nunez said, trying to hide her frustration. "Let me unlock the door."

As the gallery owner was pulling out her key, Liesel's phone buzzed with another text from Ricky.

I've got eyes on the gallery. Where are you?

Before Nunez opened the door, she handed Liesel a business card. "In case you have any further questions."

Liesel pocketed the card. "I appreciate it."

After stepping out of the gallery, Liesel scanned the street until she spotted a clearly surprised Ricky on the other side, about half a block down. She headed in the opposite direction and turned down the next street, where she stopped to wait.

Ricky joined her thirty seconds later. "Correct me if I'm wrong, but I thought our instructions were to observe and not interact."

"As you must have noticed, there was little to see from

outside."

"So, you just decided to go in?"

"With Ananke's permission."

"Oh." He frowned. "Well, crap. I should have asked her if I could have snuck into the club."

"Was the club open?"

"No."

"Then she would have told you no."

"The gallery wasn't open, either."

"No, but I had an excellent cover story." She explained how she had convinced the gallery owner to let her in. "What would you have used to get into the club?"

"I would have, um…I could have said…crap." He grimaced. "Fine."

She patted him on the back and started walking back to the hotel. "I am sure you did the best you could."

"Hey," he said, following her, "there's no need to get all condescend-y."

A GENTLE RAP on the door.

He heard it but made no move to acknowledge it.

There it was again. Still soft, but a longer one this time.

He remained still, comfortable under the sheets with a warm body pressed against him. Malaya or Mariah, he thought. Or was that the name of a girl from some other night?

A third knock, followed by the door opening.

"*Señor* Gutiérrez, it's four p.m."

Gutiérrez peeled open one eye and looked toward the doorway, where his assistant, Luisa, stood. He sighed, then pulled back the covers.

He hated mornings, even when they came in the afternoon.

Bare as the day he was born, he walked across the room to the master bath, pointing back toward the bed. "Deal with that."

"Yes, sir."

When he reemerged, showered and shaved and ready for the night, the bed was made, and all signs of his guest were gone. Luisa was very good at her job, and Gutiérrez knew his female companion—whatever her name was—would already have been escorted off the boat.

Lying at the foot of the bed was a sheet of paper, his schedule for the day. He picked it up.

He had a video conference with a client in an hour, followed by a pair of supplier calls. At seven p.m., he would be having dinner with a group that included a pair of up-and-coming models and a Colombian actor who'd made a career of playing over-the-top, rogue police detectives who would do anything to bring down the villain. The guy was too full of himself but he did bring the shine, and the shine brought the girls and the fun.

After dinner was the gallery opening for Miguel Miguel, scheduled to start at eight p.m. Gutiérrez would be fashionably late because, hey, he was Julio Gutiérrez, and Julio Gutiérrez was never first to anything where his mere presence would cause a stir. Next, it would be the after-party he was hosting at one of his favorite hot spots, Club De Gaf. Luisa was in charge of setting everything up; his job was only to smile and enjoy himself, hopefully so much that he wouldn't be heading home to the *Angelina* alone.

His life was hard.

He chuckled as he walked into his closet to choose his outfit for the evening.

The dark gray Armani suit or the beige Dolce & Gabbana?

The Armani. It was more sophisticated. To balance it with his wild side, he grabbed an apple-red, buttoned shirt.

Once dressed, he checked himself out in the full-length mirror, ran a hand along one of his lapels, and smiled.

He looked good. Flash *and* substance.

Tonight, like most nights, would be epic.

ANANKE AND ROSARIO returned to the hotel, the trunk of their taxi loaded with the results of their shopping spree. While Rosario arranged for a bellman to bring everything up, Ananke texted Liesel, Dylan, and Ricky.

Meeting in my room. 10 minutes.

By the time the others arrived at the suite Ananke and Rosario were sharing, the two women had started laying out their purchases on the living room furniture.

"What the hell's all this?" Ricky asked.

"Supplies for tonight," Ananke said.

He picked up a mauve dress that would not have covered much, even on tiny Rosario. "This is for the job?"

"Put it down, Ricky. That's several thousand dollars you're holding."

He carefully put the garment back in place.

"And yes," Ananke said, "it's for the job."

He put his hands up in surrender. "I'm not complaining. I mean, whoever's going to wear…"

A split second before Ananke glared at him, he stopped talking.

"You know," he said, "there is nothing I could say at this point that won't get me in trouble, so I'm just going to stop right there." As he backed away from the couch, he pantomimed locking his mouth.

Ananke and the other three shared surprised looks. This was not the Ricky they were used to.

Dylan said, "I take it you have a plan."

"Reports first," Ananke said. "Tell us about the boat."

"It's tied up at a dock on the far east side of the marina." Dylan looked at Rosario. "Do we have a projector?"

"Yes. Hold on."

She went over to one of the gear bags and pulled out a pair of black boxes. One was about the size of an average hardcover book, and the other was not much bigger than a bottle cap.

"Here," she said, and tossed the smaller box to Dylan.

While he attached it to his phone, she set up the larger box on the dining table and aimed the raised end at an empty section of the wall. When she toggled a switch on the side, the box hummed to life.

"All set."

A moment later, a picture of the marina appeared on the wall.

"This gives you a feel for the size of the place. I didn't count them, but I'd say there are about a hundred vessels berthed there." Dylan walked over to the image and pointed left. "The causeway to the mainland is in this direction." He touched the far-right edge of the image. "The *Angelina* is right behind this group of boats."

He changed to a picture of a large yacht and the area surrounding it.

"And this is her."

"What's that mound running down the right?" Ricky asked.

"It's the seawall. And that thing right there—that's a bridge connecting it to the dock."

He changed the picture to a closer shot of the bridge.

"It looks like you can walk along the wall," Liesel said.

"It's wide enough for a car," Dylan said. "But there's a gate where it connects with the island that keeps the public out."

"What about a sea approach?" Ananke said.

"I was thinking about that, too. I wouldn't want to try it during the day, but it should be doable at night."

Ananke nodded. "Tell us about the causeway."

The image changed to a two-lane road, with a walking path paralleling the northeast edge. Beyond the path, and even closer on the other side of the roadway, was the blue-gray water of the Gulf of Panama. "Real bottleneck potential here. Block it anywhere along this stretch and you cut off the island."

"How was traffic?"

"Not too bad."

"Any luck on getting us a boat?"

Dylan smiled. A new photo appeared, featuring a sleek, black powerboat sitting at a dock. "Meet the *Night Viper*. Nine meters of speed. It's waiting for us at the Club de Yates y Pesca. That's a yacht club about fifteen minutes from here."

"Nice," Ricky said. He held out a fist and Dylan bumped it.

"Is it small enough to get up close to the seawall unseen?" Ananke asked.

"It's got a nice low profile so it shouldn't be an issue," Dylan said.

"Nice work," Ananke said. "Liesel?"

Dylan disconnected the projector remote from his phone and gave it to Liesel. She attached it to her phone, showed her pictures as she described her visit to the gallery,

"Thank you," Ananke said when Liesel finished. "Ricky?"

The remote was passed again, and soon a picture of Club De Gaf graced the wall.

"Unlike Liesel here, I was not able to get special dispensation to enter the club."

"You didn't ask," Ananke said.

Ricky opened his mouth, clearly for some kind of retort, but stopped himself and said, "Anyway. There are front and rear entrances, both covered by cameras." He switched to the close-up he'd taken of the camera.

"X-Garo 8300s," Rosario said.

"How many?" Ananke asked.

"Four in front, three along the side, and two in the back."

"How do you get to the back?" Dylan asked.

Ricky showed them shots of the alley and the back of the club, then pulled the remote off his phone. "That's all I got." He motioned to the dresses. "You going to explain this stuff now?"

"I thought that would be obvious," Ananke said. "Some of us are going clubbing tonight."

"Some of us?"

"Liesel, Rosario, and me."

"Oh, I see. The *girls* are going clubbing."

"Unless you think Gutiérrez might take a liking to you."

"Listen, if I wanted him to take a liking to me, he'd take a liking to me."

"Fine. Then you can wear a dress and one of us will go with Dylan in the boat."

Ricky raised his eyebrows. "Whoa, whoa, whoa. Let's not get too hasty. I'm fine with boat detail."

"I thought you would be."

"Excuse me," Liesel said, looking uncomfortable. "I am

69

going clubbing?"

"We got you this great dress," Rosario said excitedly. She hunted through the packages they hadn't opened yet, and pulled out a sleek black number that had only marginally more material than the mauve dress. "You are going to look fantastic!"

"I am not wearing that."

A four-way discussion broke out between Liesel and Rosario and Ricky and Dylan over the dress's merits or lack thereof. When the voices rose, Ananke yelled, "Hey!"

The others fell silent and turned to her.

"Before we get too carried away," Ananke said, "perhaps you would all like to hear the plan."

SEVEN

"...WISH I HAD a better answer for you, but as you can see, it was out of my hands," Dominic Culpepper said over the phone as he wrapped up his overly detailed excuse. "Julio, you know me. You know I would never try to screw you."

Gutiérrez speared a chunk of pineapple with a toothpick and raised it toward his lips. "What I know is that you made a promise which you are apparently unable to keep. If that's true, I'll find someone else who can fill the order." He plopped the pineapple into his mouth.

Culpepper snorted. "No one else can pull the order together in anywhere close to the time that I'll still be able to hit, so let's not waste time with empty threats."

Still chewing, Gutiérrez said, "See, that's where you're wrong. It's not empty. I've already got a contingent deal in place with Breslan. So, you tell me, do I execute it or not?"

Silence on the other end.

"Dominic? Are you still there?"

"You talked to Breslan?"

"You didn't give me much choice, did you?"

"How long have you had this 'contingent deal' in place?"

Gutiérrez looked at his watch. "Fifteen minutes, give or take."

Another pause. "You have no wiggle room on the delivery date?"

"A deal is a deal."

A deep breath. "The shipment will be there."

"On time?"

"On time."

"Thank you, Dominic," Gutiérrez said, and hung up.

"Luisa?"

His assistant appeared in the lounge doorway. "Yes, sir?"

"Let Herrera know his shipment is confirmed, but we will release nothing until the final payment is in our account."

"Yes, sir."

"Who's next?"

"That was the last on the list, though you did receive a message from Salvador Aquino while you were on the phone. He wants to increase next week's order by five."

"Five?" Gutiérrez said, annoyed.

Aquino was another client, but his unique needs were difficult to both obtain and transport. Increasing an order on such short notice was not an easy task. Not impossible, mind you, just not easy.

"That order is being filled by…?"

"Clarke, sir."

That was good. Noah Clarke, who operated out of Indonesia, was great at supplying quantity, if not quality.

"Check with him," Gutiérrez said. "See if he can throw in five more. Tell him we'll pay the expedited shipping costs. And if he can't, check with the Americans." Dalton and Yates were pretty much the opposite of Clarke. They didn't deal in huge volume, which was why Gutiérrez hadn't bought anything from them in over a month, but their stock was typically better than Clarke's.

"I will," Luisa said. "What would you like me to tell *Señor* Aquino?"

"I'm sure someone will be able to step up. Tell him no problem."

"Very good."

He checked his watch again. If he left now, he should be able to make it to the restaurant an appropriate fifteen minutes late.

"Is the skiff ready?"

"THIS IS DYLAN. Movement on the *Angelina*."

"Copy," Ananke said. The team was using the long-range, digitally encrypted radios since they were separated by several kilometers.

Ananke, Rosario, and Liesel were still at the hotel, while Dylan was sitting in the SUV, his night vision-equipped binoculars trained on Gutiérrez's boat. Even at maximum magnification, he couldn't make out the faces of the three people who had just appeared on deck. He was pretty sure two were men and the other a woman, but he couldn't swear to that.

The two he thought were men approached the side of the boat. The shorter of the two descended a ladder over the side, to a smaller craft tied to the *Angelina*. Once he was down, the other one made the same trip.

The taller man sat in the middle of the craft. His companion moved to the back and started the outboard motor.

"Someone's heading to shore," Dylan said into his comm.

The third person disappeared back inside the *Angelina* as the smaller craft pulled away. Dylan thought it was interesting that whoever was coming ashore had decided to do so via a boat rather than walking down the long dock. Either the passenger was in a hurry or preferred saving the extra steps.

Dylan watched the craft cut through the marina, toward the dock closest to the parking area. When it was about halfway there, a light in the corner of Dylan's eye caught his attention. He lowered his binoculars. About a hundred meters away, a sedan pulled out of a parking spot and drove over to a red tile-roofed gazebo-like area, where it stopped. From his scout, Dylan knew that on the other side of the shelter was a ramp going down to the same dock the boat was heading toward.

He aimed the binoculars at the car.

A Mercedes S-Class Maybach. One hundred and seventy-five grand US at the low end.

Snazzy.

The only person inside appeared to be the driver.

Dylan turned the glasses back to the boat. Now that it was closer, he could see both occupants were men, and that the tall guy in the middle looked like Gutiérrez.

The shelter and parking area were a good three meters above water level, so the boat dipped out of sight as it approached the dock. Dylan focused on where the ramp led up to ground level.

Just over a minute went by before the tall man walked into view and headed for the Mercedes.

"It's definitely Gutiérrez," Dylan said. "He just reached shore and he's getting into a Mercedes-Maybach." He recited the license plate number and started the SUV's engine. "Commencing tail."

"Copy."

Vehicles being his specialty, Dylan was an expert at keeping the driver of whatever car he might be following from suspecting anything was up. In this case, as Gutiérrez was climbing into his ride, Dylan drove out to the road and headed northwest on the causeway, toward the mainland. He kept his speed a little under what he suspected the Mercedes's to be. When he saw the sedan's lights in his rearview mirror, he increased his pace only enough so that the Mercedes wouldn't reach him until right after the causeway ended. Once they both hit the mainland, Gutiérrez's vehicle pulled into the opposite lane and passed the SUV.

The hook had been set. The driver wouldn't suspect the car that had been in front of him was now following him.

Dylan increased his speed incrementally until he was pacing Gutiérrez from approximately four car lengths back.

"We're heading into the city. Ricky, we should be passing your position in about ten minutes."

"Ready and waiting."

Shortly before they reached the intersection where Ricky was waiting in a rented Toyota, the Mercedes unexpectedly turned left.

"Course correction," Dylan reported as he followed.

He wondered if he had been made, but instead of speeding away, the Mercedes continued at the same pace, as if traveling a planned route.

"We're on Calle 35, heading north," he said.

Calle 35 took an elbow turn to the right, then another to the left. When the Mercedes reached Avenida Justo Arosemena, it turned right. It repeated the maneuver three blocks down, then went one block and turned left.

Dylan knew he was pressing his luck, but he didn't have much of a choice. The plan had been for him and Ricky to tag team so neither would be in the sedan's view for long, but that had been thwarted.

Dylan took the left, then cursed.

"What's wrong?" Ananke asked.

"They pulled to the curb. I'm going to have to drive by."

The instant he passed the sedan, he checked his mirrors, and saw Gutiérrez climbing out of the back of the Mercedes. Dylan reported this, then said, "Ricky, I could really use your help."

"Already on my way, buddy. Two minutes out."

At the next corner was a colorfully lit restaurant, with a crowd waiting out front and music blaring onto the street. A sign above the windows read LA RIVIERA. The traffic light turned red before Dylan reached the intersection, so he stopped and looked in his mirror again.

Gutiérrez was heading in Dylan's direction. If he didn't do something, the man would walk right by him. He couldn't blow through the light, so he made a right turn.

Just before the sidewalk moved out of sight, he glanced over and saw Gutiérrez turn toward the restaurant's entrance.

"It looks like he's going into a place called La Riviera."

"You're not sure?" Ananke asked.

"I can't tell from where I am. Do you want me to go in and check?"

"One of you needs to."

Dylan saw an open spot, a block up on the other side. He zipped ahead and U-turned into the space before anyone could beat him to it.

"Heading to the restaurant now," he said as he exited the SUV.

He walked as fast as possible without drawing attention and soon was nearing the restaurant. If anything, the crowd out front had grown. He scanned the people waiting for tables but didn't see Gutiérrez.

"Ricky, are you here yet?" Dylan asked.

"Yeah, but parking sucks."

"Don't worry about parking. Just get someplace where you can keep an eye on Gutiérrez's car." He told him where it was. "I'm going inside the restaurant."

"Copy."

Dylan worked his way through the crowd until he reached a man standing behind a podium, dressed like the waiters Dylan could see inside.

"*El baño?*" Dylan said.

The man looked up and said something in Spanish. Though Dylan understood the language, when spoken at a hundred miles an hour, it was as incomprehensible as ancient Greek. Or modern Greek, for that matter.

"Sorry," Dylan said in English. "I didn't get that."

"He said the toilet is just for customers," Rosario said his ear.

As if emphasizing Rosario's point, the man at the podium said in stilted English, "Customer only. No...other people."

"I *am* a customer. I'm waiting with my friends for our table."

Now it was the man's turn to look like Dylan was speaking a dead tongue.

"Wait," Dylan said. He came around the side of the podium and looked at the list. He picked out a group of six. "Right there. See?"

The man looked at the name. "You?"

"Yeah. Well, my friend, but that's my group. Now come on, I really need to pee." He mimed the internationally recognized dance of those needing to go.

"Okay." The man pointed through the restaurant toward the back corner. "Down hall."

"Thank you."

Dylan hurried into the restaurant, then slowed after checking over his shoulder to make sure the host wasn't watching him.

The place was an amorphous whirlwind of voices and laughter and music and utensils striking dishes. It had a party vibe almost, which was probably why the place was so popular. Well, that and the food, which smelled damn tasty.

He scanned the tables as he made his way to the back of the room. Those to his left were freestanding and could be moved into any configuration. There was more of the same to the right, but also several permanently installed booths along the back wall. He finally caught sight of Gutiérrez at one of the latter, surrounded by six others.

They were being served drinks but had not received any food.

Dylan headed into the restroom. One person was inside, but the man was washing his hands and left within seconds.

Dylan said into his mic, "Found him. He's having dinner with a group of people."

"Copy," Ananke said. "How long do you think they'll be there?"

"I would think an hour at least."

"Okay, I want both you and Ricky to keep your eyes on that place. I don't want him slipping through unseen."

"That ain't going to happen, boss," Ricky said.

"It'd better not."

The bathroom door opened, so Dylan turned on the faucet and began washing his hands. In the mirror, he could see one of the men who'd been at Gutiérrez's table enter one of the stalls. The guy was a rugged fortysomething with a too-pretty face.

Bodyguard?

The man had the build for it, but Dylan didn't get that vibe. Plus, if he was Gutiérrez's bodyguard, why hadn't he been in the Mercedes?

"Dylan, did you hear me?"

Dylan blinked. He'd been concentrating on the man and had missed everything said in the last few seconds. He clicked his mic twice, for no.

"Are you in trouble?"

Two more clicks.

He turned off the faucet, dried his hands, and exited. Since no one was in the hallway outside, he whispered, "Sorry, someone came into the toilet. What was the question?"

"I just said when Gutiérrez leaves, Ricky will follow, and

you're to move on to position two."

"Copy that."

"Gentlemen, keep us posted."

AFTER CONFIRMING THERE was no back way out of the restaurant, Dylan watched the front from the corner halfway between La Riviera and the SUV, while Ricky watched the side where the Mercedes was parked.

At 8:37 p.m., the action started up again.

"Gutiérrez and his friends just walked out," Dylan said. "They've stopped on the sidewalk, talking." He watched for several moments as the group conversed, Gutiérrez doing most of the speaking. "Looks like they're finally leaving."

Gutiérrez and his friends split into three groups: rugged too-cute guy and a woman heading down the street in Dylan's direction, another man stepping into the street and waving down a taxi, and Gutiérrez and two women walking arm in arm toward the Mercedes.

"Ricky, coming your way and bringing two friends with him."

"Copy."

When Gutiérrez turned the corner, Dylan said, "I don't have eyes on him anymore."

"I got him. You head on out. I'll see you in a bit."

"Copy."

Dylan headed back to the SUV.

IT WASN'T LONG into Ricky's stint as Gutiérrez's shadow that the man finally headed toward where they'd expected him to go all along.

"Girls, looks like it's almost showtime," Ricky said. "We're about five minutes out from the gallery."

"Copy," Ananke said.

Because of traffic, it took them six. Ricky was three cars behind the Mercedes when it pulled to the curb and Gutiérrez and his two friends got out.

"You ladies had better bring your A game," Ricky said. "He's already got a pair who aren't going to give him up easily."

"We've got this," Ananke said. "It's not even a competition."

"If it was, I'd like to be considered for judge!"

"And there it is. You were doing so well."

"What? Did I say something wrong? That was nice! If I was judge, you would absolutely win."

"That does not make it better," Liesel said.

"Oh, come on now. You are being *way* too sensitive. It was just a jo—"

"Ricky!" Ananke barked. "Stop talking. Right now. Focus on the job. Got it?"

He thought about staying silent. She had, after all, told him to do just that. But he knew it was a selective command so he said, "Copy," and found a spot to pull over down the block. He looked back at the gallery. "Gutiérrez is entering the gallery now."

"Copy."

"Okay, the Mercedes is leaving."

"You got it?" Ananke asked.

"I got it."

Ricky angled onto the road and followed the sedan until it turned down a quiet street and parked.

Ricky drove by and turned down the next street, where he pulled up next to a line of parked cars. After throwing on his emergency blinkers, he hopped out, hurried back to the corner, and peeked at the other street.

The Mercedes's driver had exited his vehicle and was walking away from Ricky. Twenty meters before he reached the end of the block, the guy disappeared inside a building.

Ricky waited a minute to see if the guy would come right back out. When he didn't, Ricky pulled a magnetic tracking disc out of his pocket and strolled around the corner. As he neared the Mercedes, he confirmed he was alone and slipped the disc under the front fender.

As he headed back to his car, he checked the tracker app on his phone and verified the bug was working.

"The Mercedes has been tagged," he whispered into this

comm.

"Copy," Ananke said. "You're released to your next task."

DYLAN PARKED THE SUV three blocks from the sea, and lugged the gear bag he'd been put in charge of to the Club de Yates y Pesca marina. The *Night Viper* was tied up in a slip near the end of one of the docks. He'd been given the key when the rental agent had gone over the boat's operating procedures that afternoon.

At the time, the fuel gauge had been sitting at the one-quarter mark. Dylan had requested the tanks be filled, paying for the service on the spot. The first thing he did upon boarding the boat again was to check that the agent had done as asked. Sure enough, the gauge now read FULL.

Dylan spent the next twenty minutes familiarizing himself with every nook and cranny of the boat, and was on his knees going through a storage area on the port side when he heard, "Oooooweee! This is *nice*!"

He lifted his head and spotted Ricky standing on the dock, smiling at the *Viper*.

"Not bad, huh?" Dylan said.

"Not bad? Hell, this thing is fantastic!" Ricky started to climb on, then stopped. "Permission to come aboard, Captain."

"Granted."

Grinning wider, Ricky scrambled over the side. "I bet this thing really moves!"

"It'll do a hundred forty miles per hour in the right conditions."

Ricky's eyes widened. "Can we try it?"

"I'm pretty sure Ananke doesn't want us playing around."

"Dude, we're not going to have anything to do for the next couple hours, at least."

"That's not exactly true." They still needed to scout Flamenco Island and the seawall that sheltered its marina.

"So, you're telling me we can't squeeze out a *little* time to see what this thing can do?"

Dylan tried to resist the grin pushing at the edges of his mouth but failed. "Well, we *do* have to get to the island, and no

80

one said we have to go slow."

Ricky clapped him on the back. "Yes! That's what I'm talking about." He plopped down on one of the seats. "So, what are we waiting for?"

WHEN ANANKE, ROSARIO, and Liesel stepped out of the elevator and walked across the hotel lobby, there wasn't a single person in the room who didn't turn and stare.

"I feel stupid," Liesel whispered.

"You look gorgeous," Rosario told her.

"I do not. I look like a fraud, playing dress up."

Ananke agreed with Rosario, but knew Liesel wouldn't believe her, either.

Two doormen rushed the door, each wanting to be the one who opened it for the trio. A well-timed elbow from the older of the two won him the honors.

"May I get you a taxi?" a third doorman, stationed outside, asked after they exited.

"Please," Rosario said.

He raised a hand and motioned to a taxi parked down the street. When it pulled up, he opened the back door. "Your destination?"

"The Diego Campos Gallery."

The doorman relayed the information to the driver.

As soon as they were on their way, Rosario pulled out a compact, checked her makeup, and offered the mirror to Liesel.

"God, no," Liesel said. "I look like a clown."

Usually she wore little to no makeup, so it had fallen to Ananke and Rosario to prepare her for the evening. Despite her complaints, they had done a fine job.

"This is going to be fun," Ananke said. "You should embrace it."

"I will embrace the idea of it being over as soon as possible."

"I will bet that you get hit on at least three times tonight," Rosario said.

Liesel looked horrified. "And that is a *good* thing?"

"Depends on who it is, I guess."

Liesel groaned. "Is it too late for me to help Dylan and Ricky?"

Ananke and Rosario both said, "Yes."

They had been in the cab less than ten minutes when the gallery came into sight. A crowd filled the sidewalk out front, talking and smoking and drinking from wineglasses. Through the gallery's now uncovered windows, Ananke could see many more people inside.

The taxi had to wait for two other cabs to drop off their passengers before it could pull to the curb. Because it suited the impression they were trying to make, the women waited for the driver to open the back door for them.

Unlike in the hotel lobby, Ananke, Rosario, and Liesel weren't the only head turners present, but even so, several people gave them more than a passing glance as they climbed out of the taxi and walked to the gallery's entrance.

A buzz of voices and pop music spilled through the doorway as they crossed the threshold. Beyond stood two young men, handing out booklets.

"Welcome to the Diego Campos Gallery," one of the men said, handing Ananke a booklet.

"Thank you."

Rosario and Liesel also received copies.

They found a pocket of empty space a little farther inside and paused to get their bearings.

"I don't see Gutiérrez," Ananke said as she scanned the crowd.

"Me, neither," Rosario said.

"Maybe he left before we arrived," Liesel said. She scanned the room, then suddenly stopped.

"What is it?" Ananke asked.

"That woman in the red dress, over by the wall on the left."

Ananke and Rosario looked without making it obvious. The woman was in a group of five near one of the larger paintings. Fortyish, shoulder-length brown hair, an air of confidence. She seemed to be doing most of the talking.

"I see her," Ananke said.

"That's Carla Nunez."

The gallery owner, Ananke recalled. The plan was that if Nunez ran into Liesel, Liesel would say that Claus Schneider's flight had been delayed, and that he was still hoping to make it before the opening was over. In case he couldn't, he had sent Liesel and two other colleagues to assess the work for him.

"Let's go this way," Ananke said, motioning down the other side of the room. She wasn't worried Nunez might see through the lie, but if they could avoid her, they wouldn't even have to use it.

Ananke took the lead as they gently pushed through the crowd. More than once, men tried to lure them into conversations, but they just smiled and moved on with little more than a *sorry*.

They were near a painting of a young girl being led through an alley full of monsters when a guy swept a hand across Ananke's ass. In nearly any other situation, she would have whirled and kneed him in the groin before sending his head through the closest wall. But doing even one of those things would bring them the wrong kind of attention right now.

Instead, she turned, an eyebrow raised.

The grabber smiled. "Hi. What's *your* name?" Sixty years old at least, he sported a bushy hairstyle and a 1970s-era misogynistic attitude.

"I don't just give that out to anyone," Ananke said playfully.

"Well, I'm not just anyone, *muñeca*."

"Anyone I've only met once, I mean. Look for me later, and maybe I'll have a different answer."

He took a step closer to her, moving firmly into her personal zone. "Oh, I like you. Why have I never seen you before?"

She put a hand against his cheek, said, "Because you weren't ready," and started walking away.

He said something else, but it was lost in the cacophony.

"I would have punched him in the face," Liesel said.

"As cathartic as that might have been, we have bigger priorities than reminding lower life forms of their place."

They snaked through the other attendees, fending off more

than a few additional—albeit less overt—advances.

"Gutiérrez," Liesel said. "Ten o'clock."

Ananke shifted her gaze to the left. Gutiérrez was standing with several others, two of which Ananke guessed were the women who'd accompanied him to the opening. A man in the group, older than the rest, had the others' rapt attention.

"Everyone ready?" Ananke said.

"Oh, yeah," Rosario said.

Liesel frowned but nodded.

"Then let's get this show started," Ananke said.

With her once more in the lead, they walked toward Gutiérrez and his friends.

EIGHT

THE RAINS HAD started again about an hour before the sun went down. If it continued, the walk back to the dorm would be miserable, but for now, Gloria appreciated that the pounding noise it made against the roof drowned out the sobs of the girl at the machine behind her.

It was how others reacted when they first arrived here.

It was how Gloria had reacted.

"Stop it," someone whispered from another station. "For your own good."

The warning was so unusual that Gloria looked back to see who'd said it. She couldn't tell where the voice had come from, but saw the reason the person had spoken up. Two guards were working their way through the rows, accompanied by the Building 17 head inspector. The same three or four guards made their rounds through the room several times a day, but these guards were not them.

When the inspector pointed in Gloria's direction, she turned back to her machine and concentrated on her work.

They couldn't be coming for me. I haven't done anything wrong.

She finished the first seam on the piece she was working on, flipped the item around, and began sewing the second before a thought caused her to stop pressing down the pedal that made the needle go.

Could they know I was with Ricardo right before he tried to escape? Could they think I helped him?

Of course they could.

Her hand started to shake. She balled it into a fist, squeezing her fingers as tightly as she could.

Keep working.

Soon the guards' footsteps grew loud enough to be heard above the rain.

Keep working.

She pressed the pedal again and forced herself to push the garment she was working on under the needle.

Closer still.

And closer.

And—

The steps stopped. Not directly behind her, though.

The temptation to look over her shoulder again was almost too strong to fight.

"You are 178127?" a male voice said.

That wasn't Gloria's number.

"Yes." This voice she recognized as belonging to a man more than old enough to be her father.

"Get up."

A chair scraped against the concrete floor.

"*Get* up!"

"I am," the worker pleaded. "Please. My leg, it does not work so well."

Gloria attributed the sounds that followed to the guards grabbing the worker and pulling him to his feet. Seconds later, more steps, one set more labored than the others.

As the sounds diminished, Gloria chanced a look.

The older man was being escorted toward the exit, a guard on each arm. She had noticed the man favoring his leg in the past, but it seemed to be slowing him down even more than usual.

She had a sinking feeling this was why he was being taken away. While one didn't need both feet to operate the machines, it would certainly slow things down if he had been using only one.

"Get back to work!"

Gloria jumped, thinking the order had been aimed at her. But she realized at least a dozen others had been watching the man and the guards.

She resumed sewing and made her quota with thirty

minutes to spare.

That night, as she lay in bed, she prayed that the guards had only been taking the man to a doctor for his leg, and that he would be back in Building 17 within a few days, if not tomorrow.

But two days later, someone new was sitting at his station, sobbing at her predicament.

Gloria told herself the guards had probably moved the man to a job where his handicap would be less of a problem, but deep down she doubted that was true. The man had likely joined Ricardo in a growing pile of bodies somewhere in the jungle.

She tried to push the thought out of her mind as she moved the cloth under the needle.

Stitch.

Stitch.

Stitch.

But the image of the pile of bodies never quite left her.

Nine

"OOOOOOOOH, YEEEEEAAAAAH!" RICKY Ricky yelled as the *Viper* skipped across the bay. "Faster!"

"Are we still good?"

"What?" Ricky's job was to watch the waters in front of them through the night vision binoculars so that they didn't run into anything.

"Is everything still clear?"

"Oh. Yeah. Clear as glass!"

Dylan increased their speed a bit. He was already going faster than he should have been, but the appeal of seeing what the *Viper* could do was nearly as strong in him as it was in Ricky.

"This is a hell of a lot more fun than attending some ridiculous art show!" Ricky yelled.

Dylan let the boat run for another minute, then began throttling down.

"Ah, come on," Ricky said. "We were just starting to have fun."

"We're almost there. We can't play all night."

"Spoilsport!"

"I just raced this thing across the bay! Why all the hate?"

A pause, then, "Dylan."

"If you want to be ungrateful, that's your problem."

"Dylan."

"Don't ask me for any favors ever again."

"Dylan. Look."

Dylan glanced over and saw Ricky looking back toward shore. Dylan turned to see what had caught Ricky's attention.

Maybe half a kilometer away, flashing red lights were

moving low across the water, in Dylan and Ricky's direction.

"Is that the water police?" Ricky asked.

"The what?"

"The water police, or whatever the hell they're called."

"You mean the coast guard?" Dylan wasn't sure if it was called the coast guard here, but it was considerably better than water police.

A spotlight at the front of the other boat swung toward the *Viper*.

"Do you think they're after us?" Ricky asked.

Cursing under his breath, Dylan increased their speed again and veered the boat on a direct line to Flamenco Island.

"Why would they be after us?" Ricky said. "We were just having a little fun."

"Oh, I don't know, maybe because we were speeding through the bay in the dark, without our running lights on."

"What's wrong with that?"

"If you don't mind, how about keeping your eyes up front."

"Oh, sure." Ricky raised the binoculars. "I'd say we're about a kilometer away."

"Let me know when we're at a half."

"Aye-aye, Captain."

Dylan looked over his shoulder and grimaced. No question now that the other boat was after them, as it had matched the *Viper*'s course correction. The good thing was, the gap between them was widening, and though the spotlight was pointed toward the speedboat, he didn't think the others could see the *Viper*. Not physically, anyway. He was positive they had radar, which was why they'd been able to match the *Viper*'s path.

"Coming up on half," Ricky said.

"Hold on to something."

Dylan yanked the wheel to port, sending a spray of water over the bow, and putting them on a course toward the open ocean.

"Whoo!" Ricky yelled as a few droplets hit him. "That feels great!"

"Tell me when we're level with the end of the island."

"Ten-four, little buddy."

"You're mixing your terms."

"What?"

"Never mind."

While Ricky turned to watch the island pass off the starboard side of the boat, Dylan checked the coast guard ship, and saw that it was matching their turn. He twisted back to the bow.

"How we looking?" he asked.

"Getting close."

The boat bounced over a series of waves, nearly becoming airborne. Ricky bounced in his seat and would have fallen to the deck if he hadn't grabbed the windshield.

"Hey, man. You trying to kill me?"

"Not yet."

They plowed through two more sets of waves, not quite as big as the first, before the sea calmed again.

"Okay," Ricky said. "That's the end."

Dylan kept them on course for another minute before taking a quick turn starboard.

As they neared the island, it blocked the coast guard boat from view. Which, depending on how advanced its equipment was, hopefully meant the *Viper* had dropped off its radar screen.

Just ahead, Dylan could see the seawall that enclosed the marina where Gutiérrez's ship was docked and cursed again, knowing they should have been checking it out right now instead of hightailing it from the cops.

There were enough lights on this side of the island that he didn't need Ricky to point out the western edge. Once they'd passed it, Dylan swung the *Viper* starboard again, putting even more of the island between them and the coast guard.

He took a deep breath, figuring he'd bought them at least a few minutes. The next step on his fly-by-the-seat-of-his-pants plan had been to find someplace along the island to hide while the coast guard raced by. But the only option would have been to enter the marina, and that would be more a trap than safe haven.

Maybe if he raced along the causeway, and under the Bridge of the Americas, into the mouth of the river that served as the beginning of the Panama Canal, he could find a hiding place there. It was chancy, but it should provide more options.

"Hey!" Ricky said. "You think that's what caused those waves?"

He was pointing off the port side at a large cargo ship heading toward the canal entrance.

Dylan cocked his head. *Maybe there's a better option.*

He turned the *Viper* toward the vessel.

"It was just a question," Ricky said. "We don't need to go over and confront them about it."

"Keep a lookout for the coast guard."

Ricky narrowed his eyes, as if trying to figure out what Dylan was up to.

"Ricky! Please!"

"Okay, okay. Keep your pants on." Ricky swiveled and aimed his binoculars at the island. "It's all clear at the moment."

"The second you see them, shout."

While the deck of the cargo ship was lit up, revealing stacks of containers in tight columns, the hull wasn't much more than a dark shadow cutting through the sea.

Dylan gunned the *Viper* toward the wake a hundred meters behind the vessel.

"Um, what are you doing?" Ricky asked.

"Getting us to the other side."

"Do you see how big that wake is? You're going to swamp us."

"I'm not going to swamp us."

"You're trying to get to the other side, aren't you?"

"Obviously!"

"Why? Just pull up alongside it. They won't be able to see us, and their radar will think we're part of the ship. *Plus,* we'll be able to watch what the coast guard does."

"And what if they come close enough to see us?"

"Then we race away again. You've got way more

horsepower than they do."

Dylan studied the wake. Even if the bigger waves didn't swamp them, it would not be a fun ride. He turned the wheel and raced over to the cargo vessel. When they were about midship, he reduced the *Viper*'s speed to match it, and eased as close to the giant hull as possible.

"I sure hope you're right," Dylan said.

"Trust me."

"Yeah, because that always works out well."

Ricky snickered and lifted the binoculars again. "It does, doesn't it?"

They cruised in the cargo ship's shadow for another minute before Ricky said, "Here they come."

Dylan glanced over his shoulder and spotted the tiny flashing red lights and bright white dot of the searchlight. The other boat swung out from the island and slowed. The question now was, how good was its radar equipment?

"I think they've stopped," Ricky said.

For half a minute, neither man spoke.

"They're moving again."

Dylan tensed.

"Heading toward the island." A pause. "I think they're going into the marina…and…yep, I was right. I can't see them anymore."

Was it possible he and Ricky were actually in the clear? Dylan wondered.

"Keep watching," he said.

The *Viper* was nearing the mouth of the river when Ricky said, "I think they just came out."

"What do you mean think? Is it them or not?"

"The red lights are off, but I see a spotlight."

Ahead, on the eastern shore, was the ferry terminal. In the water near it were moored dozens of boats—a few unused ferries but mostly smaller craft. As the cargo ship passed the water parking lot, Dylan swung the *Viper* away and over to the other ships.

"What are they doing?" Dylan asked.

"Not sure. I think…yeah, they're heading away. Looks

like they're going back around the island." He looked over at Dylan and smiled. "How about that? We did it." He checked his watch. "And we still have plenty of time. Want to air it out again?"

Dylan stared at him as if Ricky had lost his mind.

"I'm kidding, I'm kidding. Sometimes you are too easy." Ricky looked through the binoculars again. "And they're gone."

"Then we should get to work."

"Aye-aye, Captain."

ANANKE SAUNTERED UP to the painting on the left of Gutiérrez's group. The sign beside the frame said the piece was from Miguel Miguel's portrait series, and entitled *Anna of Lord's Alley*. It featured a teenage girl dressed like the Madonna. Behind her was a road in a twenty-first century slum.

While Ananke could appreciate the work, she wasn't a big fan of Miguel Miguel's style. More specifically, the way he painted faces. There was something *off* about them. Like they weren't quite human. Maybe that was the point. Clearly, he was popular enough to draw this large a crowd and command the ten-grand-plus prices listed in the exhibit booklet.

She could feel Rosario and Liesel crowd in around her.

"She looks like she needs to go to the toilet," Liesel said, looking at the painting.

"And had a bad face-lift," Rosario added.

"She is a teenager," Liesel said. "Why would she have a face-lift?"

"Let's keep moving," Ananke said.

She stepped back and circled behind the larger group, purposefully brushing Gutiérrez's back with her arm as she went by. She could feel him look at her, but she kept her gaze forward.

"Pardon us," Rosario said behind her.

"I apologize," a male voice said.

Soon Ananke's friends joined her at the painting on the other side of Gutiérrez's group. It was another portrait—*Denis of Lord's Boulevard*. A teenage boy this time, shirtless and wearing a crown of thorns. The road behind him was a monument to consumerism, filled with jewelry stores and gun shops and franchised restaurants. The same oddness in the face was here, too, in this case highlighted by the boy's eyes being too close together.

"I like this one even less," Liesel said.

In different circumstances Ananke would have laughed, as she'd been thinking the same thing.

"I don't know," Rosario said. "There's a certain appeal to it."

Ananke heard the shuffling of feet and turned her head to see Gutiérrez's group separating. As Gutiérrez put an arm around a young woman, he glanced over and momentarily locked eyes with Ananke. She coyly returned the smile he gave her before returning her attention to the painting.

"I saw that," Rosario said.

"Saw what?" Liesel asked.

"Shall we look at something else?" Ananke asked.

They turned back to the room. Gutiérrez and his companions had moved over to a set of three paintings on the opposite wall.

"How about those?" Ananke asked.

"An excellent choice," Rosario said.

As they walked across the room, Liesel nudged Ananke and jutted her chin toward someone to their left. Ananke saw that Carla Nunez was also on the move, heading in basically the same direction they were. With her was a thin man, with shoulder-length black hair and a short beard. He looked young, late twenties at most. Ananke recognized him from the photo in the exhibit booklet. Miguel Miguel.

Nunez and the artist walked up to Gutiérrez. The woman gave him a hug and introduced Miguel Miguel.

Ananke smiled. "We can play this to our advantage," she whispered, then explained her plan.

They headed toward a painting to the side of Gutiérrez's group. As they neared, Ananke noticed Nunez casually glance over, like one would when someone walked by. The woman's second glance was more deliberate, a subtle double take, focusing on Liesel.

Ananke and her friends stopped in front of a wide canvas entitled *So Goes the Echo*. It was a street scene from another slum, with the road, the buildings, and the people rendered in muted tones. But the sky was a vibrant blue with billowing white and pink clouds, and the sparkling spires of an almost Oz-like city in the distance. On the gray streets, only one person wasn't muted—a girl of maybe ten, front and center, staring longingly straight ahead.

"I can feel her looking at me," Liesel said.

"I think that is the intent," Rosario said.

"I mean Nunez."

"Oh."

Ananke turned just enough to see the other group. "She is."

Nunez kept switching her gaze from Gutiérrez to Liesel, until finally she touched Gutiérrez's arm, said something, and stepped around him, coming Liesel's way. Gutiérrez turned to see where she was going, and when he caught sight of Ananke, his left eyebrow raised a little and a grin creased his face.

"Pardon me for interrupting," Nunez said.

Ananke, Rosario, and Liesel turned.

"You're the woman who was here this afternoon, aren't you? The one I showed around?"

"*Señora* Nunez," Liesel said. "Good to see you again."

"I apologize, I've forgotten your name."

"Sandra Li."

"Of course. *Señorita* Li. I'm glad you were able to make it tonight." Nunez glanced around. "Is *Señor* Schneider here?"

"Not yet. His plane landed about an hour ago, and he had to go directly into a meeting. He's hoping it will finish in time for him to make it this evening, but between you and me, I wouldn't count on it. These things have a habit of going long."

Nunez's smile faded. "Oh, that's disappointing."

"For *Herr* Schneider as well. But he has sent me with two of his associates." She gestured to Ananke and Rosario. "This is Pauline Suarez and Colette Rangel. They are familiar with his tastes."

This last bit perked up Nunez. "Are you all enjoying the show?"

"Very much," Ananke said. "The work is very thought provoking."

"*Herr* Schneider is going to be disappointed he missed this," Rosario said.

"Perhaps we can set up a private showing tomorrow. Or anytime, really. The show will run until the end of the month."

"Unfortunately, he will be flying to Mexico City first thing in the morning," Liesel said.

"I'm sorry to hear that. Perhaps you can show him the catalog. If he sees something he wants, I would happily ship it wherever he would like."

"That's very kind," Ananke said, "but won't be necessary." She motioned at Rosario and herself. "My colleague and I are authorized to purchase pieces we think he would be interested in."

Nunez's smile grew. "Let me introduce you to the artist."

She guided them over to Gutiérrez's group. "Miguel, I have some people I would like you to meet. This is Sandra Li, Pauline Suarez, and Colette Rangel."

The artist was apparently more a hugger than a shaker and embraced each woman like she was a long-lost friend, placing wet kisses on their cheeks. After a whiff of his breath, Ananke thought his enthusiasm was fueled more by liquor than a tendency to be overly friendly.

"*Señoritas* Li, Suarez, and Rangel work for Claus Schneider," Nunez said. "The German businessman."

"Is that so?" Gutiérrez said.

"Pardon me," Nunez said. "Ladies, this is Julio Gutiérrez, one of our *local* businessmen, and his friends…I'm sorry, I've forgotten your names."

"Ramona," one girl said, barely hiding her annoyance.

"Catalina," the other said, not even trying.

Ananke was positive the girls' displeasure wasn't so much with Nunez's faulty memory as with the arrival of Ananke, Rosario, and Liesel.

Handshakes this time, tepid and loose from the women,

and gentle but firm from Gutiérrez. When he shook Ananke's hand, he let his fingers linger a bit longer than necessary.

Hooked, she thought.

From there, the evening progressed in the predictable manner. After Nunez and Miguel Miguel moved on to schmooze other attendees, Ananke, Rosario, and Liesel were absorbed into Gutiérrez's group, joining him and the annoyed twins as they circulated through the exhibit, commenting on the work and telling lies about themselves.

Gutiérrez was a smooth operator, and played it cool with Ananke at the beginning. But eventually she found him more and more at her side, touching her arm when they talked, and laughing at anything she said that was even remotely funny.

As the event wound down, Ananke said, "Thank you so much for your company. We should be getting back to the hotel."

"But it's still early," Gutiérrez said. "You all must come to the after-party."

"We weren't aware there was an after-party."

"There is and I'm throwing it, so you should have no problem getting in."

Ananke laughed. "Is this a party you *just* decided to host?"

"I like you. You're smart. But while that sounds like something I would do, the party has actually been planned for weeks."

"Right. Sure, it has."

"Let me prove it to you. If it is not as I say, you can turn around and leave."

"I don't know. What do you guys think?"

Before Rosario or Liesel could answer, Gutiérrez said, "Seriously, why waste a perfectly good night in your hotel?"

"He has a point," Rosario said.

Ananke acted like she was thinking it over before saying, "Oh, why not? Let's do it."

"I'll call for my car," Gutiérrez said.

TEN

RICKY'S PHONE BUZZED with an alert from his tracking app.

"Gutiérrez's car is moving," he said, then sent a text to Ananke, telling her the same thing.

He and Dylan were near the Flamenco Island seawall. They had already practiced moving right up to it and hopping onto the rocks, and were now anchored ten meters away.

On Ricky's screen, the dot representing the Mercedes returned to the art gallery, where it stayed for about two minutes before moving off again.

Annoyed that Ananke hadn't answered him, he sent another text.

Don't know if you noticed, but I think Gutiérrez just left your party.

It was almost a minute before his phone buzzed with a reply. Instead of a text, it was a photo from a low angle of Ananke and Rosario in the backseat of a car with Gutiérrez.

He showed the picture to Dylan. "Looks like we're full steam ahead, Captain."

"Is there a book of stupid sea slang you're getting these things out of? Or is it off the top of your head?"

"It's all me, baby."

"That's what I was afraid of."

CLUB DE GAF'S VIP room wasn't really a room but an L-shaped section of a balcony overlooking the dance floor. The area was filled with purple leather furniture, round Lucite tables, and sconces projecting orange light. Scattered across the floor were white, faux-bearskin rugs.

Ananke thought whoever had designed the space should

be shot. Multiple times. The white carpets alone probably had to be replaced on a near nightly basis.

The after-party was already in full swing when Ananke, Rosario, and Liesel arrived with Gutiérrez and his two increasingly irritated companions. No doubt much of the girls' annoyance had been due to Gutiérrez sending them to the club in a taxi, while he took Ananke and her friends in his car.

Amongst the crowd were several people Ananke recognized from the art show, but she had a feeling most of the others had skipped the exhibit.

Gutiérrez escorted them to a roped-off table near the center. Before they even sat down, a bottle of Dom Perignon champagne had been poured into flutes that Gutiérrez passed around.

"A toast," he said, lifting his glass.

Ananke, Rosario, and Liesel did the same, while the sullen sisters took a moment before joining in.

"To a night of fun and new friends," Gutiérrez said.

"New friends," Ananke said, letting her eyes briefly lock with his as their glasses clinked.

She let no more than a few drops pass through her lips, and wished she hadn't even let in that much. The champagne was delicious and wasting it seemed like a sin. But work was work.

The music was pounding, making it nearly impossible to have any kind of group conversation. Gutiérrez didn't seem to notice this, however. In a loud voice, he regaled them with his love of Panama, telling them what they should see and do.

Every so often, a woman about Ananke's age would come up and have a quick whispered conversation with Gutiérrez. Ananke guessed it was a business discussion, and figured the woman worked for the club.

Gutiérrez took to whispering to Ananke, too. Innocuous things like, "How are you enjoying Panama?" and "Have you tried our *platanos maduros* yet?" eventually transitioning to, "How long will you be staying?" and "I would love to show you around my city."

Ananke continued to play it coy but not *too* coy, allowing

his hand to linger on her thigh before she casually moved her leg away, answering his questions with words and tones that could be read multiple ways, and smiling in a manner men the world over would interpret as *she's interested*.

Just after midnight, Gutiérrez leaned over to Ananke and whispered, "Have you seen the bay at night?"

"We have a view of it from our hotel."

He snorted. "Then you have not really seen it."

"We haven't?"

"No, but would you like to?"

"What do you have in mind?"

He shrugged. "I thought perhaps you might be interested in getting a tour of my yacht."

This was a raised-eyebrow moment, and she dutifully complied. "You have a yacht?"

"I do."

Ananke looked past him. "What about your girlfriends?"

He chuckled. "They are just *friends*. And unfortunately, they won't be able to join us."

"That is unfortunate."

"Does that mean you will come?"

"What about *my* friends?"

"Of course. They're invited, too."

"Can you give us a moment?"

He bowed his head, and Ananke turned to her friends, motioning for them to lean in.

"We've been invited to his boat," she whispered.

Rosario eyed her with respect. "Are you sure he wants us there, too?"

"I am sure he does not," Liesel said. "He has been…what do you Americans say? Undressing you by the use of his eyes?"

"Close enough. I said I wouldn't go without you two, and he said fine."

Rosario's eyes narrowed. "He is expecting a party."

"Probably. So, you guys ready?"

The two women nodded.

Ananke sat back up, and Gutiérrez moved his head toward her.

100

"Well?" he asked.

"We would love to see your yacht."

The smile that expanded across this face would have put the Cheshire Cat to shame. "Fantastic. Give me a moment to arrange everything."

He signaled to someone across the room, and the woman he'd talked to several times approached the table. Gutiérrez did most of the whispering this time. When he finished, the woman nodded and stepped away from the table, where she pulled out a phone and made a call.

"The car will be here in a few minutes," Gutiérrez told Ananke. "Have another glass while we're waiting."

"What a great idea." Her flute was nearly empty—for the third time—the previous contents soaking the white rug by her feet.

As Gutiérrez filled her glass and offered to do the same for Rosario and Liesel, the woman finished her call. Instead of saying anything to Gutiérrez again, she leaned down to Gutiérrez's two other companions. Both women looked confused, but soon they were on their feet, following the other woman across the room.

As soon as they were out of sight, Gutiérrez stood up. "Is everyone ready?"

Ananke, who had raised her glass to her mouth, put it back down. "Um, sure."

"Don't worry about the champagne. There is plenty more on my boat. Come. Let's get some fresh air."

RICKY HAD FALLEN asleep. But it wasn't his fault.

Once he and Dylan had scoped out the way to the *Angelina* and planned how to proceed when given the go signal, there had been *literally* nothing to do.

He'd known when he'd stretched out there was a very good chance he'd nod off. That was the reason he'd put his phone on his chest, so that the phone's rattle would wake him up.

It went off, all right, but he didn't wake up until Dylan shoved his shoulder.

"We're on," Dylan said after Ricky's eyes blinked open.

"Huh?"

"Check your phone."

Ricky blinked again and picked up the device. A message from Ananke.

On our way to the boat. ETA 35 minutes

"Oh," Ricky said, sitting up. "Hey, we're on."

"I just said that."

While Dylan moved the *Viper* back to the seawall, Ricky pulled on his stocking mask and gloves, donned his shoulder holster, put the dart gun in it, and hooked a belt containing extra darts and several prefilled syringes around his waist.

Once Dylan had the boat in place, Ricky jumped onto the sloped, rocky embankment. Dylan moved the *Viper* back a safe distance, where he would wait until he was signaled.

The slope was short, and Ricky had to take only a single step up from where he'd landed to see over the flat top. He had disembarked the *Viper* about five meters north of the bridge that ran between the seawall and the dock where the *Angelina* was tied up. Most of the bridge was out of sight from his position. It angled down to the dock, which was lower than the seawall. The only part visible was a metal platform at the top, lined by a guardrail.

Though he couldn't see the dock, he could see several of the boats moored to it, including the *Angelina*. Much of the yacht was lit up, and he counted four men moving around inside, with a fifth out on the aft deck, leaning over the onboard Jacuzzi. Preparing for their soon-to-be-arriving guests, no doubt.

Ricky scanned the other nearby boats. None of the few people he saw on them were paying any attention to the seawall. Staying low, he crept over to the platform.

The bridge to the dock was deserted, but the dock itself was not. To the south, approximately thirty meters away, two men stood at the end of another of the dock's perpendicular spurs. They were looking down the extension, but whatever held their attention was hidden behind a line of three boats, tied along the spur.

One of the men shouted something that got lost on the breeze.

"Move it," Ricky muttered. He didn't want to go anywhere until he knew what they were doing.

Finally, a third man walked out from behind the nearest boat, pulling a cooler on wheels. When he reached the two men who'd been waiting, all three started down the dock toward shore, away from the *Angelina*.

Ricky crept down the bridge and moved on to the spur the *Angelina* was tied to. A rope had been strung across the opening in the deck railing, where the gangway connected to the boat. It was more an ideological barrier than a physical one, a reminder to those who wanted to come aboard that they needed permission.

The deck on the other side was about a meter and a half wide and ran parallel to a wall, much of which was fitted with large windows. The section directly in front of the gangway had none. To the left, the passageway led to the exterior aft deck where the Jacuzzi was. And to the right it dead-ended against a section of the hull.

In addition to the windows, there were three doors along the wall. The closest was to the right, and according to the plans Ricky had seen of a similar model, it should lead into a hall that connected to the central corridor.

He crept up the gangway, stepped over the rope, and moved to the nearest door. After listening for sounds on the other side, he eased it open. The hall beyond was empty, so he slipped inside and made his way toward the intersection with the central corridor. There he paused and listened again.

All was quiet.

But as he stepped into the intersection, the door to his left started to open. This was the entrance to the large lounge, through the window of which he'd seen the four men working.

Ricky was already too far into the intersection to go back the way he'd come, so he hurried forward and stepped through the doorway that led to the engine room.

Inside was a set of steep stairs heading to the bottom deck. He moved down quietly, and found himself in another—considerably narrower—corridor. Though the space was clean, there were none of the decorative touches he'd seen on the main deck. A crew-only area.

Gutiérrez probably never came down here.

Ricky started down the hall.

The Administrator's information indicated the *Angelina* had been in harbor for at least a week. In the best-case scenario, this meant it was operating with a skeleton crew. But if Gutiérrez was planning on taking the boat out to sea anytime soon, it could be fully staffed.

Ricky reached a door leading to several toilets. The facilities were empty and clean.

Just beyond this, another hall led off to the right. If the plans were correct, there would be five crew rooms down that way. He continued straight until he reached the engine-room door. The yacht was a big vessel, but it was a fraction of the size of the cargo ship he and Dylan had hidden next to earlier, and the room on the other side would be barely large enough for two people.

He pulled out the dart gun and cracked the door open. The room was dark. Like, pitch-black. He listened for the sound of breathing, wondering if the person on duty might be taking a nap, but the only noise he heard was the mechanical hum of a small generator.

He opened the door wider, letting the hall light in, and confirmed no one was there.

He doubled back to the crew-quarters hallway and snuck down to the rooms. Two held personal possessions, but looked like they hadn't been used in days, if not weeks. The other three were definitely in use, though none was occupied at the moment. Two of these latter rooms had two beds each, and the third had three.

Seven crew members.

Ricky had seen five already. Where were the other two? Kitchen? Maybe, unless some of those he'd seen were kitchen staff. The bridge? That made more sense. A big boat like this would likely keep someone on watch whether at sea or not. Of course, if it was the captain on duty, he probably wouldn't be sleeping down here. That job came with its own cabin.

Then eight crew members, counting the captain. Ricky needed to account for all of their whereabouts before Ananke and the others arrived. He pulled out his phone to check the tracker app for Gutiérrez's car. Before he could open it, his cell buzzed.

Ananke:

On the causeway.

Ricky groaned. So much for taking his time.

He stuffed the phone in his pocket and headed back toward the stairs. As he neared the door at the top, he heard the whine of a motor on a small vessel, loud at first but quickly fading as it moved away.

He opened the door and checked the hall.

THE WOMAN GUTIÉRREZ had kept talking to at the after-party turned out to be his assistant. He introduced her as Luisa, and said she would be joining them on the trip to the yacht. This meant a very crammed car ride, which Gutiérrez set about to remedy by offering his lap to Ananke.

"Maybe you should ride on mine," she said.

"I'm okay with that," Gutiérrez said, grinning.

Soon they were on the road. Feigning messages from "the boss," Ananke was able to keep Ricky and Dylan up to date on their progress, texting behind Gutiérrez's back.

After she sent the text saying the Mercedes was on the causeway, Gutiérrez said, "Your boss is working very late."

"Our boss is working all the time. A hazard of being rich, I guess."

Gutiérrez scoffed. "I am rich, yet I am not working."

Ananke smiled playfully. "Aren't you, though?"

"This is a different kind of working."

Ananke wanted to vomit. What an asshole. But she laughed, intimating she liked the way he was thinking.

Out the windows on either side of the car she could see the ocean. To the left, back toward the shore, shined the lights of Panama City. To the right, scattered across the black sea, were sparkles from dozens of large ships, going to and exiting the canal. Gutiérrez had been right about one thing—it was beautiful out here.

They soon reached Flamenco Island. After rounding the hill where the old battery had once stood, they turned into the marina parking area and stopped next to one of the docks.

The driver hopped out and opened the back door, releasing Ananke and Gutiérrez, while Luisa, who'd been sitting up front, opened the door on the other side for Liesel and Rosario.

As they moved onto the sidewalk, a small motorboat eased through the water and came to rest next to the dock.

"Perfect timing," Gutiérrez said. "This way."

They followed Gutiérrez to the dock. The kid driving the boat was dressed in a black T-shirt and black shorts and couldn't have been a day over twenty. He helped everyone on board in a professional and courteous manner. Thankfully, there were enough places to sit and Gutiérrez's lap wasn't needed.

Gutiérrez said, "Okay, Anthony. Let's go."

The kid—Anthony—eased the boat away from the dock and piloted it toward the center of the marina.

Gutiérrez pointed to a few of the bigger boats and told the group who owned them. Ananke, Rosario, and Liesel pretended to be impressed.

"There she is," Gutiérrez said, his eyes fixed on one of the largest yachts in the harbor. "The *Angelina*. Beautiful, huh?"

"That's yours?" Ananke asked.

"You are impressed, I can tell."

"Maybe a little."

"*Angelina*?" Liesel asked. "Your wife?"

He smiled. "Hardly. An old friend."

Ananke looked at the dock and said, "Couldn't we have walked out?" She knew the answer thanks to Dylan's briefing, but her alter ego, Pauline, would not.

"This is much more...enjoyable, don't you think?"

Gutiérrez said.

"Can't argue with that."

The boat pulled up to a ladder on the side of the *Angelina*. Gutiérrez whispered something to Luisa and she went up first.

He motioned to his guests. "After you. But take care—the steps can get slippery out here on the water."

Ananke was closest, so she grabbed the ladder and climbed up first.

RICKY ALMOST GOT caught as he was about to leave the interior hall for the portside exterior walkway, when one of the doors behind him started to open. He slipped outside and closed the door a moment before he would have been seen.

His goal of locating all the crew members was not going as smoothly as he'd hoped. He'd expected to find at least a couple of them downstairs, in either the engine room or the crew quarters. Since that had been a bust, he had to make up time, fast.

In a crouch, he moved down the walkway until he was below the first window of the lounge on the main deck. He raised the camera lens on his phone just above the window frame and looked inside. There was a bar in the front corner, a curved central seating area of leather couches in the middle, and a long buffet table resplendent with fruits and desserts along the opposite side. Three crew members, all dressed in black shirts and black shorts, were moving about, making sure everything was ready for the guests.

Check that, *four* crew members. A middle-aged woman came through the door to the hallway, carrying a tray of pastries. Ricky guessed she was the one who had almost seen him.

Four accounted for, four to find.

He continued toward the stern, stopping where the cabin ended and the aft deck began.

Crew member number five was fluffing cushions on deck chairs under an overhang that stuck out a good four meters from the rear lounge. Male, probably in his mid-twenties, and dressed like his colleagues. Beyond the covered area was the open deck where a large Jacuzzi sat.

Three to find.

He thought it likely at least one would be in the kitchen, but getting a look inside without being seen would take a lot of effort and time. Best to assume a crew member was there and spend what few minutes he had left searching for the final pair.

He needed to ascend to the upper deck.

Leading up to it were exterior stairs along both sides of the covered patio. At the moment, he couldn't use either of them without being seen by the pillow fluffer.

Ricky tried willing him into taking on another task, but the guy ignored the mental suggestion, moved to the next chair, and started up with the pillows again.

Ricky crept to the waterside edge of the walkway and looked up, wondering if he could climb on top of the railing and pull himself onto the next deck. The answer was a resounding probably not.

As he turned to look for another option, one of the people in the interior lounge shouted, "Tomas!"

Ricky ducked against the wall below the window again, thinking he had been spotted. But instead of someone running toward him, he heard the fluffer walk casually across the deck and into the lounge. Ricky quickly snuck over to the nearer set of stairs and took them to the next deck, reaching the top right before Tomas, or someone, walked back outside.

The old Ricky Orbits luck kicking back in, he thought, grinning.

The upper deck had a much smaller exterior area that sat outside a smaller, window-lined room. The interior space appeared to be designed more for meetings than social events. The lights were on a low setting, and no one was inside.

This deck had no exterior walkways along the sides, leaving him no choice but to enter the room and proceed to the doors at the other end.

In addition to the conference table in the middle and two desks along the port wall, the room had a similar, though smaller, bar to the one in the space below. One of the three doors along the back wall was behind it. Figuring it probably led to a liquor closet, he focused his attention on the other two.

The first door opened into a spacious bathroom. The other proved more interesting, as beyond it was a short, wood-paneled hallway. This had two doors in addition to the one he'd just stepped through, one on the starboard side and one straight ahead. The latter had a sign attached to it that read BRIDGE, while the former had none.

He put an ear against the unlabeled door and heard nothing. He tried the handle, and when it moved, he considered pushing the door inward but decided against it.

He listened at the bridge door and heard two voices conversing.

He grinned. Here were the final two crew members.

From somewhere behind him, he heard the hum of a distant boat motor. It sounded very much like the one he'd heard a little while earlier. He returned to the conference room and crept onto the outdoor deck.

The noise was getting louder. He peeked over to the portside railing. Cutting through the water between two of the other docks was a small motorboat filled with people. Ricky used his camera to zoom in on the vessel. It was a hard to make out details, but he was able to count six people on board.

He looked around. Though he was still alone, he felt way too exposed. He spotted a ladder tucked against the wall near the conference room entrance, its width a match for the notches he'd noticed along the roof.

He removed the ladder from its hooks, mounted it in the notches, and hurried up. When he reached the top, he pulled the ladder up with him.

He had reached the very top of the ship. Given the pair of lounge chairs, he figured it was used as a sun deck. There was a short railing around the edge. Ricky crawled over to it and checked the marina again.

The small boat was close enough now for him to pick out Ananke, Rosario, and Liesel sitting on one of the benches. With them were two men and another woman. One man was Gutiérrez, and the other was piloting the boat, wearing the same type of outfit as the *Angelina*'s crew. Ricky had no idea who the other woman was. She was sitting a little off from the others and looking at her phone. She was wearing a dress, but it was considerably more subdued than the outfits Ananke and the others were wearing. He had a feeling she wasn't someone Gutiérrez had picked up at his party.

The boat approached the yacht and stopped beside a ladder mounted over the edge of the *Angelina*. The first one up was the unidentified woman, followed by Ananke, Rosario, and Liesel. Once Gutiérrez had climbed the ladder, the motorboat cruised out of sight around the bow of the *Angelina*.

Ricky could hear talking below, and caught a few words here and there, but not enough to understand what the conversation was about. After several seconds, the voices moved and then disappeared altogether, the party presumably having entered the main deck lounge.

Ricky switched to the other side of the roof and looked for where the smaller boat had gone. Turned out, it had only circled around the dock so it could be tied up on the other side. When the kid who'd been piloting it finished securing it, he walked onto the yacht.

Great, yet another one I have to worry about.

But Ricky's concern proved unfounded. A few minutes later the kid walked off the boat again, with a backpack over his shoulder, and headed to shore via the dock, looking like someone who'd finished work for the night. Apparently he didn't live on the ship or was staying somewhere else tonight. Either way, he was one fewer problem on Ricky's list.

Ricky stretched out on the roof and looked at the stars. Now he needed to wait until everyone settled in. After that, the real fun would begin.

ELEVEN

"IS HE SERIOUS?" Liesel asked.

She was holding up what technically might be called a one-piece swimsuit, but was more tiny bits of black cloth linked by narrow strips not much wider than fishing line.

"Please tell me none of these have been used before," Rosario said, gingerly lifting the top half of a yellow-striped bikini.

After Gutiérrez had suggested they move their festivities to the Jacuzzi, he'd led them to this room one deck below the lounge, in which there was a cabinet filled with swimsuits.

"Just choose something you're comfortable with," Ananke said.

"I am not comfortable with any of this," Liesel said. "It is…"

"Demeaning?" Rosario said.

"Yes. That is the word."

"I agree," Ananke said, "but we have to keep the bigger picture in mind."

"The bigger picture is if he touches me, I will kill him."

"Then we'll make sure you're not sitting next to him."

"Hold on," Rosario said. "I do not want him touching me, either."

"If you two want to stay here, I'll go out alone. I'll tell him you got sick, or fell asleep, or something. I don't want you doing anything you don't want to."

"Do *you* want to do this?" Liesel asked.

"Not particularly. But all I can think about are those one hundred and twenty-seven people, and at the moment this is the only way for us to find out where they are."

"We are not going to let you go out alone," Rosario said.

Liesel pulled out a dark blue suit. "I guess this one is not…horrible."

Rosario rummaged around and pulled out a red bikini that would cover more than the others in the drawer.

Ananke went for the lavender number that she actually thought was cute. After they changed, she retrieved the vial that had been hidden in the lining of her dress, grabbed one of the beach towels by the door, and tucked the vial into it.

"Let's get this over with," she said.

When they emerged into the hallway, Gutiérrez was waiting, wearing a gag-inducing pair of green Speedos and a towel over his bare shoulders.

"Stunning, all of you," he said.

"Convenient that you have so many suits available," Rosario said.

"I never know when I might have guests." He motioned to the stairs. "Shall we?"

He led them up to the lounge, where five crew members stood at the ready—three behind the tables of food, one behind the bar, and the other near the outer door, holding a tray of champagne flutes.

A warm breeze caressed them as they stepped outside and crossed the deck to the Jacuzzi.

"You can put your towels there," Gutiérrez said, indicating a shelf beside the spa.

Trying not to think about what activities had previously taken place in the tub, Ananke stepped into the water. Obviously the thought was on Rosario's mind, too, because Ananke was pretty sure her friend whispered, "We're all going to need shots after this."

The water was pleasant, though, and the jets felt good against Ananke's legs and back.

The crew member holding the tray had followed them out. He handed each a flute, and set the bottle in a bucket of ice on a nearby table.

Gutiérrez looked like he was about to make a toast, but stopped and said, "I almost forgot."

He touched something on the deck, next to the tub. A panel emerged from where his hand had been, and the tablet computer it held came to life. On the screen were various digital controls. After he touched one, music began playing from unseen speakers. He tapped the top of the panel and it descended back into the deck.

Raising his glass, he said, "Welcome to the *Angelina*. Whatever your desire, just ask."

WHEN RICKY HEARD Ananke and the others walk out onto the aft deck, he scooted to the edge of the roof for a look.

What the hell?

Except for a crew member toting alcohol, everyone was wearing swimsuits. But not your everyday, let's-go-for-a-dip kind. These were strip-club approved, micro garments. Though a little part of him appreciated the view they afforded, he felt…weird. Protective, even. Not that Ananke or Rosario or Liesel would need or accept his protection, but he didn't like it. If they'd put them on of their own accord, that was different, but he knew they were only wearing them because of Gutiérrez. And that made it wrong.

The fact that he was thinking this way also felt weird. He wasn't used to it, and wasn't sure he liked it. But he couldn't seem to turn it off.

"This is what working with women has done to you," he grumbled, and immediately chastised himself for thinking that. Then chastised himself again for chastising himself.

He closed his eyes.

Focus.

He needed to stay on task. Any thoughts beyond that was garbage.

He opened his lids in time to see everyone climb into the Jacuzzi. Champagne was handed out, and Gutiérrez touched something that apparently started a sound system, because all of a sudden techno music blared across the deck.

Ricky's head bobbed with the beat.

He doubted he'd have a better cue to get things started.

Keeping his movements slow, he lowered his head over

113

the edge of the roof and looked back into the conference room. Still empty.

He checked the Jacuzzi. Gutiérrez was sitting so that when he faced forward, he was angled somewhere between the bow and the starboard side. Ananke had smartly sat beside him so that when he looked at her, he was facing aft. And boy, did Gutiérrez seem to like looking at her.

Ricky quietly worked the ladder over the edge and set it in its notches. After confirming Gutiérrez was still occupied, Ricky climbed down.

As he disconnected the ladder, he glanced back, and could have sworn Ananke was looking at him so he gave her a thumbs-up. He put the ladder away and headed into the conference room.

GUTIÉRREZ WAS REGALING Ananke with a story about a party he once attended along with several top music artists, including Christina Aguilera, Ariana Grande, and Rihanna. From the way he talked, he was friends with them all, though Ananke doubted both that and the party having happened.

At one point, he said something that necessitated her laughing. When she did, she looked up, and nearly lost character. Standing on the patio of the upper deck was Ricky, holding a ladder. He gave her a thumbs-up.

She looked back at Gutiérrez and reached for her flute. It was time to get things moving. She fumbled with the stem of her glass and let the flute slip into the water, spilling the champagne.

"Oh," she exclaimed, and laughed. She fished the glass out of the tub. "Sorry. I don't know what happened."

"Do not even worry about it," Gutiérrez said. "There is plenty more." He looked across the deck toward the cabin.

"I'll get it," Ananke said. She started to rise, but Gutiérrez put a hand on her shoulder.

"I insist." Raising his voice, he said, "Tomas!"

"It's right there," Ananke said.

"And *he* is right there."

The crew member who had brought the champagne came

from the lounge and hurried toward the Jacuzzi.

"Yes, *Señor* Gutiérrez?"

Gutiérrez held up his empty flute. "More all around."

Tomas picked up the bottle and filled Ananke's and Gutiérrez's glasses.

"Ladies, anyone need more?" Gutiérrez asked.

As Tomas topped off Rosario's and Liesel's flutes, Ananke restarted the process of covertly draining her drink into the spa.

RICKY MADE HIS way back to the hallway between the conference room and the bridge, where he spent a few seconds checking his dart gun and making sure the multi-dart cartridge was securely in place.

He listened at the bridge door and heard voices again. Using the bow as his orientation point, his best guess was that one of those inside was no more than five degrees to starboard, and the other about thirty more degrees in the same direction.

He turned the handle and quietly opened the door. Before even crossing the threshold, he sent his initial dart sailing toward its target—a man in a captain's uniform—and pivoted to crew member number two.

The second man looked at Ricky as the dart flew at him, but was apparently so shocked that he didn't move until he was hit, when he crumpled to the floor, joining the captain.

The surprise for Ricky was that three men were in the room, not two. The third man was off to port, working on a computer. The guy had jumped out of his chair when Ricky took his second shot, and ducked behind the counter where the computer was.

Ricky stepped farther into the room so he could see around the obstruction.

The guy was in a crouch, tapping on a phone.

"Bad idea," Ricky said.

He pulled the trigger again.

The guy collapsed, his phone hitting the floor next to him. Ricky picked it up and checked the screen. A text had been started but not sent. He erased the message and put the phone in the guy's pocket.

Patting the man's shoulder, he said, "Points for trying, buddy."

Three plus the five downstairs equaled the eight he'd expected to find. Maybe there was no one in the kitchen. He'd have to check.

Okay, five for sure downstairs, and maybe one other.

Oh, crap. The woman who'd arrived with Ananke—he couldn't forget about her. So, six for sure, and up to seven.

Back in the hallway, he checked behind the door he hadn't opened earlier, and discovered the captain's quarters. As expected, no one was home.

He hurried through the conference room and stopped just before the outside door. From there he could see the tops of the heads of everyone in the Jacuzzi. He crossed the threshold and moved forward enough to see Ananke still soaking up Gutiérrez's attention.

While that was helpful, it didn't mean Ricky could waltz down the outside stairs unnoticed. If any crew member was positioned on the deck, that person would see him.

That left climbing over the side and dropping down onto one of the main deck walkways.

He chose the port side, as there would be less chance of Gutiérrez seeing him. Forgoing the ladder, Ricky pulled himself up onto the sundeck and moved toward the bow, until he was above the end of the passageway opening two decks below.

Taking a bundle of cord from his backpack, he doubled up the rope and tied one end to the sundeck railing. He gave it a hard yank to make sure it would hold, then rappelled over the side and through the opening onto the main deck.

He sneaked over to the lounge window. Four crew members were talking near the bar. The fifth was stationed a couple of meters outside the door, on the patio, looking toward the Jacuzzi.

Staying below window level, Ricky moved along the wall until he reached the corner where the patio started, and used his phone to look around it. The outside crew member was standing on the other side of the open doorway, hands behind his back, like a soldier at parade rest.

Attached to the wall between Ricky's position and the door was a rectangular storage box. He eyed the man, then the box, then the man again. The angle seemed favorable to the man not being able to see Ricky out of the corner of his eye.

The one thing Ricky didn't have to worry about was being heard. One of the speakers blaring Gutiérrez's music was mounted under the patio overhang, directly above the crew member.

Ricky crawled over to the box and peeked over the top. Sure enough, the crew member hadn't moved.

Dart gun in hand, he slipped around the box and crept alongside it until he reached the other side. There, he returned to the wall and stopped just shy of the doorway.

Another check with his phone's camera told him those inside the lounge were still shooting the breeze. Three of the four were facing away from the door, while the fourth was in profile and positioned so that the doorframe blocked his view of his colleague outside.

Ricky moved toward his target. Though the music was still loud, when Ricky got within a meter and a half, the man tensed and started to turn.

Ricky pulled the trigger—the sound swallowed by a thumping base line Ricky could feel in his bones—and grabbed the guy before the man could hit the deck.

He looked over the guy's shoulder toward the Jacuzzi. Ananke had a hand on Gutiérrez's face and seemed to have locked eyes with him.

Were they going to kiss?

The spots behind his ears started to burn in the way they did when he became jealous. Sure, he *knew* he and Ananke hadn't been a thing for several years. And yes, he knew they'd likely never have it again, mainly because she was way too good for him. He'd been playing so far over his head when they'd gotten together, it was surprising he hadn't died from lack of oxygen. Not that he'd ever admit that to anyone.

So, it wasn't jealousy that was causing the sensation, but

anger that this asshole thought he was good enough for her. She deserved way better.

Ricky realized he'd been standing there longer than he should have been. He lifted his unconscious companion off the deck and carried him behind the starboard-side stairs, where he laid him on the ground.

Four down.

ANANKE HAD NEARLY drained her glass again, and was about to make another attempt at getting the bottle when she saw the crew member who'd been standing on the deck go slack. Before he could fall, arms grabbed him from behind.

Ricky.

"You're empty," Gutiérrez said. "I'll get Tomas."

He started to look toward the lounge.

"Not yet," Ananke said quickly. She put a hand on his cheek, turned his head, and stared into his eyes. "I'm not quite ready."

"Is that so? Perhaps there's something else you would like."

She glanced away, acting coy, but really checking on Ricky. The idiot was just standing there, staring at her.

Dude, move it!

Eyes back on Gutiérrez, she said, "We have a whole night for that."

She could feel his breathing change. "By *we*, do you mean you and me? Or…?"

Clamping down on the bile in her throat, she said, "Oh, my friends and I do *everything* together."

He stared at her for a moment and started to laugh. "I knew you were something special when I first saw you. Perhaps we should move things inside."

Now it was her turn to laugh. "Soon." She glanced toward the main cabin and was happy to see that Ricky and the crew member were no longer there. "I think I'll have that champagne now."

Gutiérrez tried turning his head toward the lounge, but she held his face where it was. "Let me. Please."

He dipped his head. "As you wish."

As she climbed out of the Jacuzzi, she picked up her towel and wiped the moisture off her glass, while palming the vial she'd hidden in the towel's folds.

She uncorked the champagne, filled her glass, and dumped the vial's contents into the bottle.

Turning back to the spa, she said, "Anyone need a top-off?" Without waiting for a response, she carried the bottle over, and held the open end toward Gutiérrez's glass. "You look like you could use some more."

"Thank you, yes."

She filled his flute and set the bottle down next to the tub. "Better to keep it within reach, don't you think?"

"Not a bad idea." Gutiérrez lifted his glass "To an unforgettable night."

Or the opposite, Ananke thought as she smiled and tapped her flute against his.

RICKY LEANED AGAINST the wall next to the lounge door only long enough to confirm the quartet inside was still in the same positions. Staying low, he eased into the room and tucked against the wall. Since there was no way he could catch all four before they fell, he didn't even attempt to get close. He simply fired off a dart for each and watched them collapse.

Eight down.

That left only the woman who'd been on the small boat, and possibly someone in the kitchen.

He went in search of the latter first. The kitchen was empty. Not only that, there were no burners on, no food being prepped. The whole place was tidy, giving the impression that work in the kitchen had been completed.

So, his original estimate of the crew's size had been correct.

Time to find the woman.

The only deck he hadn't been on was the one where the passenger quarters were located. It seemed a fair guess that's where she was, so he descended the short set of steps and found himself in a hallway that ran almost the length of the ship.

There were nine doors, one at the bow end and four along each side.

Ricky moved from door to door, listening for activity inside. All were silent. Maybe the woman had gone to sleep. Or perhaps she wasn't on this deck at all.

If that was true, where the hell was she?

He began to check each room.

LUISA CLICKED OUT of her email program and brought up the spreadsheet again. She quickly went through the items on the active list, color coding them to update their status, and checked that all the numbers were correct. It wasn't their most profitable day ever, but it was more than satisfactory.

The coming month would be a busy one, and her boss would have to do a little less playing and a lot more paying attention to accounts. She didn't begrudge him his little pleasures—he was the one who'd built the business in the first place—but she was beginning to wonder why she didn't go into business for herself. She did pretty much everything now. It would sure be nice to do that with something she had an actual stake in.

Someday, she thought as she closed the computer. *Soon.*

She stood up and stretched. What she'd really like to do was go to sleep, but since word had not come down that Gutiérrez had turned in for the night, she needed to make sure everything topside was going well before she could even consider lying down.

After checking her makeup in the mirror, she exited her room. Too tired to take the stairs, she walked down to the most forward door on the port side and entered the two-person elevator. She pressed the button for the bridge deck, planning to start her final rounds where she always did—with the captain.

RICKY WAS CHECKING the second of the starboard-side rooms when he heard an electric motor whirl to life. He returned to the hallway and followed the noise to a door on the port side. He tried to open it but it wouldn't budge. That's when he noticed an unobtrusive button next to the jamb.

Oh, crap. An elevator.

By the sounds of it, it was moving up.

Without worrying if anyone could hear him or not, he ran up the stairs to the lounge. Since the motor was still running, he hustled out the patio door and up the stairs leading to the top deck.

GUTIÉRREZ BLINKED, AND blinked again, stretching his lids wide. Swaying a little, he said, "How's everyone doing?"

"We're fine," Ananke said. "How are *you*?"

"Me?" he asked, weaving. "I'm great. Just great."

The drug she'd put into the champagne was slower acting than that in Ricky's darts, because its purpose wasn't to knock out its victim but to make him compliant. The knockout drug would come later, and would contain a component to fog most of Gutiérrez's memory of the evening.

"Isn't it time we start having…some fun?" Gutiérrez said.

"I thought we were having—"

The sound of someone running caused Ananke, Rosario, and Liesel to all turn toward the lounge. Ricky raced out and onto the stairs to the upper deck. Gutiérrez took a moment before he twisted around.

"Hey," he said loudly. "Who's that? You're not supposed to…run on my boat. Hey! No running! Hey! Hey!"

"I think he heard you," Ananke said.

"Oh, good." Gutiérrez swiveled back to her. "Were we going to my bedroom?"

"*You* were going to finish your champagne."

"Oh, right." He tipped his glass back and finished it off. "Is there any more?"

RICKEY HEARD GUTIÉRREZ yell, but he was so focused on getting to the elevator that he didn't even try to figure out what the scum said.

He flew off the stairs and raced into the conference room.

That damn door behind the bar that he'd thought was a storage closet was an elevator. As he ran to it, he realized the whine of the motor had stopped.

He grabbed the handle, fully expecting to find it locked, but the door swung open and revealed a small—and empty—elevator car.

Oh, shit.

LUISA EXITED THE elevator as another one of Gutiérrez's techno favorites came on. He'd told her the name half a dozen times but she never remembered it. Though she tolerated techno, she preferred pop music from artists like Enrique Iglesias, Shakira, and Danny Yankee.

As she moved into the hallway to the bridge, she heard her boss yell something and figured he was asking for more of whatever they were drinking. Champagne, probably. She had a feeling he wouldn't be awake again until late afternoon, but what else was new?

She opened the bridge door. "Good evening, gentlemen. How is—"

No one was there.

"Captain Ruiz?"

She took a few steps into the room and stopped in surprise.

Captain Ruiz and Javier Morales, the first officer, lay on the floor. She dropped to her knees and grabbed the captain's shoulder.

"Captain Ruiz! Captain Ruiz!"

His eyes remained shut. She checked his pulse. It seemed okay, but she was no expert at this kind of thing.

She shook him and called his name again, but he was out for the count.

She tried Morales but didn't fare any better.

She jumped back up, but as she headed to the door, she spotted another body on the floor. It was Yañez, the new engineer's mate. He was also still breathing, so she continued on her way to find help.

RICKY FIGURED THE person who'd been on the elevator was the woman. If she had come out the back of the conference room, he would have seen her. Which meant she'd gone either into the bathroom or the hallway to the bridge.

Guessing it was the latter, Ricky hurried into the hallway and over to the bridge door. Dart gun in his free hand, he shoved the handle down, yanked the door open, and ran into the woman coming out. They fell to the deck, Ricky on the bottom.

The woman pushed off him, surprised and scared. When she tried to run around him, he grabbed her ankle.

"Let go!" she said, her voice trembling yet defiant. She pulled and twisted her leg, trying to get free.

"Stop it. I'm not letting go."

Where was his gun? It should have been right—

He found the weapon under his hip. It was built from high-quality plastic, but apparently not high quality enough to survive being crushed under Ricky's ass. The trigger guard had broken off, and there was a crack at the end of the barrel. He snatched it up anyway and pointed it at the woman.

"Hold still, or I shoot."

She thrust her free foot, heel first, at his thigh.

"Ow!"

With a twist of her other foot, she broke free and sprinted to the conference room door.

"Goddammit," Ricky muttered as he hopped to his feet.

As he ran after her, he popped the cartridge from the gun, pulled out a dart, and dropped everything else on the floor.

The woman was in the conference room, rushing toward the outside door. Ricky raced across the room and got an arm around her, two meters shy of the doorway.

She tried to break free again, but was able to jerk only once before he jammed the dart into her leg.

If not for the music, her scream would have been heard several boats away. She continued to squirm another few seconds, until the drug took her under.

He laid her on the deck and was tempted to stretch out next to her. Between forcing him to chase the elevator up and their subsequent wrestling match, she'd given him quite a workout.

But rest was something he'd have to save until later. He needed to make sure there were no other people he hadn't accounted for.

He rode the elevator down to the passenger-cabin level, and quickly finished checking all the rooms. After that, he made one more trip down to the engine-room level and searched the crew quarters.

Unless someone was hiding in a cabinet somewhere, nine was the lucky number.

TWELVE

"GIVE IT ANOTHER try," Ananke said, her arm around Gutiérrez's back. Liesel was on the man's other side, helping to prop him up.

"Whoa," Gutiérrez said, laughing as his foot splashed back in the spa. "Just a bit…too much…champagne…I guess."

"A little higher this time, and you got it."

He lifted his foot again, but it was obvious he would still be a few centimeters short of clearing the Jacuzzi.

"It…keeps moving," he said.

Rosario, who had already climbed out, leaned over and lifted his foot onto the surrounding deck.

"There you go," Ananke said. "Good job."

Gutiérrez smiled. "Nothing ever stops…me."

"I can see that."

After Rosario assisted with his other leg, Ananke and Liesel walked their host toward the lounge.

"I am not sure…I feel…so well."

"You're going to be fine," Ananke said.

"Really?"

"Trust me. By tomorrow you won't remember any of this."

He looked at her as if he didn't completely understand her. "Did anyone call the…car?"

"We're already on your boat, remember?"

"What?" He looked around. "Oh. Good. Then…we don't need the car."

"Nope."

As they neared the covered patio, Ricky appeared in the lounge. His grin morphed into one of discomfort.

"Are we good?" Ananke asked.

"All good," he said.

"There was a woman with us," Rosario said.

"Got her, too. Nine total."

"Nine? Nice work." Ananke's eyes narrowed. "What's wrong with you?"

"Me? Um, nothing." He forced a smile. "You need some help?"

She shook her head. "Just figure out where we're going to put him."

"Sure."

After Ricky retreated into the lounge, Liesel whispered, "What is with him?"

"He *was* acting weird, right?" Ananke asked.

"Very weird," Rosario agreed.

When they reached the doorway, Ricky called out, "How about this?"

He was standing in a sitting area on the starboard side, touching a cushioned chair.

"Works for me," Ananke said.

She and Liesel lugged Gutiérrez over and dumped him on the seat.

"What's happening?" Gutiérrez asked.

"Just making a stop on the way to your bedroom."

"Ah, nice." He tried to don a smile, but it came out more dopey than sexy. "You will like my bedroom."

Ananke patted his cheek, then stood up and said, "Ricky, let Dylan—" She stopped and looked around. "Where's Ricky?"

Rosario pointed back toward the patio. "I think he went that way."

Through the door, they heard someone running across the deck. Ricky reappeared, carrying the towels they'd left at the Jacuzzi. He hurried over and handed them out.

"I thought you might want to cover up. You know, in case you were cold."

"Thank you," Liesel said, and wrapped a towel around her torso.

126

"That is very kind of you," Rosario said, putting hers around her waist.

Ananke took the last towel. "Are you embarrassed by our suits?"

"What? No. I just thought, like I said, that you might be cold."

He *was* embarrassed. Ananke wasn't sure how to process that. The Ricky she knew would most definitely not have been worried about covering them up. Instead of pushing him on the subject, she said, "Thank you," and pulled the towel around her body. "Let Dylan know he can come in now."

"Right." Ricky touched his comm. "Ricky for Dylan.... Hey, bud, you still awake?.... The boss says you can join us.... Copy." He looked at Ananke. "On his way."

"The container, please," she said, holding out her hand.

Ricky pulled out from his backpack a tube about the size of a roll of Lifesavers. Inside was another vial containing a different drug from the one in the champagne.

Ananke removed the vial, unscrewed the top, and raised it to Gutiérrez's lips. "Here you go, Julio. Just a sip. It'll make you feel better."

"I like feeling better," Gutiérrez muttered.

She let about a quarter of the vial dribble into his mouth.

The drug was strong, but its effect lasted only about fifteen minutes. She wanted to make sure they had enough for multiple rounds if necessary.

They could hear the rumble of an approaching boat.

"Ricky, you and Rosario help Dylan tie up," Ananke said. "Then the three of you search for any useful information."

"Sure thing," Ricky said.

He and Rosario exited the lounge.

Ananke glanced at Liesel. "Hold his head up."

Liesel moved behind the chair, lifted Gutiérrez's chin, and anchored his head with a hand on his forehead.

Ananke slapped Gutiérrez with more force than the playful taps she'd given him earlier.

"Julio, can you hear me?"

His lids all but closed, he groaned and smacked his lips.

"I need you to focus."

Another smack was greeted with the wrinkling of his nose, and finally the raising of his lids far enough for his eyeballs to peek through.

"Hi, there," he said.

"Hi, yourself. Do you know where you are?"

He looked around. "On my boat."

"Specifically?"

"The main lounge."

"Good. And what's the name of your boat?"

"The *Angelina*."

"Right again. How old are you?"

"Fifty-one. No, fifty-two. Had a birthday last month."

These were test questions, to get him in the flow.

"What would you call the work you do?"

"Shhhh. That's private."

"You can tell me."

He grinned, then lowered his voice like he was sharing a secret. "I'm a facilitator. I get things."

"That sounds fascinating. What kind of things?"

A shrug. "Whatever my clients need."

"Legal things?"

"Sometimes."

"Illegal things?"

Another grin. "Sometimes."

"I think we might have some acquaintances in common. Do you know Dalton Slater and Leonard Yates?"

"Hey, I do. You know them, too?"

"I've met them."

"Small world."

"It is, isn't it. What do they do for you?"

For the first time, he hesitated. "Why do you want to know?"

"Let's just say I'm curious."

He let this sink in before saying, "They...suppliers."

"So, they get things for you. What kind of things?"

Gutiérrez was struggling not to respond.

"Julio, what do they get for you?"

After several more seconds of fighting with himself, he blurted out, "People."

"Slaves, you mean."

A frown. "Technically, I guess."

"Technically?"

"Well—"

"Never mind. What I'd like to know is who you sell these slaves to."

"To clients who need them."

"And do you have a lot of clients who need them?" This was her biggest fear, that the people Slater and Yates had kidnapped were now spread around among these clients.

"Not…a lot."

"How many?"

"One," he said.

Ananke's face remained neutral, but she felt a huge sense of relief. Unless that client had then sold the people to someone else, all one hundred and twenty-seven could very well be in one place. "Who is it?"

Gutiérrez did not reply.

She asked again, but he remained tight-lipped. The drug was effective, but did not work one hundred percent of the time.

She decided to come at it from a different angle.

"When was your last shipment from Slater and Yates?"

Another pause, but only so he could think. "A month ago. Or maybe six weeks."

That fit with the information the Administrator's people had dug up. "And you sold it to your client."

"Yes."

"Who are they?"

"I…can't."

Ananke had him drink another dose. After she gave it a minute to settle in, she asked, "Julio, what's the name of your client?"

"I…please…I…"

Something about this client was holding back Gutiérrez.

"Why can't you tell me

"Too…dangerous."

"You're afraid they'll kill you?"

"Or worse."

"You can at least tell me where you sent the shipment."

Gutiérrez bit his lip.

"Come on, I'm just looking for the place, that's all. Not the name of your client."

In a quiet voice, he said, "It...went to the...city."

"That's a little vague. Which city?"

"No. The city."

"Julio, I need the name of the city."

He shook his head. "No more. Please."

"Can you at least tell me—is this where all your shipments of people went?"

She thought he wasn't going to answer, but then he whispered, "Yes."

"I THOUGHT YOU guys were never going to call," Dylan said as he tossed Ricky the mooring line.

"The ladies were enjoying their time in the Jacuzzi," Ricky said, tying the rope to the dock.

"That is *not* true," Rosario said.

"All I can say is that there was a lot of drinking and laughing going on."

She glared at him. "Everything is not always what it appears." She turned to Dylan. "You have my things?"

Dylan tossed her the backpack that had been in the gear bag.

"Come on," she said. "We have a lot of ship to cover."

They started at the bow of the passenger-cabin level, in Gutiérrez's master stateroom. The only unusual thing they uncovered was a hidden camera system that could be activated from the bed.

They moved on to the other cabins, dismissing most as not containing anything useful. The one Ricky guessed belonged to the woman he'd knocked out last, however, turned into a bit of a gold mine. Using equipment from her backpack, Rosario cloned the woman's computer drive while Ricky and Dylan shot pictures of the documents they found on her desk. A search of the cabinets turned up a couple of jump drives that Rosario also copied. Once they were done, they made sure everything looked as it had when they arrived, then headed out.

They searched the crew quarters and engine room next, but found nothing important. So up they went, passing through the main deck and taking the stairs to the bridge level.

On the bridge itself, Rosario made digital copies of the navigational data, while Ricky and Dylan took pictures of several pieces of paper related to the ship's travels. Then it was on to the conference room, where they found three additional computers—two that looked like they were used as internet portals only, while the third appeared to be Gutiérrez's personal laptop. Again, clones were made of everything.

With nowhere else to check, they descended to the main deck and joined Ananke and Liesel, who were standing out of earshot of Gutiérrez. Not that they needed to worry, as he looked like he was asleep.

"Success?" Ricky asked.

"Not as much as I would like," Ananke said. "He's resisting giving the name of his client. What about you guys? Any luck?"

"We found a lot of data," Rosario said, "but I do not know what any of it is yet."

"Can you do a down-and-dirty search through it right now? See if there's anything on the shipment from Slater and Yates?"

"I can try. If there is any heavy encryption I will probably need more firepower than I have here."

"We can't leave until we have a clearer picture of what our next step will be. If I have to, I'll keep pressing pretty boy, but I'm not sure how much more I can get out of him."

"Let me see what I can do," Rosario said.

As she set up her laptop, Ricky asked, "Did you get *anything* useful out of him?"

"Not really," Ananke said. "He just kept telling me the shipment was sent to the city."

"Which city?"

"I asked the same question, but that's all he'd say."

"The city," Ricky said, mulling over the words. "Huh."

While Rosario was doing her thing, the rest of the team carried the unconscious crew members downstairs to their berths, where they stripped them to their underwear and put them under the covers. Since they didn't know who slept in which bed, they made their best guesses. They then took the captain to his room and the woman named Luisa down to hers, arranging them the same way.

There would be a lot of confusion when everyone woke up, but they would never find out what had happened.

The team wiped down surfaces any of them might have touched, and used the handheld vacuum cleaner from Rosario's backpack to suck away stray hairs.

Given that Gutiérrez had his own bedroom bugged with cameras, it was a fair bet there was also a ship-wide system. It didn't take much searching to discover the hidden cams throughout the lounge and main deck.

"They've got to feed to someplace," Ananke said. "I'll check the bridge. Ricky, see if there's anything in the bedrooms. Liesel and Dylan, check around the engine room."

Ricky drew the winning ticket. In one of the unused guest rooms, he discovered several digital storage devices, a wireless router to collect the feeds from the cameras, and a black box that he guessed was the control unit.

Rosario provided the last clue to how it all worked. When Ananke asked if she detected any other devices on board, Rosario searched the boat's Wi-Fi and discovered three iPads scattered throughout the ship. Triangulating their locations, they found the nearest one hidden inside the armrest of one of the built-in couches. An app on the tablet controlled the cameras and associated storage devices.

Rosario demonstrated what needed to be done to erase all the footage from the time Gutiérrez woke up that previous afternoon until the present, and Ricky and Dylan were given the tedious job of scrubbing the video. When they finished, Rosario programmed the system to remain off until six a.m., and returned to the task Ananke had originally assigned her.

Ananke checked the time. It was nearing three a.m.

They'd been on the *Angelina* longer than she had hoped to be. She gave Rosario another few minutes, then asked, "Have you got anything yet?"

"Like I thought, most of the data is encrypted. I did manage to find a few emails with mentions of 'the city' in them. From the context, they seem tied into the same place we are looking for. The email addresses listed are dummies, but I should be able to back trace the message to their source and find out who really sent and received them. *After* I break the rest of the encryption."

"How long will that take?"

"At least another hour."

The emails were better than nothing, and there was likely more in the data that would help. "Okay. I think we need to wrap it up here. Let's get Gutiérrez down to his room and head back to the hotel."

DYLAN STEERED THE *Viper* out of the marina, circled back around the island, and aimed for the coast.

Ananke stared out at the water, her thoughts on the hundred and twenty-seven people Slater and Yates had sold to Gutiérrez. Being African American, she was maybe more than a little touchy on the whole slavery subject, but she didn't have to be a great-great-great grandchild of slaves to know human bondage was evil.

Whatever it took, she would make sure the captives were freed.

"Oh, crap," Dylan said.

Ananke looked over. "What's wrong?"

Ricky, who was sitting next to Dylan and looking toward the coast through binoculars, said, "Our friends are back."

"Gutiérrez?" she asked, though that didn't make any sense. Gutiérrez and the others would be unconscious for the next twelve hours at least. And if someone else had come aboard the *Angelina*, all he would have found was everyone in their beds.

"If only," Ricky said. He lowered the glass and glanced at Dylan. "Maybe go east for a bit before heading into shore."

"They obviously have me on their radar," Dylan said. "We'd do better to go back around the island."

"Then maybe that's what we should do."

Ananke leaned between the two men. "What the hell are you guys talking about?"

Ricky pointed toward the shore. About a kilometer away, a boat with flashing red lights was moving toward them.

"They're coming after us?" she asked.

"I don't see a lot of other boats around," Ricky said,

"But why would they care? We're not speeding or anything."

"Not *now*."

"What do you mean, not now?" Then it hit her. *Our friends are back*, Ricky had said. "Oh, for God's sake. Were you guys racing around earlier?"

The guilt on Dylan's face was unmissable.

"There might have been a little excessive speed," Ricky admitted.

"And they stopped you? When were you going to tell me this?"

"They didn't *stop* us so there was no reason to tell you."

"Then *why* are they coming after us now?"

"There *might* have been a little bit of chasing."

"What?"

"It wasn't even a contest," Ricky said. "Dylan here did a fabulous job. They never got close enough to see us."

Ananke looked from his attempt at a disarming smile to Dylan, who was staring straight ahead. "If they didn't get close enough to see you, then why do you think they're coming after us now?"

Ricky shrugged, like a kid caught shaving the dog but acting innocent despite the electric razor in his hand.

"So, um, what should I do?" Dylan said.

"Back to the island sounds smart to me," Ricky said.

"You're sure they never saw you?" Ananke asked.

"Only as a dot on their radar."

Ananke thought for a moment. "Keep heading to shore. And act like you haven't done anything wrong."

They continued toward the coast, the boat with the flashing lights coming at them fast. When it was about a hundred meters away, its spotlight blazed on, illuminating the *Viper*.

A voice came over a loudspeaker. "Cut your engines and prepare to be boarded."

Dylan glanced at Ananke.

"Do it," she said.

Dylan killed the engine. The coast guard vessel swung around the *Viper* in a full circle before approaching on the port side.

"Maybe I should talk to them," Ricky said. "You know, *mano a mano*?"

"I don't even want you to look at them," Ananke said, then turned to Dylan. "You, neither."

"Yes, ma'am," Dylan said.

As the boat came alongside, Ananke checked her dress and moved to the edge of the boat, smiling.

"Good evening," she said. "Is there a problem?"

The three men standing along the side of the other vessel looked surprised by the presence of a tall, provocatively dressed woman.

"Uh...good evening," the one wearing an officer's uniform said. "How long have you been out on the water tonight?"

"Oh, well, I'm not sure." She turned to Liesel and Rosario. "What do you think? An hour?"

"Maybe an hour and a half," Rosario said.

Ananke turned back to the officer, and noted that bringing her two friends into the conversation had achieved the desired result. The men were openly staring at them.

"Maybe an hour and a half," she said.

"That's all?" the officer asked, trying to maintain some sense of formality.

"Couldn't have been much more than that. We were out dancing. Is something wrong?"

Uncertainty had entered the man's eyes. "There was, um, a boat about the same size as yours, moving recklessly through the bay."

"When was this?"

"Between eight and nine p.m."

"Well, that definitely wasn't us. We were still getting ready for dinner then."

"What about them?" He nodded toward Dylan and Ricky.

"All of us," she said.

"One moment, please."

The officer left his two colleagues at the railing and ran up some stairs into the boat's main cabin.

"You boys having a good night?" Ananke asked.

A nod from one, and a croaked *yes* from the other.

"It's a beautiful night, isn't it?"

No responses this time, so she gave up on the small talk.

Another minute passed before the officer reemerged and descended to the railing.

"I apologize for making you wait. Have you noticed any suspicious activity on the water?"

She pretended to think, then shook her head. "Not a thing." She looked back at her team and they all shook their heads, too.

"No boats racing around?"

"Sorry. It's pretty quiet out here."

He frowned. "Thank you for your help. You are free to go."

"Thank *you*. Hope you find whoever it is you're looking for."

As soon as the coast guard boat pulled away, Ananke said to Dylan, "Take us in."

ANANKE DIDN'T SAY another word to Ricky and Dylan until the team returned to the hotel, at which point she said, "Get some sleep, and be prepared to leave early. And *no* going back out for a nightcap. Understand?"

"Absolutely," Dylan said. "No problem. Straight to bed."

"What about a beer in the hotel bar?" Ricky said.

Ananke's eyes narrowed.

"Okay, okay. I'll just get something out of the minibar."

When the men were gone, Ananke turned to Rosario. "Unfortunately, I don't think you'll be getting much sleep. The sooner we can figure out what our next move should be, the sooner we can get out of here. And at the moment, that all depends on what you dig up. I'll stay up with you and help."

She didn't think Gutiérrez would be a problem, but there was always the chance he'd stumble onto who had done this to him. She did not want to be around if that happened. As for him paying the price for his part in the human trafficking, that would have to wait until after the team's mission was concluded.

"I would like to assist also," Liesel said.

ANANKE, ROSARIO, AND Liesel uncovered several pieces of the puzzle while it was still dark, but were unable to hammer down their next move until a good hour after the sun started shining through the hotel room's windows.

Ananke's first call was to the pilot of their jet, who told her the plane could be ready to take off within ninety minutes.

"Then that's when we leave," she said.

She called the Administrator and brought him up to speed.

"Should I divert the *Karas Evonus*?" he asked when she was done. Their floating headquarters was en route to Panama City, in case they needed its resources there.

"No reason to change until we have a better idea of what city they have been taken to."

"All right. Keep me posted."

"Will do."

Calls three and four were to Dylan and Ricky, telling them to meet in the lobby in thirty minutes. Dylan sounded like he'd been sitting by the phone. Ricky, on the other hand, was obviously still in bed. Both promised to be downstairs on time.

With all that out of the way, Ananke finally was able to take a shower and put on some clean clothes. When she reached the lobby, she found the other four already there. Rosario had arranged for a van to take them to the airport, so all Ananke had to do was load her stuff in back and climb on board.

When they arrived at the airport, they were met near the

private aircraft terminal by the jet's copilot in an airport van. They transferred all their bags aboard, and proceeded on foot into the small terminal to go through Customs and Immigration, while the copilot drove their luggage to the plane, where it would be loaded without being checked.

At 9:24 a.m., the jet was cleared to taxi to the runway.

"So, anybody want to tell D-boy and me where we're going?" Ricky said.

"D-boy?" Dylan said. "Do *not* call me that."

"What's wrong? It's the first—"

"Seriously? Haven't you a brain in your head?"

"Calm down. It's just a nickname."

"Not my nickname."

"Okay, okay. Fine. How about…Pickle?"

"Pickle?"

"Dylan. Dyl. Dill pickle. Get it?"

Dylan stared at him.

"Can someone tell Pickle and me where we're going?"

"Bogotá," Ananke said.

"Hold on," Dylan said. "I don't want to be called—"

"As in Colombia?" Ricky asked.

"Unless you know of another one."

"And what are we doing there?"

"Paying a visit to the family of a man named Simon Estrada."

"And he is…?"

The engines increased in volume, and the plane picked up speed. Ananke waited until they were airborne before saying, "He's someone who used to work for Gutiérrez."

She hit the button that changed her seat into a flat bed. Rosario and Liesel did the same.

"He quit?" Ricky asked.

"More like let go. Permanently."

"Oh. Bummer for him. So, you think his family might know something?"

"That's the idea." She slipped earplugs in and turned her back to him. "If you don't mind, some of us haven't slept yet."

Knowing Ricky, he probably asked her something else,

138

but moments after she closed her eyes, she was out.

THIRTEEN

THE MEETING TOOK place in a sleek conference room inside a shiny office building, overlooking San Diego Bay.

In attendance were Carlo Nevarez and Miko Wright of AJS International, and Bertrand Carver and Erica Munson of Nouvel Espace.

Nouvel Espace specialized in the manufacturing of knockoff clothing based on high-profile designer lines. The company was good at what it did, which was evident from the continually increasing number of contracts it received.

With that kind of success, however, came complications, such as maintaining production schedules for Nouvel Espace's customers, and delivering said product at the contracted, affordable prices. The inability to deal with these issues was the reason Carver, Nouvel Espace's founder and president, had told Munson, his VP of operations, to set up the meeting with AJS.

AJS was what its owner, Salvador Aquino, referred to as "the structure underneath." This was a fancy way of saying AJS offered services in support of other corporations—services that no one else needed to know about. They were the dirty little secret you never tell even your best friend.

"We've gone over your projections, and your schedules," Miko said.

"Then you understand the problems we face," Munson said.

"I see them more as opportunities than problems. Anything that grows your business cannot be a bad thing."

"True," Carver said.

"What you are looking for is a way to maximize these

opportunities," Miko said. "And by calling us, that is exactly what you will be doing."

"That sounds all well and good, but what we're interested in is seeing specifics on how AJS can help us," Munson said.

Miko nodded to Carlo, who removed two spiral-bound reports from his briefcase and slid them across the table.

Carver and Munson picked up the documents.

Carver hadn't even reached the second page before he looked up. "Are these numbers accurate?"

"They are," Miko said.

"How can you possibly do it for this low?"

"There's a more detailed breakdown toward the end of the report, but in brief, we can exploit economies of scale based on several accounts we work on. Plus the bid includes a new-client discount."

"Then the price will go up if we continue to use you?" Munson asked.

"It will, but only fractionally. You'll see that in there, too. In essence, the price you pay will always be at least twenty-five percent less than you will be charged anywhere else."

"Because of your economies of scale," Carver said.

"In general, yes. Like I said, there are several factors involved."

"Who are these other accounts you will balance our work with?"

Miko smiled sympathetically. "Mr. Carver, that is information I cannot now, or ever, share with you. Just like none of our other clients will ever know about you."

Carver leaned back, his eyes narrowing. "I'm not a business newcomer. I've run Nouvel Espace for over twenty years now. I know how hard it is to keep a secret. So how can we be sure no one will ever find out?"

"Because the only ones at AJS who will know who you are will be Carlo, me, and of course Mr. Aquino."

"Just the three of you?" Munson said. "How can that possibly work?"

"You are familiar with our ability to get things done, or you wouldn't have called us. Can you name one of our clients?"

Neither Munson nor Carver said anything.

"And there you go. It works because it does. But if the fact we are not more transparent is a problem for you, you are free to contract someone else to do the job. Our feelings will not be hurt. I only ask that you please return those reports to me."

He held out his hand.

"I don't think that will be necessary," Carver said.

Miko kept the smile off his face. Carver's response had been inevitable. Nouvel Espace had painted themselves into a corner, and AJS was their only way out.

"Once we sign the contracts, how long will it take before you can start?" Carver asked.

"We can begin prepping for the job the day we receive your specs and patterns. Actual production will begin as soon as the fabric arrives. Which means if you were to sign right now, we should be able to have the first shipment of finished product ready to go in six days."

Carver and Munson gawked, then consulted with each other in hushed voices. When they finished, Carver said, "Shall I use your pen or mine?"

MIKO WAITED UNTIL he'd been informed the Nouvel Espace team had left the building before he called Salvador Aquino.

"We just finished," he told his boss.

"And?"

"Everything went as we hoped. They even gave us a thumb drive with the patterns and specs. Carlo will be bringing it back to the City this evening."

"Do you foresee any problems?"

Miko was the head of manufacturing for Aquino, which meant he oversaw not only the clothing operation but also the electronics, mechanical, and the dozen or so smaller, specialized operations.

"None. Buildings 8 and 21 are finishing up that job for the Italians, and my plan is to transition them to this as soon as they're ready."

"What about prospects for future work?"

"Once they see what we can do, I have no doubt they'll be

pushing more and more projects our way." This was the pattern that had repeated itself time and again with most of their clients.

Aquino grunted his approval. "When will you return?"

"I have that meeting in Toronto tomorrow evening but will be leaving right after." That would put him back in the City by noon the following day.

"Good. Come see me when you're here. I want to discuss where we are with the expansion plans."

"Yes, sir. I will."

Fourteen

HENRIETTA AND ALFONSO stayed at Ramon's house for five weeks before the call came. She could tell from listening to Ramon's side of the conversation that this was it, but she said nothing when he hung up.

Ramon stared out the window for several seconds before he turned to her. "It's time."

"Where are they?"

"Veracruz."

She had never been to Veracruz. She had never been to most places.

On a never-used cell phone, she called the number Ramon had been given, and set up an appointment for first thing the next morning with the recruiters from Resort Staffing Opportunities, the alias the people who'd taken Gloria were using now.

When she finished, Ramon said, "Well done. Now go pack. You'll leave as soon as Pablo and Jesús can get here."

When she told Alfonso it was time, he once more tried to convince her he should come along. "You might need me," he insisted.

"I need to do this alone. You know that. You can help *Señor* Silva here."

"Doing what?"

"Whatever he needs."

When Pablo and Jesús showed up forty-five minutes later, she had to track Alfonso down in his room to say goodbye. At first he didn't even look at her, but when she turned to leave, he said, "Wait."

He ran to her and hugged her tight. "Don't go."

"I have to."

"I-I know. It's just…"

"It's going to be okay."

"You promise?"

"Yes." She could feel him holding back tears. "I love you."

One sob, and a blurted "I love you, too."

IT WAS NIGHT by the time they reached Veracruz.

The Martinez brothers took her to an apartment owned by the friend of a cousin of one of the Searchers—as the members of the group called themselves. If anyone inquired, the landlord would say Henrietta had been living in the building for six months. Several other tenants were given monetary gifts to repeat the same.

While keeping her real first name, Henrietta would use the last name Torres so that she couldn't be connected to her sister. In the weeks they'd been waiting for the call, Silva had secured enough fake documents to sell the new identity.

The Martinez brothers were put up in another apartment in the same building, where they could keep an eye on her and communicate with her without it being suspicious.

The next morning, following the instructions she'd been given, Henrietta made her way to an office not far from the harbor. The only sign on the door was a number. She wasn't sure if she should knock or walk right in. In the end, she knocked, thinking that would help sell the uncertainty of the person she was portraying, an uncertainty she actually possessed.

From inside, a raised voice said, "It's open."

She entered the office. It was a small room, with a single desk at the other end, at which sat a woman who couldn't have been much older than Henrietta. On the wall behind the woman was another door.

The woman smiled. "Can I help you?"

"I called about the ad yesterday. And was told to come in this morning."

"Of course. Your name?"

"Henrietta Torres."

She was given a clipboard with several forms. Using the information developed for her, she littered the pages with lies, most of which would pass a standard check. When she was done, the receptionist took the papers into the back room. When the woman returned, she said, "Sit tight. It shouldn't be long."

Twelve minutes later, the woman's phone buzzed. She picked it up, listened, then said, "You may go in now."

The back office was about half as big as the one in front. There were three people present—two men and a woman—all sitting on comfortable-looking chairs at a round table.

The younger man rose and came across the room, smiling. "Ms. Torres?"

"Yes."

"Thank you for coming in. Please join us."

He escorted her to the table, where introductions were made. The young man was Marco Campos, the older one Andre Serrano, and the woman Olivia Vega. They started by discussing the merits of their "wonderful" program. Talking up the "exotic locations" and the "interesting clientele," and touting the "excellent benefits" and "high pay versus low living costs."

A dream job, in other words.

"The only potential drawback is that if you are offered a position, you will have to move away from home," the woman said.

"I understand," Henrietta said.

"Will your family be okay with that?"

"I don't have any family," Henrietta said. "Not in Veracruz, I mean."

"Is that so?" Serrano said. "Where is your family?"

"I have an aunt in Monterrey, but I haven't seen her in many years."

"What about your parents?"

Henrietta looked down. "My mother passed away two

years go. My father left when I was a baby. I don't know where he is."

"Oh, I'm so sorry to hear that," Vega said.

"It's okay."

"No brothers or sisters?"

A head shake. "Just me."

"Then getting away will be a new start for you," Campos said.

"I was thinking the same thing."

They asked her about previous work experience, and probed into her social life. She felt confident she'd responded the way they were hoping.

As the interview came to an end, Vega said, "We are so glad to have met you."

"Thank you. I'm happy to have met you, too."

"One last question. The positions we're offering need to be filled immediately. If you were to be offered a job, you may have to leave on less than a day's notice. Would that be a problem?"

"Less than a day?" Henrietta said, acting surprised, because who wouldn't be caught off guard by a question like that? She pretended to think for a moment. "I guess that should be okay. My only problem might be with my landlord."

"We can help you with that, if necessary."

"Okay. That would be great."

After everyone shook Henrietta's hand, Vega said, "Keep your phone close. If you are chosen, you'll be getting a call soon."

AT 9:23 P.M., HER cell phone rang.

"Henrietta, this is Olivia Vega with Resort Staffing Opportunities."

"*Señora* Vega, it's a pleasure to talk to you again."

"I have great news. I'm calling to offer you a position."

"Really? I didn't even allow myself to hope."

"It's an entry-level position. You'll start as an assistant clerk in the reception department, but there will be opportunities to move up. The best part, the resort is on an island just off Cancun and is *very* exclusive."

"I can hardly believe it."

"Well, by this time tomorrow, you will."

"This time tomorrow?"

"Yes. Like I said earlier, we need someone immediately. We would like you to leave in the morning. If that doesn't work for you, you need to let me know now and we'll move on to the next candidate."

"No, no. I don't want to miss this opportunity. I'll make it work."

"Excellent. Will you need us to talk with your landlord?"

"Maybe. I'll call him and let you know if I have any problems."

"Perfect. As for tomorrow, a van will pick you up at our office at eight a.m. Can you be there by then?"

"Sure."

"I guess the only thing left for me to say is congratulations."

"Thank you."

Henrietta hung up, retrieved another never-used cellphone, and called Ramon.

"I got the job."

"Tell me everything they said."

WHEN RAMON AND the others had first come up with the plan to get someone taken, the big question had been how to track that person's location.

The solution was suggested by a member named Bruno Alvarado. He was a mechanic, and knew that people who could afford a tracking device would put one in their cars in case they were stolen. After much research and help from an acquaintance of Ramon's who was into electronics, they came up with something that should do the same with a person. Salvaging parts from several satellite phones, Bruno made a tracker about the width of two standard postage stamps side by side and the thickness of a pencil.

Where to put it was the next problem. They all figured their agent would be searched at some point, and any electronic devices would be taken away. The kidnappers might even take her clothes, in case something in them was trackable. So, it had to be hidden in a more permanent fashion. Again, it was Bruno who offered the answer. "They put chips in dogs, don't they?"

The chip for animals was smaller, because it was only scanned and didn't need extras like being able to receive phone calls, as the one Bruno made did. A trusted doctor had been found to implant the device when the time came. He figured out the protective material to encase the device, but warned it shouldn't remain in the host for more than six weeks.

All these details had been worked out months before Henrietta and Alfonso joined the group.

After she agreed to be the bait, Ramon had told her, "It will be inserted here," while touching the lower right side of his abdomen. "If you are ever asked, say that you recently had your appendix out."

"Will it hurt? I mean, after it's in?"

"I'm told there might be a little discomfort, but after a while you won't notice it much."

Now, a month after the procedure, the scar had faded from bright red to pink. She touched it as she dressed to leave. It barely hurt at all anymore.

When Jesús and Pablo came to her room at four a.m., she was ready to go.

The plan was for them to track her for as long as possible via the phone she'd been given, using the FindMyPhone app. Once her mobile was inevitably taken away from her, the Searchers would regularly ping the bug for its location.

"Remember," Jesús said. "We will be close, at least for a while. If you want us to pull you out, send a text, even if it's just one letter, and we will come get you."

"Thank you."

"Don't thank us," Pablo said. "We thank you for doing this."

"I hope it works."

Jesús smiled. "It will."

She wasn't sure how much he believed that, but she appreciated their optimism.

She arrived at the temporary Resort Staffing office at 7:40 a.m. The door was open, and inside she found the same receptionist from the day before, plus seven other people—five women and two men—around Henrietta's age. All seven had suitcases and expressions of excitement.

At five minutes to eight, Marco Campos, the younger man from her interview, came in through the front door, smiling. "Good morning, everyone. Big day for all of you! Let me say how glad we are that you've all chosen to join the Resort Staffing family. The van just pulled up so we'll head out in a moment. We'll be bringing your luggage in a second vehicle, so you can leave it all in here. Make sure it is properly labeled. Don't want anyone losing anything."

With the man leading the way, they exited the building and walked over to the van. Henrietta was sure none of them would ever see their luggage again. For her, that was fine. Nothing in her bag was hers in the first place. But she couldn't help feeling bad for the others, who'd probably packed some personal items they wouldn't want to lose.

She also couldn't help feeling guilty that she wasn't doing anything to keep them from getting in the van, but that would destroy any chance of finding Gloria and the others. So she climbed aboard, smiling like she was as happy to be there as they were.

The drive lasted only about fifteen minutes and ended at a building near the north end of the port.

Campos looked back from the front passenger seat and said, "There's some breakfast set up inside. I suggest you all get something to eat because you won't get the chance again until later this afternoon."

A woman behind Henrietta asked what was probably on everyone's mind. "Are we taking a boat?"

Campos smiled. "Not a boat. We're only here until our bus arrives."

They piled off the van and moved into the building. Some of Henrietta's fellow "new hires" began talking, little comments to break the ice. Henrietta avoided being pulled in. She was afraid she wouldn't be able to hide her fear and guilt.

150

Campos brought them into a large room where several long tables were set up, two of which were covered with food trays and drink dispensers. Henrietta spotted the signs for the toilets and headed into the women's room.

She entered the stall farthest from the door, locked herself in, and leaned against the wall, hyperventilating. This was crazy. What was she doing here? She was no hero. She was just a woman who, until a few months ago, had been living a simple life.

She pulled out her phone to text Jesús and Pablo, but after a few more breaths, she began to calm.

If I don't do this, I'll never see Gloria again.

As she slipped the phone back into her pocket, the door to the bathroom opened.

"Henrietta?" Campos called. "Are you in here? Is everything all right?"

"I'm fine. Just finishing up."

She flushed the toilet and, after an appropriate pause, exited the stall.

Campos was still at the door. "Are you sure you're okay?"

She smiled. "Yeah. When I get excited, I always have to…um…go."

She walked over to the sink and washed her hands.

"Totally understand. Make sure you get some food before we leave again."

"I will."

He left. Henrietta took another deep breath before following him out.

At the tables, Henrietta filled a plate with a fried egg, rice, *chorizo*, and a piece of bread, and poured herself a cup of orange juice. She took a seat near the others and dug in. After she finished the egg and was working on the rice, she noticed a couple of her companions yawning, then realized she felt a little sleepy herself.

Really sleepy, actually.

She blinked as she realized she'd been holding a piece of *chorizo* in front of her mouth for several seconds. She slipped it between her lips and chewed. Thirsty again, she reached for her glass, but misjudged its location and knocked it over.

"Oh, I'm sorry."

Though she hadn't aimed her words at anyone, a voice behind her responded, "It's okay. We can get you another."

She started to turn to see who it was but her vision blurred, and she had to grab the edge of the table to keep from falling out of her chair.

"Steady there," the same voice said. Hands were suddenly on her shoulders. "I got you."

"I...don't...feel..."

"Maybe you should rest."

Yes. That was an excellent idea. The problem was, she couldn't remember where her bed was.

She looked to her right, slowly this time. All the others had their heads on the table.

What a good idea.

She shoved her plate away, crossed her arms over the spot where it had been, and rested her head on them.

So much better.

As she was drifting off, she heard someone say, "The last one's down. We're ready to move."

She had no idea what he was talking about, nor did she care.

The only thing important...was...sleep.

PABLO MARTINEZ HAD been staring at the FindMyPhone app for what seemed like forever, so it took him a moment to realize the location of Henrietta's mobile had changed. He showed it to his brother.

"About time," Jesús muttered.

They'd been sitting in their car for nearly forty-five minutes, parked fifty meters away from the building Henrietta and the others had been brought to. The position of Henrietta's cell had changed several times in the first fifteen minutes she was there, but it had remained stationary ever since.

The information on Pablo's screen updated.

"It looks like it's coming close to the door."

Pablo sat up. The van that had brought Henrietta had left

nearly thirty minutes ago, and nothing had come to replace it.

He glanced both ways down the street, wondering if a new ride was on the way, but the few vehicles on the road were all too small for the group.

"Someone's coming out," Jesús said.

Pablo whipped his head back around to see a man come out the door, carrying a closed, microwave-sized, cardboard box. Behind him came another man with an identical box.

Pablo stared at the door, expecting more people to emerge. When several seconds passed without the door opening, he looked at his phone again. The location for Henrietta's mobile put it outside now, right at the spot where the men with boxes had been.

Looking up, he saw the men had walked over to a parked sedan and were putting the boxes into the trunk.

"Her phone must be in one of those boxes."

Jesús tensed but said nothing.

They both had known she would be separated from the device eventually. They just hadn't expected it to happen within the first hour.

After the trunk was closed, the two men drove off.

Pablo opened the app that tracked the homing device in Henrietta's stomach and had it ping her. A map popped up, with a dot glowing on it.

It was coming from the harbor but on the other side of the building, down by the water's edge.

Another ping, and the dot adjusted position and was now more dockside than on the shore.

After showing his brother the screen, Jesús started the car and tried to find someplace from where they could see that area. Unfortunately, the view was blocked by buildings and parked trucks and shipping containers.

"She's moving again," Pablo said. "Go back the other way."

Jesús made a U-turn. "Where?"

Pablo looked toward the harbor side. "Keep driving. I'll tell you when to stop." They passed several buildings and continued for several hundred more meters before Pablo said,

"Pull over here."

Before the car had come to a complete stop, he hopped out and raced across the street. The only thing blocking the view of the harbor was a chain-link fence. He checked his phone again.

A beat later, Jesús joined him. "Where is she?"

Pablo pointed. "There."

Coming into view was a medium-sized cargo ship.

Pablo turned his screen so his brother could see it. Henrietta's dot was in the middle of the harbor, right where the ship was.

FIFTEEN

The Present

THE FLIGHT TO Bogotá was not nearly long enough for Ananke to catch up on the sleep she had lost the night before, so she was still bleary eyed when they deplaned. From the looks on Rosario's and Liesel's faces, they weren't feeling much better.

They took rooms at a Holiday Inn near the airport and gathered in Ananke's room.

"Rosario, can you brief Ricky and Dylan on Simon Estrada's family?"

"Sure." Rosario opened her laptop and clicked through to the file she needed. "Estrada left behind a wife, Cecelia, age 41; and two children, Samuel, 17, and Sara, 15. They live in an area of the city known as Los Mártires, in the same building as Simon's brother, Nicholas, 48, and his family. Simon's mother lives with Cecelia and the kids, and Nicholas owns a market on the ground floor." She told them the rest of what she had found about the family, and texted everyone the building's address.

As much as Ananke would have liked to wait until the next day, they didn't know what a delay of even twenty-four hours would mean to the people they were looking for. Like it or not, she would have to rely on the two people she was least happy with at the moment.

"Rosario and Liesel, you're excused. Go get some sleep."

"I am fine," Rosario said, her eyelids drooping.

"Me, too," Liesel said, stifling a yawn.

"You're not. Either of you. I need you sharp. Now get out of here."

"You have not had any more sleep than we have," Rosario

said.

"The difference is, I'm the boss."

After Rosario and Liesel had left the room, Ananke turned her attention to Ricky and Dylan.

Ricky grinned. "I'm guessing you want us to pay these people a visit."

She took a breath. "Honestly, I would much rather be sending the two of you to your rooms."

"Oh, come on. You're not still mad about the boat, are you?"

"What do you think?"

"We were just having some fun. Right, D-boy?"

"Stop calling me that!"

"Oh, right. Sorry, Pickle." Ricky looked back at Ananke. "Those coast guard goons were uptight. We didn't hurt anyone."

Ananke closed her eyes to rein in her anger. When she opened them again, she said in a moderately calm voice, "*I* will be paying the Estrada family a visit. You two will be my backup."

"You sure you want to do that? Rosario was right—you haven't slept much, either. And, well, it kind of shows."

"I don't care if it shows," she snapped. She took another deep breath. "I am not sending you there alone. End of discussion."

"Whatever you say, boss."

"We need transportation. While you two find us something, I'm going to take a shower and change. I'll meet you downstairs in twenty."

"Got it," Ricky said.

Dylan seemed to be in the most hurry to get out of the room, while Ricky followed him at his normal, king-of-the-world pace.

Ananke shuffled into the bathroom and took a quick, hot shower. Her hope that it would wake her up proved unfounded, as she felt even more exhausted when she returned to the bedroom. According to the time on her phone, she still had ten minutes until she had to be downstairs. She pulled on her clothes, set her timer for seven minutes, and stretched out on the bed.

RICKY AND DYLAN obtained a Lada two-door SUV from the parking garage of the City Express Hotel several blocks away, and were back at the Holiday Inn with a couple of minutes to spare.

"Wait here. I'll get her." Ricky jumped out of the vehicle.

He expected to find Ananke sitting in the lobby, but she wasn't there. Figuring she was moving a little slowly, he took a seat and watched the elevators. But the doors kept opening without Ananke exiting.

He checked his watch. Five minutes past the rendezvous time. That wasn't like her. He contemplated going up to her room, but worried he'd pass her in the elevator and that would piss her off.

Three minutes later, his phone rang. He thought it was her, but the caller ID read DYLAN.

"Don't tell me I missed her," Ricky said.

"What are you talking about?"

"Ananke's with you, isn't she?"

"With me? No. I was calling to find out what the holdup was."

"She hasn't shown up yet."

"She's almost ten minutes late."

Ricky thought for a moment. "I'm going to check her room. If she shows up alone, call me."

He hung up and called Ananke's cell. Four rings, then voicemail.

He tried again and was given a repeat trip to voicemail land. He stuffed the phone back in his pocket and headed to the elevators. She couldn't get mad at him for going to check on her now. In fact, she should expect him to. Ten minutes was a long time to be overdue without some word, especially for her.

He exited on the third floor to an empty corridor. As he neared Ananke's door, he could hear a faint, repeating noise from inside, too low for him to identify.

He knocked gently. "Ananke?"

Other than the odd noise, there was nothing but silence.

He knocked again, louder. "Ananke?"

The same whole lot of zilch.

If he knocked more loudly, he would draw the attention of guests in other rooms, so he called her again. When the line rang, he could hear a low buzz inside the room that continued until he hung up.

Now he was worried. She would have never left the room without her phone. Had something happened? Someone taken her? Could Gutiérrez have woken up and somehow figured out what had happened and where the team had gone? Perhaps that was a little far-fetched, but not impossible.

He shuffled through the apps on his phone until he came to the one he'd labeled OpnSsme. It was a wireless-enabled lockpick for electronic locks. He held it next to her door, hit INITIATE, and waited for the app to do its thing. Nineteen seconds later, the indicator light flashed green, and the door clicked as the lock was released.

He eased inside. "Ananke?"

The repetitive noise was louder now. He could also hear someone breathing in counterpoint to it.

He glanced into the bathroom and saw wet spots on the floor. When he entered the bedroom, he almost laughed.

Ananke was lying on the bed, fully clothed, her mouth hanging open. On the nightstand sat her phone, its alarm ringing. He walked over and tapped STOP.

She looked so peaceful and, of course, beautiful. He had never told this to her but he'd always liked to watch her sleep. It had made him feel…content. Another thing he had never told her when they were together—or told anyone, for that matter: she was the best thing that had ever happened to him.

He blinked.

Dude, snap out of it. We got work to do.

He shook her shoulder. "Ananke? Wakey-wakey."

She groaned but didn't open her eyes.

He shook again. "Ananke. Time to go."

She turned her head away and mumbled something.

He was tempted to leave her and do the job without her.

Except, of course, she'd be furious.

"Hey," he said, shaking both her shoulders this time. "You need to get up."

She batted her eyes and struggled to focus. "Ricky? What are you doing here?"

"You were supposed to meet us in the lobby, remember?"

Her brow scrunched, then her eyes widened. "Oh, God. How long have I been out?"

"I don't know when you fell asleep, but you were supposed to meet us twelve minutes ago."

She looked at the nightstand. "I set an alarm."

"Yeah. It was going off when I came in."

"It was ringing?" she said as if she couldn't understand him.

"Maybe you should stay in bed."

"No." She pushed up on one arm and swung her legs off the mattress. She was having a hard time keeping her eyes open.

"Ananke, you're exhausted."

"No, I'm...I'm okay."

It looked like she would try to stand, but her butt never moved off the bed.

"You are *not* okay. Look, stay here. Dylan and I can do this."

"Oh, no. I don't want you talking to anyone."

"We'll just have a look around. Scope things out. That way, when you've had enough rest, we'll know what we're getting into when we go back."

She looked at him through blinking eyelids. "I don't want you talking to anyone."

"I already said we're just doing a scout."

Her eyes shut for several seconds, then popped back open. "Promise me."

"Let me help you." He eased her back down and adjusted the pillow under her head. "Get some sleep. In a few hours, you'll feel a ton better."

Her eyes started to close again, but before they did, she grabbed his arm. "Promise me."

"I promise we won't talk to anyone we don't have to."

He could see her trying to parse his words, but she finally gave up. "Don't let me sleep too long."

"I won't." When she didn't say anything else, he said, "Ananke?"

Nothing.

He pulled the cover over her, hung the DO NOT DISTURB sign on the doorknob, and headed downstairs.

"WHERE IS SHE?" Dylan said as Ricky climbed into the Lada.

"Sleeping."

"Then we're not going?"

"No, we're going without her."

Looking dubious, Dylan said, "Ananke okayed that?"

"Would I have said that if she didn't?"

"Well, um, yeah."

Ricky grimaced. "She said for us to go, okay? Now let's get this thing moving. We're burning daylight."

THE ESTRADA FAMILY lived in a neighborhood of cracked walkways, potholed roads, and rundown cars. None of the buildings lining the streets were any higher than three stories, and all looked long overdue for major maintenance. The multilevel buildings appeared to be divided into apartments on the upper floors and businesses at ground level.

The Estrada family lived in a three-story structure at the middle of their block. Balconies stuck out from the two apartment levels, both appearing to be used more as storage space than outdoor seating area. Given that each floor's balcony was undivided, Ricky guessed there was only one apartment per floor, or at least only one on the front side.

Nicholas Estrada's ground-floor market was called Abarrotes Estrada. As small markets went, it was decent sized, equivalent to a stateside 7-Eleven. Through the windows, Ricky counted five customers. The checkout counter was off to the side, preventing him from seeing who was manning the register.

The buildings around the Estradas' were shoved against

one another, with no consistency on floor height, creating a bar graphic against the backdrop of the city. The place to the Estradas' right was two stories, and to the left, one.

"Find someplace to park," Ricky said.

"Are we going in?"

"Just going to take a look around."

It was another block and a half before they found an open space.

Though Bogotá was only a few hundred miles from the equator, it was high in the Andes on a plain known as the Bogotá savanna, and was anything but tropical. The temperature seemed to have dropped a few degrees since they'd left the hotel, and if it was over sixty degrees Fahrenheit, Ricky would've been surprised. A few of the pedestrians wore light jackets, but most hadn't added any extra layers. Having lived a good portion of his life in Chicago, Ricky felt right at home in his shirtsleeves.

"What's the play?" Dylan asked.

"A little sightseeing. Get the lay of the land. We'll see where it goes from there."

They headed down the street, on the opposite side from the Estradas' building.

A couple of elderly women were coming toward them. When they neared, Dylan said, "*Buenas tardes*."

Instead of replying, the women started at them as they passed.

"Must be on the welcoming committee," Dylan whispered.

Ricky grunted. The women weren't the only ones looking at them. He'd noticed several sets of eyes pointed in their direction—a trio of young men leaning against a dented old Ford, an old woman sitting on the balcony of an apartment across the street, a potbellied bald man and his gray-haired companion in front of a store ahead.

While Ricky had some Mediterranean blood and could have probably passed for a local, Dylan's pale Irish skin was like a glowing beacon of otherness. But even if Dylan wasn't with him, the eyes would have probably still been on Ricky.

This was one of those places where if you weren't from the neighborhood, you didn't belong.

"Should we go back to the car?" Dylan whispered.

"Quiet." Ricky had a feeling speaking English would make things worse. As long as they played it cool, they should be okay.

As they neared the grocery store, Ricky slowed. A couple of female customers were exiting and a male one was entering. Otherwise, there seemed to be little change from earlier.

Ricky was hoping to get an angle on the attendant behind the counter, but checkout was too far away from the window, and all he could see was a short line of people waiting to pay.

Dylan touched Ricky's arm and whispered, "Seen enough?"

"Just chill."

Ricky studied the grocery store and snapped a few covert shots of the building on his phone before considering their next move. The truth was, without going inside, the only thing to do would be to return to the car. They could drive around the block and check for a back way into the store.

He was about to do just that, when the door next to the grocery store—the one he assumed led to the upper floors— opened. Two women exited and paused just outside.

"Get in front of me and act like we're talking," he told Dylan.

As Dylan moved into position, he said, "What do you want to talk about?"

"I don't care. Just don't say anything loud enough for anyone else to hear."

Dylan started talking in a low voice, describing the cars parked along the street.

"Perfect," Ricky said, and looked over his partner's shoulder at the women.

The younger one was probably in her mid-teens, while the older was in her late thirties or early forties. Mother and daughter?

He took a picture of them and magnified it on his screen. If they weren't related, he would eat his phone. Their eyes,

162

mouths, cheeks were nearly identical. Even their hair was the same long, thick, dark brown.

After a few moments of conversation, the younger woman disappeared into the grocery store. The older one stayed where she was.

Could they be the dead man's wife and youngest child? The ages matched.

The kid came back out seconds later with a bottle of water. When she reached the older woman, they started walking down the street away from Ricky and Dylan.

Ricky thought about following them, but before they'd gone too far, they climbed into a car parked at the curb.

"How long do I need to keep this up?" Dylan asked.

"Why are you being so whiny today?"

"I'm not being—"

"Keep at it until I say stop."

Dylan glared, then picked up the one-sided dialogue again.

Down the street, the sedan was pulling out. A Mercedes. It would have been swanky for this neighborhood if not for the fact it was at least a decade old. Ricky took pictures of it as it drove by, making sure to get the license plate.

After the car was gone, he put the phone back in his pocket. "Okay, you can stop."

"I assume it was the women you were interested in."

Ricky nodded.

"Who do you think—"

"Are you thirsty?"

"What?"

"I don't know about you, but I sure could use a Coke. Come on."

Ricky crossed the street toward the grocery store.

"What are you doing?" Dylan said, not moving.

Ricky looked back. "Were you not listening? I'm getting something to drink."

"Did Ananke say we could make contact?"

"Look around. How many people have seen us? I hate to break this to you, but we've already made contact. You can wait here if you want."

Ricky walked over to the store, Dylan catching up right before Ricky entered.

"Ricky," Dylan whispered.

"Too late to turn around now, buddy."

Ricky avoided looking directly at the counter as he moved down one of the aisles. The shelves were crammed with boxes and cans and packages of food. Along the back wall, he found two freestanding cold cabinets filled with bottled items such as soda, beer, milk, and water.

Ricky grabbed himself a Coke and a water for Dylan.

"This is such a bad idea," Dylan whispered.

"We're doing the job," Ricky whispered back. "We were told to recon so we're reconning."

As they neared the end of the aisle, Ricky got his first good look at the front counter. Behind it, on a high stool, sat a bulky man with buzz-cut hair and graying disco-era moustache. With him was a boy in his late teens, who seemed to be doing the actual clerking work.

The big man's focus was on a row of small black and white monitors showing different angles of the store. In one image, Ricky could see himself and Dylan, standing nearly out of frame. The question of whether or not the big man was paying attention to them was settled when Ricky walked out of frame and the big man turned to look straight at him.

Ricky pretended not to notice, and he and Dylan joined the checkout line. The customers in front of them finished their business and exited the store, but not before each of them shot Ricky and Dylan a suspicious glance.

When Ricky's turn came, he placed the bottles on the counter and smiled at the still staring man.

"Good afternoon," he said.

Big Man muttered what Ricky took to be a return greeting.

Ricky looked around. "Your place?"

No response this time.

Ricky hadn't planned on doing more than buying their drinks and moving on, but in all likelihood, Ananke would sleep through the night and put the mission a day behind. Just the thing she had wanted to avoid. He and Dylan had an opportunity here to keep things on track, so Ricky decided to take it.

"You wouldn't happen to be Nicholas Estrada, would you?"

The young guy froze, and Big Man's eyes narrowed.

"What are you doing?" Dylan asked in a voice so low Ricky almost couldn't hear it.

"Who are you?" Big Man asked.

"Does that mean you *are* Nicholas?"

The man put a hand under the counter, and when he pulled it back out, it was holding one of the biggest pistols Ricky had ever seen.

"I asked you a question," the man said.

Maintaining his cool, Ricky replied, "We're just two guys looking for Simon Estrada's brother."

Big Man dismounted the stool and said to the younger guy, "Clear the store and lock the door."

"That's not necessary," Ricky said.

The young guy ran out from behind the counter and began ushering people out.

"I think we might have a little misunderstanding," Ricky said. "I'm not here to cause any problems."

"Too late."

"We have a couple questions, that's all. Honestly, we can be out of your hair in ten minutes."

He heard the young guy lock the door.

"You are way overreacting," Ricky said. "Look, I know your brother got the shaft from Julio Gutiérrez. I need to find out if—"

At the mention of Gutiérrez, Big Man moved from behind the counter at a speed Ricky would have guessed was impossible. He grabbed Ricky by the neck with one hand and put the muzzle of his gun against Ricky's temple with the other.

"He's telling the truth," Dylan said. "We're hoping your brother shared some information with you that we need to know."

While Big Man didn't let go of Ricky's neck, his gun

165

swiveled from pointing at Ricky's head to Dylan's.

"We're looking for some people who were kidnapped and sold to Gutiérrez," Dylan said. "He then sold them to someone else who took them to…a city. We're trying to find out which city so we can save them. That's all."

A foot scraped across the floor at the back of the store. Ricky shifted his gaze to the side without moving his head. Standing in a doorway along the back wall was a woman who must've been well into her seventies.

"You still have not answered my son's question," she said. "Who are you?"

ANANKE'S EYES SHOT open. In the hall, outside her room, she heard the rattle of suitcase wheels, and the voices of a man and woman talking loudly in Spanish, something about not getting an upgrade that the woman thought they should have received.

Ananke grabbed her phone and checked the time—5:17 p.m. She shoved herself into a sitting position.

What the hell?

She had been asleep for nearly five hours, not the seven minutes she'd set the timer for. She opened the clock app. The timer *was* set for seven minutes, so either she hadn't started it or had turned it off without realizing it.

Even so, Ricky and Dylan should have come to find her when she didn't show up.

She opened the phone function and was about to tap Ricky's name, when she had the sudden memory of him standing next to her bed.

"Oh, crap," she muttered.

Had he really talked her into letting them go without her? What was she thinking?

She punched his name on her contacts list.

Two rings, then voicemail.

Did he just dismiss her call?

The back of her neck starting to burn, she called Dylan. She didn't even get past the first ring before an automated voice told her to leave a message. She brought up the tracking app that allowed team members to locate one another via their

166

phone signals.

"Dammit!"

The dots for Ricky and Dylan were sitting right on top of the Estradas' building.

She jumped up and called Rosario.

"Hello?" Rosario croaked, half asleep.

"Ricky and Dylan went to scout the Estradas' place by themselves."

"They what?" A shuffling of sheets from the other end. "What were they supposed to be doing?"

"They were supposed to do a scout, but with me."

"They left without you?"

"Yes."

"How long have they been gone?"

"A few hours."

Silence, then, "A few hours and you just figured it out?"

"I, um, I fell asleep."

A burst of laughter.

"Hey, it's not funny," Ananke said.

"It kind of is."

"We're talking about Ricky and Dylan. Who knows what they could have messed up?"

"We all know Ricky, but he is not going to blatantly disregard instructions, is he?"

Ananke said nothing.

"Hello? Are you still there?"

"I may have told them they could go without me."

"Sorry?"

"I was half asleep. I didn't fully realize what was happening."

"So, you are upset because they went on a scout that you gave them permission to undertake?"

"I screwed up, okay? You can give me crap about it later. Right now, we've got to get out there and make sure they haven't messed the whole thing up."

Rosario snickered. "I am sure they will be fine."

"Rosario! We're talking about Ricky."

A beat. "Give me five minutes."

Ananke's call to Liesel went only moderately better.

SIXTEEN

THE SUN WAS low on the horizon by the time the taxi dropped Ananke, Rosario, and Liesel off three blocks from the street where the Estrada family lived.

With the approaching night came a chilling of the air, making Ananke wish she had some warmer clothes. She huddled with Rosario and Liesel on the sidewalk while Rosario checked the tracker.

"They are still in the building," Rosario said, "but their phones are now on the third floor."

"Dammit," Ananke muttered. "All right, let's go."

They headed off at a brisk walk, not stopping again until they reached the block where the Estrada building was located.

"Comms on," Ananke said as she activated her set.

"Check," Liesel said.

"Check," Rosario echoed.

"All working," Ananke said. She glanced toward the grocery store. "You two wait here. I'm going to do a walk-by."

It wasn't long into her journey before she saw the market was dark. This was prime business time, when those coming home from work would pick up items for the evening. But as she neared the market's front door, she saw a sign in the window that read CERRADO, confirming it was closed.

She stopped, pulled out her phone, and called Ricky again.

Straight to voicemail.

She tried Dylan. Same.

She returned to Rosario and Liesel and told them what she'd found. "They might be in trouble. We're going to have to get inside."

Rosario worked her phone, then turned the screen so the

others could see. On it was a satellite image, focused on the roof of the Estradas' building.

"That might give us access inside," Rosario said, pointing at a dark square in the back right corner. She moved her finger to the two-story structure next door. "If we can get into this building, we should be able to climb up to it."

"But if that is not roof access, we will have wasted time," Liesel said.

Liesel was right, Ananke knew. The dark square seemed a likely way in, but they couldn't afford to lose the time if it wasn't.

"We'll go in the front door," Ananke said. She looked at the sky. The sun was setting. "Let's give it a few more minutes, wait until it gets a little darker."

Ananke spotted a nook between two buildings, almost directly across from the store, where they could wait without drawing attention. They crossed the street to the opposite sidewalk and walked toward the nook. Before they could get there, a group of five men exited a building ahead and turned in Ananke, Rosario, and Liesel's direction. The leers and catcalls started immediately, and only grew worse as the gap between them closed.

Ananke mentally forced the men to keep walking past them, but today her Jedi mind tricks weren't working.

Ananke moved to go around them, but the men were having none of it. Though she was able to get by the first two, the other three surrounded her.

"What's the hurry?" one man asked.

"Come on, baby, don't you want to talk to us?" another said.

"Get out of the way," Ananke said.

The first speaker, who seemed to be the leader, said, "You're the ones in the way. You want to leave, *you* go around us."

There was no way for her to go around without pushing through them, so that's what she started to do.

Up until that moment, there had still been a chance for all this to blow over. But one of the knuckle-draggers clearly couldn't see the bigger picture. Instead of letting her pass, he grabbed her arm.

Her hand was on his wrist before he knew what was happening. She rolled out from under him, twisting his arm as she did until she heard his elbow pop out of joint.

He screamed, staggered, and dropped to his knees, cradling his injured arm. As she'd been incapacitating him, Rosario and Liesel dealt with the two behind Ananke. Rosario yanked her target backward onto the sidewalk, and Liesel flipped hers over her shoulder, sending him to the ground beside his buddies.

The leader and the other guy still standing rushed at Ananke, arms outstretched.

A move she saw coming from a mile away.

She juked to the side and shoved the first guy in the back, adding to his momentum and sending him torpedoing straight into a parked pickup truck. He hit it headfirst with a loud thud.

The leader came next, trying to fake her out with a move to his left before swinging his right fist at her. She ducked under his arm and, as she came back up, rammed her knee into his groin. He crumpled, expelling more air than she'd ever heard anyone expel.

She toed him until he looked up at her, his face etched with pain.

"Enough?" she asked.

When he didn't answer, she pushed on his chest with her shoe.

"Yes," he squeaked. "Enough."

Ananke looked back at her friends. The men they'd dealt with were equally incapacitated.

"So much for keeping a low profile," Rosario said.

Several people had come out onto the street, and more were looking down from windows and balconies.

Great, Ananke thought. No way they could sneak into the building now. They needed to let the area cool off first.

"Let's get out of here," she said.

Before she could take a step, a voice from across the street called out, "Ananke?"

All three women turned toward the speaker.

Ricky, Dylan, and several others were looking down at the street from the third-floor balcony of the Estradas' building. A number of them, including Ananke's wayward team members, were holding bottles of beer.

"What are you doing?" Ricky asked.

"What are we…what are *you* doing?" Ananke yelled back.

"Well, we were about to have some dinner. Are you guys hungry?"

RICKY MET THEM at the street-level door and let them into the building.

"What the hell, Ricky?" Ananke said. "What are you doing here?"

"This way," he said, heading up the stairs. "Everyone's waiting."

Ricky was right about that. They entered the third-floor apartment to find eight people, including Dylan, standing inside.

"This is Nicholas Estrada and his wife, Helena," Ricky said, gesturing to the oldest man in the room and a woman who was only slightly younger. Ananke shook hands with them. "And this is their son, Roberto. We're in their apartment." He turned to a woman who was probably in her early forties, and two teenagers. "Cecelia Estrada and her children, Samuel and Sara."

Simon's wife and kids, Ananke realized, and shook with them, too.

With considerable reverence, Ricky gestured to an older woman with pure white hair and an air of hard-earned dignity. "And this is Maria Estrada. Nicholas and Simon's mother."

"A pleasure to meet you," Ananke said, shaking the woman's hand.

"I did not fully believe what your friend said about you until I saw what you just did," the woman said.

Ananke cringed. "Right. Um, they might need some medical attention."

"I am sure they can find it themselves," Maria said.

"You're not going to have any problems with them, are you? I mean, for you after we leave?"

Nicholas snorted. "No one bothers the Estrada family. And since you are our guests, no one will bother you, either." He smiled. "Shall we eat?"

Still not sure what was going on, Ananke followed the others to the dining area. The table was just the right size for the seven members of the family. With the extra five people, though, space was at a premium, making for an elbow-to-elbow eating experience.

"Would you like a beer or something else?" Nicholas asked.

"They're going to want beers," Ricky said, and jumped up. "I know where they are."

He hurried into the kitchen like this was his place, and returned with three open bottles.

"Here you go, ladies," he said, handing them out.

After that, dishes were passed around. *Empañadas* and *chicharrónes* and *papa criolla* and *chorizo* and rice. Ananke wanted to get to the bottom of how in God's name Ricky and Dylan had befriended the family, but it had been a long time since her last meal, and she couldn't resist the aroma wafting off her plate. Soon she and the others were too busy stuffing their faces to say much of anything.

When her plate was finally empty, and the offered second helpings graciously declined, Ananke leaned back and said, "Thank you. That was one of the best meals I've had in a long time."

"You are most welcome," Helena said.

"My mother has also made *cocadas blancas* for dessert," Nicholas said.

"I'm not sure I could fit anything else in my stomach," Ananke said.

"When you see it, I think you'll feel differently."

"Maybe." She shifted her gaze to Ricky, who was busy eating what might have been his third helping. "Um, Ricky?"

He looked up.

In English, she said, "So, do you want to…" She looked

around at the others, letting him connect the dots.

"Oh, right. Well, you told us to have a look around, so that's what we were doing."

"Did I tell you to knock on the door and go in for a chat?"

"Oh, no. You said don't talk to them."

"That sounds more like me. So…"

"Well, see, we decided to take a look inside Nicholas's market."

"Not *we*," Dylan said. "Don't rope me into this."

Ananke turned to him. "Did Ricky go into the store alone?"

"Um, no. But—"

"So you *were* with him."

"Okay, yes. But—"

"Then he's not roping you into anything, is he?"

"He…ah…" Dylan looked for help from Ricky, then Rosario, then Liesel. When he looked back at Ananke, he said, "No, he isn't."

Nicholas clapped Ricky on the back. "You were right. She is very smart."

To Ricky, Ananke said, "How did you go from looking around the store to dinner upstairs?"

"Simple. I mentioned Simon's name to Nicholas," Ricky said.

"And that somehow got you an invitation upstairs?"

"No," Nicholas said. "That almost got him killed."

Ananke closed her eyes and sighed.

"But *Señora* Estrada came to my rescue," Ricky said, smiling at Maria.

Nicholas and Ricky traded off telling the story, how Maria appeared from the store's back room and wanted to know why Ricky was interested in her dead son. Ricky had told her, more or less. Not only did that result in Nicholas putting his gun away, but also in the invitation to go upstairs. Where, Maria had said, they would tell him everything they knew.

"Dylan and I helped Nicholas and Roberto close the store and we all came up here," Ricky said. "We talked for a while. It got kind of late, and they asked us to stay for dinner. We were just sitting down to eat when we heard your admirer screaming outside."

"So, you've already talked about everything," Ananke said.

"I wouldn't say that. Honestly, we got sidetracked into some of Maria's stories about Nicholas and Simon when they were kids. Let me tell you, they were troublemakers. Am I right, Nick?"

Nicholas grinned sheepishly. "Perhaps."

"We were going to really get into things after we finished eating," Ricky went on. "Which, I guess, is now."

Ananke didn't know what annoyed her more—Ricky flouting her orders again, or the fact that nearly every time he did, it worked out for the best.

While the kids cleared the table, the adults adjourned to the living room.

"How exactly can we help you?" Maria asked in Spanish.

"I'm not sure how much Ricky has told you," Ananke said, answering in kind, "but—"

"He has told us you are looking for several people who were sold by Julio Gutiérrez. And you think that my Simon helped Gutiérrez with similar transactions in the past."

"Okaayy," Ananke said. "That's pretty much correct."

"If you are concerned that you are painting an unflattering picture of my son, you are not. He painted the picture himself. While I will not say we did not benefit from his association with Gutiérrez—this building, for instance, that he bought for Nicholas—my son paid for what he did with his life. And by losing him, we all paid the price for ignoring how he had made his money. We are not proud of this."

"We all do…things we regret," Ananke said.

Ricky snorted.

Ananke raised an eyebrow. "You have something to say?"

"What? Oh, no. That? That was just an automatic response. I actually agree with you."

She blinked, surprised and unsure how to interpret his answer.

"If we can do something to help make right even a little of

what Simon did, we will," Nicholas said.

"I've got to say, I did not expect to get this reaction from you," Ananke said. "And I can't tell you how much we appreciate your willingness to help. I guess we should start with how much you know about what he did."

"Almost everything," Nicholas said.

"Really? I assumed since you said you were ignoring what he did, you might not have...well, you know."

"*They* were ignoring," Nicholas said, looking at the rest of the family. "Up until a year before he was killed, I worked for Simon."

"Closely?"

"Very closely."

"Then you're aware Gutiérrez sometimes deals with human cargo."

Nicholas nodded solemnly.

"And Simon was involved with this also?"

Another nod.

"What about you?"

"Not directly. Simon kept me out of that aspect. He thought of it as a stain, and I think he didn't want it to get on me. But I would overhear things, and sometimes he would talk to me when he became too frustrated."

"Okay, well, what we're interested in is the client Gutiérrez sold to. What we know is thin at best. There are several mentions of people he sold being taken to a place referred to only as 'the city.' The way we've seen it used made it seem like the city's name should be obvious. But we have no idea what it is."

"It's not *a* city. It's *the* City. That's what they call it," Nicholas said.

"Are you saying it's not really a city?"

He nodded. "It's a giant labor camp, hidden in the jungle."

"Which jungle?"

"Unfortunately, I have no idea."

"None at all? Not even a hint?"

"I wish I knew more, but—"

"*She* would," Simon's widow, Cecelia, cut in.

"She?" Ananke asked.

"Tell her," Cecelia said to her brother-in-law.

Looking uncomfortable, Nicholas said, "There is someone who probably knows which jungle."

"Who?" Ananke asked.

"Simon's girlfriend," Cecelia said.

UNLIKE THE ESTRADA family, Lola Pérez had not chosen a life of contrition after Simon was killed. Nor did she live the same, middle-class lifestyle.

Simon had bought a luxury condo in Cartagena, overlooking the Caribbean Sea, which he'd put in her name at her insistence. According to Nicholas, Simon had also given her a generous monthly allowance, showered her with expensive jewelry, and indulged her massive shopping habit.

It was no wonder the Estrada family lived a simpler life. The head of their family must have given the largest portion of his ill-gotten gains to his paramour.

When someone like Lola gets used to being treated like a queen, the mere thought that her lifestyle would go away was unacceptable. Nicholas said within weeks of Simon's death, she had become the girlfriend of a sixty-five-year-old shipping magnate named Bertrand De Soto, who split his time between Miami, where he had moved his family years ago, and Colombia, where the majority of his business was still based.

It was a sweet deal for her. She would accompany De Soto whenever he was in the country, which was usually no more than a couple of times a month, and take foreign trips with him on rare occasions. Otherwise, she was on her own.

"And you're sure she'll know about the City?" Ananke had asked.

"He told her everything. So, yes, I'm sure she will know."

"Do we just go to Cartagena, knock on her door, and she'll let us in?" Ricky asked.

Nicholas snorted. "No. She will never willingly talk to you."

"It wouldn't be the first time we've had to deal with someone like that."

"De Soto has given her a couple of bodyguards. I have no doubt he told her it was to protect her from being kidnapped, seeing how he is such a rich and famous man. But I am equally sure it's his way of making her stay true to him."

Ananke leaned back. "That doesn't worry me. I assume you have her address?"

"Of course."

"We could use as detailed a description of the building as you can give us."

"Of course, I—"

"There is an easier way to get to her," Maria said.

They all turned to Nicholas's mother.

"You will go with them," the woman said to her son. "She will meet with you."

Nicholas frowned. "I don't know if that's a good idea. The last time I saw her was not…pleasant."

Cecelia cleared her throat. "Then I will go."

The attention shifted to her.

"She may not be happy to hear from me," Simon's widow went on, "but she will not refuse me."

"That's not a good idea," Nicholas said. "I'll go with them. I can get Lola to talk."

"She has no reason to tell you anything," Cecelia said. "Maybe you can get close to her, but I do not think you can get her to open her mouth."

"I…I can," he said, a little too defensively.

Cecelia started to protest again, but checked herself when Maria rose from her chair.

"You will both go," the old woman said. She looked at Ananke. "It is a long trip, but Nicholas knows the way. You may take our car if you do not have one."

"Actually," Ananke said, "it would probably be quicker if we took our jet.

SEVENTEEN

CARTAGENA SAT ON the northern coast of Colombia, beside the Caribbean Sea, where it enjoyed the hot tropical climate Bogotá lacked. This was evident from the moment they walked off the plane at ten p.m., when the temperature was considerably warmer than midafternoon Bogotá.

Ananke had contacted her assistant, Shinji, when they were in flight, and had him arrange for transportation to be waiting upon their arrival. An SUV could have fit all seven of them, but Ananke worried it would have been too conspicuous. Instead, she'd requested two nondescript sedans. Shinji had delivered a Renault Sandero and a Hyundai Creta.

Ananke, Nicholas, and Cecelia rode in the Renault with Dylan driving, while Liesel drove the others in the Hyundai.

Nicholas, acting as navigator, guided them into a high-rise-filled section of town he called Bocagrande. He eventually pointed and said, "That one."

Ananke leaned between the seats to get a better look. "The oval-ish building?"

"Yes. Lola lives three floors from the top."

The building was about twenty stories high and constructed with no visible sharp angles. Like many of the buildings in the area, it was dramatically lit by powerful low lights shooting up the sides.

"Take us by, slow," Ananke said.

On the seat beside her, Cecelia tensed.

"You okay?" Ananke asked.

Cecelia nodded, but said nothing.

"Is this your first time here?"

"Yes. I have…only seen pictures."

"But you *have* met Lola before, right?"

A deep breath. "She is my cousin."

Oh. Crap.

Confronting a dead husband's lover was bad enough. Throw in the fact the lover was family and you had the makings for all out nuclear war. But bringing Cecelia had been Maria's decision, and Ananke had taken a real liking to the elder Estrada.

Ananke studied the building as the sedan drove past, noting that the areas between it and the high-rises to either side were covered by multilevel, concrete patios. Scattered across these were tables and chairs and cement benches and identical large planters. If there was an underground garage, the entrance must have been on the other side, because there was no opening here. Then again, as close as the building was to the water, maybe they couldn't build one here.

"Primarily residential?" she asked Nicholas.

"If I remember correctly, there are business offices on the first three or four floors, but after that, yes, residential."

"Tell me about the lobby. Can you just walk up to the elevators? Or do you have to check in with a guard?"

"During the day you can just walk in, and at night you must sign the book first. I'm not sure what time the change occurs."

"Cameras in the elevators?"

"I don't know about that. But I would assume so."

The building receded behind them.

"What about Lola? Does she like to stay out late? Go dancing? Party?"

"At one time, yes. Now…maybe? It depends on if De Soto is in town, I would think."

De Soto's whereabouts was something Rosario was working on at that very moment.

Ananke caught Dylan's eyes in the rearview mirror. "Find someplace to park."

He nodded. Two minutes later, he pulled the sedan onto a sandy strip between the road and a temporary wooden wall surrounding a construction site of yet another tower. Liesel pulled the Hyundai in behind him.

"You two don't mind waiting here for a moment, do you?" Ananke asked Nicholas and Cecelia.

"No problem," Cecelia said.

"Dylan, with me."

Ananke and Dylan climbed out of the Renault and walked back to the other sedan. Ricky and Rosario rolled down their windows so Ananke and Dylan could lean in.

"You have a location on De Soto yet?" Ananke asked.

"He is in London," Rosario said, her computer in her lap.

"Is he alone?" The fly in the ointment would be if this was one of those foreign trips Lola sometimes accompanied him on.

"His wife is with him."

"Good. Then Lola is in town?"

"According to her credit card, she had dinner two hours ago at Ivonne's. That's a restaurant about ten minutes from here."

"Any idea if she was by herself?"

"I checked for cameras, but either the restaurant uses a closed system or they don't have any. The bill was large enough for at least three people, though."

"What about her building? Were you able to scan it when we went by?"

"I was. I picked up over twenty Wi-Fi signals, none of which appeared to be too terribly secure."

"Nicholas says Lola lives three stories from the top. What I'd like to know is if she's home right now or not."

"There is no way a building like that does not have security cameras. I should be able to determine when she left and what time she came back, if she did. All I need to do is get within signal range so I can hack in."

"Ricky, take over for Liesel and drive Rosario wherever she needs to go. You'll be her lookout. Liesel, you'll come with us. And bring gear bag number two."

"Wait," Ricky said. "What are you guys going to do?"

"What we came here to do."

She started back for the other car.

"Hey," Ricky called out, "I'm the one who made this happen. I should go with you."

She opened the door and climbed inside without looking back.

RICKY COULDN'T BELIEVE he was being aced out of the big prize. Sure, he knew it was because he'd bent the rules a bit. Okay, he broke them, but no one could argue with his results. If he hadn't made contact with the Estradas, he and the rest of the team probably would still be in Cartagena. But Ananke hadn't been open to even discussing his inclusion.

Why did it feel like he was perpetually in the doghouse?

Again, he knew the reasons, but the punishment always felt greater than his crimes.

"Anywhere around here should be okay," Rosario said.

"Huh?"

"That spot up there," she said, pointing. "Grab it."

He pulled to the curb and killed the engine. They were two buildings down from Lola's.

"There is a booster in the bag," Rosario said, her focus on her laptop screen. "I need you to get it as close to the building as possible. Make sure you turn it on first."

"Yes, ma'am," he said, willing himself to not be too annoyed.

As he opened the door, she said, "Turn on your comm. We will use channel two. And Ricky?"

He looked back at her.

"Do not go inside the building. Plant the booster and come straight back here."

He shut the door a little harder than he needed to and retrieved the booster from the trunk.

The pleasant night did little to temper his mood. What did he have to do to get any respect around here? It seemed he was doing more than his fair share of the work for the team. Not that anyone else was slacking, but he'd gone above and beyond.

Hell, on the last job he'd even gotten himself kidnapped, putting him in the perfect inside position to help take down those sickos in Bradbury. Okay, yes, Rosario had *also* been kidnapped with him, but he'd been the one to take the initiative, man. He deserved a little recognition for that, didn't he?

"Have you planted it yet?"

He snapped his head up and realized he'd almost walked by Pérez's building.

He clicked on his mic. "Looking for a place now."

"Hurry it up."

He turned his mic off. "Yes, sir, Colonel."

A LEGO-like path of concrete slabs, each a bit higher than the last, led up to the building's entrance. Not far beyond the glass doors, he could see a guard station, though no one appeared to be there at the moment.

Look at that. The perfect opportunity to make an unseen entrance.

Not counting the potential camera problem, of course, but Rosario could neutralize that in a hurry, and he could be on his way to Pérez's floor without anyone being the wiser.

Ah, well, what could have been…

He walked along the darker side of the building, and behind one of the cement benches, he found a notch big enough for the booster.

He turned the device on, slipped it into the hole, and clicked on his mic. "You should be good to go."

"Let me check…yeah…okay. Got it. Good work. Come on back."

"On my way."

He was halfway to the front of the building when he heard the main entrance open and someone step outside. Ricky scampered back and ducked behind a planter. Peeking between the bushes, he spotted a security guard walking slowly toward the road. Upon reaching it, the man stopped and looked in each direction, his back to Ricky.

Ricky waited, thinking the guy would return to the building, but the guard just stood there.

What the hell, dude? I don't have all night.

After another minute passed, Ricky decided to go the long way. Crouching, he moved to the back of the building. Another road ran behind the property, only it was a little farther away than he'd expected. Cutting across the property from the road to the building was a downward sloping driveway that ended at the entrance to the subterranean garage. Instead of a standard gate, the entrance was completely blocked by a wire mesh curtain. A few meters in front of this, sitting next to the driveway, was a keypad on a stand.

Ricky shot pictures of the area and continued to the road.

ANANKE HAD DYLAN park half a block away from Lola's building, where they waited to hear from Rosario.

"Is that Ricky?" Dylan said, a few minutes after they'd stopped.

Ananke zoomed her camera in on the shadowy form moving down the street, but it turned toward the building and disappeared. The size of the shadow and the way the person was walking seemed right, though.

She clicked on her comm. "Ananke for Rosario. Is Ricky with you?"

"I sent him to plant a booster near the building. If you need him, he's on channel two."

"Copy," Ananke said. So, it was Ricky. At least he was following orders and not on another rogue mission.

Two minutes later, Rosario's voice came back over the comm. "Booster's up."

"Give me some good news," Ananke said.

"Checking now."

Dylan leaned forward. "Security guard."

A man in uniform was walking down the path from the building toward the street. When he reached the curb, he stopped and stood there.

Ananke frowned. "What's he doing?"

"Nothing, from the looks of it."

For several minutes, the man just stood there, seemingly without a care in the world.

"Car stopping," Dylan announced.

There was plenty of traffic on the road, but up to this point, all vehicles had sped by. Now, a battered Toyota van was pulling to the curb right where the guard was standing. When it stopped, the guard stepped up to the passenger-side window and leaned in.

The interior of the vehicle was too dark for Ananke to see what was going on, but within a few moments, the guard moved back onto the pathway, holding several bags.

"Looks like someone ordered takeaway," Dylan said.

As the van drove away, the guard headed back to the building.

That was the extent of the excitement until Rosario announced, "I have the woman leaving the building at 8:22 p.m. She has not returned yet."

Exactly what Ananke had hoped. "Building security?"

"Three guards. Two in the lobby and a third on rounds, currently on the fifth floor."

From the background of Rosario's feed came Ricky's voice. "Forget the lobby. Use the—"

"Channel one," Rosario said.

Still sounding distant, Ricky said, "What? Oh, right."

A click.

"Ananke?" Ricky again, now on the correct setting.

"You were saying something about the lobby?"

"Yeah, you don't need to use it. There's an automated entrance to a parking garage in the rear. I didn't see any guards there."

"Cameras?"

"I saw at least one, but—"

"I am checking," Rosario said. "There are two covering the entrance to the garage."

"What about inside?"

"More there, too."

"Can you black them out, or loop them or something?"

"No need. The guards are monitoring everything on two TVs at their desk. One of the screens is showing a constant feed from the camera at the front door. The other is cycling through all the building's other cameras, at…hold on…five seconds per feed. Unfortunately for them, they are using an old Mahado system."

"Which means?"

"Which means I can control which cameras they see, and which they do not. They will never even realize they are not

185

seeing everything."

"That works for me. Can you control the gate, too?"

"You are seriously asking me that?"

THEY LEFT THE car parked along the road behind Lola's building, and walked toward the garage entrance.

Ananke said to Cecelia and Nicholas, "Now's the time to back out. If you'd rather not go with us, we'll understand."

"We're coming," Cecelia said without hesitation.

Nicholas looked uneasy, but he said nothing.

As they descended the ramp, Ananke said into the comm, "We're getting close."

"I see you," Rosario said.

The gate rose, and the group walked in.

Following Rosario's instructions, they found the elevator and took it to the seventeenth floor.

"Which way?" Ananke asked Nicholas when they stepped out of the car.

"To the right. It's down at the end."

Whoever had been in charge of decorating the hallway had obviously been a big fan of the 1970s. The walls were painted dark brown on the bottom third, tan on the top third, and covered by mirror tiles in the middle, each section separated from its neighbor by a wide stripe of gold metal. The only things missing were disco balls hanging from the ceiling.

There were only four doors along the corridor. The residents were apparently allowed some individuality when it came to their personal entrances. One person had gone with a dark wood monstrosity that looked like something out of *Game of Thrones*. Two of the others had gone with brushed aluminum—one door was blue and the other silver.

The final door—Lola's—was bright pink plastic.

"That wouldn't have been my choice," Dylan said as they stepped up to the woman's door.

"Scanning for alarms," Ananke said.

She tapped the scan app on her phone and moved it up and down the door. The screen displayed the message: ALARM DETECTED. She touched the warning and the message switched

186

to one revealing the details on Lola's system.

"She has a Benchly XR33."

"Put your phone close to the door again," Rosario said.

Ananke did so.

"Okay, give me a moment." Keyboard taps drifted over the line. "It should be disarmed now."

Ananke scanned the door again and received an all-clear message. She traded her phone for her lockpicks and set to work.

"Car entering the garage," Rosario said.

Ananke paused. "Lola?"

"Could be. There's a woman in the front passenger seat, but she was looking down when the car passed the camera."

Ananke freed the deadbolt and started in on the lock in the handle.

"They just got out of the car. I think it might be her. Sending you a picture."

"How many is 'they'?"

"Four, counting the woman."

Ananke's phone buzzed as the last tumbler fell into place. She pulled out her mobile and opened Rosario's message. The security camera image wasn't the best quality, but it was good enough to make out the features of the blonde woman in the center.

She turned the screen to Nicholas and Cecelia. "Is this Lola?"

It took Nicholas only a glance to say, "Yes."

Cecelia nodded her agreement.

"Then I guess we should get inside."

EIGHTEEN

LOLA WAS FEELING pretty fantastic. Perhaps it was the cocaine talking, but she hadn't had much. Bertrand would be flying back in a few days, and he hated it when she was high, so it was always best to taper off before he came to town.

The real reason she felt so warm and fuzzy was sitting behind her in the backseat of her BMW. A young man named Juan.

It *was* Juan, wasn't it? It didn't matter. She'd call him Juan and if he wanted to have fun, he'd answer to it.

The BMW's tires squealed on the concrete ramp leading down to the parking area. Being on one of the upper five floors meant her parking spot was on the garage's top level, so it was only a few more moments before her bodyguard Mateo pulled the sedan into her assigned spot.

Felipe, her other bodyguard, exited the back, opened her door, and helped her out.

"*Gracias*," she said, smiling at him.

Though she had very little time for most of the people beneath her, she was always nice to her bodyguards, even buying them trinkets they could give their girlfriends. These favors were paid back by Mateo and Felipe not reporting to Bertrand that she enjoyed a plaything or two when he wasn't around.

She felt a hand slip into hers and looked over. Juan. Right. She'd momentarily forgotten about him. Boy, did he have sweet eyes. That could be a problem. People with eyes like his were the kind who often wanted more than just a tumble in the sheets. If she didn't set him straight before she sent him on his way, he'd probably call her and send her notes and flowers and

God knew what else. But she could worry about that in the morning. Right now, all she needed to think about was the fun they were about to have.

She snuggled against him as they followed Felipe across the garage and onto the elevator. Mateo entered behind them and pushed the button marked 17.

"You're not tired, are you?" she whispered to Juan.

He smiled. "I could stay up all night."

She let her hand skim the front of his pants. "I hope that's true."

When the doors opened, Mateo exited first, looked around, and nodded for the others to follow. She liked when he did that. It made her feel important.

At her door, Mateo deactivated the condo's alarm and Felipe unlocked the locks.

"Some wine before..." Lola cooed into Juan's ear.

"How about after?" he replied.

Oh, was she ever glad she picked him out of the crowd tonight.

She peeled her gaze off him so she could lead him to the bedroom, and smacked right into Mateo's back.

"What the hell?" she said. "Move."

But the beefy bodyguard remained where he was. "Something's not right."

"What are you talking about?" She looked around. Everything appeared fine to her.

"Get back," he said, pushing her behind him while reaching into his jacket with his other hand.

A metallic click from the darkened doorway of the guest room.

Mateo yanked his gun out, but before he could point it at anyone, there were two more clicks, from behind them this time.

Lola looked over her shoulder. A man and a woman stood on either side of the doorway, one pointing a gun with an extra-long barrel at Felipe's head, and the other at Mateo's.

"Guns on the floor," a female voice said from the guest room.

Mateo hesitated before tossing his on the carpet.

"Your friend's, too," the woman said.

Mateo glanced back at Felipe and nodded.

As Felipe reached under his jacket, the voice said, "Slowly."

Felipe carefully withdrew a pistol, holding the grip by two fingers. He dropped it near his feet.

The woman at the door stepped over and kicked the gun out of his reach.

"Wh-wh-what is this?" Juan said.

"Shut up," Mateo hissed.

"You can't talk to me like that. I'm—"

"Shut up," Lola said.

He gawked at her, but mercifully said nothing more.

She had never shared Bertrand's fear that she might be kidnapped, but now, as panic rose in her chest, she realized how wrong she'd been. She knew with sudden certainty she would be taken into the jungle and stowed away in some dark shack until her boyfriend came up with the ransom, at which point there would be as much chance of the kidnappers killing her as returning her.

As she started to hyperventilate, a tall black woman walked out of the guest bedroom, holding a gun similar to those of the two at the door.

"Why don't we all have a seat," she said, motioning to the living room.

Lola's feet felt glued to the floor. Apparently Mateo and Felipe were experiencing the same sensation, because neither of them moved.

"I insist," the woman said.

"You'll never get out of the building," Mateo said.

"We got in. We'll get out."

"Not with any of us."

She snorted. "Why would we want to take any of you?"

Lola's blood turned cold. If they weren't here to kidnap her, they must be here to kill her.

She didn't want to die. She was *way* too young to die. Her life was too good for her to die.

"There's-there's jewelry in my bedroom," she blurted. "And I have some cash, too. You can have it all. And-and anything else you want."

The woman walked toward Lola. "The only thing I want right now is for you all to have a seat."

Mateo looked back at Lola, as if asking for permission.

"If she wants us to sit, we should sit," Lola said.

They moved into the living room.

"*Señorita* Pérez, why don't you sit on the couch." The woman looked at Mateo and Felipe. "And you two can sit there." She pointed her gun at the love seat.

The bodyguards jammed themselves into the smaller sofa, while the Caucasian man moved into position behind them.

"What about me?" Juan asked.

The woman scrutinized him. "You're not a bodyguard, are you?"

"Me? God, no."

"Then who are you?"

"I'm Lola's…uh, date. Javier."

Javier, Lola thought. At least she'd gotten the first letter right.

"You're her boyfriend?"

"No. No, not at all. We, um, just met tonight."

The woman looked at Lola. "Is that true?"

Lola nodded.

"It's your lucky day, Javier."

"I can leave?"

"No. But you don't have to hang around for the festivities."

The other woman—who was Asian, or mixed, now that Lola got a good look at her—stepped in behind Javier and jabbed something into the base of his neck.

"Ow!" Javier exclaimed. "What are you…do…ing…"

His whole body went slack. The woman grabbed him and dragged him to the side, where she laid him on the floor.

She then joined the man behind Mateo and Felipe.

"Gentlemen," the black woman said to Mateo and Felipe, "consider yourself off duty tonight."

191

The duo behind them produced syringes and stuck them into the bodyguards' necks. In short order, the men slumped together, out for the count.

The leader moved in front of Lola and looked down at her. "Hello, Lola."

Lola clasped her hands together to keep them from shaking. "What do you want?"

"Just to talk."

"About what?"

"I'm not the one who's going to talk to you. My friend is." The woman looked across the room.

Lola assumed she was talking about one of the others, but then two new people walked into the room. A man and a woman, older than the three who'd taken Lola hostage.

It took her a second before she realized the man was Simon's brother, Nicholas. What was he doing here?

And then she took a longer look at the woman. Though she hadn't seen her in years, Lola knew her, too.

"Hello, Lola," Cecelia Estrada said.

Lola felt the blood drain from her face.

AT ANANKE'S DIRECTION, Dylan brought over one of the dining room chairs and set it in front of the couch so Cecelia could sit face to face with her cousin.

Ananke had thought Lola was a bit drunk when she walked in, but from the way Lola's eyes were dancing around, it was a good bet there was more than alcohol flowing in the woman's veins.

"Would you like some water?" Ananke asked her.

Lola jerked her head, as if she'd forgotten Ananke was in the room. "What?"

"Are you thirsty?"

"Water, yes. Please."

Ananke glanced at Liesel, who headed into the kitchen.

Lola's gaze continued to flitter about, looking everywhere except at her dead ex-boyfriend's wife.

"You have a beautiful home," Cecelia said, unsmiling.

Lola allowed herself a quick look at her cousin. "It's mine.

You can't have it."

"Is that why you think I'm here?"

Lola's brow creased before a wave of resolve tried to wash it away. In a voice more tentative than she likely intended, she said, "I don't care why you're here. You need to leave. This is my home. You are trespassing."

Cecelia stared at her.

With each passing second, Lola grew more and more uncomfortable. "Stop looking at me like that."

"It was all about the sex, wasn't it?" Cecelia said.

"What?"

"I can't see any other reason why Simon would have found you interesting."

Looking offended, Lola said, "He liked a lot of things about me."

Cecelia laughed quietly. "No. He didn't. He liked a few things, at most."

"He loved everything about me, unlike how he felt about—"

Ananke loudly cleared her throat.

Cecelia glanced at her, mouthed *sorry*, and turned back to Lola.

"To answer your question," she said, "we are not here about your home, or to debate Simon's feelings about you."

"He did love me," Lola mumbled.

A restrained smile from Cecelia. "We are here because you have information my friends here need to know."

Confusion again. "What information?"

Nicholas said, "About things Simon told you."

Lola's gaze shifted to him before taking in Ananke, Liesel, and Dylan. "He's dead. I don't remember anything he told me."

"I'll bet you remember more than you realize," Ananke said.

Lola shifted on the couch, grimacing but not saying anything.

"You remember Julio Gutiérrez, don't you?" Nicholas said.

Though she replied, "Barely," it was clear from her eyes

she remembered more than that.

"There was a certain product Simon used to help Julio with," Nicholas said.

"He helped Julio with all kinds of things."

"I'm talking about people."

"No," she said way too quickly. "I don't remember anything like that."

"Lola, I think you're failing to understand the position you're in here." Nicholas gestured at Ananke. "These people are not going to leave until you tell them. And if Cecelia and I can't get you to talk, then they will, and trust me, you don't want that."

"I don't know any—"

"Enough lies," Ananke said in a commanding voice. "We all know you know exactly what we're talking about."

Lola made no protest this time.

"These people were taken to a place called the City," Ananke said. "You will tell us where this is."

Lola's head shot up again and her eyes widened. "No. No, I-I-I don't know about that."

Ananke motioned for Cecelia to move to the side, then stepped directly in front of Lola and crouched down. "You do know. And you're going to tell us."

"I-I can't."

"Why not?"

"If they realize I know, they'll kill me like they killed Simon."

"Gutiérrez killed Simon," Nicholas said.

She shook her head. "Only because they gave him no other choice. Simon threatened to expose them, so they ordered Julio to get rid of him."

"How would you know this?" Cecelia asked, surprised.

"It…happened on Julio's yacht. They thought I was asleep in our cabin, but I heard the fighting so I was listening at the door when Julio told him."

"You're worried that Gutiérrez's clients are going to kill you at some point if they find out you told us?" Ananke shook her head in pity. "If you don't tell us what we want to know, we'll have to kill you *tonight* so that no one will ever find out why we were here." She looked back at Liesel. "A syringe, please."

"What? Wait! No." Lola looked at her bodyguards. "You didn't kill them."

"They don't have the information we need, so we only used something to knock them out. For you, however…"

Liesel set the syringe kit on the coffee table, untied it, and unrolled the multi-pocketed sleeve. She selected a syringe and handed it to Ananke. Like the others, it was filled with Beta-Somnol and would knock Lola out for several hours, but would not kill her unless they gave her several doses.

Ananke held it up and pushed the plunger to let a drop trickle out.

"I would much prefer if you tell us," Ananke said. "But I will not hesitate to use this if you insist on remaining unhelpful. So, I'll ask you one last time—where is the City?"

Lola's eyes welled with tears. "Please."

"If that's your decision, then that's your decision," Ananke said. "The good thing for you is, other than a little prick when the needle goes in, you shouldn't feel any pain."

As she moved the syringe toward Lola's arm, Lola scooted along the couch, trying to get away. But Dylan grabbed her by the shoulders.

"Sorry, darling," he said. "But that's not how it works."

He pushed her back to the center and held her there as Ananke moved the needle toward the woman's arm again.

"No, please. Don't!" Lola said.

Ananke stopped the syringe a centimeter above the woman's skin. "The only way I stop is if you have something useful to tell us."

Lola took a stuttering breath. "I do. I-I do."

Ananke pulled the needle back but made a point of not returning it to its holder.

"The-the-the City," Lola said. "It's in the jungle."

"We know it's in a jungle," Ananke said. "You need to be more specific than that."

"In, um, in Venezuela."

Ananke groaned inwardly. Of course it would be Venezuela, where the late, mad dictator Hugo Chavez had been replaced by a less charismatic knockoff. "Venezuela is a big country. Where in Venezuela?"

"I don't know! I've never actually been there."

"Simon must have told you more than just which country it's in."

Lola stared at the floor, her eyes wide in desperation. "Wait. He did say once that it was near Guyana. I think his plane would actually land in Guyana and he'd take a boat in from there."

A small airport near the border with a river that crossed into Venezuela—those were things they could search for.

"How big is the City?"

"I told you I've never been there. How should I know?"

Ananke started to move the needle back toward the woman.

"Okay, okay. Let me think." Lola was silent for several seconds. "I don't know for sure how big, but-but Simon did say there were at least a thousand workers."

"You mean slaves."

A pause. "Yes."

Dear God. A thousand? This had just turned into something a lot more insane than Ananke already thought it was.

"And they use these slaves to make…"

"Anything they need. Clothes, luggage, electronics."

"How do they get the products out?"

"I have no clue. Simon never talked about that."

"How often did he go there?"

"Four times that I know of. When he came back, he was always…agitated."

"You said earlier that he had decided to expose them."

Lola nodded. "He said he couldn't live with himself if he didn't do anything. I told him he should forget it. That it wasn't worth it."

"I don't understand," Cecelia said. "How did these people find out what he was going to do?"

196

"Gutiérrez told them, and they told him to take care of the problem."

"So, you're saying Simon told Gutiérrez?"

Lola half nodded, half shrugged and looked away.

Ananke's eyes narrowed. "Simon didn't tell Gutiérrez, did he?"

Lola kept her eyes glued to the wall.

"*You* told Gutiérrez," Ananke said.

"I-I-I didn't say that."

"You didn't have to." Ananke grabbed the woman by the jaw and turned her face forward so she could lock eyes with the woman. "Why would you do that?"

"You're hurting me."

"Answer my question."

Lola tried to pull free, but Ananke held on. Frustration peaking, the woman said, "Because he was going to ruin everything! If he exposed the people in charge of the City, then all of this would disappear!" She gestured at the room.

"Let me guess," Ananke said. "Gutiérrez promised to take care of you for helping out. I'll bet he's the one who introduced Bertrand De Soto to you, isn't he?"

Lola didn't answer, but she didn't have to. The truth was branded on her face.

Cecelia tapped Ananke on the shoulder.

"May I?" Cecelia said, nodding toward Lola.

Ananke let go of Lola's jaw and stepped away. Cecelia then slapped Lola so hard, the other side of Lola's face imprinted itself on the leather couch.

"For once, Simon was going to do something good and you stopped him," Cecelia said, seething. "You *knew* what would happen if you told on him. You knew he would be killed."

Hand cradling her cheek, Lola said, "You would have done the same in my position."

A dozen comebacks ran through Ananke's mind in that instant, but Cecelia had something else in mind. She punched Lola in the face, sending a river of blood flowing from Lola's nose into her mouth, and knocking the woman unconscious.

"I'm sorry," Cecelia said, holding her hand. "I didn't mean to hit her that hard."

"It's okay," Ananke said. "I think we got pretty much everything we were going to get out of her."

She laid Lola on the couch and elevated her head, so the woman wouldn't drown in her own blood.

"You are more restrained than I would have been," Liesel said. "I would not have stopped with one punch."

"I would have hit her again, but…" Cecelia rubbed her red knuckles.

"We should put some ice on that," Dylan said, and hurried into the kitchen.

While Dylan and Liesel helped Cecelia, Ananke motioned Nicholas over.

"Did what Lola said ring true with you?" she asked.

"Yeah. I remember Simon making a few trips to Guyana. I just didn't realize it was for this."

"Is there anything you may have heard that could add to her info?"

"Nothing I've heard, but…what she said about taking a boat across the border. The biggest river in that area is the Orinoco. The main channel doesn't cross into Guyana but there are many tributaries. And if the City is off one of them, then a boat could easily make it back to the Orinoco and out into the Caribbean Sea. And from there, anywhere."

"How big a boat?"

"Depends on the tributary. Some of them could handle a pretty large one."

"Like a cargo ship?"

"Definitely. If I'm not mistaken, one of the larger tributaries runs near the coast and does cross the Guyana border. I don't remember the name of it, but if we look at a map we should be able to find it."

"You wouldn't happen to know anyone who lives in that part of the country?"

"Unfortunately, no. But it's possible I know someone who does have contacts there. I can make some calls."

"We'd appreciate it."

FROM THE SWELLING of Cecelia's hand, Ananke thought it likely that the woman had broken at least one finger, but the woman didn't seem to mind. Her only concern was that Lola hadn't paid enough for depriving her of a husband and Simon's kids of their father.

"We can take care of that," Ananke said. "I'm sure her current boyfriend would be very interested to know the truth about how Simon met his end. I doubt he's interested in dumping more money into someone who so easily turns on the one providing for her. And without his protections, I have a feeling law enforcement will become very interested in her. In fact, I can guarantee they will."

"You can do that?" Cecelia asked.

"Oh, sweetie. That's child's play. You should see what we can do when things really get difficult."

Ananke had Liesel give Lola a dose of the Beta-Somnol to make sure she stayed out. They then made their way out the same way they'd come in, Rosario once again dealing with the cameras on their path.

A doctor was found to discreetly treat Cecelia's hand, and arrangements were made to take Cecelia and her brother-in-law to a local hotel, where they could get some sleep before catching a flight back to Bogotá in the morning, courtesy of the Committee.

Ananke gave Nicholas her phone number, instructing him to let her know if he discovered someone who might be able to help them.

"Thank you again," she told him and Cecelia. "Your assistance has been invaluable."

She offered her hand to Nicholas, but he pulled her into a hug. Cecelia did the same, but before she let go, she whispered to Ananke, "Find the people who have been taken and set them free."

"That's the plan."

Cecelia pulled back, her eyes locked on Ananke's. "I mean all of them."

All Ananke could manage was a noncommittal smile. "Take care of that hand."

Back in the car, Dylan said, "Where to?"

"The plane," Ananke replied.

"And then?" Ricky asked.

An excellent question for which she didn't have an answer yet. "Let's start with the plane."

STANDING ON THE tarmac next to the jet, Ananke called the Administrator. "This problem is a *lot* larger than we realized."

"Are you concerned you won't be able to deal with it on your own?"

"It's certainly in the back of my mind, but we won't know until we get a look at the place."

"I understand, but you do realize that while we can provide supplies and weaponry, pulling together more personnel to help you will take time and may not even be possible."

"I know, and I'm not saying we should delay. I'm just expressing my concern. We'll figure out a way to deal with it."

"I'm sure you will. And if you need anything short of calling in the Marines, let me know and we'll get it for you."

"Well, now that you mention it, there is one thing that might help."

"Of course. What is it?"

"Tell me—where exactly is the *Karas Evonus* now?"

NINETEEN

GETTING TO THE portion of the Rio Orinoco they needed to reach would not be easy.

From the giant delta through which the river drained into the Caribbean Sea to the point where crossing from Guyana no longer made sense, there were only small villages and tinier settlements, most only reachable by boat.

The few landing strips within the targeted area were too short for the team's jet. But even if it weren't, all of the strips were privately owned, very likely by the kind of people who wouldn't appreciate Ananke and her team dropping in.

The only real option was to take a boat.

Before leaving Cartagena, Rosario and Shinji worked on locating a vessel the team could use. Shinji ended up having better luck. The only problem was, the boat he found was on the island of Trinidad, just off the coast. It would mean several hours at open sea before they reached the river, but no other vessels nearby could get them there as quickly.

So off to Trinidad they flew, landing in the capital city of Port of Spain first thing the next morning. They hired a van to take them south to San Fernando, where a fishing trawler called the *Green Eyed Dawn* waited for them.

When Ananke laid her eyes on it, she thought Shinji had rented them a dud. The boat looked rundown and a whole lot slower than what they needed.

She sent Dylan on board to check everything out.

When he returned, he was smiling. "She may look like an ugly duckling, but I doubt she's done any serious fishing for years."

"Then it's even worse than I thought?"

"That's not what I meant. She's got serious firepower under the hood, and the hull is in a lot better shape than it appears from here. That there's no fishing trawler. It's a smuggler's ship."

Apparently, Shinji had known what he was talking about.

Ananke wanted to push off right away, but the captain had other ideas.

"Six p.m., no earlier," he told her.

"You get that we're in a hurry, right?"

"Feel free to find another boat, but if you want to actually reach your destination, we leave at six. This way we travel in the dark. Go any earlier and the coast guard will intercept us, maybe even shoot you when they find out you are American."

"I never said I was an American."

He shrugged. "So, what? You're Canadian? Maybe they'll just throw you in prison for a few months."

His point was a valid one, so the departure time was agreed to.

The team spent the rest of the day in a pair of hotel rooms, mostly catching up on rest. When Ananke could sleep no more, she hopped on her computer and pulled up the most recent satellite images of the area between the Rio Orinoco and the Guyana border. There were dozens of tributaries in that region, though most were too small to support the kind of operation the City supposedly was running. She was sure the City was on a spur both wide and deep enough for cargo ships to pass.

Out of the handful of choices, one stood out above the rest, a tributary called Rio Barima. Its size was right, as was the fact it crossed into Guyana. It was also near the coast like the tributary Nicholas had mentioned. She sent him a text, asking if the Barima was what he'd been thinking about.

What she didn't find were any signs of a substantial dock where large boats could load cargo. Maybe Ananke was wrong. Maybe this wasn't the jungle where the City was.

Not ready to give up, she increased magnification of the satellite image to maximum and scrolled down the Barima, kilometer by kilometer.

She was so focused on the search that when Rosario said,

"What are you doing?" from right behind her, Ananke jerked in surprise.

"For God's sake, make some noise or something," Ananke said.

"I thought you were supposed to be a spy or something. Are you not supposed to sense when someone else is around?"

"I was an assassin, and you would do well to remember that."

Rosario huffed a laugh, then leaned over Ananke's shoulder and looked at the screen. "Seriously, though, what are you doing?"

Ananke explained her search of the tributaries and how she'd come to focus on Rio Barima. "The problem is, I can't find anywhere to dock a large ship, let alone any of the equipment needed to move cargo on board, and there are no signs of the City in the surrounding jungle."

"May I?"

Ananke pushed her chair back. "Be my guest." She stood up and stretched.

"This may take a few minutes," Rosario said as she sat. She glanced back at Ananke. "Maybe you should take a shower."

"Why?" Ananke lifted her arm and sniffed. "Do I need one?"

Rosario shrugged and set to work.

Ananke gave herself another sniff, and decided her friend was right.

If the hotel had hot water, someone else must have used it all, because the water Ananke managed to coax out of the pipe could be called only tepid at best. She dried off, pulled on some clean clothes, then saw she'd received a text from Nicholas.

Yes. The Barima. That's it. I'm waiting to hear back from a contact who might know someone in the area. Text you again as soon as I do.

Ananke returned to the bedroom.

Liesel was up now, sitting with Rosario. She turned, and upon seeing Ananke, hopped out of her chair. "My turn."

She grabbed a pile of clothes and headed for the bathroom.

"Don't expect any hot water," Ananke called after her.

Either Liesel didn't hear her or didn't care.

Ananke walked over to Rosario. "Any luck?"

"You tell me."

Ananke looked at the computer over Rosario's shoulder. The top half of the screen was taken up by water, while in the bottom half was a curving, vegetation-filled shoreline.

"Where is this?" Ananke asked.

Rosario clicked a few times and the image pulled out, revealing that the close-up had been of a portion of the Rio Barima, approximately twenty kilometers northwest of the border with Guyana. She zoomed in again.

As far as Ananke could tell, there was nothing special about it. It looked just as wild and unapproachable as the areas she'd been looking at earlier. In fact, it *was* one of the areas she'd looked at earlier.

"I'm not sure what I'm supposed to be looking at."

Rosario moved the cursor over a small area of the shoreline and circled it several times. "Right here."

Ananke wasn't seeing—

She cocked her head. There *was* something different. It was so subtle she almost missed it.

"Is that a…corner?"

Rosario looked up and grinned. "Very good."

In the center of the circled area, a small part of the shore stuck out at a perfect right angle. The feature could have been naturally made, but it seemed unlikely. Whatever the corner was connected to was obscured by the jungle.

"Now here," Rosario said.

She moved the image until the river disappeared off the top of the screen. When she stopped, she circled an area of the tree-covered land.

"And here."

She circled another area.

In each circle, there was a small section not covered by the jungle canopy, revealing something on the ground that was either black or in shadow.

"It's a paved road," Rosario said.

Ananke's brow furrowed as she leaned closer. "How can you tell?"

After pointing out several other spots of black, Rosario clicked a tab. A pair of parallel red lines overlaid the image, starting at the top of the frame where the river was and moving down through the jungle to the bottom of the image. While the lines curved slightly here and there, they basically traveled straight from one end to the other. Every spot of black Rosario pointed out was contained within the area between the two lines.

"Okay, but that doesn't automatically mean it's a road," Ananke said.

"A, those black patches appear nowhere else for at least five kilometers to either side."

"Yeah, but it still—"

"And B…" Rosario copied a section of the parallel lines and pasted it over another area. "Are you watching?"

"I'm watching."

Rosario increased the transparency of the copied section, until it was at fifty percent. While the red lines shifted slightly as the lines on the image beneath it became more prominent, the jungle covering didn't.

At all.

It was as if the two areas of canopy were clones of each other.

"Whoa," Ananke said.

Rosario moved the copied section to another area along the outlined corridor. Another perfect fit. She shifted the picture down until the river's edge came back into view, and moved the transparent piece over a portion of the image close to the angled object she'd first shown Ananke. Again, the covering was the same.

Ananke's first thought was that someone had doctored the image, but that didn't make sense. Like almost everywhere else on the planet, this area was probably being photographed on a regular basis. If there was something to hide, whoever had changed this image would have had to do so to all the images, on a daily basis.

"Camouflage?" she asked.

Rosario nodded. Moving the cursor along the shore, she said, "It goes from here to here, more than enough to hide a dock of sufficient size."

Ananke stared at the shoreline. "How far does the road go?"

Rosario smiled and pushed out on the image, until they could see the starting point of the red lines at the dock and the end point in the middle of what looked like nowhere, about twenty kilometers from the river.

"Please tell me there's more camouflage where the road ends," Ananke said.

Rosario clicked another tab, and an amorphous, green-outlined blob appeared over the image right where Ananke had asked for it.

"It's a mix of actual foliage and more of the fake," Rosario said.

"That's...a huge area," Ananke said.

"Approximately a square kilometer."

AS THE TEAM was leaving the hotel for the *Green Eyed Dawn*, Ananke received another text from Nicholas.

> There is a settlement along the Rio Barima called
> San Christophe. My contact says to look for a man named
> Angel Largos, and he should be able to help you.

This was followed by a text with the coordinates of the settlement. As they drove toward the boat, Ananke had Rosario put the information in the map. San Christophe was about ten kilometers west of the hidden dock, making it an excellent place from where to stage their operations.

If this Angel Largos could help them.

They arrived at the harbor at a quarter to six p.m. and shoved off right on schedule.

The sun set around the time the *Green Eyed Dawn* rounded the southern end of Trinidad. They killed their running lights and charted a course just inside international waters, parallel to the Venezuelan coast. They could see only hints of the dark mass of the continent in the distance, off to starboard.

Ananke, with Liesel, watched from the bridge, while the rest of the team endured the voyage below deck. Now and then they spotted the lights of freighters in the distance, and more commonly, those of smaller fishing boats, working the sea.

Dylan's prediction that the *Green Eyed Dawn* could carve a quick path through the water proved accurate. But the engines weren't the only nonstandard equipment for a vessel of its type. The *Green Eyed Dawn* also had a sophisticated GPS system and a long-range radar.

At half past one a.m., the captain gave the order to turn toward shore and took over monitoring the radar. Though Ananke guessed most of the blips on the screen were fishing vessels, the captain made sure the *Green Eyed Dawn* never came close to any of them.

Thirty minutes on, as the GPS showed they were nearing the mouth of the Orinoco, the captain gave the order to stop.

The sound of the engine died, and their steady forward motion turned into more of a diagonal drift.

"What is it?" Ananke asked.

The captain stared intently at the radar screen. Ananke shifted her position to see what he was seeing.

Among the stationary dots was one that was speeding just offshore, on a path that would have collided with theirs if the captain hadn't ordered the stop.

"Coast guard?" she asked.

The captain nodded without looking up.

Once the coast guard ship was a good kilometer past the *Green Eyed Dawn*'s intended route, the captain gave the order to proceed.

They made it into the delta without incident and headed to the entrance of Rio Barima at the southeastern end of the bay.

Before leaving Trinidad, Ananke had asked the captain if he could take them to San Christophe. He seemed reluctant to go that far down the river, but in the end, he'd agreed. As they entered the Rio Barima now, he seemed more and more tense.

She asked, "Do you think there's more coast guard here?"

He shook his head, grim-faced. "No coast guard here."

"Something's bothering you."

He glanced at her, then away. "It's nothing."

It wasn't nothing, but obviously he wasn't going to share it with her.

Five minutes later, the reason presented itself in the form of a spotlight that suddenly lit up a boat coming toward them from upriver. Its beam swung to the *Green Eyed Dawn* and illuminated the bow.

The captain snapped an order, and one of the crewmembers grabbed Ananke and Liesel by their arms.

"What the hell?" Ananke said, pulling from his grasp.

"Go with him," the captain shouted. Ananke took from his tone that things would not go well if she refused.

She motioned to the crew member to lead the way, and she and Liesel followed him down into the interior of the ship. When they reached the small mess area where Rosario, Ricky, and Dylan sat, the man said, "They come, too."

"Grab everything and follow us," Ananke ordered.

"What's going on?" Ricky shouted.

"I think we're about to be boarded."

Ricky and Dylan grabbed the gear bags, while Rosario scooped up her computer and backpack, and they fell in behind the others.

The crew member took them all the way down to the engine room in the bottom of the ship. There, he said something to the crew in the room. Three of the men began pulling up floor panels, revealing a narrow space that smelled of brine and rot.

"In, in," their guide said.

Ananke motioned for Ricky and Dylan to go in first, and then she and Liesel handed them the gear bags. Next Rosario slipped through the hole, followed by Liesel. Ananke climbed in after them.

The crew then replaced the panel, sealing them in darkness.

Ananke didn't like this one bit. By all appearances, the

captain was acting in their best interests, but what if he was stashing them here so he could sell them out to whoever was on that other boat? She'd paid him enough, but maybe he thought he could make a little more on top of it.

"Pass out the guns," she whispered.

Ricky turned on the flashlight on his phone, unzipped one of the duffels, and passed weapons around.

"Suppressors?" he asked.

"No," she said. Suppressors would only make their pistols' barrels longer, and in their confined space, it was better to shoot a gun that made a lot of noise and risk going deaf than getting it caught on a support beam while trying to aim it.

Ricky turned off his light and they lay at the bottom of the boat, waiting.

For the first few minutes, there was only the sound of the engines. Then, with a fading whine, the motors wound down. Not long after that, something thudded against the *Green Eyed Dawn*, rocking it slightly.

Ananke listened for voices, but there was too much boat between her and the main deck, where the action was happening.

More time passed, marked only by the occasional sound of one of the engine-room men moving around.

Her internal clock told her they had been hiding for just over six minutes when they heard several people enter the engine room. As the footsteps drew closer to the panel above her, Ananke placed both hands on her gun, positioning it in case the cover moved.

More voices, right above her now. Close enough that a few words leaked down. *Time* and *trouble* and *start* and *morning*. Not enough to know what they were talking about.

The shuffle of a shoe, so close that if there had been a hole in the floor, she could have touched its sole.

Then, as quickly as they had arrived, the visitors exited.

The boat creaked in the silence that followed.

Five minutes.

Ten.

Another thud, this one not nearly as loud or disrupting as

the last, followed by the sound of a motor whirling to life. From somewhere off to the side, beyond the *Green Eyed Dawn*.

The sound faded as it moved farther away. Before it was completely gone, the *Green Eyed Dawn*'s engines churned back to life, drowning everything else out.

"We're moving," Dylan said. "That's got to be a good sign, right?"

"Depends on who's in charge of the ship," Ananke said.

"Right. There's that."

Because of the motor noise, Ananke didn't hear anything else until the panels above started moving. She raised her weapon.

"Shit!" a man screamed.

Since Ananke's eyes had adjusted to the dark, all she could see was a silhouette, surrounded by bright light, jumping out of the way. She squinted as another shadow leaned over the opening.

"It's okay," a different voice said. "They're gone."

Slowly, the face of the crew member who had escorted them down came into focus.

Ananke sat up, bringing her head above floor level, and looked around. The only other people in the room were the men who worked on the engines. She lowered her gun.

The man held out his hand, and she let him help her out.

"You can put that away," he said, nodding at her weapon.

Ignoring him, she asked, "Who came on board?"

"The captain will tell you. He wants to see you." He looked past her to the hole where Liesel was climbing out. "All of you."

THE CAPTAIN SCOWLED as Ananke and her team walked onto the bridge. She could see the boat's pace was extremely slow, almost like it was just holding its position against the flow of the river.

"You owe me another thousand dollars," the captain said.

The implication was he'd had to pay someone off. She was sure the bribe was only half as much, but she said, "No problem. Who were they?"

"No one I want to deal with again."

"As soon as you drop us off, you can be on your way home."

He snorted and shook his head. "You're getting off here."

Ananke looked outside again. There was no dock, no buildings, not even a footpath as far as she could tell, only the darkness of the jungle. "We had a deal to take us to San Christophe."

"You can either leave here or come back with us to Trinidad. But if we are stopped again, I am not going to hide you."

Ananke pointed at the shore. "We're supposed to just walk through that? That will take forever."

A twinkle grew in his eyes. "For another thousand, you can have the lifeboat."

They stared at each other. Ananke could tell he'd been rattled by the boarding. If the visitors hadn't been the coast guard, then who were they? Local thugs? Pirates?

A private patrol for the City?

Whoever they were, their proximity meant she couldn't get the captain to travel the final few kilometers to San Christophe.

"Deal."

He held out his hand. "A thousand for the bribe, and a thousand for the boat."

"I'd like to see this boat first."

TWENTY

THE LIFEBOAT TURNED out to be a Zodiac. While it wasn't new, it looked in fairly decent shape. It came with an undersized outboard motor that would be sorely lacking in the speed department. After contentious but quick negotiations that saw an extra five hundred dollars added to the tab, several extra cans of fuel and four wooden oars were thrown in.

Once payment had been made and the Zodiac put in the water, Ananke's team climbed on and shoved off.

Behind them, the *Green Eyed Dawn* began swinging around to head back to the sea.

"I am not leaving them a good review on Yelp, I'll tell you that much," Dylan said as he fired up the Zodiac's motor and pointed it upstream.

Ananke was pleasantly surprised to find they were traveling faster than she thought they would. Not by a lot, but at least they weren't crawling.

Above them hung the star-filled sky, and to the sides the dark curtains of the jungle, from which came the occasional calls of unknown animals.

"Am I the only one getting a serious *Apocalypse Now* vibe?" Ricky asked.

"Apocalypse what?" Rosario said.

"Do not tell me you haven't heard of *Apocalypse Now*. You have, right? It's only one of the greatest war movies of all time."

Rosario wasn't the only one staring blankly at him.

"Marlon Brando? Martin Sheen? Robert Duvall and the helicopters with speakers blaring 'Ride of the Valkyries'?"

Still nothing.

"What about the book *Heart of Darkness*? You've heard of that, right?"

Dylan's eyes lit up. "Oh, sure. Had to read it in school, I think."

"The movie's based on that."

"Something about a hunt for a crazy guy who thinks he's a god, right?"

"Colonel Kurtz," Ricky said. "Or at least he was a colonel in the movie. He had his own little empire set up deep in the jungle. Like this place."

"What happens to him?" Rosario asked.

"He gets killed."

"That is not a good omen," Liesel said.

"We wouldn't be Kurtz in this scenario. We're more like...whatever the hell Martin Sheen's character was called."

"And does Martin Sheen die, too?"

"No." Ricky paused. "Though I do think he went a little crazy at the end."

Liesel raised an eyebrow. "And this is a better omen?"

"Quiet," Ananke said. She tilted her head. "Is that a motor?"

Dylan cut back on the outboard and everyone listened for a moment.

"A big one," Rosario said.

The sound was coming from where they were headed.

Worried that it might be another patrol boat, Ananke scanned the nearby shore. There wasn't a beach they could disappear onto, but she spotted brush overhanging the water in several areas.

She pointed and said to Dylan, "Take us over there. Hurry."

He veered the Zodiac toward shore.

Ananke searched the waters behind them for the other vessel. "Anybody see it?"

"I got nothing," Ricky said.

Liesel shook her head.

"It must be running dark like we were," Rosario suggested.

As soon as the Zodiac was right up to the brush, Dylan killed the engine. Without needing to be told, everyone ducked below the mass of vegetation and grabbed branches, pulling the lifeboat underneath the covering.

"This should be good," Ananke whispered once they were all the way under.

Ananke adjusted her position to see the river above the boat's pontoon sidewall. If the other vessel was the one that had stopped the *Green Eyed Dawn*, she would have seen it by now. Though the noise had grown louder, there was still no sign of it.

"Maybe it's a ghost ship," Dylan whispered.

"There is no such thing as ghosts," Liesel replied.

"Obviously, you've never visited Ireland."

"No talking unless you see something," Ananke chided them.

For nearly a minute, the only sound other than the approaching rumble was water lapping against the Zodiac.

"There it is," Ricky whispered, pointing downriver.

At first glance, Ananke couldn't see anything, but then she realized a shadow was moving toward them. A *huge* shadow.

As it came nearer, she noticed a halo of orange light leaking through a window, about twenty meters above water level, near the back end of the shadow. The bridge?

Now that the ship was nearly parallel to them, its shadowy form separated more from that of the jungle, allowing Ananke to make out several structures on board. In addition to the wide tower the light was coming from, there were at least two other structures midship, made up of several interconnected beams, creating what she guessed were cranes used for the loading and unloading of cargo.

This had to be one of the ships that picked up the goods produced at the City. She and the team were on the right track.

The ship had probably entered the river as soon as it had gotten dark, loaded up, and was now on its way out so that it would be at sea again before the sun came up. To maintain its anonymity, the City would not want any vessels near its dock in daylight.

The team waited until the ship had moved several hundred meters downriver before maneuvering the Zodiac out from under the brush. Dylan started the motor again and aimed them upriver.

"How much farther?" Ananke asked.

Rosario, who was monitoring their position on her satellite phone, said, "San Christophe is about two kilometers ahead."

"And the dock?"

"You mean for the City?"

"Yeah."

"Another eighteen beyond that."

Ananke stared at the river.

"What are you thinking?" Rosario asked.

Ananke watched the water for another few seconds before saying, "I'm thinking that if there's another ship being loaded right now, it would be a good opportunity to see these people in action." She turned to Dylan. "How long should it take us?"

"Not more than an hour. As long as there aren't many more ships we need to hide from."

Ananke nodded. "Let's pay them a visit."

THEY HAD TO hide two more times, in both instances from patrol ships similar to the one that had stopped the *Green Eyed Dawn*. A kilometer shy of the dock, they turned off the motor, switched to the paddles, and rowed along the same side of the river the dock was on.

Four hundred meters away, Ananke caught sight of the ship tied to the dock and motioned for everyone to stop paddling.

The vessel was maybe half the size of the one that had passed them earlier. She could see motion on the ship and the dock, but it was difficult to make out any details. The reason had to do with the lights illuminating the area. Not only were they very dim, they were also tinted blue. This should have made it impossible for any work to get done, but she could see one of the cranes hoisting a shipping container off the dock and swinging it toward the deck of the boat.

The crews must be wearing some kind of night vision

eyewear, she thought. A remote area like this blazing with light would draw unwanted attention from passing aircraft, whereas the blue lights they were using would likely go unnoticed.

They paddled on until they found a small open stretch of shore a few hundred meters from the ship. After disembarking, they tied up the Zodiac under some more brush. Ricky handed out pistols while Liesel distributed comm gear. After making sure they were all keyed into the same encrypted channel, they slipped into the jungle.

Though they didn't have far to travel, the going was difficult, and several times they had to double back when the way forward proved unpassable. Finally, the brush thinned, and Ananke could see the blue glow beyond. She motioned for the others to huddle around her.

"Liesel, Ricky, head south a hundred meters or so, then turn east and scope out the road. Rosario and Dylan, you're with me."

Liesel and Ricky headed off, while Ananke led Rosario and Dylan to just shy of where the jungle stopped and the dock started.

There were about twenty people on the land side, and around half as many visible on the ship. As she'd suspected, all were wearing goggles strapped around their heads. A shipping container was being lowered into the hold. Only three more were waiting, so it appeared the operation was nearing its end.

Ananke studied the dockworkers. There were two distinct groups—the ones doing the actual work, and the armed personnel watching over them. The former group was uniformly dressed in tan T-shirts and matching pants, while the guards wore army camouflage and carried assault rifles. The men on the ship were dressed in clothes that made her think they were part of the vessel's crew.

Ananke noted the name of the ship—the *Sebastian Cole IV*—so she could pass that on to the Administrator. She hadn't been able to get the same info on the other cargo vessel, but could give an approximate time it had sailed into the sea. Hopefully it would be enough for the Administrator's researchers to find it.

At the *Sebastian Cole IV*, the empty crane lines rose and moved back over the dock. As they lowered to the next container, Ricky came over the comm. "We're at the road."

Ananke was too close to the dock to risk talking, so she clicked her mic once to indicate she understood.

"Get this," he said. "Rosario was right. It *is* paved. I mean, like a real highway. It's wide enough for probably three lanes, too. It must have taken a hell of a lot of work to rip the path through the jungle and put it here."

She clicked again.

For the next few minutes, she, Rosario, and Dylan watched as the cargo lines were connected to the next container. Once everything was set, the box was lifted into the air. At this pace, the ship would be loaded and ready to go in the next ten minutes.

Ananke caught Rosario's and Dylan's attention and motioned that they were done here. She led them around toward the road. "Ananke for Ricky or Liesel, what's your exact position?"

No response.

"Ricky, Liesel. Come in."

"Sorry, boss. We're here."

"I need your location."

"We, um—" He fell silent. When he spoke again, his voice was barely audible. "Give us a minute."

Ananke exchanged looks with Rosario and Dylan. All three picked up their pace.

THE ROAD STRETCHED from the back of the dock—a hundred meters to Ricky and Liesel's left—to where it disappeared into the jungle to the south, cutting a line through the vegetation like a fire break.

Rosario had said it was paved, but Ricky hadn't really believed that until he laid eyes on it. Three lanes of thick asphalt, missing only the lane lines.

Almost as strange and out of place as the road itself was the camouflage canopy stretched a dozen meters above it, blotting out all but a few stars.

After reporting to Ananke, Ricky checked both ways down the road. He could see some of the blue glow toward the dock, but there were no people or vehicles in sight. He started to step out from cover but Liesel grabbed his arm, giving him a what-are-you-doing look.

"It's okay," he whispered. "Just a quick check."

She frowned.

"There's no one around," he said. "Nothing's going to happen."

She hesitated before letting him go.

Ricky crouched and crept out to the center of the road. He leaned down until his face was hovering above the surface. There were tire-sized grooves in the asphalt, telling him the vehicles that used it were a) heavy, and b) fond of driving the exact same path over and over. He scanned the road. Two sets of dual grooves, one per direction, he guessed.

He looked toward the dock, envisioning the trucks coming and going. In order to load two cargo ships, there had to be a whole mess of vehicles bringing the containers to the river in a steady stream.

Unless…

He looked toward the dock again.

Huh.

About twenty-five meters short of where the dock began, there appeared to be a wide break in the jungle, on the eastern side of the road. He'd missed it the first time he looked that way, his gaze taken in by the blue glow.

He waved to Liesel to follow him and scooted into the jungle on the other side of the road.

"What are you doing?" she asked when she caught up to him.

"I think there's something up ahead."

Before he could take a step, Liesel grabbed his shoulder.

"What something?"

"I saw some kind of opening down there."

"Opening? What kind?"

"*Some* kind."

He calmly removed her hand from his shoulder and started

moving again.

This part of the jungle had been partially cleared, so it was easier to pass through than the area where they'd come ashore. Probably kept that way to prevent the brush from growing out onto the road.

In just over a minute, they reached another clearing, this one extending perpendicularly to the road.

Ricky scanned it from the cover of the brush. To his left was the break he'd seen, connecting it to the jungle highway. The opening was plenty wide enough for fully loaded trucks to pass through. Judging from the handful of shipping containers stacked near the far end, this was a storage and staging area. There was even a high-tech rail system on which containers could be manually transported to the docks. So that meant the trucks could deliver the containers during the day, before the boats arrived.

No trucks were here at the moment, but there was a bus, which Ricky guessed was worker transportation. There would also have to be some living quarters in the area. With all the expensive equipment and stored containers around, they'd be crazy not to have a twenty-four-hour security presence. The only place where that could be was to the east side of the dock.

He looked at the bus. Like the whole area, it was illuminated by only a bit of the blue light seeping through the trees. If the vehicle *was* for the workers, and there was no reason to think it wasn't, then it would be heading back to the City when things wrapped up.

And if that was the case, it might be a way for one of the team members to get inside the place.

"I'm going to check the bus out," he whispered.

"What? No. That is a terrible—"

Before Liesel could grab him, he moved out from the trees and sneaked across the clearing. He could sense her following but didn't look back.

It was an old tourist-type bus, with three hatches along the bottom that opened to luggage space. If the space wasn't used, someone could covertly travel in there. He pulled on one of the handles but it was locked.

Liesel poked him in the back as he went to try the next one. She looked at him like he was crazy and pointed toward the front of the bus.

He frowned, not understanding.

She led him to the front corner and gestured for him to look around it. He leaned out and spotted a pedestrian passageway through the brush that appeared to lead to the dock. And within the passage was the silhouette of a man heading toward the clearing, the red glow of a cigarette hovering by his side.

"Ananke for Ricky or Liesel," Ananke said over the comm. "What's your exact position?"

Ricky pulled back around and looked at Liesel.

Ananke called again.

Ricky whispered, "Sorry, boss. We're here."

"I need your location."

"We're, um—" He heard a step coming from around the bus, toward the passageway. Taking his volume down even more, he said, "Give us a minute."

He could now hear steps in the clearing, moving toward the bus at a steady but unhurried pace. "Rigo!" someone shouted. "Rigo, wake up!"

A bump from inside the bus.

Ricky and Liesel ducked as the driver brought his seat back to its normal position and opened the bus's door.

"I'm up, I'm up," the driver—Rigo—said.

The other man stopped walking. "Fifteen-minute warning."

"Got it."

Ricky led Liesel around the back of the bus. It had no rear window, just a ladder attached to the back, leading up to a large luggage rack on the roof. Looking under the vehicle, he watched the other man walk back to the passageway.

The bus's engine rumbled to life.

There was opportunity here that would be a shame to waste. But as much as Ricky thought hitching a ride would be a good idea, he knew he couldn't do anything without getting Ananke's okay first.

"Come on," he whispered.

He headed back until he was sure he and Liesel couldn't be seen in the shadows, and turned for the jungle.

When they reached it, he flicked on his comm. "Ananke, where are you?"

"At the road. Where the hell are you?"

"We'll be right there. Meet us seventy-five meters back from the dock."

ANANKE, ROSARIO, AND Dylan repositioned to the approximate meeting point, and waited.

Ananke expected Ricky and Liesel to appear from within the jungle around them, so she was taken off guard when Dylan said, "There they are," and pointed at the road, where Ricky and Liesel were emerging from the other side.

"What were you doing over there?" she asked when the two reached her.

"Look, we've only got a few minutes so you've got to listen to me," Ricky said.

"What do you mean we've—"

"Ananke, please. I promise I'll tell you everything."

She took a breath. "Okay, talk."

He briefed her on what he and Liesel had found and explained his idea. When he finished, no one said a word.

He looked at Ananke. "Well?"

"You know there's an excellent chance of getting caught," she said.

"I don't intend to let that happen."

"But you don't even know what you'll be getting yourself into."

"Which is exactly why we need to do this."

He was right. At some point they would have to scout the City, which would mean a twenty-kilometer hike through the jungle. "The signal amplifier is back at the boat," she said. "We won't be able to get it in time, so you won't be able to reach us."

"Then set a pickup time. Say, tomorrow night after it gets dark. Seven thirty."

She considered it, then nodded. "Okay. But don't go inside the City. Stay in the jungle around it. The moment you think there might be trouble, you get out of there. Promise me or you're staying here."

"I might need to get closer. We need to know what we're up against."

"I said promise me."

He frowned. "Okay, I promise."

"I have something that might help," Liesel said. She pulled off her backpack and handed it to him. "The drone, plus some food, a knife, and matches..."

The drone was a high-end stealth model—small, with a high-res camera, and rotors that ran near silently.

"Is the drone a good idea?" Ananke asked.

"I'll only use it if it's safe."

"Don't take this the wrong way, but I'm not sure you know how to judge that."

He snorted. "Don't worry. I'll apply the Ananke Rule."

Her eyes narrowed. "What's the Ananke Rule?"

"Simple. I ask myself, what would Ananke do?"

"You should do that with everything," Rosario said.

Back toward the dock, they could hear the bus's engine rev.

"I need to get a little farther down, I think," he said.

Together, they jogged just inside the jungle until they were nearly two hundred meters from the dock.

Ninety seconds later, the bus pulled onto the road, heading their way, headlights on but much dimmer than standard ones. Ricky stepped to the edge of the jungle.

"Hey," Ananke said.

He looked back.

"Thanks for asking instead of just doing it on your own."

"See, sometimes I can learn."

Seconds later, the bus's headlights lit up the brush near them as it passed.

The moment their surroundings fell back into darkness, Ricky sprinted from the brush to the back of the bus. At first it looked like he wouldn't be able to catch it, but he stretched out a hand, grabbed the ladder on the back, and pulled himself up.

Ananke and the others watched until the bus disappeared.

TWENTY-ONE

HOLDING ON TO the ladder was not as difficult as Ricky had feared. The road remained relatively smooth, offering up few bumps or dips that might knock him off. The driver kept his speed slow enough that even if Ricky had fallen, he probably wouldn't have suffered more than a few cuts and bruises.

Okay, *maybe* a broken wrist.

Since there was no rear window through which someone might see him, he considered climbing onto the roof where he could stretch out on the luggage rack. But he was concerned his presence on the roof might be heard. So he hugged the rungs, shifting his weight between his arms to keep either from getting too stiff.

Kilometer after kilometer, the scene around him remained an unchanging corridor of dark jungle to either side and opaque netting above, making him fight hard to keep from zoning out.

Around what he figured was the fifteen-kilometer mark, the bus slowed. He crept up the ladder and peered over the roof.

Dammit.

Sitting at the left side of the road, about a hundred and fifty meters ahead, was a hut. Two floodlights pumping out blue light—like at the dock—were mounted atop a pair of poles on either side of the asphalt, across which were four wide metal pillars sticking up about a meter high.

As the bus neared the roadblock, two armed guards wearing goggles exited the hut and took up positions beside the road.

Ricky knew his current location was untenable. If the guards didn't perform a walk-around of the bus when it stopped, they'd at least glance at the back as the vehicle drove off and see Ricky hanging there.

He had only two choices. The first was to hop off and slip into the jungle, then hope he could sneak around the roadblock and jump back onto the bus as it drove away. But that would only occur if everything went his way, *and* the guards didn't happen to be looking when he climbed back onto the ladder.

Or he could ignore his earlier concerns and climb onto the roof, lie as flat as possible, and hope the guards would check things only at ground level. At least with this method, when the bus drove away, the luggage rack would hide him.

Going with option two, he waited until the bus was almost at the roadblock—so that the guards' view of the top would be obstructed—before crawling onto the roof. He scooched as far forward into the luggage rack as he could and flattened himself against the surface.

The bus came to a halt in a whoosh of air brakes. The hut's door opened, and Ricky heard voices talking to someone inside the vehicle. After a laugh and a bit more talking, the door closed again.

The guards walked back to their hut. A few seconds later came the distinct squeal of a hydraulic system in operation, which Ricky interpreted as the lowering of the posts blocking the road. The bus moved forward again.

He turned his head to see through the opening at the back of the rack. When the hut came into view again, the guards were nowhere in sight.

Ricky peeked over the front of the rack. Except for what the bus's feeble headlights lit up, the road was dark again.

He made a pillow with his arm and settled in for part two of his night ride.

WHEN ANANKE AND the others reached the Zodiac, she asked, "How many signal amplifiers do we have?"

"Four," Rosario said.

"Let's hide one near where the road meets the dock." If they or Ricky returned to the area before the other, this would help them make contact.

Rosario pulled an amplifier out of one of the duffels, and

with Liesel accompanying her, disappeared back into the jungle.

By the time they returned, Ananke and Dylan had moved the Zodiac out of its hiding spot and swung it around so that it pointed downriver. Dylan had also topped off the outboard motor's fuel tank.

The team paddled away, a job made considerably easier now that they were going with the current.

When she felt they'd gone far enough, Ananke gave the order and Dylan fired up the motor.

IT STARTED AS a dim blue glow in the distance. At first, Ricky wondered if he was seeing things, but the halo of light continued to grow.

Had he come the final five kilometers? Or was this another checkpoint?

The closer he got, the more individual lights he could see stretching out into the jungle.

This must be it.

The City.

He crawled back onto the ladder but remained near the top so he could watch ahead. When the bus was about half a kilometer from the first light, Ricky climbed down, took a deep breath, and dropped onto the road. The instant his feet hit the asphalt, he tucked and rolled, then bounced to his feet. A quick assessment revealed a small cut on his left elbow, a few spots where he'd probably have bruises later, but nothing too bad.

He sprinted to the edge of the clearing and jogged toward the lights.

Ahead, the bus's brake lights flashed as it neared the end of its trip. Ricky could barely make out the shadow of someone standing at the side of the road. Another guard, likely. The bus was waved through and drove out of sight.

Ricky continued along the edge of the road until he was about two hundred meters away from the lights. He stopped and used his camera to get a better look at the area. In addition to another set of hydraulic posts in the road, there was also a metal gate, currently pulled to the side. He couldn't see anything beyond the lit area, as the road appeared to take a ninety-degree turn about fifty meters in.

Where there was a gate, there was usually a fence. The question was, did it extend around the whole damn City?

He took a few pictures of the entrance, shoved the phone into his pocket, and slipped into the jungle. He angled his path so he should reach the fence about a hundred meters east of the gate, if it extended that far.

Turned out, it did. And it was a big one, too. Close to seven meters high, with four strands of razor wire across the top.

That was kind of a bummer, especially if the thing encircled the whole compound.

But that sure seemed like a waste of materials. The jungle was these assholes' friend. There was nothing but misery and death for hundreds of kilometers.

Well, except the north side, where Ricky was, which faced the river. He could understand a fence along here. Hopefully that's all there was.

He wasn't going to find out which it was just standing there, so he began following the fence into the brush.

THE FIRST RAYS of light were tickling the eastern sky by the time Dylan guided the Zodiac up to the pier used by the residents of San Christophe. It was an old thing, patched together with odd scraps of wood to create a surface that was surprisingly sturdier than it looked. Two boats were tied to it, neither large enough to carry more than four people. Whoever used them was nowhere to be seen.

The only visible structure other than the dock itself sat just up the bank, and was little more than a roof hoisted on four posts above a concrete foundation.

Beside it ran a path into the jungle. Since there didn't seem to be any other options, the team headed down it, Ananke leading and Liesel bringing up the rear.

After about three minutes they found the settlement, situated in what was more a thinning of jungle than an actual clearing. There wasn't much to the place. Six buildings, the largest two about the size of a single-wide mobile home back in the States. The others were smaller, from a half to a quarter of the size of the larger structures. Between two of the buildings was a fenced-in area where a couple of goats and some chickens roamed.

According to Nicholas's contact, Angel Largos lived here.

Ananke could hear movement coming from the big building on the left, and thought it was as good a place to start with as any.

She told the others to hang back, to avoid overwhelming whoever might answer the door, and approached the entrance. Before she reached it, the door to another building opened, to her right. An older man stepped out from one of the smaller huts and froze, staring at her.

Taking a step toward him, she said, *"Buenos días."*

He blinked but said nothing.

"We're looking for Angel Largos," she continued in Spanish. "Do you know where we might find him?"

A woman around the same age as the man appeared in the doorway, her expression stern. "Who are you?"

"My name is Ananke. My friends and I are looking for Angel Largos."

The man's gaze whipped over to Rosario, Dylan, and Liesel, apparently just realizing Ananke wasn't alone. The woman seemed unfazed.

"Angel isn't here," she said.

"Do you know when he'll be coming back?"

"No time soon. He's dead."

"Oh. I'm…I'm sorry."

The woman made no reply.

"Is there somewhere we might rest?" Ananke asked.

"Do you see a hotel here?"

Ananke frowned. "I'm sorry. Have I done something to make you angry?"

"What are you doing here?"

"We're just passing through."

"From where to where?"

"We're…looking for some friends."

"Angel is dead. I told you already."

"Not Angel."

"Who?"

There was no way the people here weren't aware something bad was going on upriver. They might not know specifics, but the comings and goings of the cargo ships and patrol boats along the Barima would clue them in that not all was right in their little piece of paradise. It was likely they'd had interactions with City personnel, too. But if the people running the City were paying off the residents here to guarantee their silence, Ananke couldn't see evidence of it. While none of the buildings looked like they would fall apart in the near future, they had all been repaired multiple times, in the same use-what-one-could patchwork fashion as the dock.

No, she thought. *These people aren't seeing any benefits from their neighbors.*

She decided to take a chance. "I'm guessing you've heard about the City. That's where our friends—"

The man backed into the doorway, nearly running over the woman. Once he was inside, the woman shoved the door closed.

"That didn't quite go as planned," Dylan said.

Ananke was more convinced than ever that thugs from the City had been here, probably more than once, and used intimidation instead of cash to keep the locals' mouths shut.

Hoping that someone else might be a little more receptive, she took another step toward the door she'd originally been heading toward.

Somewhere behind her, the sound of a rifle bolt being locked into place cut through the air. Two similar sounds followed, joined by the *cha-chunk* of a shotgun being racked.

"Hands in the air," a voice called.

RICKY'S INSTINCTS HAD been correct again.

The fence continued for four hundred meters into the wild, where it ended at a near vertical drop-off into a ravine. The bottom was a good eight meters down and covered with slimy-looking rocks. The other side of the gap was almost twice that

229

distance away, but no fence was there.

To prevent anyone from swinging around the end of the fence from one side to the other, strands of barbed wire were looped around the final post. Even if someone avoided getting cut, the person would still likely fall to the rocks, where the best outcome would be dying instantly from brain trauma.

Ricky knew the fence wasn't electrified. Even ignoring the fact it was missing the conductors and telltale hum, having juice run through it in the middle of the jungle would be a nightmare of constant repairs. The weather was too damn wet, plus who knew how many times it would be shorted out by a wandering animal committing unintentional suicide.

He pulled off Liesel's backpack and looked through it for anything that might help him. The closest he got was the knife. Its blade was pretty badass, but it wouldn't cut through the mesh.

He looked at the top of the barrier. The knife *might* be able to cut the razor wire.

He pulled on the fence to make sure it was solid enough to climb, and headed up one of the posts, knife between his teeth, commando style. Securing himself at the top was a little dicey, but after carefully wiggling an arm between the end of the mesh and the bottom of the lowest strand of razor wire, he was able to hold himself in place.

He started with the top strand where it met the post. He assumed he would have to saw at it for a while to get through, but Liesel kept her blade a lot sharper than he'd realized. With only a few back-and-forths, he was able to slice the wire free.

One by one, he worked his way down until the only wire still up was the one hovering above his stabilizing arm. He pulled his arm out, grabbed onto the mesh, and cut through the final wire.

When it fell free, he pulled himself onto the other side, and climbed down to the City side of the barrier.

He proceeded toward what he assumed was the heart of the City, picking out a point that would provide cover, moving to it, and repeating the process. If it had still been the dead of night, it would have been a much more difficult task, but the sky had lightened, helping him see his surroundings better.

He'd advanced in this manner for nearly ten minutes when he heard a horn blare, not only ahead but to the left and right, too. Like a schoolyard horn, prerecorded and amplified. The sound lasted for approximately fifteen seconds.

He started forward again, but couldn't have gone more than a dozen meters when the jungle thinned. He crept forward until he saw the wall of a large building. He was dangerously close to breaking his promise to Ananke, so instead of continuing forward, he moved left, following a gentle rise in the jungle floor. He came upon a group of trees that had collapsed upon one another. Some of the trees were still alive, but most were not. From the looks of it, a storm must have uprooted a couple of them and sent them into the others, creating a ramp that rose several meters above the brush.

Ricky crawled up one of the trunks until he was about three quarters of the way to the end, where he could hide behind branches on one of the living trees. He shifted around until he felt stable and peeked through the leaves.

Holy crap.

Stretching before him was the City, or at least part of it. He counted eleven buildings nestled among the jungle. Several meters above them was more of the camouflage canopy. The structures were all pretty much clones of one another—each about as big as a decent-sized barn, sided with wood and topped with corrugated tin. The windows he could see were long horizontal slits, maybe half a meter tall. The biggest variations between the building were the numbers painted on each.

As if the dreary structures weren't weird enough on their own, the area between them held what appeared to be a giant cage. It stretched across every inch of open space he could see, chain-link on top and presumably along the sides.

He pulled out the drone and sent it aloft, guiding it so that it would blend in with the jungle. When he found a good vantage spot, he let it hover, zoomed its camera in on the cage, and hit RECORD.

His first impression hadn't been entirely correct. The area underneath the chain-link top wasn't just one big open space.

Rather, chain-link walls were built throughout, creating long, alley-like sections no more than three persons wide.

He saw something else, too. Along the top were planks of wood laid out to create pathways people could walk on.

He panned the camera across the entire area, first with no magnification, then zooming in. In the middle of his final pass, the horn blared again, this time in three short blasts. This allowed him to pick out the speakers on the sides of several of the buildings.

They weren't the only things that caught his attention.

Eight men appeared on the pathway on top of the cage, coming from an area hidden from Ricky's view by the jungle. Each carried an assault rifle and a pistol holstered on his hip. They dispersed over the cage to cover essentially equal areas, and looked down through the chain-link, their rifles following their gaze.

Ricky wanted to recall the drone, but was afraid someone might notice. So, he let it hang in the air where it was.

The horn again. One blast.

All at once, doors on four of the buildings opened, and people shuffled out into the caged lanes.

"Damn," he muttered under his breath. There had to be a couple of hundred, if not more.

Everyone was dressed in the same drab clothing the dockworkers had worn. But there were women here. Ricky's unscientific sampling led him to believe there were considerably more women coming out of the buildings than men.

With the drone still recording, he watched the groups proceed down their different lanes. These walkways weren't as straight as they had first appeared. They turned to either side, always at right angles, like a maze but with no alternate paths to take.

Two of the groups looked like they were on a collision course. He focused the camera on them. Right before the first group reached the point where the two paths intersected, the people in front stopped walking.

As far as Ricky could tell, no order had been given. They

had halted as if they knew what to do. As if it was something they did every day.

Interestingly, the second group stopped short of the intersection, too. The guard above them moved a radio to his mouth. A moment later, two sections of chain-link rose through the top of the cage with a loud rattle, sticking up like tabs poking out of a file. When the first group began crossing the intersection, Ricky realized the two raised sections had been blocking their way. Sure enough, after the last of the group passed through, the guard spoke into his radio again and the sections dropped back down. After a beat, two more sections rose, allowing group two to pass.

It wasn't just a damn maze. It was a *moveable* damn maze.

Ricky guessed the overlords could send people anywhere they wanted without two groups ever coming into direct contact with each other. It was both ingenious and horrifying.

Less than a minute later, the cages were empty, and the guards up top had disappeared the way they'd come.

Ricky recalled the drone and stored it in his bag.

He had no idea where the prisoners had gone. None of their paths had led to any of the buildings he could see. They'd kept moving until their routes became obscured by the jungle.

He waited another thirty minutes to see if anything else would happen, but it was like a ghost town. So, he descended to the jungle floor, and went to see what else he could find.

ANANKE, ROSARIO, LIESEL, and Dylan sat on chairs in the middle of the only room in one of the settlement's two large buildings. Their weapons and gear bags sat on a table at the far side of the space.

Between them and the table stood seven people, each armed with a hunting rifle or shotgun or, in one case, a Colt .45 pistol.

The woman who had questioned them at the house was among them, but it was a man about a decade younger who appeared to be in charge. He'd given the order to take the team's guns and search the bags, something that had caused quite a stir when the arsenal inside was discovered. He'd also been the one who decided to move everything inside.

"You should not have come here," he said, addressing them for the first time.

"We don't mean to cause you any problems," Ananke said, acting as nonthreatening as possible. "We were just—"

"There is an agreement."

"An agreement?"

"We have lived up to our end. No one has said anything."

"I'm not sure we're who you think we are."

The man's eyes narrowed. "We all heard you. You told Marta that your friends are with the City."

"No, I said our friends are *at* the City. I didn't say they are *with* the City."

That knocked the man off balance for a moment, but then his jaw tensed again. "You're lying."

Ananke took a breath and stood up. The man's friends aimed their weapons at her. "I appreciate your caution," she said. "In your position, I might react the same way. But I honestly don't have the time or patience to deal with this right now. All we were looking for was someplace we could do some work and get a little rest. Obviously we were wrong to think we'd find that here. If we're going to get our friends out of there, we need to find someplace a little more welcoming, fast. So, if you'll excuse us." She started walking toward the table.

"If you do not sit back down, we will shoot you!" the man said.

As she neared the line of gun-toting locals, she said, "If you could please step aside."

Apparently thinking his Colt made him invincible, the guy directly in front of her pointed his weapon at her forehead.

"You don't want to do that," she said.

"Victor said, sit down," the guy replied.

She rolled her eyes. "And I said, I don't have time."

She ripped the gun from his grasp, jammed her shoulder under his arm, and flipped him onto the floor behind her.

His friends backed away, their guns temporarily forgotten. Ananke pointed the Colt at Victor, then flipped it around so she was holding the barrel and handed it to him. "Tell your people

234

to put their guns down before they hurt themselves."

Victor hesitated before he motioned for the others to do as she suggested. They complied.

"Thank you," she said.

As she turned back toward the table, someone behind her said, "Wait."

She looked back and saw it was the youngest of the posse, a girl who couldn't have been much more than twenty.

"You said you were going to get your friends out of the City?"

"Now, see, *that* is what I said."

"They are…workers?"

"You mean slaves."

The girl nodded. "And you are going to break them out."

"I feel like we've already been over this. Do you have a point?"

The girl stepped over to Victor and whispered to him. A few of the others joined in, seemingly arguing with her.

Ananke exchanged glances with Rosario, Liesel, and Dylan, who were all on their feet but still by the chairs. They looked as clueless about what was being discussed as she was.

Finally, the huddle broke up.

"You need to wait here," the girl said.

"I told you guys, we don't have time. We're sorry we ruined your morning but—"

"No. You must wait here. I have to…get someone. You will want to talk to him."

"Does he know something about the City?"

"You will want to talk to him. I will be back as fast as I can." She rushed out the door.

Ananke turned to Victor. "What the hell is she talking about?"

"It will be easier to understand when she returns. Until then, you are welcome to rest here. And if you are hungry, we can bring you something to eat."

IT WAS NEARLY two hours before the girl came back. With her was a middle-aged man. Though he radiated a sense of determination, he didn't look like the type who would try to make a life in the depths of the jungle.

"You're the one who knows something about the City?" Ananke asked him.

"In a sense, yes," the man said. His accent was not like the others. He sounded Mexican.

"What does that mean?"

He eyed her cautiously. "Why exactly are you here?"

"There are people there we know, and we're going to get them out."

"Relatives?"

"No."

"Friends, then?"

"Look, I don't have time for this."

"Please. It is important."

Ananke took a deep breath. "We don't know them, exactly. We took down the people who originally sold them. We're here to get them free."

Her response surprised him. "You are…police?"

She almost laughed. "Not police. More of a private organization. Now you tell me, can you help us or not?"

"I believe we can," he said, and held out his hand. "Ramon Silva."

She looked at it for a moment before taking it. "Call me Ananke."

TWENTY-TWO

"LIESEL FOR RICKY," Liesel said for at least the twentieth time.

She had started trying to reach him when she and Dylan were still about five kilometers from the docks, but so far hadn't had any luck. She hoped it meant he was still making his way back to the river and wasn't in range of the booster yet. Otherwise, this might have to turn into a rescue mission.

From ahead, she picked up a dull hum. She lifted the binoculars and, after a quick scan of the river, whispered to Dylan, "Boat."

As he'd done three times since leaving San Christophe, Dylan swung the Zodiac toward shore. Like elsewhere, brush overhung the river, only here the gap between the bottom branches and the water was too small to maneuver the boat into. He settled for snuggling up against it, and he and Liesel lay flat.

As the other boat passed, Liesel snuck a peek at it. A fishing boat, about twice the size of their craft, making its way slowly toward the delta. Two men were on deck, working on equipment.

While Dylan steered them away from shore, Liesel tried the radio again.

There was a crackle in her ear, then, "...or...icky."

"This is Liesel. Can you hear me? Are you at the dock?"

"...ink I...ilo...way."

"Repeat, please."

"I'm...kilo...away."

"Your signal is weak. Not getting everything."

Static.

"Ricky?"

She heard him say something again but couldn't work it

out.

"We should be at the dock in…" She looked back at Dylan, who mouthed the number ten. "Ten minutes."

Nothing.

"Ricky?…Ricky?"

IT HAD BEEN an interesting day, to say the least.

By noon, Ricky had a pretty good idea of the size of the City. He counted forty-seven buildings in and around the jungle, almost all connected to the cage maze. He was pretty sure the half dozen or so unattached ones were used by security and admin personnel.

It wasn't long before he noticed similarities between the structures attached to the maze. Each about the size of a standard barn, the buildings could be divided into two subgroups: ones with high, narrow windows; and ones with large side panels propped open to let air in.

He figured the first group was where the captives slept. It consisted of the type of buildings he'd seen the slaves exit after the horn at sunrise. He guessed they could hold anywhere from fifty to a hundred people each, depending on how things were laid out.

There were twenty of these buildings.

Twenty.

Of course, he didn't know how many were being used, but even if it was only half, that could mean a labor force of a thousand.

Dear God.

From the sounds coming out of the second type of buildings—the ones with the side panels—they had to be the workhouses or factories or whatever they called them. Though he couldn't get very close to any of them, either on his own or with the drone, every single one he saw had its panels open and bled the sounds of machines in action.

Near the main gate, on either side of the road, were two buildings unlike all the others. They were long and tall and wide. The first word that came to mind when he saw them was warehouses. Beside them, under a tin roof, were at least twenty big rigs attached to flatbed trailers designed to carry shipping containers. This had to be where the goods started on their way to the river.

Ricky spent a fair amount of time probing the perimeter of the City for cameras and other security devices. He didn't discover any cameras but found two sets of trip wires, about three meters apart, that basically encircled the City. The interesting thing was that the wires were set very close to the buildings built at the edge of the City, like they were meant to be triggered by someone moving away from the City toward the jungle, not the other way around.

That seemed to be pretty much the theme of the place. There appeared to be very little worry about incursions from beyond the City's limits, while there was great concern about anyone on the inside getting out.

Just after two p.m., when he was a quarter of the way around the west side, he heard the rattle of several diesel engines starting up. He worked his way back toward the sound.

A couple of the trucks had moved out from the covered parking area and were on the road, facing the front gate. The lead truck was idling between the warehouses.

As Ricky watched, an automated hoist carried a shipping container out of the western warehouse and positioned it over the big rig's trailer. The hoist ran on a railing system that exited the warehouse near roof level and passed over the road into the other warehouse.

At a signal from a man standing next to the trailer, the container was lowered into place. Other workers moved in and quickly secured it to the trailer. The now empty hoist line rose back up and the entire apparatus returned to the interior of the building.

The loaded big rig rolled forward through the main gate, headed down the road toward the river, and disappeared from sight. The process then repeated itself with truck number two, during which another truck moved onto the road behind it. When truck two left, truck three moved forward, and truck four turned onto the road.

It took two hours before the twentieth, and last, truck was

loaded and sent on its way.

Clearly, the process had been planned by a logistics genius, because as that last big rig passed through the gate, the first truck returned, empty now. It entered the City, turned around in the parking area, and returned to the spot outside the warehouse, at which point the process started all over again.

Seeing no need to watch the dance replay itself, Ricky went back into the jungle and finished his scout.

At 6:20 p.m., with the sun hanging low in the sky, he returned to the jungle near the entrance. As he'd hoped, not all the big rigs had been loaded yet, though it did look as if the process was nearing the end. One truck was being loaded, and three sat waiting in line. The other returned trucks were being parked where they had originally been.

Ricky hurried through the jungle to the river road, far enough down that he would be hidden by the growing darkness from anyone back at the gate, and hunkered down.

A few minutes later, two trucks zoomed by—an empty returning, and one of the final four heading to the river. The next loaded one came by five minutes later. He thought about jumping on the back of it, but knew it would be best to wait for the last one.

The third full one came by six minutes after that, followed by another empty headed back to the City a minute later.

Five minutes passed with nothing.

He cursed. Was he wrong about the fourth truck?

Three minutes later, he was beginning to believe he was. But then, back toward the City, he saw a set of the dim headlights.

He moved as close to the asphalt as he dared and visualized grabbing the back of the container and pulling himself onto it.

A rumble from the other direction caused him to glance around. A pinpoint of light down the road toward the docks. One of the returning empties.

You've got to be kidding me!

He gauged the timing of both vehicles. His intended ride would arrive first, but he would have no more than thirty seconds to get onto the back before the other drove by. Not to mention the risk of the returning driver looking in his rearview mirror and seeing Ricky hanging off the back of his colleague's vehicle. Ricky would just have to deal with that if it became a problem.

When his ride rolled past, he ran out behind it and sprinted toward the back. Instead of closing the gap between them, Ricky was barely keeping pace. The truck's driver apparently hadn't gotten the memo about keeping his speed slow and steady.

Ricky dug deep, moving a little closer, but not close enough.

Come on, come on!

Another half meter and he was pretty sure he could jump for it. But the thought had barely crossed his mind when the headlights of the oncoming big rig shone on the jungle to his left.

He looked at the shipping container just out of reach in front of him, and at the light on the brush.

Cursing under his breath, he broke off pursuit and rushed into the jungle to his right and ducked behind some bushes.

Back at the road there was a crescendo of diesel engines and lights. Then, as quickly as they had approached, the vehicles drove off in opposite directions.

He moved back onto the road and started walking. Seventeen minutes later he heard another vehicle coming from behind him. He rushed into the brush again.

When he caught sight of the vehicle, he smiled.

Ricky, you are one lucky son of a bitch.

Coming down the road was what appeared to be the exact same bus he'd ridden in on. Getting on it was even easier than the first time, but instead of hanging on to the ladder, he proceeded straight to the roof and lay down.

He didn't realize he'd fallen asleep until he heard Liesel in his ear.

He blinked and pushed himself up enough to look around. For a moment he was worried he'd reached the dock, but the bus was still moving.

"Go for Ricky," he said.

"Ricky? This is Liesel. Can you hear me? Are you at the dock?"

He checked the time and did a quick bit of math. "I think I'm a few kilometers away."

"Repeat, please."

"I'm a few kilometers away."

He waited for her to respond.

"Liesel?"

Nothing. Whatever problem she was having with the comm, apparently he was experiencing it, too.

He rolled onto his stomach and looked ahead. At first, he thought there was only darkness beyond the reach of the truck's headlights, but when he caught movement a few hundred meters ahead, he realized he was wrong. The headlights had blinded him to the blue glow coming from the lights of the dock.

He wasn't a few kilometers away. He wasn't even one.

He scrambled down the ladder and dropped and rolled again.

He worked his way through the jungle until he was near the rendezvous point. Instead of going straight there, he took a detour over to the bushes surrounding the dock, wanting to get a picture of the cargo ship if it had arrived. It had. The boat's name was the *Wideroe VII*. Surprisingly, a few of the forced laborers were already there, getting things set up for the loading session. They must have been transported by some of the trucks.

Ricky took pictures of everything, and was about to head off to find Liesel when he heard steps on the pier, very close by.

A teenage boy shuffled into view. Minus the rotting flesh, he looked like an extra from a zombie movie—thin, slack face; emotionless, dead eyes; arms dangling as if he'd temporarily forgotten about them.

Behind him came one of the guards.

"There," the guard said, tapping the end of his rifle against the boy's arm and pointing it at a pile of rope. "The top one."

When the kid didn't seem to hear him, the guard flipped his rifle around and whacked him in the back with the stock. The kid flew forward and fell on the pile.

"The top one," the guard repeated.

A voice in Ricky's head—Ananke's, if he was being honest—said, *Don't you do it.*

He wanted to obey, but couldn't have stopped himself. After checking to make sure no one was looking in this direction, he grabbed the guard from behind, yanked him into the jungle, and slammed him to the ground. He followed this up with a powerful uppercut to the guy's jaw, knocking the guard out.

Ricky had had his fill today of watching the horror happening at the City without doing anything about it. His fury needed its release.

He looked back through the brush. The kid had regained his footing and was slowly lifting the top coil of rope off the stack, apparently not having noticed his escort had disappeared.

Trying to emulate the guard as best as possible, Ricky said in Spanish, "Leave it and come here."

The kid hesitated.

"Do you want to eat the ground again?" Ricky asked.

The coil fell back on the pile, and the kid walked to the edge of the concrete slab.

"In here," Ricky said, staying out of sight. "Now."

A flash of fear in the kid's eyes, making Ricky feel like crap.

After another pause, the kid pushed a branch away and entered the brush. When he reached the unconscious guard, he stopped and stared.

Ricky grabbed him around the chest and put his other hand over the boy's mouth. The kid tensed but didn't struggle, giving Ricky the impression the boy had lost all his willpower.

"I'm not going to hurt you," Ricky whispered in his ear. "I'm going to get you out of here."

Apparently Ricky had been wrong about the willpower thing, because his words had the opposite effect of what he'd expected. The kid started to struggle as if his life depended on it. He was stronger than he looked, but not strong enough to break Ricky's grip.

"Calm down," Ricky said.

The kid was not listening.

Ricky removed his hand from the kid's mouth, wrapped his arm around the boy's neck, and squeezed until the kid passed out.

Okay, smart guy, what now?

He was not going to leave the kid there, and the only way Ricky would leave the guard behind was if he killed him. That would be wasting a good resource. The problem was, Ricky couldn't carry both of them.

He touched his comm. "Ricky for Liesel. Are you here yet?"

"Yes," Liesel said. "Come to the water. Same place as before."

"Um, yeah. Sounds great, but before that, I'm going to need someone to give me a hand."

"A hand with what?"

IT WAS NEARING ten p.m. when one of the villagers stuck his head inside the building and said, "Boat coming. Sounds like your friends."

Ananke stepped outside and listened. The hum of the Zodiac's motor was low but growing stronger.

She headed down to the river, ostensibly to hear what Ricky had learned as soon as possible, but in reality to make sure he was okay. She had approved his mission, and would be responsible if something had happened to him.

She was standing on the dock when the Zodiac emerged from the darkness. Upon seeing three silhouettes on board, the tension in her chest eased. He'd made it out.

As Dylan brought the boat alongside the dock, Liesel tossed a mooring line to Ananke, who tied it to one of the posts.

She started to say, "Welcome back," but noticed the two bodies lying in the Zodiac. "Who the hell are they?"

"My fault," Ricky said. "But before you get mad, let me explain."

244

He did so, but while his story of saving one of the prisoners was admirable, it didn't keep Ananke's anger at bay.

"Now they're going to be searching for them," she said. "They'll probably come here! Dammit, Ricky, do you ever think?"

She expected him to use some lame excuse to justify his actions, but he said, "You're right. I wasn't thinking. All I can say is that I'd just spent the whole day spying on the nightmare those assholes are running in the jungle, and when I saw this guy—" He gestured to the kid wearing captive garb. "I just acted. I shouldn't have. It was stupid. But I couldn't stop myself."

She frowned. The truth was, under the same circumstances, she probably would have done something, too. "What's done is done. If the others do come this way, they'll be looking for anything unusual. The Zodiac will be a magnet. Dylan, Liesel, get it out of the water and stow it in the brush somewhere it'll be hard to see. Ricky, let's get your friends to the village."

Though the kid who'd been held captive was light enough to be carried, the guard was not. They left the boy on the dock while they lugged the guard into San Christophe.

This garnered the stares of several settlement dwellers, one of whom ran off into one of the buildings and returned with Victor.

"Is…is he from the City?" the man asked.

"Apparently," Ananke said.

"What happened to him? What's he doing here?"

"That's a long story."

"You can't bring him here. They'll come looking for him!"

"I'm a little worried about that, too. So I'm open to ideas, if you have someplace we can hide him."

"Hide him? No, no, no. Take him back. He can't be here."

"Well, he's here now and he's not going back. Which reminds me. Can you have two of your people go to the river and get the other one? He's lying on the dock."

"The other one? There are two?"

"The other one was one of the slaves."

That drained some of the anger out of the man. "A-a slave?"

"Victor, please. I'm sure there's something better he can be lying on than a few planks."

Victor called out to one of his fellow residents, then the two of them headed toward the river.

"Good to see Nicholas's tip paid off," Ricky said.

"Not quite in the way we expected, but yeah." She nodded toward the big building the team had co-opted for their headquarters. "That one over there."

ANANKE ENTERED THE building first, going backwards as she held the guard's feet. Ricky followed, holding the other end of the man.

The only one inside was Rosario. She looked up from her computer. "Who's that?"

"Ricky decided to bring a couple friends back."

Rosario rose to her feet. "Is that one of the guards?"

Ananke and Ricky laid the guy on the ground. Ricky checked the cord he'd used to tie up the man's hands and feet while on the Zodiac. Everything was still nice and tight.

"I take it you ran into some problems," Rosario said.

"Not really," Ricky replied. "This was kind of a last-minute thing."

"Did you get all the way to the City?" Ananke asked.

He nodded. "And pretty much all the way around it."

"So?"

He took a breath and pulled the backpack off. "Easier if I show you."

As he was removing the drone, the man Ananke had called Victor and his friend entered the building, carrying the rescued worker.

They started to lay him next to the guard, but Ricky said, "No. If he wakes up, I don't want that son of a bitch to be the first thing he sees."

They carried the boy over to some open space near Rosario and put him down.

"They can't stay here," Victor said. Ricky figured he must be the mayor or whatever the equivalent was here. At least that was the way he was acting. "They'll kill all of us."

"If they come," Ricky said, "it won't be for a few hours. Hell, they might not even realize anyone's missing yet. But even if they did, they were just starting to load a ship, and that's going to take precedence over any search party."

"But they *will* come."

"And we'll deal with that when it becomes necessary," Ananke said, calm and firm.

"But...but—"

"If everything goes right, the City isn't going to be a problem for you ever again."

"But if it goes wrong, we will pay the price."

"I know there's a part of you thinking that maybe it would be better if everything stayed as it has been. But the status quo is over, and whether you help us or not, we *are* going in and things *are* going to change. If I were you, I'd want to be on our side. And I'm telling you right now, we don't let things go wrong."

He considered her words. "You really will make sure nothing goes wrong?"

"It's what we do."

He seemed to come to some decision. "There is a building farther in the jungle. It has a hidden space underneath where we sometimes...put things we don't want found. If they come, you can all hide there."

"See, it's better when we work together." She smiled at him. "You might want to have a couple people watching the river from now on. We don't want to be taken by surprise, do we?"

Eyes widening, he said, "No, we don't," and rushed out of the building.

Rosario inserted the memory disk Ricky had given her into her computer, but Ananke had her wait until Liesel and Dylan arrived before hitting PLAY. Ricky narrated what they were seeing, every so often supplementing the video with clips and pictures he shot on his phone.

"What's your assessment?" Ananke asked Ricky when they were through.

"That place is massive. And I counted fifty-eight guards, but I'm sure there were others sleeping, and more inside the building who I couldn't see. The thing is, their efforts are all focused inward. I got the sense they think their location is all the outward defense they need. Honestly, I don't think it's going to be easy with just the five of us, but we can take them."

"Glad to hear that. But it's not going to be just the five of us."

Ricky frowned. "You mean Victor? He doesn't seem so keen on getting his hands dirty."

The others shared glances, making Ricky feel like he'd missed some kind of inside joke.

"One of you want to tell me what's going on?" he said.

"There's someone you need to meet."

Ananke waved for him to follow her and led him out of the building to one of the smaller structures, closer to the river.

She knocked and said, "It's Ananke."

The door was opened by a young woman.

"Is Ramon here?" Ananke asked.

"Just a moment."

A few seconds later, a middle-aged man came to the door.

"I wanted to introduce you to the fifth member of our group," Ananke said.

The man smiled. "So, you're Ricky."

While Ricky took the man's hand and shook, he was still confused. "Yeah, but who are you?"

"This is Ramon Silva. He's from Mexico. His daughter and son-in-law are being held in the City."

Ricky looked at him, then at Ananke. "One more is better than none, I guess."

"There are fifteen others with me."

"Fifteen?"

"Have you heard from them?" Ananke asked.

Ramon nodded. "They should be heading this way in the next couple of hours."

"You might want to tell them to hold where they are for

now."

"Did something happen?"

"Not yet, but there's a pretty good chance this place is going to get a visit from the City soon. A guard and prisoner went missing. It'll be tough enough hiding those of us here already."

Ramon looked confused. "How would you know they're missing?"

"Because they're in the big house right now."

Ramon blinked. "I'll call my people."

"When you're done, gather your things and join us. Victor says he has a place to stash us when the patrol shows up."

Ramon nodded, then retreated inside.

As Ricky and Ananke walked back to the other building, Ricky said, "When I said we might need more people, I didn't mean a bunch of out-of-shape, middle-agers."

"First off, Ramon's the oldest. The others are mostly in their twenties and, from what he tells me, in good shape. And second, they *all* have someone in the City so they are very motivated."

"That's better, but they're still amateurs. They're liable to get themselves, or one of us, killed."

"I'm not planning on putting them on the front lines."

Ricky played scenarios through his mind until he realized what her plan was and smiled. "You want them to be shepherds."

"Exactly."

TWENTY-THREE

FOR THE NEXT four hours, the team reviewed Ricky's footage, and discussed different ways they could tackle the problem of the City's large security force. Ramon had joined them not long after they started, and while he threw in a suggestion here and there, for the most part he just listened.

Ricky had been involved for the first ninety minutes, but having gone well over twenty-four hours with no more than the nap he had atop the bus finally caught up to him. When Ananke noticed he could barely keep his eyes open, she'd ordered him to get some rest.

"I'm fine," he'd protested, without much enthusiasm.

"To bed. Now."

Dylan had put an arm around Ricky's back. "Let me help you." He guided him to one of the cots at the far end of the room, and the moment Ricky's head touched the pillow, he was out.

The hours of work had paid off. The plan was gelling into shape, and Ananke felt considerably more confident than she had when they first arrived in the area. The City being focused more on keeping people in than out was its Achilles' heel. She was about to ask Rosario to play the last clip again, to double-check the placement of one of the lookout towers, when the door burst open. Fara, one of the San Christophe residents, rushed in.

"Alejandro spotted a patrol boat on the river, heading this way. He says they'll be here in ten minutes."

"Let's move," Ananke ordered.

Most of their gear was back in the duffels, sitting by the door, ready to go. Rosario shoved her computer into her backpack, while Liesel and Dylan cleaned up the food they'd been munching.

Ananke went over to the cots. "Time to get up," she said as she shook Ricky.

He woke with a start. "What? Huh?"

"The patrol's coming. We need to hide."

"Oh, right." He pushed himself off the cot.

"I need you to carry one of the duffel bags." She nodded toward the door, then hurried back to where the others were. "Dylan and Liesel, if you two can carry the guard, I'll get the other guy."

"No problem," Liesel said.

"Rosario, you and Ricky are on the bags."

"Got it," Rosario said.

Ananke slung the freed prisoner over her shoulder. In anticipation of the patrol's arrival, he and the guard had been drugged to ensure they remained unconscious.

She carried him to the door, where Fara was waiting. "Okay, where are we going?"

The girl led them out of the building and onto a narrow path into the jungle. They wound through the brush for several minutes, ducking beneath low branches and swatting at mosquitos, until they reached the old shack Victor had told them about.

Fara held the door open. "Hurry."

Once they were all inside, she grabbed a flashlight off a table along the wall, turned it on, and shut the door. If not for the light, they would have been plunged into near total darkness. The place was used as a storage shed, with shovels and sledgehammers and various other tools leaning against the walls or lying on shelves. What Ananke didn't see was any place they could hide.

"Move back," Fara said to Liesel and Dylan.

As soon as they were out of the way, she grabbed the edge of one of the floor planks and pulled the board up. She repeated this with three more planks, creating a hole more than wide enough for a person to slip through.

She pointed her flashlight through the opening. "See

that?" she said to Ananke.

In the center of the beam was a rock sitting on the dirt. Ananke nodded.

"There's a handle underneath it. Pull it up. There's a cellar. After you close it again, I'll cover it with dirt."

Ananke laid down the guy she was carrying and dropped through the hole. She moved the rock and brushed away dirt. Not only was there a handle underneath, inset in a metal panel, but also a latch that could be padlocked to prevent anyone from getting in, *or* out. She pulled the panel open as far as it would go.

A black hole, from which wafted the smell of damp dirt and stale air. She could just make out the first steps on a set of stairs.

"There's another flashlight at the bottom of the steps," Fara said.

That was nice, but it wouldn't help Ananke on the way down. She pulled out her phone and turned on its light.

At the bottom of the stairs was a single room, no larger than the interior of the smallest house in San Christophe. It would be cramped, but hopefully they wouldn't have to stay here long.

She went back up the stairs, and had Rosario and Ramon lower the unconscious kid to her. She carried him down, and the others followed. When everyone reached the bottom, Ananke went back up and grabbed the hatch.

"Don't forget about us," she said to Fara.

She meant it as a joke, but the girl looked deadly serious when she said, "We won't."

The second Ananke closed the panel, she could hear Fara pushing the dirt back over the top. When the sound stopped, she went back down to join the others.

VICTOR HAD BEEN too nervous to deal with the searchers from the City, so the task fell to Juliana, a woman who had lived in San Christophe for fifteen years.

To avoid any suspicion, she set herself up on an old chair near the river end of the village, where she worked on mending one of the fishing nets.

It wasn't long before she heard the boat approach the settlement's dock and its engine turn off. She acted like it was just another day living along the Barima.

Though she heard the footsteps moving down the path, she waited until the first of the City patrol emerged from the brush before she looked up.

"You," the man in the lead said, pointing at her. "Have two people come through here in the last few hours? One would be wearing clothes like mine." He was dressed in the same camouflage uniform the men on the patrol boats wore.

"There hasn't been anyone new here in weeks," she said.

He eyed her suspiciously. "What about boats on the river? Have you or anyone seen any go by today?"

"Yours is the first I've heard. I don't know about anyone else."

He walked up to her. "You know who we are, don't you?"

"You-you're from the City," she said, letting just the right amount of fear into her voice.

"That's right. So you need to tell us the truth."

"I *am* telling you the truth. If we had a visitor, I'd know it. We don't get many."

He stared at her for a moment, his mouth a slit. Then he looked around. "Take us to the others. We want to talk to them."

"O-okay."

She led him into the settlement, where they went from house to house, each time the patrol receiving the same answer Juliana had given them. When they reached the final door at the end of the village, and were once again told no one had been seen, the guard asked Juliana, "We were told you have a storage hut somewhere."

"About a hundred meters farther back, but no one lives there."

"Show us."

As she turned toward the path, she caught sight of Fara. The glance Fara gave Juliana said the visitors had been safely stowed away.

When they reached the hut, the City guard asked, "When was the last time someone was out here?"

"I don't know for sure but probably earlier today. We keep many of our tools here. Somebody's always needing something."

"Wait here."

The patrol approached the hut. With two men standing off to either side of the entrance, the lead man put his hand on the knob and thrust the door open. Everyone hurried inside, guns drawn. When they found no one, they came back out.

"Are there any more buildings?" the leader asked.

"This is it," Juliana said.

The men hunted around the structure for another few minutes before the leader told her to take them back.

In the village, they insisted on looking through every building, but again found nothing.

"If *anyone* comes through here, you will inform us," the leader said.

"For how long?"

"Until we tell you to stop. You will tell everyone this."

"Okay."

With that, the patrol took the path back to the dock, and a few minutes later, the boat motored back into the current. Juliana ventured down the path to make sure they hadn't left anyone behind, but she counted all five patrol members on the receding boat. She waited until they disappeared, then returned to the settlement.

"No problems?" Victor asked her. He'd been in the building he shared with his wife, acting sick in bed. He had only ventured outside when the boat's engine was heard in the village.

"None."

"And they won't be back?"

"I don't think so. Not unless we call them."

He didn't look convinced, but she didn't care. She spotted Fara across the way and headed over to her before he could ask anything else.

ABOUT TWENTY MINUTES after they'd entombed themselves, Ananke and the others had heard faint noises from above. Soon, however, the commotion was gone. After that, the only sounds were whispers of the team as they honed their plan. Finally, the door opened again.

"You can come out now," Fara called down. "They're gone."

Ananke went up first, alone, in case it was a trap and the settlement dwellers had sold them out. But Fara was alone.

The decision had been made to leave the guard in the cellar. The kid Ricky had freed was hoisted out and taken back to the main building with Dylan, Ramon, Rosario, and Ricky.

Ananke and Liesel also remained in the cellar, where they propped the guard up on a chair and tied him to it with some rope they found in the room. Ananke administered a shot of wake-up juice into the guy's vein and took a step back.

She counted off eight seconds before the guard's eyes shot open, and he jerked in his chair as if waking from a dream about falling. He looked around, disoriented, but all he could see was the flashlight Liesel had trained on his eyes.

He tried to raise his arms to block the beam and realized they were tied to the arms of the chair.

"What the hell?" He yanked his arms against the restraints, but they weren't going anywhere.

He squinted against the light.

"Who's there? What the fuck is going on? Why am I tied up?"

Ananke took a step forward, partially blocking the light.

"Who are you?" he snapped.

She stepped over to him, placed the sound suppressor attached to her pistol against his right index finger, and pulled the trigger.

His scream filled the confined space.

"Let's get one thing straight right from the beginning," she said. "You don't ask anything. Nod if you understand."

Whimpering and panting, he nodded.

"What's your name?"

"Hugo…Reyes."

"I'm going to ask you a few questions, Hugo. Some of them I already know the answers to, some I don't. If you give me the wrong answer to something I know, I'm going to pull the trigger again. Got it?"

He nodded again. "My finger. It's bleeding."

"Let no one say your observation skills have been compromised."

"I need to tie it off! I need to stop the bleeding!"

"If you give me some useful answers, maybe I'll consider it. Here's my first question—how far is the City from the river?"

"I...don't know what you're-you're talking about."

"Oh, come on, Hugo. Is it worth losing another finger on the very first question?"

"T-t-twenty kilometers."

"Very good. How many workers do you have imprisoned there?"

"I don't know."

Ananke pressed the gun against the index finger of his left hand.

"I don't know!"

"Make a guess."

"Twelve hundred?"

She pressed the gun down harder. "Is that your final answer?"

"Between twelve hundred and fifteen hundred. That's as close as I can get. I swear to God."

She pressed down for a moment longer before easing up. "And how many security guards?"

Indecision fluttered in his eyes.

"Don't lie to me," she said.

"Around forty."

Ricky had counted more than that. "You're about to lose another finger."

"On day shift. Forty on day shift. Fifteen on night."

"Wrong answer." She pulled the trigger again.

Hugo howled.

Ananke set the gun down and grabbed the wads of cloth

she'd prepared ahead of time. She cleaned the man's wounds and bandaged the injuries with narrower strips of cloth, cinching them tight.

She picked up the gun again and placed it against the next available finger. "How many security personnel?"

The guard was hyperventilating and seemed not to have heard her.

"Pay attention, Hugo, or I'll take number three."

Wincing, he tried to focus.

"How many?"

"I think sixty...five on day. Twenty-five on night."

She was pretty sure he wasn't lying this time, but he also wasn't telling the complete truth. "What about at the pier? How many are there?"

His head sagged. "Twelve permanent. Sometimes a few extra come from the City when they are loading."

"And the patrol boats?"

"I don't deal with the boats, so I have no idea how many. Honest! Please don't shoot again."

She believed him.

Without the boats, his numbers added up to one hundred and one security staff. But she knew that wasn't the whole picture.

"How many who are not security?"

"What?"

"The people running the place, not the ones guarding it. How many?"

"I'm not sure. An inspector in every shop. A few more in administration."

"Which totals what?"

"Another thirty or forty, I guess. I never thought about it."

"You're doing great, Hugo. Well, you *have* lost two fingers, but for the most part, great. I just have a few more questions."

"Please, I need a doctor."

"I can't disagree with you there. So, how often do ships pick up cargo? Every night?"

"Not...every night. Many."

257

"Do you know the schedule?"

He winced as a wave of pain rushed through him. "Please. My fingers."

Ananke twisted the suppressor against his knuckle. "The schedule, Hugo."

"I...I...only know the next few...days."

"That's perfect. I'm only interested in the next few days."

THE OTHER MEMBERS of Ramon's group arrived via a trail through the jungle, three hours later. They had been staying at an abandoned settlement about ten kilometers downriver, having been directed there by the more sympathetic residents of San Christophe.

It would have been faster to come by boat, but they wanted to avoid being spotted by the City's frequent patrols, especially now that there was additional security personnel searching for the missing men.

As promised, most of the fifteen were in their twenties, brothers and sisters and close friends of the missing. The three not in that age group were a pair in their late thirties and a teenage boy.

"Alfonso Ortega," Ramon told Ananke when she asked about the boy. "He has two sisters at the City. The oldest, Henrietta, is our person on the inside."

He had earlier explained how they had set about getting Henrietta kidnapped so they could track her by a makeshift bug inserted under her skin. It was because of her that Ramon and the others had come to the Barima over a week ago. They had been trying ever since to figure out a way into the City.

Part of that effort had included scouting missions through the jungle to the edge of the City. The information they'd gathered didn't add much to what Ananke and the team already knew, but it did jibe with what Ricky had found and what Hugo the guard had told them.

Ananke's team, Ramon and his people, and a few people from San Christophe talked late into the evening. Ananke, with assistance from Rosario and Ricky, laid out the plan, emphasizing the roles she wanted the nonprofessionals to play and avoiding the details they didn't need to know.

There were a few grumbles from those expressing a desire to be more involved in the meat of the operation, but Ananke knew that was only their anger and concern talking.

"I doubt any of you have come this far only to get yourself killed before you can be reunited with your loved ones. My friends and I are trained for this. If you come with us, you'll only get in our way. And *that* could be the difference between success and catastrophe."

This quelled any further objections.

"I suggest everyone get some sleep. Tomorrow we'll go over everything again as many times as necessary until everyone knows exactly what he or she is doing. And tomorrow night, we do this. Sound good?"

She was answered by nods and words of assent, as excitement rippled through the room. This was what they had come for, what some of them had been dreaming about for more than a year. Ananke couldn't imagine the despair that must have been ruling their lives.

The group trickled out, to their assigned spots in the other buildings as guests of the San Christophians. If another City patrol showed up, they'd been instructed to go at least a kilometer back down the trail toward the abandoned settlement and hide there until they were given the all-clear.

"I'll take first watch," Ananke said.

"I will take second," Liesel said.

Dylan raised a hand. "Put me down for third."

"Hey, I can take a watch," Ricky said.

"You still need to catch up on your sleep. You're going to be our guide tomorrow night, and we need you bright-eyed and clearheaded."

She left them to get their rest and headed to the dock to keep an eye on the river.

After finding a comfortable spot, she called the Administrator on her sat phone, and brought him up to speed on Ricky's scout and the discovery of Ramon and his people.

"We're planning to go in tomorrow night," she said. "You should know it could get a little messy."

"That's the kind of thing we brought you and the others together to handle."

"I mean messier than anything we've done for you so far."

"Understood. We trust you will do what is necessary."

"There is a way to make it a little less so, but that will depend on you."

"What do you mean?"

She explained.

"Let me see if I can make the logistics work on that. The *Karos Evonus* is halfway through the Panama Canal as we speak, and I've been told it should be in the Caribbean in about four hours. So, it is definitely a possibility."

"That would be great. Oh, one more thing."

"Yes?"

"I have a feeling we might need the ship, too."

TWENTY-FOUR

GLORIA CURSED TO herself. She'd screwed up another one of the pieces she'd been assigned that day. That made seven so far. She'd never messed up more than a couple in one sitting. But given the reason she was having such a terrible time concentrating, it was a wonder she hadn't screwed up more.

Two nights ago, as she had been returning to her dormitory from the factory, she had glanced at one of the groups passing by in a neighboring caged walkway. Like those in her group, most of the workers were shuffling along, gazes on the ground, zombies waiting for the moment they could fall on their mattresses and pass out.

As she was about to look away, a woman in the other corridor caught her eye. Instead of staring at the dirt, the woman was looking around, allowing Gloria to see her profile.

It can't be.

But the more she stared, the more she couldn't help thinking the woman was her sister. But how could Henrietta be here?

She wanted to call out, but knew the guards above the cages would close in to see what was going on. If it was Henrietta, Gloria didn't want anyone to find out. She imagined the guards separating them so that she never saw her sister again. And if it wasn't Henrietta, Gloria would bring problems on herself for nothing.

She had watched the woman until she disappeared, still unsure if it was her sister or not. She had clung to the possibility, though, and the next night searched the other cages for the woman again. But she hadn't seen her.

And now it was nearing quitting time once more,

presenting her with another opportunity to catch sight of the woman. Only Gloria would have to stay late if she couldn't sew another five perfect pieces by the time the bell rang.

She willed herself to concentrate and banged out three more. She grabbed the two halves that would make up the fourth and ran them quickly through the machine, dumping the finished item into the bin. As she was pulling up the parts for the fifth, the bell started ringing.

The rule was, when the bell sounded, the machines were to be turned off, but Gloria shoved the pieces under the needle and finished a split second after the bell stopped. As she pulled the finished garment out and cut it free, she noticed a couple of the stitches weaved slightly from the prescribed path.

Another mistake that should go on the reject pile, but she put it in her completed bin, burying it under a few other pieces.

She looked around to see if the inspector had noticed her, then breathed a sigh of relief when she realized no one was paying attention to her.

Tonight, her row was the last to be checked. When the inspector finally reached her bin, Gloria kept her face forward like she was supposed to and prayed he would approve her work.

He rifled through the pieces, stopping a couple of times to examine different samples. When he finished, he wrote something on his clipboard and said, "You're dismissed."

Relief flooded through her as she rose from her chair and headed toward the door. Since she was one of the last to leave, she was worried she would miss the other groups, but upon stepping outside she saw the other corridor filled with workers.

She searched for the one who looked like Henrietta. But like the night before, she didn't see her.

"Gloria."

The whispered voice had come from behind her.

Gloria looked back.

It was the woman. It was *Henrietta*.

Her sister was walking next to the fence separating the two pathways. Gloria dropped back and matched Henrietta's pace.

Keeping her head down and her lips as unmoving as

possible, she whispered, "What are you doing here?"

"Are you okay?" Henrietta asked. "Have they hurt you?"

"I'm as well as can be, I guess. You didn't answer my question."

"I've come to get you out."

"What? How?"

But they were approaching a spot under one of the guards, so Henrietta didn't answer. When they passed him, she said, "Be ready."

"For what?"

Again, her sister didn't reply. Gloria glanced over and realized the other corridor had taken a ninety-degree turn away from Gloria's. She tried to spot Henrietta, but she was gone.

Be ready.

She had no idea what she was supposed to be ready for, but for the first time since she'd arrived here, she felt a small flicker of hope.

TWENTY-FIVE

BY MIDAFTERNOON, RAMON'S people had been drilled with their responsibilities until each could explain, without hesitation, what he or she was supposed to do. Liesel, who had handled most of the instruction, expressed cautious optimism to Ananke that most of them wouldn't screw up too badly.

The rest of the team split time between divvying up the gear and watching the river in case the City security forces returned. The three different patrol boats passed San Christophe a total of eleven times, but never once did they slow. Normal patrols, Ananke surmised. As for the smaller boat being used by the search party, it had not made a reappearance. It was probably still downriver, looking for the missing men.

That morning, the Administrator had confirmed he could fulfill Ananke's request, and just after four p.m., he notified her it would be arriving within the next ten minutes.

She and the others moved out into the clearest area in San Christophe and turned their gazes to the sky.

"There is it," Rosario said, pointing to the west.

A blotch of gray on an otherwise clear day. A long-range drone, similar to the type used by the military, though not quite as large. It flew several hundred meters above the trees. As it passed over the settlement, its cargo detached and deployed a parachute that matched the color of the sky. This made it hard to follow the package's descent, but the person remotely piloting the drone was clearly skilled, because as the craft began its return trip to wherever it had come from, the package landed a mere ten meters from where Ananke and the others stood.

The box was designed to absorb the impact of the low-level drop, so the vials of Beta-Somnol, the one hundred twenty-five empty syringes, and two hundred empty darts arrived undamaged. The packages of zip ties in the box would have survived whether the impact had been soft or not.

The team spent the next hour preloading the syringes and darts.

It wasn't because Ananke had a distaste for killing that had caused her to ask for the extra supplies. Up until about a month ago, she had been a professional assassin. If anyone deserved to die, then it was the people who ran and protected the City. But this mission was all about stealth, and, for that purpose, the drug would be more effective than a bullet.

By 7:20 p.m., Ananke, Dylan, Ricky, and Liesel were at the river, hidden in the brush near where the Zodiac was stashed, watching the water.

According to Hugo, only one cargo ship was due tonight. It was expected at the dock by eight p.m. Which meant it would be passing San Christophe soon.

Sure enough, seven minutes after they'd settled in, Liesel whispered, "I hear something."

Ananke heard it, too. The deep rumble of large engines, accompanied by the soft swoosh of water being displaced. It was another minute before the shadow of a cargo ship sailed into view. At the pace the ship was moving, it should arrive at the City's dock right on time.

Trailing the ship was the smaller silhouette of the patrol boat Ricky had dubbed Meeny. Eeny was still downriver somewhere, while Miny was in the opposite direction, back toward the dock. Moe was what they were calling the search party's craft.

As soon as both boats passed out of sight, Ananke said, "Let's do this."

They hoisted the Zodiac back into the water, climbed aboard, and rowed into the current, letting the water help them move downriver.

In a mission filled with potential obstacles, the first to resolve had been how to get twenty-five people—Ananke and her team, Ramon's group, and the settlement residents who had

265

volunteered to help—from San Christophe to the area near the City's dock without being caught by one of the patrols.

There was only one guaranteed solution, which was why Ananke and most of her team were on the Rio Barima.

Twenty minutes went by with only the empty water surrounding them. Then Ananke heard another engine, not as big as the cargo ship's but still powerful.

Dylan moved them toward the river's southern edge, getting them as close to the overhanging jungle as possible. Soon Eeny appeared out of the night, about a hundred and fifty meters away. There were lights on in the cabin and a few more on the deck. The spotlight near the bow, however, was off.

Using her night vision binoculars, Ananke counted three people on the deck, and at least two more in the cabin where the boat's controls would be. Though Hugo hadn't known how many were on the boats, the residents of San Christophe had told Ananke they'd never seen more than seven on a patrol boat.

"How do you want to handle this one?" Ricky asked.

They had come up with several plans, depending on the situation.

This one seemed pretty straightforward, so Ananke said, "Nice and quiet," using the name they'd given to one of the options. She glanced over at Dylan. "Wait until they're about seventy-five meters away to make your move. Comms on, everyone."

She pulled out her pistol, clicked her suppressor into place, and made sure a bullet was in the chamber. She then checked her dart gun.

The patrol boat continued to motor against the current, in no real hurry. She could see now that the three people outside were talking to one another. One laughed, the sound drifting over the water.

"Here we go," Dylan whispered.

Once more using the current as their engine, Dylan aimed the Zodiac toward the middle of the river, on a collision course with the patrol boat. The others all ducked to minimize their profile. Ananke found a position from which she could watch the men on deck. They remained relaxed and unaware of the smaller boat approaching them.

Right before the Zodiac reached Eeny, Dylan adjusted their path so that they ran alongside the vessel, though going in the opposite direction.

Right on cue, Ricky stood up, with Ananke and Liesel bracing him from below, and tried to hook the pre-looped end of a mooring rope around anything he could find. His first two attempts were busts, but he managed on his third try to get the loop around a cleat.

He dropped back down to a crouch before the rope went taut. When it did, the Zodiac jerked violently as it began moving in the opposite direction. The bigger problem was its pontoon side sliding across the water toward the patrol boat. But they'd prepared for this. Everyone but Dylan reached over the pontoon and put their hands on the side of the City's vessel, using their arms as shock absorbers to stop the two boats from smacking together. Once the momentum had dissipated, they eased up and let the Zodiac settle gently against the patrol boat.

Ananke went up and over the side first, followed by Ricky then Liesel. Dylan would stay on the Zodiac in case they had to make a hasty getaway.

The three split up, Ricky and Liesel heading toward the foredeck, and Ananke to a door to the ship's interior. She placed an ear against the surface, and when she heard nothing, eased the door open.

A large room, with a table and built-in benches. A dining area by the looks of it, probably also a place to hang out. No one was using it at the moment.

At the front end of the room was a door that could lead to only one place.

A click came over the comm, indicating Ricky and Liesel were in position. Ananke clicked twice, telling them she wasn't ready yet.

She crossed the dining area to the door and listened again. No voices, but there was the sound of music. She opened the door far enough to confirm she had found the bridge, and clicked her mic once.

A single click answered.

She responded with the three clicks that would set things in motion, and quietly opened the door all the way. The two men present were sitting on cushioned chairs in front of the bow-side window, looking out at the river. Both were wearing the same uniforms she'd seen on the guards at the City's dock, and in the drone images Ricky had brought back.

She fired her dart gun twice, each shot hitting its mark. The two men slumped onto the floor.

She walked up to the window and looked out at the deck. The three men who'd been standing there had been similarly dealt with.

Ananke backed down on the throttle so that the boat was basically treading water against the current, and returned to the common room. There, she located the stairs down into the guts of the ship. She found bunks and a storage room and the small engine room, but no other people.

"We're clear," she said into the comm. "Get the Zodiac on board."

THEY EACH DONNED one of the unconscious men's uniforms, then Dylan took charge of the bridge while Ananke, Liesel, and Ricky took up positions on the foredeck.

Dylan swung the vessel around and headed toward the delta. As they plowed through the water, everyone kept an eye out for Moe, the search party's boat.

"I see something ahead," Liesel said after they'd been going for nearly half an hour. "Near the shore off to port."

Ananke raised her binoculars and spotted a boat moving in the same direction they were, almost two hundred meters ahead. She smiled. Five men were on board, all in City security uniforms.

After they closed the gap to almost one hundred meters, one of the men on Moe pointed a flashlight at the patrol boat and flashed it twice.

"Return the signal," Ananke said.

Since Liesel was closest to the spotlight, she fired it up, flashed it twice, then left the beam shining at the other boat.

One of the men on Moe shouted across the water. "Hey, turn that off!"

Ananke said. "Dylan, take us in."

"Copy."

He steered their boat to the other vessel and reduced the speed so they could ease up alongside.

When they were approximately seven meters away, Ananke said to Liesel, "You can douse the light."

The spotlight winked out, and the men on the other boat lowered their arms and hands from in front of their eyes. As Ananke had anticipated, from the way they were blinking, they were temporarily blind.

"Your turn, Ricky," she whispered.

Ricky stepped up to the edge of the boat and looked down at the other vessel. "You can stop looking. They found the missing men."

The guy in the middle said, "We haven't heard anything."

"Radio silence. Management's worried someone might have helped them escape and could be listening in. They're conducting a sweep, trying to see if they can find him."

"Where?"

"About five kilometers from the dock. We've been ordered to bring you back so you can help. Come aboard and we'll tow your boat."

One of the men tossed Ricky a line, which he tied to a cleat. He then dropped a rope ladder over the side.

The first of the men handed Ricky his rifle and climbed onto the patrol boat. As he stepped onto the deck, he was greeted by Ananke and Liesel pointing their pistols at him. Ananke held a finger to her mouth and motioned for him to move to the side and sit. Looking confused and scared, he complied.

One by one his colleagues followed in a similar manner.

The last man to board was the one who had been sitting in the middle. Unlike the others, he possessed an additional firearm, a pistol in a holster at his waist. The moment he realized something wasn't right, his hand moved toward it.

"I wouldn't do that," Ananke said.

He pretended to comply, then quickly moved sideways and pulled his gun out.

Ananke's and Liesel's bullets hit him in the chest within a few centimeters of each other, dropping him to the deck.

Ananke looked at the four sitting nearby. "Any of you want to try something?"

There were no takers.

THEY RETURNED TO San Christophe, where they unloaded the prisoners and took them to the storage hut in the jungle. All the stuff that had been inside the cellar had been cleared out by Ramon's people, so it was now only a concrete box. They put the men inside and locked the latch.

The team—less Rosario, who was in charge of making sure Ramon's people would be ready to go when the time came—returned to the patrol boat.

Leaving Moe behind, they headed out again, this time going upriver.

Fifteen minutes later, they caught sight of one of the two remaining patrol boats as it headed toward the delta.

The radio crackled in the control room. "This is Watch Three, is that you, Watch Two?"

Ananke nodded at Dylan.

He picked up the mic. "This is Watch Two. Confirming."

"Who is this speaking?"

"Largos," Dylan said, using the name of the team's dead, would-be contact at San Christophe.

"Where is Mendoza?"

Dylan took a moment to think before saying, "Below deck. Would you like me to get him?"

"We're coming alongside."

"Crap," Dylan said under his breath. He pushed the talk button. "Okay. Reducing speed." He put the mic down and looked at Ananke. "He knows something is up."

"You think?" Ananke turned to the others. "Ricky, you're going to have to act as decoy. Liesel man the big gun." She had a feeling this was one of those situations they couldn't resolve with their darts. She glanced at Dylan. "If I tell you to get us out of here, punch it."

"Yes, ma'am."

While Liesel and Ricky took up their positions on the foredeck, Ananke grabbed one of the rifles and an extra clip they'd confiscated earlier, and climbed on top of the central cabin, where the antenna was located. She stretched out across the roof and snuggled the butt of the rifle against her shoulder.

Four men stood on deck of the other ship as it approached, their rifles ready. A fifth man was behind them, and a sixth was at their big gun. If the no-more-than-seven rule held, the only other man would be piloting the boat.

Ricky raised a hand as the two vessels neared each other. Two of the riflemen swung tires, which were tied to the hull, over the side to act as bumpers. Their pilot maneuvered the boat closer until it was a meter and a half off the port side.

"Where's Captain Mendoza?" the man standing behind the riflemen asked, his voice matching the one that had come over the radio.

"He's down below," Ricky said and touched his stomach. "Something he ate."

"Who are you? I don't recognize you."

"Me? Oh, um, Banderas. I'm new."

"Put your hands up!"

The men aimed their rifles at Ricky.

"What? Why?"

"Liesel, you've got the guys at the railing," Ananke said.

"Copy."

"Put your hands up or you *will* be shot!" the man on the other boat said.

When Ricky began to raise his hands, Ananke said, "Now."

As Liesel opened up on the riflemen, Ananke put a bullet into the man at the big gun and adjusted her aim to the guy who'd been doing the talking. She had no need to pull her trigger, though. Some of Liesel's shots had caught him, too.

The engine on the other boat revved up.

Before it could pull too far away, Ricky jumped the gap and grabbed the railing on the other vessel. He scrambled onto the deck and raced to the bridge. For a few seconds, the boat continued to veer off, then the engine wound back down.

"Boat secured," Ricky said over the comm.

THE FINAL BOAT was the easiest of all. Correctly assuming its call sign was Watch One, Dylan had called it, saying Watch Two was experiencing engine trouble, and asked for assistance.

The team hadn't needed to fire a single dart or bullet.

They took their six new prisoners and all three boats back to San Christophe.

The river, as of 10:20 p.m., was free of City patrols. The team had captured or killed twenty-four City security personnel. While eighteen were permanent patrol-boat personnel and not part of Hugo's estimate, six—Hugo and the search party—were part of the land-based security, leaving approximately ninety-four to deal with.

TWENTY-SIX

THEY USED THE two patrol boats that hadn't been shot up to transport everyone to the same spot where Ananke and the team had gone ashore their first night on the river. The boats could get close to the water's edge, but there was still enough of a gap that they had to use the Zodiac to get everyone on land.

Six people—three from San Christophe and three of Ramon's people—had been preselected to stay with the boats, three on each, and had been outfitted in security uniforms before they left San Christophe. They took the boats back into the main channel and went upriver, to positions from where they could watch the dock and report back to Ananke.

As for those who had been put on shore, Dylan and Rosario were tasked with escorting the bulk of the group to a staging point fifty meters from the dock, while Ananke, Ricky, and Liesel went off to deal with the next phase of the operation.

The route Ananke's group took went directly to the brush surrounding the dock, where they hid.

"I count seven guards and twenty-three prisoners," Ananke said.

"I count the same," Liesel said.

"Agreed," Ricky said.

There were also seven containers on the dock, in line to be loaded.

"Let's see if there are any more containers waiting to be brought out," Ananke said.

They moved through the jungle until they reached the road.

"I've got four more guards," Ananke said. The men were standing in the roadway, about three meters away from the dock, facing it. Probably a safeguard in case any of their prisoners tried to sneak off in that direction. Using her binoculars, she looked through the gap on the other side of the road, into the area where containers were stored. "I see another ten containers in there, but there's no one around trying to move them out."

"Can I see?" Ricky said.

She handed him the glasses.

"Those are the same containers that were there last time we were here," he said. "Maybe they're empties or waiting for a different ship."

"Are you sure?"

"Hold on." He pulled out his phone and sifted through photos. He stopped on one and showed it to her. "These look the same to you?"

Ananke looked at the photo, then through the binoculars again. The containers were too far away to make out the numbers on them, but several had big logos on their sides. The logo pattern matched exactly the pattern on the containers in the photo.

"Yeah. They're the same."

That meant only seven containers to go.

Make that six, as one was now being swung over the boat.

Ananke and the others moved parallel to the road until they were about fifteen meters past the guards stationed there, then quietly out to the middle of the asphalt. After Ananke indicated which guard was each of their responsibility, they crept forward and raised their dart guns. With her free hand, Ananke counted backward from three. When her last finger went down, three darts flew down the road, with a fourth from Ananke's gun following a second later once she'd adjusted her aim for the final guard.

The men dropped without a word.

After carrying the guards into the jungle and zip-tying them, Ananke, Liesel, and Ricky headed across the road into the storage area.

No guards here, but there was someone in the area who needed to be taken care of.

Crouching, they crossed the darkened clearing to the prisoner bus.

Ananke let Ricky handle this one, but was right behind him as backup. Liesel stayed by the front of the bus in case anyone showed up.

The door was closed, and through the window they could see the driver's seat was empty. Ananke raised a questioning eyebrow and Ricky shrugged.

He carefully pushed the door. It moved easily. He ascended into the bus and peered down the aisle, then gave Ananke a thumbs-up and pointed farther inside. As he sneaked down the aisle, Ananke stepped on board.

The driver was lying across two seats, his feet sticking into the aisle. Ananke could hear his deep, rhythmic breathing.

Ricky put away his dart gun and pulled out one of the syringes he'd been allocated. The driver woke up as the needle pierced his arm, but the drug quickly pulled him back under.

Ricky and Ananke carried the driver off the bus and laid him near the shipping containers, where he'd be out of sight. He, too, received the zip-tie treatment.

With Liesel joining them, they moved over to the footpath cutting through the jungle that connected the storage area with the dock. They stopped at the other end.

A watchtower rose above the path's exit. It was an enclosed space about two meters square, sitting on four telephone pole-like legs. Attached to one of the back legs was a ladder.

After motioning for the other two to keep an eye out, Ananke climbed the pole until she was just below the floor of the crow's nest. Three of the four sides had a half wall on the bottom and nothing on top, but the back side was completely open.

Ananke edged up to peek over the floor. One guy inside, sitting near the front, watching the dock. From his body language, he looked bored. She raised the dart gun over the lip and shot him in the base of his neck.

He let out a little cry before he slumped forward. Though it wasn't loud enough to worry her, she was concerned he might tumble over the half wall and fall to the dock. But his shoulder caught on the top, keeping him from the long drop. She zip-tied him to the chair, and propped his head up as best she could, so that anyone looking up would think he was still working.

A palm-sized metal box sat on the small counter that ran along the sides of the space. It had a button on top and a wire running out the back. An alarm button. Working fast, she opened it with her multi-tool and disabled it.

When she got back to the ground, she and the others split up, each finding a spot from where they could cover a specific section of the dock. Ananke had two guards and seven prisoners in her zone. She visualized what she needed to do as she waited for the time to come.

Finally, the last shipping container was lowered into the cargo ship, and the vessel pulled away from the dock.

Ananke clicked her mic once. Single clicks from Liesel and Ricky came back right away. Ananke clicked three times.

A second later, Darts flew across the docks, three in the initial volley, three in the second, each striking one of the guards.

Most of the prisoners continued whatever task they'd been assigned, not even registering what was going on around them. A few, though, were looking around, confused.

"I'm clean," Ananke said.

"Me, too," Liesel chimed in.

When Ricky came on, he was breathing hard. "I've got a jackass who made a run into the jungle but I'm on him. My other two are down."

Ananke cautiously rose to take a better look around. All the guards save Ricky's runaway lay unmoving on the dock.

She looked over at Liesel and said over the comm, "Check to make sure none of them are going to jump up and surprise us."

"Copy."

While Liesel checked the guards, Ananke noticed more of the prisoners had stopped working and were openly staring at the unconscious guards. Some were looking around, clearly fearing they would be next.

"Ananke for Rosario."

"Go for Rosario."

"It's time."

"Copy. On our way."

Liesel came on a moment later. "We're all good."

"Then I'm going to see if I can find that building Ricky thinks is here," Ananke said.

"Copy," Liesel said.

As Ananke headed to a path leading away from the east side of the dock, Rosario and the first few members of Ramon's people arrived and approached the prisoners.

Ricky's instincts were dead-on. There was indeed a building about thirty meters beyond the dock—a two-story, tin-roofed, cinder-block structure that looked like it had been thrown together in a hurry. Power lines ran up the side from a pair of diesel generators sitting next to the south wall. At the moment, they seemed to be powering only a pair of lights shining through windows on the ground floor. The second floor, at least from the front of the building, was completely dark.

Ananke moved up to the door and tried the knob. Locked. Not surprising. Being the only building in the area, weapons would likely be stored inside, and the last thing the City assholes would want was for one of their slaves to sneak in and get his hands on a rifle.

She pulled out her lockpicks and disengaged the lock. Beyond the door was a deserted hall, with doors off each side, and a stairway to the second floor at the other end. One of the lights shone through one of the doors, into a small, unoccupied mess hall, and the other into an equally empty bathroom. After searching the rest of the rooms on the ground floor and finding no one, she headed upstairs. Most of the beds were empty, but three were not. The first two were in a room near the middle of the building, and the last in one at the far end. She figured these were the men assigned to keep watch on the dock during the daytime.

Using her syringes, Ananke gave a dose to each man, then zip-tied them and left them where they lay.

She touched her mic. "Dorm is clear. Three sleeping. Ricky, how's it going?"

RICKY WAS ANNOYED at himself for missing the target. It wasn't *really* his fault. His dart would have hit home if the target hadn't jerked to the left upon seeing one of his buddies go down. Ricky had to give the guy credit. The jerking might have been reflexive, but the immediate sprint into the jungle showed some pretty quick thinking.

Ricky fired again but it was another miss.

Dammit!

"I'm clean," Ananke said over the comm.

Ricky jumped up and raced across the dock. "I've got a jackass who made a run into the jungle but I'm on him. My other two are down."

He weaved around the prisoners and rushed into the jungle. Ahead, he could just make out the silhouette of the guard barreling through the brush. He raised his gun but lowered it again when his target took a hard right, behind a wall of trees and bushes.

Though Ricky couldn't see the guard, he could still hear him, and veered his course toward the sounds. He followed the man deeper and deeper into the jungle, until suddenly he couldn't hear him anymore.

As Ricky skidded to a stop, a bullet slammed into a tree an arm's length away. He dropped to the ground and crawled through the brush, working his way in an arc that he hoped would put him behind where the guard had apparently decided to make his stand. Every few meters he would stop and listen. At first, there was only the ever-present soundtrack of the jungle, but as he drew nearer to where the gunshot originated, he could hear the man's choppy breathing.

Ricky chose his steps carefully as he circled behind the guard.

Ananke's voice came over the comm. "Dorm is clear. Two sleeping. Ricky, how's it going?"

He clicked his mic twice, letting her know he was not in a position to talk.

"Do you need backup?"

Two clicks, this time telling her no.

"Copy."

He inched closer and closer, stopping when he could see the guard three meters ahead.

Ricky raised his dart gun and shot the guard in the back. The impact not only knocked the guard onto his rifle, but also caused his finger to pull the trigger, which sent a bullet into the ground half a meter away.

Ricky walked over and toed the man's leg.

He turned on his mic. "I'm clear."

BY THE TIME Ananke returned to the dock, both patrol boats had moved alongside it, and a few of Ramon's people were helping tie them in place. The rest of Ramon's group were rounding up the workers, half of whom looked confused, and the other half suspicious of all these new people.

Once the boats were secured, the workers were guided toward them. This sent a ripple of fear through the group.

"Where are we going?" someone said in Spanish.

"Where are you taking us?"

"What's going on?"

Ananke was about to say something, but Ramon jumped up on one of the mooring posts at the edge of the dock.

"Please, everyone," he said in Spanish.

The rumbling quieted.

"If you can understand me, raise your hand."

One by one, all the workers raised a hand.

"Good," Ramon said. "Everything is going to be all right. We've come to take you home. But you have to get on the boats first."

Ananke saw the realization dawn on many of the faces, but not everyone was ready to embrace the possibility yet.

"It's just another trick," one man said. "You're going to kill us, aren't you?"

"No, we're not," Ramon said. "We're here to save you. We're going to bring everyone out."

"It's a test," another man said, looking at the others. "If

279

we get on the boat, we won't see anyone ever again."

Ananke's chest tightened. Being beaten down so badly that they saw evil in everything spoke to how hellish this whole situation was.

But time was being wasted. "Look around you," she called out. Everyone turned to her. "You see the guards who have been watching you? Do you think they're pretending?" She walked over to one of the bodies and pushed it with her foot. "If this was a test, why would we do this to our own people?"

Silence.

"Now, please, get on the boats. The more time it takes, the less time we'll have to free the rest of the prisoners."

There was a beat during which no one moved, then a few people started walking toward the boats, and soon everyone, even the doubters, joined them.

When everyone was on board, the boats pulled away and began the journey to San Christophe, where they would stay until the City was taken down.

Ananke turned away from the river, but before she could give her next order, Ricky appeared out of the jungle, carrying a guard over his shoulder.

"Glad you could join us," she said over the comm.

"This guy needs to go on a diet."

Ricky laid the guy on the ground next to one of the other guards.

"Okay, everyone who is going to the City, follow me. The rest of you, tie the guards up and move them over to the container storage area. At least two of you stay with them and keep an eye out for trouble. Hopefully the next time we see you, there will be a whole lot more of us."

TWENTY-SEVEN

THE TEAM AND five people from Ramon's group boarded the bus and headed toward the City, Dylan driving.

When they spotted the lights of the checkpoint at the thirteen-kilometer mark, he slowed to a crawl and opened the door, allowing Ricky and Liesel to exit.

They moved around the back of the vehicle and climbed onto the same ladder Ricky had clung to the night of his scout. Ricky knocked twice on the bus, and Dylan picked up speed again.

Tonight's ride on the back was short compared to Ricky's previous journey. When the bus slowed again, he and Liesel dropped onto the road and slipped into the jungle. Moving quickly through the brush, they made it behind the guard hut moments before the bus arrived.

Like before, the hydraulic posts were up, and the two guards were standing outside.

Dylan had pulled his security hat down so that the bill obscured most of his face. It wouldn't keep the guards from realizing he wasn't the regular driver, but with his uniform, he'd encounter more questions than concern.

The moment the bus stopped, one of the guards headed to the bus's door, while Ricky and Liesel slipped around the hut and behind the guard standing at the side of the road. Ricky wrapped an arm around the guy's chest and slapped a hand over the guy's mouth. Liesel injected the drug, and by the count of three, the guard was slack in Ricky's arm.

They laid him in the road and crept past the front of the bus in a crouch. The open door blocked all but the other guard's feet from view.

"So, he stayed at the dock?" the man was asking Dylan.

"Yeah, he wanted to lie down. Said he thought he'd feel better in—"

Ricky and Liesel moved around the door and dealt with the second guard the same way they'd dealt with his friend.

When the guard lost consciousness, Dylan said, "I thought you guys were going to make me talk to him all night."

Ricky flashed him a smile. "Sorry. We'll try to be faster next time."

He and Liesel moved both guards to the floor of the hut. After the men had been zip-tied, Ricky punched a button on the wall. As he'd hoped, the hydraulic road barriers dropped into the ground.

Before getting back on the bus, he and Liesel removed the bulbs from the brake and reverse lights on the back of the vehicle.

"Punch it, Pickle!" Ricky said after he and Liesel hopped back on.

Dylan shot him a glare as he shifted into drive.

GLORIA WAS DEAD tired. The ending bell, which normally sounded at ten p.m., didn't go off until nearly 10:45. That sometimes happened. It was never explained to the workers, but she figured the extra time was added because there was a deadline to meet, or they were behind, or both.

Whatever the case, her fingers ached more than normal, and it took extra effort to stretch them out. The small of her back was not happy, either. As she stood after being dismissed, she almost had to grab the chair to keep from falling back down. The hope of seeing Henrietta again was the only thing that kept her moving.

She exited the building and stepped into the chain-link corridor, worried that her shop had been the only one to have worked overtime and she had missed her chance to see her sister. But when she looked over at Henrietta's passage, she saw her sister walking very slowly next to the fence, surrounded by the others from her group.

Gloria had to stop herself from crying out in relief as she

moved over to the fence and walked next to her sister.

"What did you mean when you said, 'be ready'?" she whispered.

Henrietta put a finger briefly to her lips and glanced upward.

A guard was on the roof, about five meters away, walking in their direction.

Not again, Gloria thought.

She had so many questions. How did Henrietta get here? Had she been here long? What building was she in? And most importantly, how was she going to get Gloria out?

They passed under the guard but were still too close to him to talk. And with the bend in Henrietta's passageway coming up, it looked like they wouldn't get the chance to speak tonight at all.

Gloria's heart sank. At this rate, it would take months just to have a short conversation.

"Hey," Henrietta whispered so low it almost sounded like an expelled breath.

Her fingers were skimming the chain-link, waist high.

Gloria moved her hand parallel to her sister's, and for an instant, their fingers touched.

Gloria's breath caught in her throat, and it was all she could do to keep from crying.

"Soon," Henrietta whispered, then she took the turn and was gone.

HENRIETTA'S HEART ACHED. She wanted to cut through the fence and fold Gloria into her arms, but she knew even the act of whispering a single word could get them separated. She had forced herself to stay strong.

Touching fingers had been dangerous but she'd allowed herself that one indulgence, if only to prove to both herself and Gloria that neither was seeing things.

She probably shouldn't have told Gloria the other night that she had come to free her, but it had just come out. As the word *soon* had tonight. She had no idea how long it would take. She had no idea if the bug in her arm had worked and Ramon even knew where she was.

But she had to believe. For Gloria. For herself. She had to.

She entered her dorm, grabbed her box of dinner, and retreated to her bunk. After she finished eating, she lay in her bed, staring at the mattress above her, sure she wouldn't be able to sleep.

But the work she did, assembling metal pieces for God knew what, had worn her out, and it wasn't ten minutes before she drifted off.

A KILOMETER PAST the checkpoint, they killed the bus's lights. Ricky, the resident expert, flew the drone fifty meters ahead of the bus, utilizing the camera's night-vision function to guide them past any obstructions.

Three kilometers on, he said, "Stop here."

Dylan lifted his foot from the accelerator and let the bus roll to a stop as Ricky showed the camera feed to Ananke. Lights twinkled down the road, about half a kilometer away.

"That's it?" she said.

Ricky nodded.

Ananke faced the rest of the bus. "Okay, everyone. This is it. Where are my radio folks?"

Ramon and two others raised their hands.

"Go ahead and turn on your comms now," Ananke said. "Make sure you're on channel three. If we need you, that's where we'll come to find you. If, and only if, you spot someone headed your way, or you have some other emergency, then one of you can switch to channel one and call us. Otherwise stay off both that and channel two. Do not even switch to those channels just to listen in, no matter how tempting that might be. Doing so could interfere with our communications. Am I clear?"

"Yes," Ramon said.

The other two nodded.

Ananke glanced at Dylan. "Do it."

Dylan executed a series of back and forth turns until the bus was sitting across the road, blocking all but a meter of asphalt on either side. He set the brake and killed the engine.

Ananke and her team pulled on their backpacks.

"If one of us radios and tells you to bug out, turn the bus around and get back to the pier as quickly as you can," Ananke said to Ramon.

"We will."

"I'll try to check in every hour, but we might get a little busy. If two hours go by and you haven't heard from me, you can try channel one. If you still get nothing, consider that a bug-out order."

"What if you need help?"

"If we're unreachable, the kind of help we would need would not be something you could give us." She could see this didn't help at all. "But that's not going to happen. I'm sure it will all be fine."

He smiled, but she could tell he was forcing it.

She turned back to Liesel, Rosario, Dylan, and Ricky. "Okay, gang. Time to hit it."

THE TEAM MOVED through the jungle, just off the road.

When they were about a hundred meters from the gate, Ricky said, "We'll cut in here."

He led them on a diagonal to the tall chain-link fence that fronted the City, and followed it west for a while.

Finally Ricky said, "This is far enough."

Ananke looked at Liesel. "Get us through."

Liesel removed her backpack and pulled out a pair of bolt cutters. Rosario pulled a small bundle of folded cloth from hers. As Liesel put the jaws around the first link, Rosario wrapped the end of the tool and as much of the wire as she could with the cloth. It didn't completely muffle the sound when Liesel cut through the metal, but someone would have had to be pretty close to have heard it.

They continued to work, up and across, creating a door-like flap. When done, Liesel handed the bolt cutters to Rosario and pushed the flap open, holding it until everyone had passed through.

MIKO WRIGHT RAN a hand through his hair and sat back, ready

for a drink.

After returning from his very successful sales trip for the City, he'd immediately been summoned to Salvador Aquino's office. He had gone in thinking it would be the standard updating of the plans for expanding the City. Though it'd started out that way, it soon turned into an accusation-filled tirade about why the project hadn't even started yet. It didn't matter that Aquino himself had requested changes to the plans at the previous meeting, pushing the schedule back. No, it was all Miko's fault, and unless he did something about it right away, he would be replaced.

Miko knew Aquino had only been in one of his infamous moods so it was an idle threat, but that didn't mean Miko could ignore his boss's orders. So, since that meeting, Miko had been finalizing the plans and figuring out the construction schedule, a project he'd just completed.

Barring any other tangents from Aquino, the clearing of the land they were expanding into would commence in two days. And three months from now, they should be able to bring in a large group of new workers, upping their total to around eighteen fifty.

He saved his files, closed his computer, and headed home. As the number-two man at AJS, he had his own standalone building within the complex that contained the administration facility and all the staff quarters. He checked his watch as he headed outside. Just after midnight. Late, but not as late as the previous night. And tomorrow, he should be able to call it quits early.

One of the guards on night watch was walking along the same path as Miko but coming from the other direction.

"Good evening, *Señor* Wright."

Miko nodded but said nothing, not wanting to encourage conversation.

As Miko neared his house, he heard something behind him. Figuring it was the guard clearing his throat, Miko didn't even look. He entered his house, poured himself a glass of whiskey, and went up to his bedroom.

"SEE THAT?" RICKY said.

The others were gathered around him, looking at a feed from the drone on his screen. The image showed a watchtower similar to the one at the dock.

"There are three total," he said. "One man in each." He remotely tilted the camera to show more of the buildings in the compound below the towers, and the chain-link system that connected them to one another. "Those are the cages. I counted over three dozen guards patrolling the top when I was here before, but that had been daytime. I doubt there'd be even half that this late at night."

"So, the rest will be in one of the dormitories," Ananke said.

He nodded. He had already told them about seeing what looked like dorms in a section of the City that appeared to be used only by those who ran the place.

"Take care of the watchers in the towers first?" Ananke said.

"That would be my call."

Unlike at the dock, one of them couldn't climb up any of the towers without being seen by one of the men walking the cages. That was unfortunate for the men stationed there, as it meant a longer-range solution was called for, one that would not involve the tranquilizer darts.

Inside Ananke's backpack was a compact sniper rifle, a laser-enabled sight, and a large suppressor. She found a spot as far from the first tower as she could get and still have a good view, and assembled the rifle. Through the scope, she studied the top of the cages directly below the crow's nest, estimating sight lines of the guards in the area, then examined the nest itself. Not only would she need to do this with one shot, she once again had to keep her target from tumbling out of the tower.

She adjusted her position a meter to her left, checked again, and made another, smaller move before she was satisfied.

"Here we go," she whispered into her mic.

She pulled the trigger.

The muffled shot was loud enough to cause several birds in nearby trees to call out in complaint, but not loud enough to be heard by the guards on the cages. The bullet hit the target exactly where Ananke had planned, knocking him sideways so that he slumped onto the floor of the nest.

She swept the cages again, but none of the other guards showed any sign of suspecting something was up.

"Tower one complete."

The other two towers went almost as smoothly. The only real problem had been finding a viable firing spot, far enough away from the last crow's nest that no one would hear the shot. She ended up having to climb a tree and balance on a limb, but in the end, the result was the same.

She returned the rifle to her pack, exchanged it for her dart gun, then she and the others made their way to the administrative area.

There were eight buildings in all. Three smaller ones that looked like houses, four two-story rectangular structures Ricky identified as the probable dormitories, and one three-story building sitting away from the others that he thought was some kind of headquarters. Pathways ran between the buildings, lit every seven meters or so by shin-high lights in the ground.

"Guard," Rosario said over the comm. "Southwest quadrant, walking between the last two dorms."

"I've got one, too," Dylan reported. "In front of the office building, moving toward the edge of the clearing closest to us."

Ananke spoke up. "Guard number three, center, straight back. North end."

"If it's the same as the other night, that should be it. Do you want to do a drone pass to check?"

Ananke thought for a moment. "Yeah, send it up."

A few seconds later, the drone rose from the brush and flew over the area, just below the camouflage canopy. Ricky stopped it at the approximate center point of the clearing and let it hover.

"Looks like just the three," he said.

"Liesel, you've got number one," Ananke said.

"Copy."

"Rosario, number two."

"Copy."

"I got three. Ricky, watch our backs."

"Copy that."

"All right," Ananke said. "Move out."

While Liesel headed to the right, Ananke and Rosario crept out of the cover of the brush to the back side of the headquarters building. Rosario went right, to circle around the near end in her pursuit of the guard in front. Ananke went left and stopped at the far corner, where she had a direct view of the three smaller buildings and the guard walking from there toward the headquarters. The buildings were definitely homes, with balconies on the second floors and porches out front. She assumed these were where the bigwigs lived.

"We've got a new player," Ricky announced. "Just exited the headquarters. Doesn't look like a guard, though. No gun, no uniform." A pause. "He turned down the same path Ananke's guy is on. They should pass each other."

Ananke watched the path until she saw both men. They were no more than half a minute from passing each other. Ricky was right about the new guy. Not only was he not wearing a uniform, he looked like he was in his forties at least. None of the guards they'd seen were anywhere near that old.

Staying low, she moved from the back of the building to some bushes about twenty meters away, closer to the path. Through the branches, she watched as the two men passed each other, the guard saying something, but the other not responding. The older guy then took a fork leading to the small buildings.

That might mean he was someone important, but Ananke would worry about him later.

She turned her attention back to the guard, who had just passed Ananke's position. She crept out and moved in behind him. Holding a syringe in one hand, she grabbed him around the throat with her other arm and plunged the needle into his neck. He tried to yell, but managed only a muffled yelp.

When he slumped forward, she whispered into her comm, "Guard three neutralized."

"Two is down also," Rosario said.

A brief pause before Liesel said, "Okay, one is out."

"Ricky, how we looking?" Ananke asked.

"All clear."

"Excellent. Everyone, rendezvous at the dorms."

After zip-tying the guard, Ananke jogged toward the buildings, doing some quick calculations in her head. So far, they had removed six guards here in the City, sixteen at the dock, and the two at the checkpoint. Wait, she couldn't forget the five members of the search party and Ricky's friend, Hugo. They weren't normal patrol boat personnel. So, thirty total.

That left the off-duty guards, the forty to fifty administrative personnel, and the guards patrolling the cages, of which she had counted fourteen when she was taking out the watchtowers but knew there were a few more. Make it a hundred and fifteen to a hundred and twenty-five left, give or take. That seemed a crazy amount, but after all they'd done so far, not so much.

She reached the dorms at about the same time as Rosario and Liesel. Ricky and Dylan arrived about thirty seconds later.

"Darts if they're moving, syringes if they're asleep," Ananke ordered before they entered any of the buildings.

They started on the ground floor of the dorm farthest to the east. It was divided into four rooms with six beds each. Ananke chose one of the rooms, and they slipped inside. The beds were all in use, their occupants asleep. Before anyone on the team could administer a shot, though, Ananke motioned for everyone to stop.

The sleepers did not look like guards. Like with the man who'd been walking to the house, most were a bit too old and, at least the one she was looking at, too out of shape.

Ananke signaled everyone out of the room.

Huddling near the front door, she whispered, "I don't think any of them is with security." She explained her reasoning, and the others nodded. "Dylan, Liesel, check the other rooms on this floor. Rosario and Ricky and I will take upstairs."

Ananke led the other two to the second floor, where they

found more of the same. Ananke checked several of the cabinets that lined the walls in each room. No uniforms or anything else she would associate with security.

The team reconvened outside, where Ananke whispered, "Admin staff."

"Definitely," Liesel said.

"I found an empty bed," Rosario said. "Anyone else?"

Dylan raised a hand.

Liesel said, "I found two."

Forty-four beds occupied.

"That's right about how many people our friend Hugo said were in non-security positions," Ananke said. "If he wasn't lying, then that should be the lot of them."

They moved to the next building. Five beds per room here for a total of forty. All four rooms upstairs and one on the ground level were empty, though there were items in the cabinets indicating they were all claimed. Of the rooms that were occupied, those sleeping there definitely fit the profile for security. That led Ananke to guess the empty beds belonged to the night crew.

The team entered one of the rooms in use, where each took one of the sleepers and stuck a needle into the base of the neck. A couple of the guards snapped awake when pricked, but they were quickly returned to dreamland. Wrists and ankles were tied to the bed frames, leaving each man spread-eagled on his mattress. Then it was on to the next room.

The process worked as well in building two, where all forty beds were occupied.

"Man, I could do this all night," Ricky whispered as they moved to building three.

Ananke rolled her eyes, but kind of felt the same.

The final security dorm turned out to be slightly different from the other two. Here, there were only four beds per room, but what was surprising was that all the beds on the ground floor weren't being used. The lack of bedding and anything at all in the cabinets indicated they were waiting to be claimed.

They moved upstairs. Also four beds per room, but occupied. The team worked its way from room to room, and within five minutes, the remainder of the off-duty security staff had been neutralized.

Seventy-five more to add to the out-of-commission list.

"So, who's next?" Ricky asked. "Guards on the cages, or do you want to go back and take care of the admin staff?"

"The guards," Ananke said. Best to deal with the ones with guns before worrying about the sleeping desk jockeys. "Can you give us a sneak peek?"

Ricky grinned. "Absolutely."

He pulled out the drone and sent it skyward until it hovered below the artificial canopy. The tricky part was flying it through the grove of trees that separated the administration area from the rest of the City, many of which passed through holes in the canopy to tower above it.

The team gathered around Ricky and watched the camera feed as he guided the tiny craft between branches. When it reached the edge of the trees, he stopped it and let it hover.

From this vantage point, they could see about a quarter of the forced labor camp area. Though no one was in the mazes, floodlights on the sides of the building kept the cages illuminated, presumably so any unauthorized entry would be detected by the guards patrolling on top. The camera showed six men, each appearing to cover a specific, non-overlapping zone.

"Show us the other areas," Ananke said.

Ricky flew the drone to one of the crow's nests, from where they could see a second, smaller slice of the compound. More guards and lit up, empty cages. Only three men here.

Ricky maneuvered the drone through three more stops, until the entire City had been covered. Nineteen guards were walking the cages. With the three in the crow's nests Ananke had taken care of and the three who'd been patrolling the admin area, this equaled the twenty-five empty beds in the dorms.

"We'll start with the nearest group and work our way to the back," Ananke said.

She pulled out her dart gun, double-checked that the magazine was filled, and led her team across the grounds toward the trees.

TWENTY-EIGHT

MIKO HAD HOPED the whiskey would relax him enough to fall asleep, but his mind was still filled with estimates and schedules and to-do lists that refused to let him nod off.

Annoyed, he returned to the kitchen and poured himself another drink, a double this time. When he returned to his bedroom, he grabbed a cigar and headed out onto the narrow balcony.

He eased into his deck chair, set his whiskey down, and used the cutter already on the outdoor table to clip his cigar.

Sitting out here at night, with a smoke and a drink and the sounds of the jungle, was one of his favorite things to do here. He could almost imagine he was at a resort someplace else, enjoying a quiet night after a day filled with massages and cocktails and—

He blinked.

Across the clearing, five people were running toward the operations building. His first thought was that they were guards responding to some kind of trouble. But only three were assigned to this area.

He went inside and grabbed his own radio. "Wright calling night ops commander."

"This is Badia. How can I help you, Mr. Wright?"

The man sounded calm, even bored.

"Is something going on?"

"Going on, sir? What do you mean?"

"A problem, or something unusual."

"Nothing that I'm aware of. Why?"

"I just saw five guards rushing across the compound over here."

"Five? There's only three over—"

"I know there's only three! That's what caught my attention."

"Let me check," the man said, with only a bit more enthusiasm. "Give me a couple minutes to get back to you."

THE FIRST GROUP of guards was the six the drone had shown in the area just on the other side of the small slice of jungle. Ananke decided the easiest way to get them would be from the trees. Each team member chose one close to his or her target and scaled it.

The only change from what they'd seen on the camera feed was that one guard had left his area and was talking with Ananke's target. In his hand was a radio. Everything else was status quo, though.

"I'll pick up the extra guy," Ananke whispered into her mic. "Everyone else set?"

Four single clicks.

"All right, then. Three, two, one, fire."

Darts sailed out of the trees toward the guards.

"Missed shot," Dylan said.

Ananke, who had dispatched her two darts for clean hits, saw Dylan's target turning toward the trees and raising his weapon. She adjusted her aim and pulled her trigger again. Hers was not the only projectile flying toward the guard, however, as the other four had fired also. The man was able to fend off one of the darts, but not the rest, and was soon lying on the chain-link with his colleagues.

The team held its position for several seconds in case reinforcements showed up.

When no one came, Ananke said, "On to the cages."

MIKO FROWNED, TOOK another sip of whiskey. Badia's couple of minutes had already come and gone. He picked up his radio. "Wright for Commander Badia."

No response.

He checked to make sure he hadn't accidentally turned off the device. Nope.

"Miko Wright for Commander Badia. Come in, please."

Still nothing.

"Does anyone know where Badia is?" he asked.

A few beats of continued silence, then a tentative voice said, "He's, um, in Section A."

"Then send someone over there to check on him. He was supposed to get back to me."

"Yes, sir."

The skin at the base of Miko's neck began to tingle. He looked toward the narrow jungle barrier that separated the admin zone from Section A—in the same direction the running silhouettes had been heading.

He didn't like this. Not at all.

ANANKE AND THE others zip-tied the guards where they lay. Then, dart guns reloaded, they headed along the top of a narrow section of the maze lined by jungle that led toward the next group of guards.

Before they were halfway there, two guards appeared at the other end, coming toward them.

"Rosario and Dylan, they're yours," Ananke said quietly. "But wait until you're sure of your shot."

"Hey, I was sure of my shot earlier," Dylan said. "He just turned a little and the damn thing hit the buckle on his rifle strap."

"You keep telling yourself that, Pickle," Ricky said.

"My name isn't—"

"Enough," Ananke said.

They continued down the passageway. The guard uniforms they were wearing prevented the two approaching them from realizing something was up, until Rosario's and Dylan's darts were racing toward them. By then, all they could do was open their eyes wide as their bodies became human pincushions.

"THIS IS WRIGHT looking for an update on Badia," Miko said, five minutes since he'd last talked to anyone.

No answer.

"This is Wright requesting update on Badia."

Silence.

He hurried downstairs and input the combination that opened a panel near the front door. Inside was a single button.

He pushed it without hesitation.

THE TEAM HAD reached the end of the narrow corridor. Ahead were the three guards covering the area, which was surprising. Ananke had assumed the two they'd just taken out were part of this group, but apparently they had come from one of the groups farther on.

"Liesel, Ricky, and me, left to right," she said.

After Liesel and Ricky indicated they understood, the three of them headed out onto the widening roof, relying once more on their uniforms to get close to their targets. But when they were only steps beyond the passageway, a loud alarm blared from the speakers and floodlights mounted high in the trees switched on.

Ananke, Liesel, and Ricky rushed forward and pulled their triggers, downing the three guards as the men were looking around in surprise at the alarm.

Ananke shoved her dart gun in its holster and pulled out her 9mm pistol. Darts would be lousy in a shootout, and with the remaining guards now on alert, that seemed a likely situation.

The rest of the team followed suit.

GLORIA WOKE WITH a start.

A *whoop-whoop-whoop* screamed from the speakers outside the dorm. As she sat up, she could see bright light leaking in through the narrow windows at the top of the walls. Inside the room, it was still dark.

Others were sitting up and looking around.

"What's going on?" a girl on a nearby bunk asked.

Gloria had an idea but kept her mouth shut, worried she might be wrong.

"I've come to get you out," Henrietta had said.

Could this really be it?

While the alarm continued outside, a prerecorded voice came over the dorm's interior speaker. "Stay in your beds. Anyone found in the aisle will be shot. Stay in your beds. Anyone found…"

The people who had gotten up rushed back to their mattresses, but Gloria didn't think they had been in danger. As far as she could tell, there were no guards in the room.

HENRIETTA HAD ALSO been startled from her sleep by the alarm. Unlike Gloria, she *was* sure this was Ramon's rescue attempt. But instead of it giving her hope, she took it as a sign something had gone wrong.

Before she'd allowed herself to be kidnapped, she had asked Ramon several times how he was planning to get her and Gloria out.

His standard response was always some variation of: "It will depend on where you are. But don't worry—we *will* get you."

She had worried. A lot. But she also knew this was the only chance of freeing her sister so she'd ignored her concern as best she could.

Now, it was pressing down on her, full force.

Something must have gone wrong. Maybe Ramon and the others have been captured. Or maybe they're dead.

If either was true, she and Gloria might never get out of here.

RICKY AND DYLAN led the way into the next area. Three soldiers had been present when the drone flew by, but now there was only one. This had to be where the two extra guards had come from.

The man remaining had a panicked look as he circled around, scanning for trouble. When he spotted Ricky, Dylan, and the others, relief washed over his face.

"Do you know what's going on?" he yelled. "Is there an es—"

His gaze had flicked past Ricky and Dylan to Ananke, Rosario, and Liesel. Though they were in uniform, in the halo of the floodlights there was little chance they'd be mistaken for men.

He fumbled with his rifle, but before he could aim it at the team, Ricky shot him in the chest. The guy flew backward and crumpled against the chain-link.

Twelve cage guards down. Seven to go.

AS SOON AS he activated the alarm, Miko ran out of his house over to where his boss lived and pounded on the front door.

Aquino soon yanked the door open. "Is it an escape?"

"I-I'm not sure. Something's going on. The guards aren't responding, and I saw a group of hostiles crossing the compound." The last was a bit of a stretch, as he didn't know who the group was.

"Not responding? Then who set off the alarm?"

"I did."

Aquino stared as if he didn't understand.

"I'm going to find out what's going on," Miko said. "Stay inside until I come back."

Aquino started to close the door, but stopped. "Make it fast. I want to know what this is all about!"

"Yes, sir."

With no one answering the radio, Miko had to go to the cages, but there was no way he was going to do that alone.

He hurried over to the closest security dorm building. When he came around the front, he was surprised to see people standing outside the administrative dorm but no one outside any of the security ones.

A sense of dread building, he went inside. The guards were all there, still in bed. Each and every one was unconscious and restrained to his bed frames.

He tried waking one of them, but no matter how loudly he yelled or how hard he shook him, the man didn't stir.

Miko tried a few others, but they were just as out of it, so he grabbed three rifles from the cabinets and went back outside. Assuming the guards inside the remaining two security dorms were in a similar state, he sprinted over to the administrative quarters and pointed at two of the largest, most in shape men.

298

"Both of you, come here."

The men looked reluctant, but Miko was the boss so after a brief pause, they obeyed.

He handed each a rifle.

"What are we supposed to do with these?" one of the men asked.

"You're coming with me, and if I tell you to shoot something, you shoot it!"

He turned and ran toward the cages.

ANANKE HAD TO admit they'd had a pretty great run up to this point. That's what happened when you had a good plan and executed it well.

But few plans were ever perfect, and the longer they took to complete, the more chances for Murphy's Law to kick in.

Case in point, the alarm.

Still, that hadn't kept the team from quickly eliminating the first group of guards they had encountered after it went off. Unfortunately, the second group was not as easily fooled.

The moment Ricky and Dylan ran out from behind the trees that had masked the team's approach, the guards opened fire. Ricky and Dylan skidded to a stop and scrambled back to safety.

"Still just the three of them?" Ananke asked. When the drone spied on the area, it had shown three guards, with the final four in the last area, about a hundred meters beyond this one.

Ricky nodded.

Ananke looked back at Liesel and Rosario. "See if you can find a way around through the jungle."

The two retreated down the pathway.

Ananke turned back to Ricky. "Get the drone up."

"THAT'S GUNFIRE," SOMEONE said, a few beds away from Gloria.

"Someone must be trying to escape," another suggested.

"I've never heard that much shooting before," a third voice chimed in.

Gloria had counted five booms before the guns fell silent. Two or three hundred meters away. Close, but not right outside their building.

She leaned over the end of her bed and looked down the main aisle. Still no guards. She pulled back and thought for a moment.

"To hell with it," she said under her breath.

She slipped off her mattress and crept toward the wall.

"What are you doing?" a girl she passed asked. "You're not supposed to leave your bed."

Gloria ignored her and continued on until she reached the bunk closest to the outside wall. Using the ladder attached to the side, she climbed past the middle bunk to the one on top.

A man jerked in surprise as she appeared over the side of his mattress.

"What are you doing?" he asked.

"Shhh," she told him, and climbed onto his bed.

The man pulled back from her as if she was going to attack him. Ignoring him, she stood on the end of his mattress nearest the wall, high enough to see out the window. The bunk was positioned nearly a meter from the wall, however, and she couldn't see down onto the cages.

She looked back at the man. "I need your help."

"What?" he said, eyes wide.

"Come here. I need your help."

Though he looked like he wanted to do anything but what she asked, her commanding tone compelled him to crawl over to her.

"Hold me," she said and touched her hips. "Right here."

"Why?"

"I'm trying to reach the window."

"You're planning on jumping out?" Fear still coating his words.

"What? No. I just want to take a look."

Dubious, he nevertheless grabbed on to her.

"Don't let go," she said.

She took a deep breath, leaned over the gap, and reached for the window frame. She was able to hold on to the ledge and peek out at the cages. The area looked weird, all lit up and devoid of people.

No. Not devoid.

A guard was lying on his side on top of the cage. His hands were behind his back, his wrists pressed together. He appeared to be asleep, but if he was, he wouldn't have been able to hold his hands that way.

She scanned the cages and spotted another guard also lying on his side.

She could hardly believe what she was seeing. "Pull me back."

As she pushed off the wall, the man yanked her toward him and they almost fell onto the mattress.

"Well?" a woman on top of the next bunk over asked.

"I think someone's taken the guards out," Gloria said.

"Taken them out? What does that mean?"

"Knocked them out or killed them. There are two guards lying on the cages, both looking like they were tied up."

The questions came at her a mile a second, everyone wanting to know exactly what she'd seen. Before she could answer more than a couple, the sound of wood scraping on the concrete floor drowned everyone out. Three other prisoners were shoving their heavy bunk against the wall.

After that, a stream of people made their way to the top to see for themselves.

RICKY SENT THE drone all the way up to the canopy, and positioned it directly above the guards. The three men had retreated behind one of the buildings and were using the corner to watch the spot where Ricky and Dylan had made their earlier appearance.

"No way we can get out there without them getting a shot at us first," Ricky said.

That was what Ananke thought. She clicked on her mic. "Liesel, Rosario, any luck?"

"Give us another minute," Rosario whispered.

"Copy," Ananke said, then looked back at Ricky. "Let's see what the last group is doing."

The drone swept over the passageway to the final part of the City. Like the areas they'd already been through, this one had several of the large, tin-roofed buildings. What was different, though, was the large amphitheater-like area, its slope partly covered by more cages, with an unrestricted area where the stage would be.

"I didn't see any of the guards," Ananke said.

"They've got to be there somewhere," Ricky said. "Hold on."

He flew the drone through the zone, more slowly this time, checking around each building. As he circled it around a building on the east side, the picture shook and the drone dropped from the sky.

"Dammit!" Ricky said.

"What happened?" Dylan asked.

"Someone shot me!"

"Then there's at least one guard still there," Dylan said.

"Excuse me if I don't celebrate that."

The radio crackled. "Rosario for Ananke."

"Go for Ananke."

"Just saw the drone go down. We have the guards in sight. They're tucked against the back of a building with the number 32 on it. But we only have good angles on two of them."

"Ricky, back up the footage and show me where that is," Ananke said.

He scrolled through the video from the drone until he found a shot of Building 32. "Should be about there," he said, pointing at an angle through the trees. "Sixty meters out."

Ananke moved down to the last tree before the end of the passage. "Rosario, give me a countdown and take the shots."

"Copy. Three. Two. One."

At the unspoken zero, Ananke stepped out from the tree, her gun aimed at Building 32. Less than a second later, the third guard rushed from behind the structure, flushed out by Rosario's and Liesel's shots.

Ananke picked him off before he made it five steps.

"I got the runner. How did you guys do?"

"Do you even need to ask?" Liesel said.

"Four left, then, but no drone to tell us where they are."

"Except somewhere in front of us," Ricky said.

"Except that. Okay, Ricky, Dylan, and I are going to head to the building the guards were behind. You two keep a watch out for anyone trying to take a shot at us."

"Copy," Rosario said.

UPON ARRIVING IN Section A, Miko discovered all six of the guards assigned to the area laid out with their hands and feet bound. He didn't even try to wake them. Instead, he and the two men he'd dragooned headed to Section B.

In the passage on the way there, they found two more unconscious and bound men.

The story was repeated a third time with the three guards in Section B.

Miko's anger was becoming tinged with panic. Maybe he should be worrying about getting the hell out of there rather than tracking down whoever these people were.

Ahead, he heard rifle fire from the kind of weapons used by his people. Hoping the intruders were finally losing their advantage, he said to his companions, "Hurry," and ran toward the noise.

They found another downed guard in Section C, only this one wasn't unconscious but dead from a bullet to the chest. Miko's companions both looked as if they were going to flee.

"If you run, I'll shoot you in the back," Miko said.

As they neared Section D, he saw someone move from the trees, right where the passageway stopped, into the open area, out of his sight.

Miko sprinted to the end and halted next to the last tree. Glancing around the trunk, he saw three people in guard uniforms huddled by Building 32, one of the workhouses. At first, he thought they were his men, but then he realized one was a woman.

There were no female guards at the City.

He motioned for his men to join him.

"There are three hostiles next to Building 32," he whispered. "We're going to step out and shoot them."

303

"I-I-I don't know if I can," one of the men said.

"If you don't, I'll practice on you two first then take care of them myself."

Both men indicated they'd do as he asked.

"HOW'S IT LOOKING ahead?" Ananke asked.

"You're clear to the next building," Rosario replied over the comm.

Ananke moved to the corner to get a look at the route before she, Ricky, and Dylan repositioned.

As she leaned her head out, a *boom-boom-boom* shattered the night behind her. At nearly the same instant, a shower of splintering wood burst from the wall they were standing against. They dove to the ground and looked back.

Three men holding rifles were standing near the trees Ananke, Ricky, and Dylan had been hiding behind moments before. As she and her guys raised their guns, the two men farthest from the trees dropped their rifles and raised their hands.

The third guy, however, dove behind the trees, out of sight.

"Do we shoot them?" Ricky asked.

She was sorely tempted to say yes, but the men weren't wearing uniforms. And from how badly they'd missed and then thrown down their rifles, she didn't think they were serious threats.

"Kick your weapons toward us," she yelled.

The men complied.

"Now tell your friend to come out from behind those trees."

Both men looked toward the passageway, then the one who had been in the middle said, "He's not there."

"Where is he?"

"Running."

The guy seemed too scared to be lying, but she wasn't about to believe him. "On your stomachs, hands behind your backs."

The men dropped to the chain-link.

To Ricky and Dylan, Ananke said, "Go wide and come around to the trees. Check if you can see the other guy behind them."

Ricky and Dylan jumped to their feet and sprinted to the left. They circled along the edge of the area, slowing when they neared the trees. After several seconds, Ricky rounded the last tree and checked down the passageway.

When he looked back, he waved to Ananke. "All clear."

She jogged over.

"Please," one of the guys said as Dylan zip-tied his hands. "We didn't want to shoot."

"I've never even held a gun before," the other said.

"Then why did you try to kill us?" Ananke asked.

"I didn't!" the first said.

"Me, neither! It was Mr. Wright. He made us do it."

"Mr. Wright?" Ananke said.

"The man with us. He ordered us to help."

"Is Mr. Wright your boss?"

"He's our boss's boss's boss."

"So he's important."

"Yes," the first guy said, clearly wanting to be as helpful as possible. "Only Mr. Aquino is more important."

"Is that so? And where is Mr. Aquino?"

"I-I assume back in his house at the operations compound."

"Unless…" his friend said.

When he didn't go on, Ananke said, "Unless what?"

The two men shared a look. "The company helicopter," the second man said.

"There's a helicopter here?"

Both men nodded.

Ananke shot Ricky a look. He shrugged in a way that told her he'd tried to see as much as he could on his scout, but he wasn't perfect.

"And he knows how to fly it?" she asked the men.

"I don't think so," the second man said.

"But Mr. Wright does," the first added quickly.

Crap.

The goal of the mission was to free the prisoners, not keep the people who ran the City from getting away, but letting any of them slip through their fingers, especially those at the very top, did not sit well with her.

"Where is this helicopter?"

"Behind the operations section."

"That's the section where you all live?"

"Yes. There's a path through the jungle on the south side."

"It's my screwup," Ricky said. "Let me go."

She nodded. "Take Dylan."

As her two friends raced into the passageway, Ananke pulled out a pair of syringes.

"Wait," the first guy said. "What's that?"

TWENTY-NINE

THOSE IDIOTS!

Miko was burning mad. Obviously, he'd chosen the two most inept people to accompany him. They hadn't even shot straight. His was the only bullet to strike anywhere near where the intruders had been. And then, at the first sign of trouble, they had both thrown down their rifles and surrendered.

Miko had had no choice but to run. And not just from the intruders. The City was on the brink of falling, so he was getting the hell out.

He'd known from the beginning this place couldn't last forever. That's why he had a contingency plan. From now on, he'd be living in Indonesia as a retired tech investor from Canada. He had an impeccable set of documents for his new identity, and a house waiting for him in Bali. He just needed to fly the helicopter to the airstrip in Guyana, where he'd have the company's private jet take him to Lima. From there, he would catch the first available commercial flight across the Pacific.

He needed to grab a few items from his house first. Most were packed in the bag in his closet, so he should be able to get in and out in under a minute.

He sprinted through Sections C, B, and A, and descended the stairs back to the jungle floor. As he hurried into the operations section, he saw that the people who'd come out of the admin dorm were still there, most looking nervously toward the rest of the City.

Miko kept to the edge of the jungle and made it undetected to the private residences. He rushed inside his house and up the stairs to his bedroom, where he retrieved his bag from the closet, shoved in a couple of items from his desk, and grabbed the envelope containing his fake passport from the underside of the dresser drawer to which it was taped.

He all but flew back downstairs and out the front door.

"Miko?"

Miko stopped. Standing on the balcony of the next house over was Aquino.

"Did you find out what's going on?"

"It's nothing. Security has it under control."

"I heard gunshots."

"A couple of the laborers tried to break out, that's all. It's taken care of."

"Then why is the alarm still going off?"

"They just haven't gotten around to turning it off yet. I'm sure it'll be soon." Miko started walking toward the path to the helipad.

"What do you have there? Where are you going?"

Miko paused. "I'm too awake to go right back to sleep. Thought I'd take care of a few things since I'm up. You should go inside, though. Everything's going to be fine."

"Is that a travel bag?"

Miko ran.

RICKY AND DYLAN descended the cages and hurried over to the clearing where the administrative buildings were located, and stopped a few steps beyond the brush to scan the area.

A couple of dozen people were standing outside the dorm at the other end of the clearing. They had to be members of the operations staff. Ricky's first thought was that this Mr. Wright had headed over to them in order to lose himself in the crowd. But then Ricky heard voices to the left, and spotted Wright standing between two houses, holding a bag he hadn't had before, and talking to an older man on the balcony of the biggest house.

Aquino? Seemed like a fair guess.

The conversation appeared to end abruptly, with Wright running toward the back of the houses.

"I've got the helicopter. You get the guy in that house," Ricky said to Dylan, and took off.

As they neared the homes, the older man yelled down, "Hey, you! What's going on out there?"

Ricky ran by without looking up, but behind him Dylan said, "I was just coming to brief you."

When Ricky reached the rear, he turned right, in the direction his target had gone. The man was nowhere to be seen. Ricky kept going.

About thirty meters on, a gap opened on his left, wide enough for a small car. He swung around the corner and raced through it.

For the first twenty meters or so, he could see nothing but jungle. Then, at the same time a bit of sky appeared not too far ahead, he heard the sound of a powerful motor winding up.

ANANKE RENDEZVOUSED WITH Rosario and Liesel near where the cages narrowed to a single corridor, leading to the final area.

"Did you see any other way to get there?" she asked.

The guards would know they were coming and, unless the security people were completely incompetent, have the other end of the corridor covered.

"There is a stretch of jungle we could probably work our way through," Liesel said. "We'd just need to figure out a way back on top of the cages."

"The amphitheater," Rosario said. "If we can reach the open area at the bottom, it should be easy enough to scale the fence there."

"I like it," Ananke said. The amphitheater route would have the added benefit of bringing them in behind the last known whereabouts of the guards.

Liesel led them back to a point where the jungle looked thin enough to navigate. They climbed down the side of the cages one at a time. Ananke, the last to go, tossed down their bags before joining her friends.

The brush cooperated for the most part, forcing them to backtrack more than a few meters only once. The path Liesel was able to pick out brought them to the edge of the jungle, at the west end of their target.

It really was an amphitheater. The caged area on the slope was divided into more than a dozen large pens, which, unlike the cages in the rest of the City, had no chain-link roofs. Between the pens were narrower corridors that *were* covered, probably where guards patrolled when the area was in use.

Must be where the City's overlords brought everyone to address them at once, Ananke thought. Of course, they also had the speaker system for that.

She pointed to the back of the stage area, where a long building sat across it, the structure's side acting like a backdrop.

Liesel guided them through the vegetation to some bushes on the other side of the building. Wanting to make sure no guards were hiding inside, Ananke sneaked up to the door along the back and tested the handle. It was unlocked.

She raised her gun and pushed the door open.

The interior was silent and pitch-black, so she pulled out her flashlight. As she swept the beam, her jaw tensed.

Across the back wall were five, steel-bar jail cells. All were empty, but she had no doubt they'd seen plenty of use. The rest of the room held a collection of whips and straps and spikes and knives and other torture devices.

She had a pretty good idea now what the amphitheater's purpose was. Discipline one prisoner in private, and only he learns the lesson. Discipline him with all the City's other slaves watching, everybody does.

She stepped back outside and nodded toward the cages.

Time to finish this.

MIKO RAN ACROSS the concrete pad and yanked the helicopter's door open. After tossing his bag onto the other seat, he climbed in.

His heart pounded as he prepped the aircraft for takeoff and flicked on the ignition. He couldn't help but grin when the motor came to life and the rotors started to turn.

He gripped the stick, ready to lift off as soon as the blades were ready, but something punctured the window beside him, missing him by millimeters. He swiveled his head and saw one of the intruders race out of the jungle, his gun aimed at the helicopter.

Miko checked the gauges. He was at the very low end for a safe ascent, but that would have to do.

He pulled back on the stick and the chopper rose.

"OH, HELL NO," Ricky said as the helicopter's skids lifted off.

He stopped, adjusted his aim, and emptied his magazine.

MIKO SMILED, SURE he'd made a clean escape.

Then the helicopter jerked to the side and the engine sputtered.

He pulled on the stick but it was no use.

Something banged in the engine compartment, and the rotors slowed.

"Oh, shit."

RICKY WATCHED AS the helicopter dropped hard back to the pad, landing at a forty-five-degree angle. One of the blades slammed into the ground, its lost momentum transferring back down the rotor shaft and flipping the cabin.

It was more dramatic than he'd planned when he sent bullets into the vehicle's engine, but Ricky was fine with the results.

Once the dust settled, he walked over and stuck his head through a broken window. Wright was hanging in his chair, moaning and eyes half open.

"Hey, buddy," Ricky said. "Welcome back."

DYLAN RAN UP to the house, tried the knob, and knocked loudly when he found the door locked.

From inside, he heard footsteps heading his way. "Hold on!"

Seconds later, the door was opened by the older man Dylan had seen on the balcony.

"For God's sake, tell me what's going on out there," the man said.

"Someone has been trying to free the prisoners," Dylan

said.

"Someone from the outside?"

"Yes."

"Were you able to stop them?"

Dylan grimaced. "Well, see, that's the problem."

"What do you mean?"

"I'm actually one of those people from the outside." He pulled out his dart gun and shot the man in the chest.

The guy staggered back and wobbled. Dylan grabbed him before the man could fall. After laying him on the floor, Dylan went back outside and jogged over to the group in front of the non-security dorm.

He pointed at the first two he saw. "You two. I need your help."

They looked at him, confused.

"Let's go," Dylan said. "We don't have all day."

He started running back toward the houses, confident the uniform he was wearing would make the men follow. Sure enough, when he glanced over his shoulder a few seconds later, they were doing just that.

Upon reaching the big house, Dylan headed straight inside, but the other two hesitated to even climb onto the porch.

"Hurry it up," Dylan called from inside.

They came in, but stopped the moment they saw the man on the floor.

"Is that Mr. Aquino?" one asked.

"You tell me," Dylan said.

They didn't need to do that, though, as the answer was written on their faces.

"What happened to him?" the other one asked.

"Not feeling well, I guess," Dylan said. "I need you two to pick him up."

"What?"

"How else are you going to carry him?"

"Why do we need to—"

"Do it!" Dylan barked.

The men jumped at his tone and lifted Aquino off the floor.

"Are we taking him upstairs?" the first one asked.

"Nope. Follow me."

He led them outside and back to the area in front of their dorm. Several of the others looked over as they arrived.

"Lay him right there," Dylan said.

"On the ground?" one of his helpers asked.

Dylan stared at them without replying, and they put Aquino down.

Dylan looked over at the others. "Everyone, please gather around."

The crowd moved toward Dylan.

Once they were all there, Dylan said, "Good evening, gentlemen. Can everyone in the back hear me? Am I talking loud enough?"

"Yes," a man at the rear of the crowd said.

"Great. Now is this everyone? Or are there still people inside? Because I just want to say this once."

As the men looked at one another, Dylan counted them and came up with a total that matched the number of occupied beds he and his friends had seen inside the admin dorm.

"I'm guessing you're wondering what's going on," he said.

A chorus of assent.

"First, I need you to—"

A crash roared from the jungle, in the direction where Dylan guessed the helicopter was.

The men all jerked in surprise.

Several yelled variations of, "What the hell was that?" while others looked around as if expecting another similar sound.

Dylan whistled loudly. "Everyone, calm down."

It took a few seconds, but finally the men were all looking at him again.

"I need everyone to sit down."

A few did as he asked, but most remained on their feet, confused.

"That was not a suggestion." He unholstered his dart gun.

The rest of the crowd complied.

"Gentlemen, the good news is, you're all getting the day off tomorrow."

More confusion.

"Actually, that's kind of misleading. You've all been laid off because the City is officially closed."

An uproar of questions that went silent the moment he swept his gun over the crowd.

"Better," he said. He worked off his backpack, set it on the ground, and pulled out three packets of zip ties. He tossed one each to different sections of the group. "Those contain plastic zip ties. I want you to use them to tie each other's hands together. Make sure they're nice and snug, right around the wrists."

"You're not security, are you?" one of the larger men asked.

"I'm afraid not."

"Then who are you?"

"Consider me your new, temporary boss."

"What happened to the guards?" another man asked.

"I wouldn't worry about them."

The large man jumped to his feet and started running away.

"Seriously?" Dylan said. He put a dart in the guy's back. The man continued for another few steps before nose-diving to the ground, where he lay unmoving.

"Someone else want to run?" Dylan asked.

The men who held the zip-tie packages opened them and passed out the strips.

THE GUARDS HAD been smart enough to spread out, each taking a position either behind or on top of one of the buildings. Unfortunately for them, they expected the threat to come from the passageway.

Ananke, Rosario, and Liesel each chose a guard, this time with Rosario drawing double duty, and crept toward their targets. Before the team reached them, one of the boards Ananke stepped on emitted a low groan.

Her target turned, whipped his gun around, and shouted,

"They're behind us! They're behind us!"

Ananke pulled her trigger. Her rushed shot hit him in the shoulder and sent him flying back into the wall he was standing beside. He tried to return fire, but his shots sailed wildly into the air. Ananke tucked and rolled to her left, out of his line of fire, popped back into a crouch, and fired again.

This time she did not miss her mark.

From back the other way, she heard more gunfire, both rifle and the muted shots of her team's suppressed pistols.

"I'm clean here," she said. "Who needs help?"

"I'm good," Liesel replied. "My guy is pinned down."

"Hold on," Rosario said.

Ananke heard a muffled double tap from one of the pistols.

"Okay, one down," Rosario said. "I do not know where my other guy went."

Ananke circled around the building behind which her target had been hiding, and peered across the cages in the direction Rosario had been covering. She didn't see the missing guard, but could hear someone running. The sound wasn't the clank of chain-link, however, but of dirt under boots.

"I think he went down into the cages," she said and ran toward the noise, scanning the corridors below her.

Rosario sprinted out from behind another structure ahead. "I see him!"

Ananke ran after her.

"Stop!" Rosario yelled.

She pointed her gun into the cages and pulled her trigger three times, but from her reaction, Ananke knew she'd missed.

"We have a problem," Rosario said. "He went into a building."

"Liesel, what's your status?" Ananke asked.

"This guy is not going anywhere, but he is also not giving me anything to shoot at, either."

"Tell me exactly where he is." Once Liesel relayed the information, Ananke said, "Get over here and help Rosario get through the cage. I'll take care of your friend."

Ananke weaved around two buildings and jumped onto

the roof of the third. Not a particularly difficult task, given that the cage's roof already put her nearly five meters above the ground.

She slunk up the tin roof to the apex and peered down the other side. Liesel's target was right where she'd promised, hiding on the roof of a nearby building, using a water tank as a shield. Ananke's vantage point gave her enough of an angle to see his shoulder and a bit of his neck. She retrieved her sniper rifle and snapped it together.

She placed the man in her crosshairs and pulled the trigger.

"Target neutralized. How we doing on the cage?"

"Working on it," Rosario said.

Ananke slid down the roof, not worried about the noise now, and ran back to the others. Liesel had her bolt cutters out and had cut a hole nearly big enough for them to fit through. When she made the last clip, a section of the chain-link flapped down, and the trio dropped into the caged corridor.

Rosario led them to the building the guard had disappeared into and pulled the door open.

"Go away or I'll kill them all," a male voice yelled from inside, stopping them from entering.

There were gasps and cries from inside. Prisoners.

Ananke looked at Liesel and whispered, "See if there's any other way to get inside."

Liesel nodded and left.

"Did you hear me?" the man shouted. "I'm not kidding! I *will* kill them!"

Ananke closed her eyes and took a deep breath. When she opened them again, she said, "I don't think you appreciate the situation you're in. You're the last member of the security force standing."

"Bullshit!"

"Don't you think someone would have stopped us long before we reached you if you weren't?"

"You're lying!"

"We *could* wait and see if someone shows up to help you, but I'm telling you now, no one's coming."

No response.

"Why don't you put your gun down and come out here? The sooner you do that, the sooner we can help those people get home to their loved ones."

A murmur from inside, loud enough to let her know the guard had more than a few hostages.

"What's it going to be?" she asked.

"No! No, you're just trying to get—" The sound of movement. "Hey! Get back! Let go of that. Hey! Hey!"

The rifle boomed.

"No!" the man yelled.

More movement. Then silence.

"What's going on?" Ananke asked. "Did you hurt someone?"

Steps moving toward the door, then the sound of a magazine being pulled out and pushed back into a rifle.

"Are you really going to take us home?" The voice was female, older, and just around the doorway.

Ananke and Rosario shared a look.

"We are," Ananke said.

"Let me see you."

Before stepping into the doorway, Ananke removed the security hat she'd been wearing and took off the shirt, leaving her in the tank top she had on underneath.

A woman with salt-and-pepper hair wearing prisoner garb stood two meters away, a rifle tucked against her shoulder. Huddled farther in the room were at least fifty others, all eyes on Ananke.

"What's your name?" the woman asked.

"Ananke. What's yours?"

"Mariella. Have you really taken care of all the guards?"

"All except the one who is in here with you."

"He is…unconscious."

"Then, yes. All the guards have been taken care of."

The woman stared at her over the barrel for a few more seconds before lowering the gun and handing it to Ananke.

"We are ready to go home now."

THIRTY

ANANKE KNEW THERE was one group that still needed to be dealt with, so she wasn't ready to lead the former prisoners to safety yet.

Mariella wasn't pleased that she and her people couldn't walk out right then and there, but when Ananke returned the rifle to her and said she'd leave the door to the building open, the woman agreed to stay.

It turned out Ananke had been wrong to be concerned about that final group. When she, Rosario, and Liesel returned to the administrative section, with the intent of corralling the non-security staff, they found all the admin workers sitting outside their dorm, their hands zip-tied.

"It was mostly Dylan," Ricky said when Ananke asked what had happened.

Dylan shrugged. "I thought it was better than letting them wander around."

Aquino was on the ground, unconscious and also cuffed, with Wright stretched out next to him, wincing in pain. There had been no need to zip-tie Wright. His broken leg and dislocated shoulder were more than enough to keep him from going anywhere.

Ananke had Liesel, Dylan, and Ricky check through all the administration buildings to make sure they hadn't missed any stragglers. While they were doing that, she sent Rosario into the main building to collect any information and computer data she could find. "Pay special attention to anything related to organizations these people have done business with— shipping companies, clothing companies, things like that. And they must have a few employees who work elsewhere, selling their business. It would be good to get their names, too."

When she was alone, she switched to channel three on her comm. "Ananke for Ramon."

"Yes. Hello. This is Ramon."

"You can bring the bus in now."

"Really? You-you did it?"

"We did it."

"I SEE SOMEONE coming!" a woman shouted, looking out the window from the rearranged bunk.

Gloria ran over to the wall below the woman.

"Who is it?" someone else asked.

"I can't tell. They're in the cages."

"There's more than one?"

"Yeah."

Thirty seconds later, the lock on the other side of the main entrance rattled. This was followed by metallic sounds and a loud clunk. By the time the door opened, Gloria and the rest of her building mates were standing together in the main aisle.

Four people walked in—two men and two women—none wearing security uniforms.

"Hello," the oldest of the group said. "My name is Ramon Silva, and my friends and I are here to see that you get home."

For a few seconds, there was only silence. Then it was like someone had flipped a switch and everyone started talking at once.

Everyone but Gloria. All she could do was smile.

AS EACH DORM was emptied, the people inside were escorted to one of the warehouses near the entrance of the City. The space quickly became a madhouse of confused, happy, wary, excited former prisoners. Ananke had to use the public address system to get everyone to settle down.

"We will be transporting you to the pier in a bus and inside shipping containers we've attached to two trucks. But it's going to take several trips to get you all out of here, and we need you to be patient."

Knowing that riding in a closed shipping container

wouldn't make anyone comfortable, Ricky and Liesel had found pieces of extra canopy in one of the warehouses, then stretched them over the open doors of the containers. The occupants would be able to see outside but not feel like they might fall out.

Pablo, one of Ramon's people, was assigned to drive the bus, while Dylan took charge of one truck and Ananke the other.

"Everyone ready?" Ananke said over the comm, once the first group of passengers had been loaded.

"Ready," Pablo said.

"Me, too," Dylan said.

Ananke gave the air horn a couple of yanks, then shifted her rig into gear.

THE BUILDING WAS massive, but Gloria knew Henrietta was there somewhere. She worked her way through the crowd, searching the faces she passed.

"Gloria?"

The voice had come from her left, but it wasn't Henrietta's.

She turned, and blinked. "Alfonso?"

They hurried through the crowd toward each other, too slowly for Gloria's liking. When they finally reached each other, they fell into each other's arms, hugging as if they'd never let go.

Tears flowed down Gloria's face. "What are you doing here?"

"We came to get you out."

"You were in the City, too?"

"What? Oh, no. Only Henrietta. It's because of her we found you."

The only reason they stopped hugging was to search for their older sister.

"There she is," Alfonso said a few minutes later, pointing across the room.

They hurried over, not calling out her name until they were almost to her.

More hugs and tears.

"I told you we were going to get you out," Henrietta said. "I told you."

Gloria wanted to say thank you over and over and over, but her tears and happiness were so overwhelming that she couldn't have said anything if her life depended on it.

THERE WERE OTHER reunions, in the warehouse and more on the pier, as Ramon and his people found their friends and relatives.

"I'm sorry," Ramon's daughter kept saying as she clung to him and her husband. "I'm so sorry."

"No," Ramon said more than once. "I'm sorry I couldn't get you out sooner."

SHORTLY BEFORE DAWN, the *Karas Evonus* arrived at the pier.

Though it was a good-sized ship, transporting over a thousand people in a single trip was beyond its capabilities. Even two trips would be difficult. Luckily, each voyage would take less than half a day, so a little overcrowding would be acceptable.

The group was divided in half, with Ananke, Rosario, Liesel, Ricky, and Dylan remaining behind with those going second.

They spent a hot day under the canopy, nourished by water and food meant for the City's non-prisoner workers. Liesel, Ricky, and Dylan had made the rounds of the security guards who'd been drugged and given them each a booster shot to keep them under until well after everyone was gone.

Ananke had taken a ride down the river, back to San Christophe, where she told the residents what had happened.

"What about the men we're holding in the cellar?" Victor asked.

"Someone will come for them soon," she said.

"How soon?"

Ananke was so tired she almost snapped at him, but she simply said, "Soon."

Using one of the City's patrol boats, she transported the

prisoners who had been loading the cargo ships back to the pier. She then gave the boat to Julianna, one of the San Christophe residents who'd joined them on the mission. "It should make a good fishing boat. Though you should probably get rid of the gun on the deck."

It was nearly two a.m. when the *Karas Evonus* returned, and another hour and a half before everyone was on board and settled in the holds.

After they left the delta of Rio Orinoco, Ananke, who wanted nothing more than to go to her room and pass out, dragged herself into the conference room, where she initiated a video call with the Administrator.

"We're entering the Caribbean now," she said, stifling a yawn.

"Then I will have our contacts inform the Venezuelan Army they have a present waiting for them on the Rio Barima."

"And you're sure they won't try to cover this up?"

"They might try, but I think we've ensured they won't succeed."

The team had left behind everyone associated with the running of the City, save for Aquino and Wright, both of whom, the Administrator had assured her, would be held accountable for their crimes.

As for the former prisoners, the first group was waiting in a pier-side warehouse in Trinidad. Once the second group had joined them and the *Karas Evonus* and Ananke's team were miles out to sea, the local authorities would announce the rescue to the world, claiming credit for the operation—in cooperation with Venezuelan authorities, of course. The Trinidadian government would see that the freed all found their way home, posthaste.

Perhaps a few of the former captives would tell a different story, but it would lead to nothing, as the Administrator's people were already working to cover any trace of the Committee's involvement.

All nice and—

Ananke sat up. "Gutiérrez. We need to—"

"He's already been dealt with," the Administrator said.

"As soon as you told me the mission had succeeded, I had a freelance team snatch him and his assistant off his boat. They are on their way to the States right now, where they will soon find themselves in the company of the US government, along with records of their activities."

Ananke relaxed again. "If the feds need any help interrogating him, I'm happy to volunteer my services."

"I'm sure you understand that we can't let that happen."

"It was just a thought."

The Administrator smiled. "How much recovery time do you and your team need before the next mission?"

She yawned. "Seems to me our recovery time from the last mission was cut short to undertake this one."

"True. Then how much time off would you like?"

She leaned back in her chair to think about it. *A few days would probably be enough. But a week would be better. Maybe two. Yeah, that's a...that's a...*

And with that, she fell asleep.

Made in the USA
San Bernardino, CA
19 November 2018